I couldn't have been in the office all this time with a murderer!

It was indefinable, a whisper-soft brush of sound, eerie, but no hallucination. Someone was out there...

The faint sounds of stealthy movement were almost inaudible over the pounding of my heart, but he was coming this way. I couldn't chance a wild dash to the storage room to lock myself in. He'd catch me the second I stepped out into the hall. Looking around frantically for a place to hide in here, I saw just as little hope. The desk was open in the middle and not wide enough to conceal me. There was no escape either unless I jumped out of the fourth story window. The only alternative was to barricade myself. My hand was out to slam the door shut but I had waited too long.

"Good evening, Mrs. Gordon. Working late tonight?"

His words held the ring of deadly irony. It was the most frightening thing I'd ever heard. My body seemed frozen in response, until he touched me on the arm.

"No!" I shrieked.

My panicked repulse moved me out the doorway, leaving the body in clear view...

Bare Acquaintances

Karin Berne

Popular Library

An Imprint of Warner Books, Inc.
A Warner Communications Company

Popular Library books are published by
Warner Books, Inc.
666 Fifth Avenue
New York, N.Y. 10103

W A Warner Communications Company

Printed in the United States of America

First Printing: April, 1985

10 9 8 7 6 5 4 3 2 1

To Gordon

Chapter 1

"You look like shit."

"So what else is new?" Brushing back a strand of lifeless hair, I rubbed one furry bedroom slipper against the other and let Betsy in.

"Never fear." She patted my sticky cheek. "I have the answer to your problems right here in today's paper. And none too soon." Holding her contaminated hand away from her body, she grimaced. "Having a hot fudge pick-me-up before dinner?"

"I wasn't eating. I was reading."

The telltale spoon disappeared behind my back, but not before Betsy's experienced nose led her right into the kitchen, where my perfidy was exposed. A chocolate-stained bowl with a few dabs of whipped cream dribbling down the side sat on the table. I raced for the paperback, but Betsy got to it first.

"Notorious Criminals and How They Did It," she read

aloud. "A great self-help book. What are you doing between mouthfuls of junk food, plotting Dan's gory end?"

I sank my fat into a chair and licked the spoon openly. "Not a bad idea. How should I do him in: gun, knife, or poisoned daiquiri?"

Betsy fixed me with a pair of expressive blue eyes that were not exactly sympathetic at the moment. "You divorced him. Isn't that enough?"

To Betsy, a career woman who never considered the idea of marriage, one ex-husband was a trifling matter; but the only rug I'd ever known had been pulled from under me, and the floor felt damn hard. Here I was, Eleanor Gordon, a nice, middle-class housewife, now abandoned and left to moulder in a fully furnished, luxuriously carpeted tri-level, only an hour from Los Angeles and thirty minutes from Disneyland. Paunchy, balding Daniel Gordon, with his endless supply of unmatched socks and stale jokes, had moved out of the up-and-coming suburb of Casa Grande, and into a swinging bachelor's pad that featured mixed doubles in tennis and hot tubs. The divorce decree followed shortly after.

Betsy took the spoon out of my hand and put it on the table. "Why are you still in that ridiculous muumuu? I thought we were going to the club for dinner?"

"Yes, I did accept your kind offer; however, I've had second thoughts since then. Nothing personal, but this muumuu you seem to despise is the only thing in my closet that fits anymore, and rather than embarrass you in public, I thought it might be better to forego the pleasure of an evening in your company. I considered wearing my bathrobe, but I outgrew it last week. You needn't look so pitying. These red hibiscus all over the front bring out the gray highlights in my wispy hair."

Another expletive burst forth from my friend, and I graciously ignored it. What Betsy failed to appreciate was that the muumuu's bright colors and gargantuan proportions hid a lady who was in a decline. If I had been a Victorian, I could have lain on a fainting couch and quietly faded away. The twentieth century provides a more active approach to self-destruction. Some take to drink. I haunted pizza parlors and took corned beef sandwiches to bed. Having achieved my goal of fat and slothful, I was now toying with the idea of a nervous breakdown.

Betsy put on a pot of coffee, then checked the freezer. I bit my tongue as she commandeered the last of the jamocha almond fudge and dumped it down the disposal. A half-eaten quarter-pounder from the refrigerator followed.

"No wonder you smell like yesterday's hamburger," she snorted. "Why don't you snap out of this? You can't drown your sorrows in special sauce. Keep eating three Big Macs a day along with the other crap you stuff in your mouth, and you'll weigh two hundred pounds before the month is out." She poured a cup of sobering black coffee and set it in front of me. "Drink! Maybe this will cut through some of the cholesterol that's clogging your brain."

"Pass me the sugar."

Betsy flipped me a package of artificial sweetener, got herself a cup of coffee, then sat down. She crossed one long, elegant leg over the other, tilted her perfectly coiffed blonde head, and glared at me. Only the fact that she had been my best friend for twenty years kept me from spilling my coffee all over her lap. Even in college, Betsy Hanson impersonated a Nordic goddess while the rest of us thought it was enough to look intellectual.

"It pains me to say this," she began predictably, "but you are the biggest farthead I've ever known. From a reasonably attractive, fairly perceptive woman, you have become a mindless blimp. I know how much fun you're having, wallowing in this horse manure, but Ellie, my friend, all good things must come to a screeching halt, and today Hell has frozen over. Luckily for you, though, I brought a pick with me."

"Sit on it. You have no sympathy or understanding. What you see before you is the natural devastation wrought by a faithless husband, rejection, and divorce. You think I enjoy being so miserable?"

"Of course you do. It's very convenient," Betsy answered. "It saves you the trouble of having to cope with an identity crisis. Shall I tell you what your real problem is?"

"No."

"Dan did not break your heart when he absconded with his secretary. He scared the crap out of you." She leaned forward and pushed my coffee cup away, as if I couldn't hear her over the rim. "You're hiding in the kitchen like a congealed ball of fat because your mediocre marriage self-destructed, and you don't know who you are without it. Dan was your identity, your security blanket. He provided the house, the cars, the income, the status, so you think without him you're a nonentity. It's not quite true yet, but keep it up, and you will disappear. Face it, Ellie, those aren't tears of unrequited love. You're suffering from withdrawal."

Betsy had a wonderful knack for telling me things I didn't want to hear. Not that this was a startling psychological discovery; I knew what was going on. Calling it withdrawal symptoms was like explaining the pain in your mouth when a bad tooth is extracted. Only, the old ache was easier to live with.

That was my situation. Our marriage had been decaying, slowly but persistently, over the last few years. When the discomfort became noticeable, I merely took an aspirin and hoped for temporary relief. Lots of couples go through patches of boredom and irritation with each other; some live that way indefinitely. So I wasn't the most satisfied wife in the world. This was my niche. Dan may have become a habit, but I assumed the attachment was mutual. It took our second honeymoon in Hawaii to show the flaw in that theory.

I came home from the trip and called Betsy to say that our journey to paradise had felt more like serving time in purgatory.

"Dan insisted on going deep-sea fishing. I was bored and sick for eight hours. Have you ever spent eight hours puking over the side of a boat? I don't recommend it. Furthermore, I got to spend only one tantalizing hour at the Bishop Museum. Dan had to get back to see some underclad beauties wiggle their bottoms in the Tahitian hula."

Her answer was pragmatic, as usual. "Why didn't you stay at the museum and let Dan ogle in peace?"

"Why didn't we just take separate vacations? Married couples are supposed to do things together, or hadn't you heard?"

"Fine. Then you should have been very happy being miserable together."

Happy—no. Miserable—yes. Dan and I had rented a beachside bungalow on Maui for our last two nights. The lush scenery and ocean view made a beautifully romantic setting, and when I suggested we go skinny-dipping in the moonlit waves, he was all for the idea. I hoped that making love on the beach would rekindle the passion between us. Those scenes always look so erotic in the movies.

The reality was a little different. It took a half-mile walk down the beach before I settled on a reasonably secluded spot and fifteen minutes until I worked up the nerve to undress. Dan complained bitterly at the delay, but when we finally got down to business, we made the disillusioning discovery that sand and salt water are not aphrodisiacs. With every thrust, Dan grunted and I moaned, but not in passion. All I felt was sand . . . everywhere . . . scraping, cutting, digging into the most tender parts of my body, outside and in. I squirmed to get away, while Dan growled for me to help him. At my lack of response, he started pinching a nipple in his sandy fingers until I clawed his hand away. Then he went limp and rolled off me.

If we had managed to laugh it off, agreed that a sandy beach was no fit place for anything but crabs to cohabit, then tried it again on the king-size bed in the bungalow, we might have had a chance. But this episode was an all-time low, and we didn't have enough highs to compensate. Inevitably we carried all sorts of recriminations back to the mainland, where they turned into outright hostility. Finally Dan broke the news that he'd found someone more appreciative of his efforts in the bedroom . . . and elsewhere.

It was a boringly familiar script, but we acted it out with all the acrimony and fervor of the original story. My *shtick* was, "I've given you the best years of my life." Dan's answer was the unarguable, "So what have you done for me lately?"

That's a fairly common epilogue to a marriage turned stale, where neither partner has done anything but keep up the status quo. For a somewhat bright woman, I had let things slide past stupidity, all the way to irretrievable. That's why I chomped away on triple-decker club sandwiches and giant orders of fries. Every calorie consumed fed my resentment. Oh, sure, I condemned Dan for taking the coward's way out, but my anger was really sheer envy. Big-mouthed me, with all my fine talk—I didn't even have the guts of a lily-livered used car salesman. I wanted out of the coop just as badly, only I was too chicken to do anything but squawk.

Why couldn't Betsy let me suffer in peace? Dan was slipping and sliding his way through his midlife crisis on his nineteen-year-old secretary's black satin sheets. My son had left to take a summer job in L.A. and had forgotten my telephone number. So if I chose to be a Desdemona tightening a three-foot salami around my own neck, that was the only fun I had these days.

Betsy was regarding me with fierce determination, her jaw out. Once set into motion, my calm, collected friend was quite a bulldozer and she had only begun to push. "I don't want to hear any more wisecracks or lame excuses. You have to get out of this house. If you don't have anything to wear, I'll buy you a tarpaulin. But Ellie, it is time to move."

"Thanks for the tip, but where am I supposed to go? While you were forging a career, making yourself indispensable to the world at large, I was entertaining the Roto-Rooter man and soaking dirty diapers in the toilet. Don't you understand that I'm thirty-eight years old, and for almost half that time I've been nothing but a supportive wife and mother? I'm a statistic now—a displaced homemaker. *Knishes* are my specialty, only the market is depressed at the moment."

"That's no great loss. *Knishes* are fattening anyway. But this displaced homemaker business . . . how often did you scrub floors, wash windows, bake bread, knit booties? Come on, Ellie, you sat on every committee in town, from art auctions to that ridiculous drama festival. You were only a homemaker part of the time, so how displaced can you be?"

"I don't care if I homemade three hours a week; that's all I'm trained for."

"Really? What about the high school whiz kid who won a college scholarship at sixteen, kept a four-point average for four years, and graduated *summa cum laude?* She can do something else."

"I'll send my application to NASA tomorrow."

"Didn't I warn you to switch to a more practical major than Elizabethan drama?" She sidetracked.

"It was English Lit, and I did switch—to marriage. Look where that got me."

"It got you Michael, so stop bitching. But procreation did not atrophy your brain. You can still get a job."

"Betsy, stop dreaming. Tall, blonde, beautiful women engineers who can command forty thousand a year are in greater demand than short, dumpy, ex-housewives. All I can do is sell fat dresses in a fat store to other fat ladies. So I can quote Shakespeare?" I shrugged. "So who cares?"

"Funny you should ask, my erudite munchkin, but somebody out there loves you."

With a smug look, Betsy pulled out the newspaper and pointed to a front page photograph of Phillip Devereaux Abbotts. What, the headline asked, could a candidate for Congress gain by delaying the trial of a notorious criminal? Phillip Abbotts owed the public an explanation. His law partner, the much-publicized feminist, Katherine Busch, had filed another postponement on the Mannie Blanco case, only no one was saying why. Did it have anything to do with the upcoming primary?

Under Mr. Abbotts's dignified pose was a snap of the lady in question and a mug shot of Mannie Blanco. The combination was eye catching. Ms. Busch looked petite and businesslike. Her client looked like a hood.

He had appeared quite ordinary until the State Crime Commission discovered that he was running a commercial gambling racket under the cover of a home improvement company. Now, the formerly respectable, if colorful, Mr. Blanco was exposed in all his villainy and being represented by the firm of Abbotts, Devlin, and Busch, Attorneys-at-Law.

I read the article with mild interest, but when I turned to the inside page, I forgot all about it in an instant. Instead, I gave a cry of disgust. "That pig! He ought to be banned, defrocked, run out of town on a rail!"

"What are you raving about?" Betsy asked.

"The self-styled prophet of reactionary cretinism. The Rev. Billy Joe Ritchie. Listen to this. 'Feminism is a greater threat to the American Way than Communism. Birth control is the tool of Satan.' How dare they print this garbage?" I pointed at the picture of Ritchie, with his pop eyes, three-piece suit, and smile of pure beatification.

Betsy took the paper out of my hand. "He does look like a self-satisfied hog, doesn't he?"

"How can you be so cool about it? This guy would have us all back in the kitchen if he had his way."

"Really? So where are you, liberated thinker? I thought you just told me this was your favorite room in the world. No matter that hubby and kiddy have waved bye-bye, you're going to remain the great unwashed dishwasher out of sheer cussedness. Ritchie could use you as a walking billboard for his politics. The Lady Who Knows Her Place in This World: Down and Out."

"You're a Fascist pig," I grunted.

"Well then, my dear Ellie Gordon, you can prove I'm wrong by removing your carcass from that chair and asking Phil Abbotts for a job."

"Are you joking? He won't hire me. I was a volunteer worker when he ran for the State Legislature, and he can still get people for free."

"Probably. But you were his publicity coordinator. You were the one who knew what corporate doors to knock on, who could help him map out ad agency propaganda, and set up television advertising. You had all that experience from running the annual Art Show, organizing the Shakespearean Drama Festival. Abbotts knew he had a winner in you, and now that he's running for Congress, he needs you even more. Don't shrug your shoulders. Listen to me. All those skills you used as a volunteer can be turned into a money-making career. Try it. Go ask for your old job back, but with a salary this time."

I shook my head. "It won't work."

"How do you know? Besides, he owes you a favor. If he won't hire you for the campaign, he has a big law practice too, remember. Someone in that crowd he employs must be quitting, having a baby, retiring. Remind him what a help you were before, and what an asset you can be now."

"So I should take Mr. Abbotts on a jaunt down memory

lane, then stick him with a little moral blackmail. Political payback. I helped you, therefore you owe me one.''

"Don't make it sound like extortion. You'll only be selling yourself. If he buys, great. If not, it's good experience for you. I may be able to give you a boost too. Katherine Busch's husband works at Di-Con, only a floor up from me, and we cross paths every so often. He'll put in a word for you if I ask him.''

"Wonderful," I said sarcastically. "And don't forget Mr. Abbotts's other partner, Mark Devlin. I met him at the victory party three years ago, where I refilled his glass of punch expertly. He'll be more than happy to give me a glowing recommendation.''

"Will you stop being so negative! Do you want to spend the rest of your life in a muumuu stuck to that chair?''

We both knew the answer to that, but if I did crawl out of the pit I'd labored so hard to dig, what would happen to me if I didn't like it out there? What if nobody liked me? As long as I was bestowing my favors gratis, there was no room for complaint. However, taking money under false pretenses is frowned on, and I just might not be able to hack an ordinary job. The brash kid with the oversized I.Q. had long since faded into obscurity, and I cringed at the thought of taking my Shakespeare quotes out of mothballs, then tripping over the words. Yet, the only alternative was to pretend I was still Mrs. Daniel Gordon. That was no great shakes either. If a wife's credentials rest on her husband's laurels, that made me a reflection of Dan's mediocrity. I could do at least that well on my own.

"All right," I sighed. "What do you want me to do? Sign up for a six-week rejuvenating course at the gym and give up jamocha almond fudge for life?''

"Exactly! Put yourself in my hands for a month, and I'll have you looking like the girl who stole the captain of the football team from me in '59. She was short too, but slim and very unfrumpy, if you remember."

"Alas, poor Yorick. I knew her . . ."

"Don't worry. You'll know her again. Start by thinking of all those available men out there, waiting to be knocked off their feet by a pocket-sized brunette with big boobs."

"The problem is not getting but keeping," I said cynically.

"Keeping? What's the rush? After all those years of suburban togetherness, you need a fling or two. Who knows? You might like the single state as much as I do."

"You're conditioned to it," I replied glumly. "I'm used to having a warm body next to me in bed."

Betsy burst out laughing. "So am I."

Chapter 2

It took two weeks of desperate effort before I had the courage to try for a job, two weeks in which I crash-dieted back into the largest of the clothes hanging in my closet.

Betsy started me off by dragging me to her aerobic dancing class that met every Monday and Wednesday at 5:30 P.M. I puffed and panted and sometimes lay like a beached and moribund whale as more lithesome bodies pranced around me. That first week Betsy called three times a day to give me pep talks and check on what I was putting in my mouth. Not much, believe me.

The second week Betsy began appearing on my doorstep at the unconscionable hour of 6:45 A.M., demanding that I jog with her. And no excuses were accepted. I came up with a sinus headache, arthritic knees, and a heart condition, and that was just the first day. Betsy gave me a fishy stare with her bright blue eyes, and I found myself following her down the block, my baggy gray sweatsuit in lamentable contrast to her Frank Shorter running gear. As I admired the muscle definition in her thighs, I despaired of ever possessing such sinews. It took an hour in a hot tub when I got home before I could move. After that, the torture became more bearable, though I didn't stop bitching for weeks.

The next step in my transformation was a trip to the Hair Lair. Mr. Frank took charge of my neglected locks, clucking sadly that I had stayed away too long. He cut most of my hair off, then gave me what he claimed was a body perm, which turned out to be a mop of curls. Crowning his masterpiece with a rinse to hide the gray and bring out some golden highlights in my boringly brown tresses, he finally pronounced me ready to whip out my Master Charge. Mr. Frank didn't hold himself cheap, but the results were worth the big bucks, if I got the job. Big if.

On the day of the interview at Abbotts, Devlin, and Busch, Attorneys-at-Law, I jammed myself into a girdle, the mark of desperation in California's sunny heat, and just managed to squeeze into my best ladies'-luncheon-type dress. It was a crisp brown and white cotton with a flared skirt that could accommodate hips one size larger than the rest of me. A last glance in the mirror showed a marked improvement over the woman who had belted malteds like whiskey and dressed in a one-size-fits-all bedsheet, but when I finally arrived at the doorstep of Casa Grande's most prestigious law firm, I had a sudden urge to run for the beckoning golden arches around the corner. In that haven I could eat my way through the next hour, then report to Betsy with all honesty that Mr. Abbotts never got a chance to see me. Only the thought of her wrath, when she called his office to check up on that lie, pushed my dragging feet over the threshold.

Two Twenty-One Wilshire Lane was an impressive building of cream stucco with a genuine imported Mexican clay tile roof. It was authentic California, from the palm trees in front to all the Mercedes parked in back. The law firm owned the property and leased out the offices on the lower three floors, taking the fourth for themselves. The tenants used a separate lobby on the other side of the building, while Abbotts, Devlin, and Busch were reached through their own private entrance, next to their own private parking lot, and by way of private elevator. They avoided the traffic that way.

I was relieved to note when I got upstairs that the hum of voices was at a decent conversational level. Sometimes the hushed sobriety of my gynecologist's office made me feel as though the patient before me had died with her feet in the stirrups, and I have arrived just as they're pulling the sheet the rest of the way down. At this office, a perky young thing took my name, told me to wait in the lounge, and suggested that I might like to read the latest copy of *Women in Business*. Good guess on her part; or there was a certain aura about females who came job hunting as opposed to those who were buying the goods and services.

The lounge was screened off from the main part of the office by a dividing half-wall and several hanging plants. The color scheme was the tasteful blend of earth colors and brown leather so favored by those who drive unobtrusively elegant cars. The owner of one of the Mercedes parked outside was a middle-aged man heavily engrossed in the *Wall Street Journal*. He looked up briefly when I sat down, then went back to Dow Jones. The only other occupant of the room was a vaguely familiar looking woman, with a petulant *möue* on her lips. It took me a moment to place her. She was Carolyn Brewster, heiress to a cattle ranch kingdom and in the process of suing either her husband, or her sister, for stock manipulation. It had made hilarious headlines for a few weeks. When the receptionist called for me first, Mrs. Brewster flashed both of us a dirty look. I smiled back.

As I followed one of the secretaries down a plushly carpeted hallway to the rear of the suite, I got my first lesson on the working woman. This one was about six years younger than I, highly confident, as indicated by the swagger of her walk, and more than willing to let me know that they had no earthly use for me in this office.

"Maybe it's the way I smell, but how do you know I'm looking for a job? The receptionist outside seemed to pick up the same scent."

She tossed her gypsy mane. "It's an attitude you learn to recognize. Women like Mrs. Brewster sit back and wait for you to come to them. The rest of us have that eager look...you know, eyes bright, mouths open in anticipation, purses clutched in tight little fingers." She laughed. "You can tell the ones who've made it. They carry briefcases. The *Gucci*-er the better."

I determined to go out tomorrow and buy the most ostentatious attaché case I could find. "Any other tips?" I asked.

She stopped in front of one of the closed doors and knocked, giving me a last-minute onceover before walking away.

"Get some new clothes."

Who says women are catty? This one was a tiger. Yet even taken as insults, real or implied, her advice was sound, and not much different from the basic *do*'s for a successful volunteer worker, except brown and white afternoon tea dresses were out, and briefcases in. Hoping Mr. Abbotts would take my improvement on faith, I sucked in my gut and stepped into his office.

He was overjoyed to see me. Immediately coming from behind his long walnut desk, he greeted me warmly, shook my hand, set me down in one of the deep cordovan leather armchairs, and insisted that I have something to drink, either from his well-stocked bar or the built-in coffee service next to it. This was the kind of reception guaranteed to win friends and influence people, though Phillip Abbotts had won me over long ago. It was a relief to see that, in turn, he still felt the same. He even looked the same.

Mr. Abbotts was one of those men who combine a reassuring maturity with youthful vigor. It was hard to believe he was on the wrong side of fifty. Even the salt and pepper hair added to his appeal rather than diminished it. That's the way it is with men. They get craggy. Women get wrinkled.

"Eleanor, it's marvelous seeing you again. I missed you at the county convention. Weren't you a delegate?"

I explained the upheaval in my life and the change in marital status. Mr. Abbotts was consolingly sympathetic but had little to say, as he hardly knew Dan. Instead, we spent the next few minutes chatting about the good old days.

One thing for sure, the man was made for politics. Not only did he remember names and faces and shake all the right hands, Mr. Abbotts looked directly into a person's eyes when he spoke. He never searched the room for a more influential backer, then smiled and stared over your shoulder while you were dishing out compliments. He always appeared to be giving his undivided attention to the slightest comment. Politically, he was one of the few hometown boys to achieve statewide recognition. A following had gathered around him eight years ago when he was appointed to fill the temporarily vacant State's Attorney's post. After honorably finishing the term, he was prepared to come back home and take up his regular law practice again, but the party bosses liked his style and persuaded him to run for the State Legislature. He won that election easily, with my modest help, and was now preparing to enter the primary next spring as a candidate for Congress. The polls predicted he'd have no trouble with that either.

Naturally, he assumed I had come to volunteer my services once again, but when I explained that necessity had driven me into the work force, he was truly apologetic.

"Nothing would please me more than to have you back on my team, Eleanor," he said in his velvety baritone voice. "Unfortunately, we haven't set up campaign headquarters yet. In fact, the organization is quite loose at the moment. We plan to gear up come September. Check back with me and perhaps I can find something for you then.''

"That sounds wonderful, and I truly appreciate it; but I'm afraid I can't wait that long. My immediate problem is a son who is going to college this fall. Need I say more?'' I smiled ruefully.

"Of course not. I understand. But I'm going to miss you. Not everyone has your excellent rapport with the press, and at the moment, I could use your winning smile with Steve Tedesco. Have you been reading the garbage he's putting out for the *Chronicle*? I've spoken to the editor several times, but apparently Steve has carte blanche. I don't recall his being so vicious about me in the past, but now he just won't let go of my neck.''

"It's nothing personal. Steve's always in search of a hot headline, and if he can't find one, he invents his own. I almost came to blows with him once over a column he wanted to write, suggesting that you bought your way into politics. It's his proletarian soul. Steve doesn't believe that anyone who's not a bona fide member of an oppressed minority has any redeeming virtues.''

Mr. Abbotts smiled slightly, but his expression was thoughtful. "You did a lot of ground work for me that went unnoticed. I'm beginning to think I owe you a larger debt of gratitude than I realized.''

Betsy would have kicked me in the rear for not pressing that, but even though Mr. Abbotts was my best shot at getting a job, I didn't like the idea of political patronage. "You don't owe me anything.'' I demurred. "I worked for you because I liked your stand on the issues. Maybe I'll have some time to do a little campaigning again, voluntarily.'' On that gracious note, I started to rise from the chair, but Mr. Abbotts stopped me.

"I realize," he said slowly, as though the idea were developing at that very moment, "that your experience is mostly in public relations, but do you think you could adapt it to an office job?''

''I imagine so.'' Careful, I warned myself as I breathed in deeply. He may not be leading up to what you think.

But he was. ''Eleanor, we could use someone with your qualifications right here in the office. Truthfully, I'd like to take advantage of your organizational abilities, and we need an office manager. You wouldn't be a secretary, as such, but more a liaison figure to deal with the staff and make sure clients aren't being kept waiting. All you'd need is a general knowledge of office procedure. Would you be interested?''

Only because I had such control of mind and spirit was I able to answer with a restrained, ''Yes, I think so.''

Without further ado, Mr. Abbotts got down to the business of hours, wages, and insurance benefits. I asked twice before finally accepting his word that he wasn't doing me a special favor, but rather the reverse. It was a heady thought. He needed me. I knew that for certain when he pressed the key to the ladies' room into my hand, but I felt absolutely cherished at being assigned my own parking space. What a career I was going to have. Sailing out of his office on winged feet, I made sure to wave good-bye to the glamorous secretary with the helpful tips. When she asked how the interview went, I told her I was off to buy an entire new wardrobe . . . and a briefcase.

Of course, I didn't get her reaction until the following Monday when I showed up at eight-thirty sharp and was introduced to everyone by Mr. Abbotts as the new office manager. She seemed to approve of my simply cut linen suit, though not of the woman inside. It wasn't until a few days later that I found out the job should have gone to her, by rule of seniority. Not that anyone in the firm had ever considered having an office manager, but Barbara Beauchamp felt abused.

There's often a private clique among office personnel that can effectively shut out a newcomer. The other two girls had no grudge against me, but for the sake of loyalty they copied Barbara's aloof attitude. One of them said outright that she didn't realize political pay-offs could be so profitable, but then apologized for the nasty crack. Eventually the hostilities wore themselves out from lack of retaliation. I was too busy brushing up on my rusty typing, learning to subdue the man-eating word processor, and referring to the legal dictionary I carried with me at all times. The public part of my manager's job took up less time than Mr. Abbotts thought. Nitty-gritty help was what this office needed. When the girls realized I was ready to nit and grit with the rest of them, a tentative truce was called. When they discovered the unique advantage they had over me, fraternization began in earnest.

These three were a walking encyclopedia of the brave new world of the single woman. Details I had always considered too intimate to discuss came pouring out of them as naturally as their multiple orgasms. Now, I never pretended to be a virgin when I got married. I just never said I wasn't. They said, did, explained, and accepted constructive criticism. I tried not to blush the first time I heard one of their confabs on how long foreplay should last prior to oral sex. But after that, it became a game with them to try and shock me. And they succeeded so well.

When I was nineteen, I was heavily into iambic pentameter. At the same age, our secretary-receptionist, Josie Faria, was heroically coupleting two boyfriends. Brown haired, blue eyed, and exuberant, she seemed to find work a boring interlude between stanzas. Maggie Connell was slightly older and much more polished. She had that finishing school flair, although in her case it was Hollywood High. Long, lithe, with creamy skin and honey coloring, Maggie added a touch of class to her kiss and tells. She omitted the names.

The last of the titillating talebearers was Barbara. Supremely confident of her voluptuous charms, she always saved the best parts of her morning-after stories until I was free to listen. We snatched these moments of private conversation during five-minute lulls throughout the day, when we could stop to grab a cup of coffee. All drinking was done in a small alcove next to the lounge, and all talking dropped to a quiet murmur as certain subjects were brought up. I couldn't say that Barbara and I became best buddies at these bull sessions. Her aim was to embarrass me, maybe rub in a little superiority too. She was divorced, but had a cynical live-in relationship with her ex, which included dating other men. Barb claimed the arrangement was on her terms—the knock being that I couldn't even keep a husband on his.

I described this trio to Betsy as the titty-tats. She said there were loads of them in her office. She called them Siamese sex kittens. If they didn't report back to each other, how could they know they were doing it right? I thought there was a bit more one-upmanship in my crew, if not toward each other, at least toward me. When I needed to touch base with normal old-fashioned, I ran to Nancy Weaver. The bookkeeper had a cubbyhole next to the storage room, where four days a week I could bring my snatched cup of coffee and listen to fond grandmother stories. She had seven little Weavers to report on, and their achievements were endless.

There was one other female in the office, but, not unnaturally, she kept a friendly distance from the rest of us. Katherine Busch wasn't just a boss, but a two-briefcase woman, both cases bulging with important papers. She wouldn't consider indulging in girlish gossip. By virtue of her status, she created most of it.

Ms. Busch was the prototype success story as featured by *Cosmo*, *Ms. Magazine*, and the National Organization of Women. Just past thirty, she had already achieved prominence by being selected as a partner in a distinguished law firm, and was on her way to becoming a noted feminist. Katherine Busch was vocal, media oriented, and controversial. Not only was she representing a colorful crook like Mannie Blanco;

she had a running and much-publicized dispute going with the unctuous Reverend Ritchie. He called her liberated views sacrilegious. She accused him of giving God a bad name. So far their argument had been from afar and through newspaper quotes. Now it was taking on harsher overtones, and I figured it wouldn't be long until Mr. Abbotts's name cropped up. Ritchie was one of those zealots who believed freedom of religion meant the divine right to take over the American political system. If he didn't approve of Ms. Busch, he couldn't be in favor of a man who supported her. And he'd preach that in the pulpit, on the radio, on TV screens, in front of any audience that would listen. Pretty soon feminism wouldn't be the issue, but whether Phillip Abbotts believed in God. It worked in the Salem witch trials; why not now?

I applauded Katherine Busch for taking on such a heavy adversary, but to her it was just another feather in her modish white felt hat. She did so many things so well. Her husband obviously doted on her, and didn't mind having to wait outside her office on evenings when she was working late inside it. The tall, blond, precise engineer made a perfect foil for his wife's petite vitality. He had the looks in the family, as Katherine Busch was only passably pretty, but she had the animation. I admired her from afar, as it were, though the titty-tats were less appreciative. They thought she was a snob. I thought they were delinquents, so it kind of evened things out.

On the male side of the office staff were Andy and David, both part-time clerks and full-time law students. When they weren't attending classes or doing research for the firm at the law library, they furthered their education with the titty-tats. Since everyone was having such a good time, I ignored the goings-on at the water cooler, as long as the work got done. But when Dennis Devlin tried to include me in the fun and games, I didn't find it so pleasant.

I should explain that there were two Devlins at Abbotts,

Devlin, and Busch. Mark Devlin was the partner in the firm; Dennis, his nephew, was an associate. Admittedly, I had a soft spot for Mr. Devlin, Sr. Everyone did. Forty-five years old, with dark, wavy hair and green eyes, he had enough Irish charm to join his partner in politics and knock 'em dead. He preferred instead just to practice law and take an official position as an appointee to whatever board he chose. His reputation as a criminal lawyer had brought him more cases than he could handle; hence, the addition of Katherine Busch to the firm. But what made Mark Devlin so unusual, as if the above accomplishments weren't enough, was that he did it all from a wheelchair.

A car crash ten years before had left him with a pair of useless legs, yet he not only got around with ease, but also seemed to have no hang-ups about his disability. Mr. Devlin was unfailingly cheerful, quick to joke with the girls about their various boyfriends, and never asked for special treatment. That alone won him everyone's devotion, mine included.

I gave him extra points for surviving the tragedy ego intact, because shortly after his accident, his wife left him. The reasons were made clear when Maggie said taking dictation on the lap of this particular boss wasn't possible. At first I thought she meant the wheelchair would get in the way, a small obstacle for Maggie's dexterity, but then I realized that Mr. Devlin was disqualified from their games. It was a pity too. His looks were undamaged and his droll sense of humor irresistible.

I had dashed into his office one morning to give him a brief he had requested. "Don't forget," I reminded him, "Mrs. Brewster is coming in today at four, after all. And Mr. Johnson called three times this morning. I think he may be ready to settle out of court. The messages are on your desk. Did you get them?"

"Yes, ma'am. I always read my messages from you. They're masterpieces of English syntax and grammar, properly punctuated and spelled. Believe me, Mrs. Simons, I would never dare neglect such communications.''

I looked at him doubtfully, but the twinkle in his eyes was reassuring. "Just doing my job," I said.

"And very well," he responded, grinning.

That was Mark Devlin.

Dennis, his nephew, was hatched from another egg. He was the junior member of the firm and apparently felt obliged to strike a balance with his uncle. While Mark Devlin was hard working, fair minded, clever, and an asset to mankind in general, Dennis was a prick.

He had been passed over last year when Katherine Busch was made full partner, and he had continued to pout about it ever since. He must have placed a lot of weight on nepotism if he even dreamed he had a chance of winning that race. While Ms. Busch worked for her promotion, Dennis spent most of his time playing with the titty-tats and taking very long lunches. If he had put some of that energy into practicing law, he might have had a chance. He was perfectly competent, one might even say reasonably bright. Sometimes.

The day I had to slap him in line was not a good one from the start. Maggie Connell and Katherine Busch were each home with the flu, Mr. Devlin was in L.A., Mr. Abbotts was speaking at the Rotary Club; and by four-thirty, I felt put upon, overworked, and bitchy. Dennis caught me in the storage room as I was impatiently feeding default judgments to the copy machine. The door clicked shut behind me, and I turned to see him leaning against it, a silly grin on his lecherous face.

"I was hoping to get you alone one of these days. It's time we got to know each other better."

If the situation weren't so surprising, I would have laughed out loud. Shiny-faced Dennis Devlin was posing as Burt Reynolds. His voice was low and suggestive, but his line was pure corn. Forgive me, Burt, the slur was unintentional.

"Please, Mr. Devlin, I'm very busy. Would you just unlock the door and go away?"

"It's not locked . . . yet." He smirked.

"Good. Then you can turn yourself around and march right out of here."

Dennis was uncertain about his next move. There was just enough age difference between us to make my command seem like an order from mommy. His instincts prompted him to obey, but his ego fought on.

"What's the harm in a little fun?" he asked.

"None at all. But not here. Not now. And not with you."

What was the matter with him? Surely he preferred the young and eager to the old and sagging. Dennis didn't lack for females in his life. He was good looking and had some degree of intelligence, although possessing no charm that I could see. So he wasn't desperate to be making a pass at me, just degenerate.

"This is your last chance, Denny dear. Either get the hell out of here, or I vomit all over you."

To show him I meant business, I grabbed the papers from the machine and moved toward the door. In his haste to sidestep me, his foot caught under my shoe and we both stumbled against the wall, with Dennis's hand accidentally brushing across my breast.

His face turned white. "Honestly, it was a mistake. I didn't mean to touch you."

"Just try it again," I fumed, "and I'll slap a sexual harassment charge on you so fast, you won't have time to cry 'uncle.' "

Leaving him with that threat to mull over, I stalked to my desk, dumped the papers on top, and took my purse out of the bottom drawer. Josie and Barbara watched as I tramped into the ladies' room; and not twenty seconds later, Barbara was hot on my heels. I was sitting on the pink velvet vanity stool applying lipstick when she burst through the door.

"What happened?"

"Nothing," I answered before blotting my lips.

Her black-fringed eyes scanned me for signs of ravagement. "I just saw Dennis, and he wouldn't even come out to go to the elevator until he checked that the coast was clear. Are you sure nothing happened?"

"Cool it, Barb," I said irritably. "The little fart made a pass at me. That's all."

"Jesus! You acted like you were ready to call in the National Guard. I thought maybe he pulled a gun and tried to rape you. A pass?"

Here was more fuel for the titty-tat information forum. Tomorrow they'd take an impartial survey of storage room seduction techniques, and make a personal probe of the office manager's overreaction. From the look on Barbara's face, it appeared her in-depth study was going to start now.

"Did he unzip his pants?" She smirked.

"No, and neither did I undo mine. It was a chance encounter, Barb. Two ships passing in the night—a fleeting brush of gossamer wings. You'd better get outside. Josie's alone in the office."

"Yes, ma'am. I'm sorry to have intruded, ma'am." Her wide red mouth was sulky. "A regular virgin, aren't you? Didn't you ever do anything when you were married, or does it have to be legal before you put out?"

"Are you selling me on Dennis?" I snapped.

"You better find somebody, toots. You need it." She flipped the mane of black hair over her shoulder and sauntered out, hips swinging.

Chapter 3

I may have been a slow learner about a lot of things in my life, but at work I was moving to the top of the class. Not only had I made some very visible improvements in the office, noted and commented upon by Mr. Abbotts, I also became privy to the details of the Mannie Blanco case. To a mystery lover, it was sheer whodunit.

For weeks the story had been splashed all over the papers that the irrepressible Mr. Blanco was a gambling operator who used his home improvement company as a front. Now that he had been put out of both businesses, everyone was waiting anxiously for his trial to begin so they could hear who his best customers were. A few fines would be dished out, and some heads would drop in embarrassment, but the brunt of the punishment would fall on Mannie. He didn't like that idea.

The media's innuendos and outright suggestions about why the trial was so long in coming all skirted the truth but missed the focus. It had nothing to do with plea bargaining or political maneuvering on Mr. Abbotts's part: Mannie Blanco himself was working a deal. He claimed to know every nook, cranny, and rat hole of the underworld crime syndicate in California; and in exchange for immunity from prosecution, he'd pass on the information. Detente was not running smoothly, because every week Mannie thought up a new demand. Right now, it was that all seventeen charges against him be dropped and that he get a hundred thousand dollars, a new identity, and a plane ticket to South America. This largesse was beyond the bounds of generosity possible for our small District Attorney's office, so it brought in the Federal Witness Protection Program as well as the State Crime Commission, who had nabbed Mannie in the first place.

All these agencies would have been happy to work out a suitable arrangement with him, if just to get him off their necks, but Mannie refused to talk until they signed on the dotted line. In turn, they weren't going to part with a cent of the taxpayers' money until he said something worthwhile. Up to now, all he'd done was a lot of bragging.

This standoff had brought things to a standstill. Because of the danger to Mannie from the mob if word leaked out about the proposed trade, he had sealed himself away in his beachfront villa, defended by a ten-foot wall, several growling Dobermans, and four husky weight lifters. The only time the press could get near him was when he came into town to see his lawyer.

This was also when the intrepid boy reporter, Steve Tedesco, came sniffing around. He was positive a hot story simmered behind the trial postponement; and on the basis of the First Amendment, he wanted to lay it bare. The hell with prejudicing a jury when it came to freedom of the press.

Steve had another pet project too. Now that the Reverend Billy Joe Ritchie and his Church of the Essential Truth had made a public stand on the evils of the E.R.A. and other assorted atrocities, Steve wanted the feminist viewpoint in rebuttal. That gave him a second reason to chase Katherine Busch. One morning he caught me.

"Ellie Gordon! Holy shit, is that you?"

I was about to enter the lobby when Steve's unmistakable voice rang out from across the street. There was no pretending I hadn't heard him. Everyone on the block had. I turned around as he dashed from his car and made a reckless sprint through traffic. It was the same old impetuous Steve, charging in front of a bus and giving the passengers a heart attack.

He trotted across the parking lot with a cheerful grin on his square face, his hair shooting out in seventeen different directions. I could have sworn he was wearing the same plaid sports jacket I had last seen him in, and no question those were his old baggy pants. Steve would probably look disheveled in a tuxedo. Nothing could help his short, stocky build or the freckles on his nose; though if he brushed his hair and shined his shoes, it might improve matters.

I waited until he caught up with me. "I see your vocabulary hasn't improved any more than your wardrobe," I observed.

He gave one of his full-throated laughs. "And you're still sucking a lemon. Jesus, you look great, Ellie. I haven't seen you around lately."

I broke down and smiled at him. "It's been a while. Have you missed me?"

"Damn right, I have. Nobody knows how to put up a fight like you do." He nodded toward the building. "Back on the campaign trail?"

"I'm actually employed these days. Meet the new office manager."

Steve's impudent eyes traveled down the length of me and came up impressed. So he should have been. I had always fought the battle of the bulge, but now I was sixteen pounds lighter, six below the weight I used to carry, and decked out in a style I had never worn before. The emergence of the new

Ellie Gordon had begun at Nieman-Marcus's summer sale two weeks ago. Bored with the few conservative navy blue and black dresses I had bought to start work, I splurged on a cranberry silk blouse reduced to bargain basement price. That was the breakthrough. Charge card in hand, I then poked through suits, sportswear, shoes, and the Ms. dress department. Steve was now enjoying the effect of the silk blouse worn with a white skirt and jacket. There was still some weight to come off on the hips and thighs, but the overall picture couldn't have been framed better.

Once Steve had feasted his eyes, he got down to his favorite subject. "Hey, Ellie, I'm having trouble getting in to see Katherine Busch. Not the Blanco case this time. I want her reaction to Reverend Ritchie's new line on affirmative action. You know, *The Ultimately Liberated Woman Demands Equal Opportunity for Rebuttal*. She'll like that. Come on, Ellie old pal, do me a favor. Sneak me past the receptionist."

"Forget it, Stevie old pal. You're *persona non grata* around here as long as you keep bringing up the Blanco case. All slant and no substance make for no soliciting. You'll just have to take your yellow journalism somewhere else."

"It's pure white," he denied. "Besides, 'the less we know, the more we suspect.' "

"If you're going to sink to homilies, try 'suspicion is far more apt to be wrong than right.' "

"Okay. Tell me the truth, and I'll print it."

"Talk to Ritchie," I said. "He'll give you the truth in Roman typeset from his direct pipeline to God. Why do you think he's the only ordained minister in the Church of Essential Truth? Nobody else has his connections. Go ask, my son, and he shall tell."

Steve's face broke into a grin. "How come you're picking on the Reverend Billy Joe? He only wants to put women back in the bedroom where they belong. Hey, I'm only kidding. Put that purse down." He pretended to cover his face as I swung the bag in warning. "Your boss turned you into a red-hot feminist too, huh? I always said you had dangerous tendencies." He gestured toward my whole getup. "What does hubby say about the militant Ms. Gordon? He like it?"

"There is no hubby anymore."

The smile faded. "Why didn't you call me?"

"Why should I? You would have just made another headline out of it."

"Like 'The brainy and beautiful, but uptight Eleanor Gordon is available, but all lines form behind Steve Tedesco.' Has a nice ring, doesn't it?"

"So does 'Steve Tedesco is an outrageous flirt and all married women beware.' "

"You're not married anymore," he said quietly.

My stomach gave one nervous quiver before I could manage a retort. "But you are. Don't get carried away out of old times' sake, Steve. You know how I feel about cheating on an unsuspecting spouse. That's what ended my marriage, and I think it's a dirty trick. Besides," I tried to lighten it up, "I still disapprove of your paparazzi methods. What you call news reporting, I call an invasion of privacy."

"I can't see what infidelity and investigative journalism have to do with each other, but can we argue the issue in bed?"

The direct question brought me up short. Three years ago Steve had asked the same thing, and my answer was no. Even then he was honest about what he wanted—to screw around on the floor of campaign headquarters. However, much as I was flattered that a younger man wanted me for my body, especially since it wasn't doing much for Dan anymore, I couldn't unlock the chastity belt welded by marriage vows, Jewish guilt, and plain old scared-to-death. Besides, sex without love seemed hypocritical, although it didn't appear to bother me with Dan. My scruples also failed to check my response to an unexpected kiss in the dark.

One night, near the end of the campaign, I had come back to headquarters to drop off a box of brochures. The secretary was just leaving. She had two young children at home and a babysitter who couldn't stay later than nine o'clock. Her pretty face fell when she saw me come in with more work, but I shooed her off, promising I would put the promotion material into delivery packages for each precinct so that they could be picked up early the next morning.

Grabbing her jacket, she dashed out the door as Steve Tedesco came sauntering in. He was more crumpled than ever at that time of night, and I put him to work in the back room with me dividing the brochures. Of course he had something to say about my clever publicity.

"What the hell does this mean? 'Phillip Abbotts has your best interests at heart. He will fight for more stringent pollution standards, improved public housing, and lower taxes.'" Steve shot me a sarcastic grimace. "I guess that means that his opponent wants smog, rat-infested tenements, and a fifty-percent surcharge on income. Come on, Ellie, you can do better than that."

"Shut up and tape that box. People have to know what a candidate is going to fight for, and they have to be won over." I tossed him a marking pen. "Here. Write the precinct number on top."

"I could be stripped of my typewriter and byline if it got out that I was helping Abbotts's campaign," he said, stacking the packages against the wall.

"Don't worry. I'd never admit to using a biased reporter who endorsed the incumbent. What are you doing here anyway? Isn't it time for you to be putting the newspaper to bed, or whatever you do with that rag?"

"I'll ignore the slur on the *Casa Grande Chronicle*, and instead take you up on your offer of bed. Let me remind you that your job is to seduce the press, not insult a prominent member of the corps."

I rubbed my tired head absently and tucked a loose strand of hair behind my ear. "All right, prominent member, we're finished. Turn out the lights back here while I make sure everything's put away in front."

"Marjorie Abbotts is married to the guy. Let her clean house."

For the hundredth time since I'd met the maddening Steve Tedesco, I turned on him in irritation. "Why don't you go uncover a scandal someplace! There's nothing here to interest you."

"How about the exhilarating wit of a certain publicity coordinator? I find it stimulating to have my ethics, journalistic procedure, and spelling all ground into the dust by one persnickity woman."

Against my will, a smile tugged at the corners of my mouth. "When you develop some redeeming features, I'll be kinder."

The office was in order, and I waited at the front door for Steve. He reached me just as I turned out the overhead light, leaving us in shadow.

"I do have some redeeming features," he murmured. Then he took my face in his hands and kissed me. What may have started as a joke caught fire immediately, and the next thing I knew I was in his arms, giving back as good as I was getting.

"Oh, God," he whispered against my lips. "Go to bed with me."

"No!" I pushed him away and straightened my sweater with shaking hands. What in hell happened? What was I doing?

Steve had a ready explanation. "Jesus, you turn me on," he said in a husky voice.

"Then you can just turn off," I snapped, more embarrassed at my own reaction than angry at him. "You have a wife at home, and, if that doesn't mean anything to you, I'm a married woman."

"Obviously an unsatisfied one." He saw the expression on my face even in the dim light and was immediately contrite. "Sorry. That was a cheap shot."

I turned my back on him and bent to retrieve my purse from where it had fallen on the floor. "It's no more than I've come to expect from you."

"Hell, it is!" Steve grabbed me by the shoulders and forced me around to look at him, though there was little I could see in the dark. His anger I felt through the strength of his fingers digging into me. "I know I'm an uncouth lout, and you wouldn't give me the Pulitzer Prize if I were the only one in the running," he panted, "but under my black heart, I do have some integrity. If you'll notice, I did not check out the state of your marriage before I kissed you, and I did not take advantage of your virtue when you kissed me back."

"So you are a gentleman *and* a terrible writer. Anything else?"

"You better believe it. I'm so horny right now from touching you, I don't care what you think. All I want to do is rip off those pants and fuck the hell out of you."

As a declaration of passion, that was a winner. "Thanks for the compliment," I managed. "No one has offered to rape me in years."

"Oh, Ellie, Ellie. How can you make lust sound so cold when I'm so hot?" His voice was a groan as his hands slid across the front of my sweater. "Can't you feel it?"

I felt it all right, and took a step back. "No, Steve. This isn't for me. Not when it's just sex."

"I happen to think," he said with a spark of his old raillery, "that sex is a hell of a good reason to go to bed with someone."

There was a certain logic in that, but not one I could accept. "Steve, you're an incorrigible brat."

"Are you going to slap my face?"

He was so straightforward about everything, I had to

laugh. "No. How could I slap a guy for offering himself body and soul?"

"Not soul," he said lightly.

"Good. That makes it easy." My foot was out the door when he stopped me.

"Hey, Ellie, I respect the fact that you're faithful to your husband, but if you ever change your mind, I want to be the first to know about it."

We parted on that vague prospect, but, truthfully, I never even thought of Steve again. One mad kiss was simply the result of proximity, surprise, and an unhappy marriage, on my part anyway. As for Steve, he was just one of those men who's always out for a piece of ass. That hadn't changed either. Here we were, three years later, and he was still coming on—at 9:00 A.M. yet.

"Not the slightest bit tempted?" he asked ruefully.

I put my hand on his sleeve. "How about humbly flattered?"

At that moment Mr. Abbotts drove up in his powder blue Cadillac. He got out and locked the car, walked across the parking lot and passed by us without a word, only nodding his head at me. I snatched my hand away from Steve's arm. When the doors to the lobby closed, Steve began to chortle gleefully.

"Consorting with the enemy. Holy shit, Ellie, you should see your face. What's the matter, Abbotts swear you to a vow of nonfraternization? Just tell him you were doing some PR."

"That's exactly what I'm doing, for your information, so shut up."

"You call turning down my dishonorable proposal good PR? Okay, okay, joke's over. But if you really want to do your boss a favor, get him off the hook."

"What do you want, Steve, a copy of his last year's income tax return?"

"I want to know if Blanco is ever going to come to trial. Don't give me that closed-face stare. The public has a right to know if Kathy Busch and her partner are staging a preelection performance. You understand me. I think Mannie's working a deal for immunity, except the grand announcement isn't going to be made until a few weeks before the primary. Then Mr. A. will look like a crusader against crime instead of a lawyer who gets crooks off on a technicality.''

"In case you've forgotten, Mannie's attorney is Ms. Busch—not her partner.''

"She'll do whatever Abbotts tells her. And Mannie won't have a word to say about it either.''

"That's filthy, Steve, accusing Mr. Abbotts of using a client for political expediency. You're just looking for an excuse to blast him, and, believe me, the public is not entitled under the First Amendment to hear your prejudices. Besides, I know Mr. Abbotts wouldn't abuse his position.''

"You don't know a damn thing, Ellie baby, but I love your body anyway.''

Chapter 4

I repeated this edifying conversation to Betsy early the next morning while we were jogging. It was a mistake.

"You're ready for a date now."

"No," I puffed.

"What's the point of self-improvement if you don't benefit from it?"

"I'm benefitting, believe me. I'm earning my living. Isn't that enough?"

"There's a guy I know who'd be great for you. His name is Barry Janish and he—"

"Forget it," I broke in. "No men. I'd rather have a pet boa constrictor."

"Aha! Watch those Freudian slips. A snake—"

"All right already. If you say one word about phallic symbols I'll hit you."

Betsy was grinning. "The old unconscious. You can't keep it down."

"Betsy, I'll tell you when I'm ready. Okay?"

Betsy being Betsy, she didn't give up, just tried another angle. Instead of nagging, she offered a further boost to my morale by planning a visit to La Cosmetique after work on Thursday.

Mme. Denaud charged a month's rent just to allow you to enter her sacred portals and then added to the pain by dumping you straight from a sauna into a freezing bath. The only gentle treatment found there came after the masseuse stopped pounding, if you were still breathing, when it was time for the famous strawberry facial. Betsy swore on her life the results were guaranteed: instant and unforgettable beauty. I asked if it would be as unforgettable as the bruises on my fanny.

Unfortunately, the comparison test was called off this particular Thursday night. Ms. Busch asked me to stay late and help her clear up some work that had accumulated when she was out with the flu. I didn't have the heart to refuse, though I thought wistfully of the canvas tote bag that I had schlepped along today. Needless to say, Betsy took the news poorly. The receptionist at Mme. Denaud's wasn't thrilled either to have an appointment cancelled at the last minute. The only one who got any joy from my change of plans was Katherine Busch.

"You're an angel," she thanked me. "I hate to ask you to give up an evening, but I really need help."

I heartily agreed. Even without three days' backlog to take care of, Ms. Busch was a busy lady. The number of criminal suits filed, wills drawn, civil cases, property liens, and fore-closures that went through our office was staggering. All the attorneys were kept jumping, but Ms. Busch had to cope with the Rev. Billy Joe Ritchie too.

When he came in earlier that afternoon for his appointment with Ms. Busch (he called her Mrs.), all of us were primed for his visit. Steve Tedesco had run his column on women's rights that morning, using old quotes from Ms. Busch, and the nine o'clock edition was barely out when Ritchie called, irate, disgusted, and eager for a private showdown. I didn't blame him. It was much less embarrassing to be cut down to size in the privacy of an office than on every newsstand in town.

Ritchie came in angry, but after ten minutes alone with Ms. Busch, he burst out of her door with his pitchfork and tail ablaze. Josie turned up the Musak for the benefit of our clients, while I stood at the top of the hallway to bar the view of him shaking his fist at the unmoved Katherine Busch.

"God is not mocked!" he bellowed. "You dare say the Bible is wrong?"

"No, just unverified," was her cool reply. "You have your interpretation, and I have mine. Let's call it a toss-up."

His face was bright red, but when he glanced over and saw me, he lowered his voice. It still wasn't what I would call a moderate pitch. "You are blasphemous," he rumbled majestically. "But remember, 'the wages of sin is death.'" With that, he crammed his Panama hat on his head and stalked down the hall, brushing past me in a pious rage. His exit was spoiled by his having to wait for the elevator. Such an anticlimax to a magnificent performance. He would have done better to use the fire escape.

If that weren't enough for one day, Mannie Blanco had swaggered into the office around four o'clock, his bodyguard muscling along behind him. The contrast was ludicrous. Mannie was barely 5'7" and weighed about 130 pounds, while the blond gorilla looked as if he had spent the last five years swinging from trees. While waiting for Ms. Busch, the firm's most celebrated client had a wink and a joke for everyone in the office. He even stopped by my desk long enough to invite me to come home with him and try out his jacuzzi. As I politely declined, I wondered if Mannie had ever tried that line with his attorney. She'd break his nose.

When Ms. Busch was ready to see him, she buzzed me and

asked for the tape recorder in the conference room. All her sessions with the garrulous Mr. Blanco were recorded for posterity, and, if no one cared, at least it was a convenient way to weed out the irrelevant and get his more pertinent remarks on paper. Barbara used to sit in on the sessions and take it all down in shorthand, but Mannie spent more time ogling her boobs than making sense, so she was replaced by a flat-chested cassette recorder. Barb continued to do all the transcriptions, but when Ms. Busch found out I had been an English major, she assigned me the job of editing Mannie's prose style and putting it into readable copy. Barbara made a few snide comments about favoritism and apple polishing, then settled into her normal mild resentment of me. She had no cause, really. I had made life a lot easier for her by reorganizing office procedures and filling in wherever any of the titty-tats needed help. But I guess virtue was going to be my only reward.

It had been impressed on me that the information on the Blanco tapes was strictly confidential and not to be discussed—in the office or out of it. Actually there was nothing to discuss. The meetings had been pretty thin of content, as he still hadn't revealed a thing of the slightest importance. Today when he left, gorilla in tow, Ms. Busch seemed worried, and I figured he had finally come through with something interesting if troubling.

Apparently so. She went right to Mr. Abbotts's office, where they spent a heated twenty minutes discussing it. In spite of the excellent soundproofing, their raised voices were audible, though I don't think anyone could actually catch the words. Later Maggie told us that Mr. Abbotts had questioned the way Ms. Busch was handling the Blanco case.

I didn't believe that for a second, but Katherine Busch did look unusually tired this evening, almost frazzled. Who wouldn't after Ritchie and Blanco both on the same day? When I suggested we have a cup of coffee before starting work again, she was all for the idea and invited me to put my feet up in her office.

The liberated lady with the oversized glasses on her under-sized nose eased off her shoes and stretched her legs out. "How can you stand sitting behind a desk all day?" she asked me. "Sometimes I think I'm going to scream if I don't get out of here."

"Actually my job is more running than sitting, but I know what you mean. This place can tie you in knots. Have you taken your vacation yet this year?"

One side of her mouth turned down in a funny smile. "Not yet, thanks to Mannie Blanco." She took a sip of coffee and looked over her horn-rims at me. "What do you think of him?"

I answered with all the certainty of a good guess. "He has a Napoleon complex." That drew a real smile from her. "Other than that, he's just a slimy worm who gets his kicks from breaking the law and propositioning secretaries."

"That sounds like the Mannie we know and love," she said. "I'm ready to tear his hair out."

"Mmm. I can always tell that you've had it when the tape clicks off in the middle of a sentence. Are you sorry you took his case?"

She took off her glasses and rubbed her eyes. They looked oddly defenseless when not surrounded by frames. "Not really. It's a challenge. The trouble is that Mannie spends all his energy thinking of angles. He knows just enough law to think he knows it all, and he refuses to take my advice. I'm merely a woman, and he's a big-time crook. Besides, he wanted Phil Abbotts, but was talked into taking me. So he's playing around, hoping I'll get discouraged and drop him back into Phil's lap. I'd like to drop him in the Pacific, to tell the truth. But he's hanging on. And this new garbage he's up to . . ." She shook her head.

I nodded in commiseration and glanced at today's tape

sitting on her desk. "What's his latest demand, serial rights to his autobiography? I know Mr. Abbotts wasn't overjoyed when you told him about it."

"You heard us?"

"Oh, no. I just saw the scowl on Mr. Abbotts's face afterwards." I couldn't very well tell her that the titty-tats were listening through the walls.

"Yes, well, he wasn't pleased. But it's not important." She sighed and laid her head back against the top of the chair. "Thank goodness Howard will be back tonight from his two-week stint in Seattle, not that I'll get much sympathy from him. He didn't want me to take the Blanco case to begin with. If I start crying about Mannie again, all I'll get is a 'I told you so, and why did we have to cancel our vacation when you don't even like what you're doing?' But I do like it, at least, career-wise. It isn't often a woman who's relatively new in the field gets a case like this. It's unusual for a woman, period. I know that's why Mannie is being such an asshole."

A fairly apt description of the man, I concurred. "Just give it to him the way you did the irreverent reverend this afternoon. That perked up my whole day."

She turned her head to me. "Do you know what I said that blew the cover off his bland bigotry? I quoted Ambrose Bierce, for one thing, that old devil's disciple, and I told Ritchie that the only Essential Truth of his religion is 'explaining to Ignorance the nature of the Unknowable.' I thought he was going to hit me."

"He cursed you nicely, though," I offered in compensation.

"Yes. That's what worries me. Not that I may be cast into everlasting hell, but Ritchie has a large pulpit; I don't want him to preach against Phil because of me. Maybe I went too far with him." Her hand reached for the gold silk Givenchy scarf around her throat and loosened the tie.

Rather than add to her woes by confessing I had the same thought, I gave the old pep rally cheer. "Don't look so glum.

Ritchie will talk himself right out of business. The cowgirls with the white hats always win.''

"You're sure about that."

"Absolutely. You're just feeling the effects of a long day and coming back to work too soon. Flu can really knock you out. I think you should have stayed in bed a few more days."

She gave me another funny smile, then sat up and put her glasses back on. "As long as I don't lose my fighting spirit."

I collected the dirty cups and picked up the Blanco cassette from her desk, as she was already starting to go through some papers. At the doorway, I turned. "You are okay, aren't you?"

She lifted a tired face, but the eyes sparkled. "I'm in great shape now. Thanks for the company."

The pile of work on my desk wasn't nearly as inviting as staying to talk to Ms. Busch some more, but I prodded myself onward with the promise that after I did the filing and indexing, I could run over to Barney's for a quick salad before tackling the typewriter and the Xerox machine. Transcribing Mannie Blanco's latest bombshell would be dessert.

An hour later, I was more than ready for bran and alfalfa sprouts, but Ms. Busch buzzed me on the intercom.

"Would you please put a call through for me to my husband's office in Santa Monica? I'm holding on another line and I can't click off."

"Sure thing." How I wished it were. The superefficient Ms. Busch would be surprised to know that after nearly two months in the office, I still didn't completely understand the phone system. It was one of those futuristic models, with buttons all over the place, a separate column for transferring calls, and hookups for a five-way intercom. That didn't include the setup in the conference room. Normally it was Josie's province, and I seldom had to use it. Here was my big chance.

Di-Con's telephone number was indelibly inscribed in my

memory because I called Betsy there so often, but I had to check the revolving card file on Josie's desk for Howard Busch's extension. Number in hand, I was set to go.

The first outside line was already connected to extension 20 on Mrs. Busch's phone. It must have been left open today if she dialed the call herself. Usually, all lines were turned on and off at the switchboard. No problem. I opened a second outside line and made the call to Di-Con. Their operator had just begun ringing Howard Busch's office, when a third light in front of me flashed on.

I wanted to take the chicken's way out and ignore the incoming call, but as long as Howard Busch hadn't answered yet, I might be able to work a bit of legerdemain. Putting the call to Di-Con on hold, I quickly pushed into the third line. It was my seldom-seen son.

"Michael? Good grief. I don't hear from you for two weeks, and you pick this minute to call. Hang on a second, hon."

Putting him on hold, I hooked into line two again, where luckily, Howard Busch's phone was still ringing. Timing perfect so far, I buzzed Ms. Busch and transferred the call to her office on extension 21. Not bad for a novice. There were three outside lines going on the switchboard, and I had handled two of them without blacking out all of Southern California. Hoping my luck held, I got back to Michael.

"Mom, I'm calling from L.A., but I charged it to the house. I found an apartment on Fairfax, right next to a bagel factory. The neighborhood's not so fancy, but the food's great. Can I take it?"

"Yes, I'm feeling fine. So nice of you to ask."

"Sorry," he said impatiently. "So what do you think? The rent's only two hundred dollars a month and it's furnished."

"Did you ask your father? He's—" I was momentarily diverted when one of the lights on the switchboard blinked off. It was Ms. Busch's first call. "Michael, listen to me. Check with your father before you sign any lease."

"I got the okay from him this afternoon. Say, Mom, did you know he tried some pot? It made him sick." Michael laughed.

"Well, when he recovers, ask if he'll pay your rent. As soon as I sell the house, I'll be able to help out too." Feeling magnanimous, I swiveled around in Josie's chair to stare out the window. "Will a hundred dollars a month keep your tab at the bagel factory within bounds?"

"Yeah, thanks. And Mom, when you pack all the stuff in my room, be careful of my records."

"Your records," I said clearly, "will be given to Goodwill in a paper bag unless you come home and pack them yourself. This weekend is a good time to start, in fact. Do you realize the accumulation I have to go through? And that's besides the furniture, the books, the linens, the silver, the—"

"Mom! I can't come home this weekend. Don't you remember? I'm going back-packing with Jerry."

Who says children are a comfort in your old age? I wasn't counting on it. Michael had taken the divorce with uncommon coolness. Or maybe it was such a normal occurrence these days he had no idea how traumatic the experience could be. Even the sale of the family homestead was no cause for a nostalgic tear. Michael's reaction when I told him was the felicitous suggestion that I move into a singles condo. At least he was well adjusted, I consoled myself.

After extracting a promise that he'd be home the following weekend to help me, I hung up and got my purse. It was almost six o'clock and before Ms. Busch could give me another call to make, I walked down the hall to tell her I was leaving for a dinner break. The door of her office was open, and she was sitting at her desk, facing the window.

"Howard, please. Meet me here at eight and we'll go to Antonio's for crab legs. It's not so bad," she said in a beseeching tone. "Afterwards we can go home and make love all night."

She looked up and saw me then, her eyebrows shooting up in inquiry. Embarrassed, I pretended I hadn't heard a thing, but apologized for interrupting her and said I'd be back from Barney's in about a half hour. As I passed the telephone console on my way out, I noticed the red disconnect light flashing from her first call. Reaching down, I flicked it off, leaving only one little beacon glowing. Maybe I'd remember to disconnect the line to extension 20 when I got back. I was a pro at the switchboard now.

What an accomplishment, I thought cynically, riding down on the elevator. At almost two score, I had learned how to push buttons. Katherine Busch was so many light years ahead of me, I'd never catch up. If I had started when she did, I might have a tenured position at U.C.L.A. by now. Eleanor Gordon, gentlewoman and scholar, saying sweetly to her husband, "Not tonight, dear. I have these term papers to grade." If the husband were anything like Howard Busch, he'd answer, "But darling, your poor eyes. Please, let's go to Antonio's for crab legs, and after we make love all night, I'll help you." Now that's what I called a real marital problem. Ms. Busch should only know how lucky she was.

So was I, in some respects. When I arrived at Barney's, it was only full, not packed. Happy hour was just over, but the dinner crowd hadn't come yet. Although Barney's specialized in barbecue and steak, the main attraction was an extra dry martini with two olives. It was recommended with brunch, lunch, dinner, and snacks. The food wasn't so bad either. It wasn't a classy restaurant, the booths decorated in basic black naugahyde and the waiters in white aprons, but it was cheerful, convenient, and had the added inducement that Barney himself would stop by the table for a chat. The rotund little owner had an inexhaustible supply of jokes, and liked to be on a first-name basis with all his regulars.

The hostess found a small table in the corner for me, and though the aroma of barbecue got all my glands racing, I ordered the vegetarian salad. Five more pounds, then I could gorge on ribs . . . maybe even a martini, but with only one olive.

I'd developed a technique for eating out alone. Take a book along. Otherwise, there's nothing to do but stare at the other people in the room and then pretend you aren't, when they catch you at it. The other ploy is trying to act as if you're waiting for Robert Redford to join you, but that's difficult to sustain for thirty minutes.

My latest mystery kept me company, but after three chapters the crowd and the cigarette smoke were thickening to alarming proportions. When the waitress came by for the third time with a coffee refill, it was clearly a hint to get back to work. My supper break had taken nearly forty minutes, though I figured I still would be done and out of the office by the time Howard Busch arrived.

Bookmark in place, I edged through the crowd waiting to be seated and stepped into the cool summer dusk. It was blessedly quiet after the noise inside the restaurant. Except for the cars driving up to Barney's, there wasn't much traffic, though I did have to wait in the middle of the street for a couple of seconds, until the blue Cadillac parked in front of our building pulled away. For a moment I thought it was Mr. Abbotts, but Thursday nights were his weekly commitment to executive fitness. He played racquetball at the Sports and Sorts Health Club. Then I saw a car I did recognize, and almost tripped over the curb trying to avoid it. Dennis Devlin and his flashy yellow Corvette. What a madman. He must have had the accelerator down to the floorboard, and he was driving out of our parking lot, straight for me. I jumped out of the way as he made a ninety-degree turn onto the street, but he never even looked.

Damn that idiot! I glared at the disappearing taillights, and cursed the exhaust fumes shooting in my face. What did he do, leave his raunchy little black book in the office and race back to copy down a particularly juicy number? Grumbling to myself all the way up in the elevator about Dennis Devlin's general imperfections of character, judgment, and sensitivity, I tossed my purse on the desk and marched straight back to the storage room. Remembering Dennis's equally disgusting conduct in here did not improve my mood.

"I'm back, Ms. Busch," I called out. "Have these copies ready in a minute." In keeping with my luck, I discovered that a page was missing, and, after checking my desk, the file, and the pile of papers on top of the copy machine again, I still couldn't find it. "Ms. Busch, do you have page three?" I piped.

When she didn't answer, I stuck my head outside the storage room and saw that her office door was closed. Dashing down the hall, I knocked once before opening it. "Ms. Busch," I took a step in, "do you have . . ."

The words died on my lips. Katherine Busch was lying on the beige carpeting, her legs sprawled apart and her Givenchy scarf tied in a deadly knot around her throat.

Chapter 5

At first nothing penetrated. I stood rooted to the spot in numb disbelief. That couldn't be Katherine Busch lying there. When I left her a little while ago, she was fine.

Not anymore. Coming to my senses with a start, I rushed across the room, only to turn away gagging at the sight. It was grotesque. Her face was contorted beyond all recognition, eyes bulged open, tongue gaping out. I stumbled back to the door with hands pressed against my mouth.

Fighting the nausea gurgling in my throat, I also fought the urge to run into the street screaming. I had to be calm, call the police, the rescue squad, somebody. It was a slim hope, but maybe there was still a chance to save her.

Then again, maybe there wasn't even a chance to save *me*.

I froze into a sickly statue and listened again, praying it was my imagination, my stomach. That couldn't have been the rustle of paper coming from the front of the office. No, not paper anymore; now it was indefinable, a whisper-soft brush of sound, eerie, but no hallucination. Someone was out there.

Please, dear Lord. Not him. I couldn't have been in the office all this time with a murderer. Why hadn't he escaped while I was in back? Huddled in terrified stillness, I gave him a perfect opportunity to leave now. He didn't take it.

The faint sounds of stealthy movement were almost inaudible over the pounding of my heart, but he was coming this way. I couldn't chance a wild dash to the storage room to lock myself in. He'd catch me the second I stepped out into the hall. Looking around frantically for a place to hide in here, I saw just as little hope. The desk was open in the middle and not wide enough on either side to conceal me. File cabinets and cupboards were built-in, bookshelves too narrow to squeeze behind. There was no escape either unless I jumped out of the fourth-story window. The only alternative was to barricade myself. My hand was out to slam the door shut, only I had waited too long. We saw each other at the same time.

"Good evening, Mrs. Gordon. Working late tonight?"

His words held the ring of deadly irony. It was the most frightening thing I'd ever heard. My body seemed frozen in response, until he touched me on the arm.

"No!" I shrieked.

My panicked repulse moved me out of the doorway, leaving Katherine Busch's body in clear view. Mark Devlin looked past me and saw her, but before I could scream again, he shot into the room, wheeling by me as though I didn't exist. I watched until he leaned over and took her hand, then I turned away, covering my mouth again.

"How did this happen?" he rapped out. "Who did it? Answer me! Were you here? Do you know anything about this?"

I could only shake the back of my head at him, but now when he came up behind me, I recognized the muffled sound of the wheelchair. This time, when he touched my arm, no blast of trumpets; I just flinched.

"All right, Mrs. Gordon, calm down," he said in a tightly controlled voice. "Have you called the police yet? No, I didn't think so. Come on, let's get out of here. Can you walk?"

Marginally. I tottered down the hall without collapsing, but once at my desk, I flopped into my chair like an unstuffed rag doll. Sinking into a mindless stupor, I only vaguely listened as Mr. Devlin made his call from the switchboard.

"I can't even guess. Doesn't look like a robbery. What? Hell, I don't know. Seems our office manager just walked in and found her." His voice lowered and I missed the next part. ". . . sure, I'll try. How long will it take your boys to get here? All right. See you in a while."

There was that strange, disembodied sound again. Crazy how it seemed so terrifying before. It was just wheels rubbing on carpet.

"Mrs. Gordon, are you feeling better? The police will be here soon, and they'll have to get a statement from you. Up to answering any questions yet?"

Trying to shake off the lethargy that was putting everything into the background, I felt a spurt of nausea again. Mr. Devlin looked pretty gray himself, but at least he could talk without upchucking. There was every chance that if I did get one lucid word out of my mouth, the contents of my stomach would spill out with it.

I swallowed hard. "Sorry to be such a basket case, Mr. Devlin. I shouldn't have screamed at you . . . but the surprise . . . I thought . . . well, yes . . . I am feeling better now, thank you." That was a lie, but getting the apology out restored some of my composure. "Ms. Busch and I were working late tonight. I left a little after six to take a dinner break at Barney's and came back about forty minutes later." Pressing icy fingers to my middle helped me through the next part. Mr. Devlin was very patient.

"Was anyone here with her when you left?"

"No. She was on the phone with her husband. I waved good-bye."

I didn't mean to sound allegorical, but it silenced both of us. Mr. Devlin went back to his office to make a few more calls, and I blew my nose. It was the last moment of quiet we had. Almost immediately, sirens began blaring.

Three police cars pulled into the parking lot downstairs, followed by a crowd of people who came pouring out of Barney's to see what the excitement was. Two patrolmen set up a blockade at the curb to keep them away; the four others came up here. A half hour later, the office was filled with police photographers, lab technicians scraping the walls for samples, fingerprint crew, and medical investigators. I made myself concentrate on whether or not to call Police Chief Matthew Steunkle by his first name.

We'd met a couple of years ago at a dinner party. My interest in police procedure had drawn a host of stories from him, and we spent the better part of the evening comparing fictional detectives to the real thing. He still looked like a basset hound with a peptic ulcer. Retirement had been on his mind then; now, with his whiter head and sadder eyes, he no doubt felt it to be "a culmination devoutly to be wished."

That brief acquaintance notwithstanding, I felt more secure when Mr. Devlin agreed to stay with me while I gave my statement. A policeman began writing the moment I opened my mouth to answer Chief Steunkle's questions.

He was polite and matter-of-fact, but the whole scene was too intimidating to try for a personal note. As a mystery buff, I should have been prepared for the repetition, the constant checking and reading back of what had been said a minute before. Only this was no straightforward statement of my actions. Matt Steunkle wanted a chronicle of the entire day:

who came to see Ms. Busch, who called, and any unusual occurrences. It was an action-packed tale I recounted.

"You say Reverend Ritchie was angry?" Steunkle asked again.

"Isn't he always? I don't know what went on inside her office, but when he warned her that the 'wages of sin is death,' he was ready to swing at her."

"And Mr. Blanco," he repeated. "That was another heated meeting."

Another sounded as though Ms. Busch did nothing but argue with people all day. I disliked the inference, but was forced to add to it. In my play-by-play coverage of Thursday the eighth of August, I had to report a third altercation. The titty-tats were bound to mention it when they were questioned, but at least I was able to say, with the authority of having discussed it with Ms. Busch, that Mr. Abbotts was angry not with his junior partner, but with her temperamental client. I was discreet about the facts, though it helped that I didn't know much either.

Then came the final tally. With Mr. Devlin staring straight at me, it wasn't easy to inform the police that I had seen his nephew tearing out of here only moments before I found Katherine Busch. I took particular pains to stress that I had only seen Dennis driving off the parking lot, not leaving the building. But where could he have been coming from, a hot and heavy necking session in the back seat of his car? I kept that bit of sarcasm to myself.

Matthew Steunkle went over everything with exasperating thoroughness, but I still couldn't remember if the blue Cadillac on the corner were a two door or four, if the driver were male or female. As for the license plate, that was definitely a lost cause. Finally I reminded him that Howard Busch was due shortly, and he sent a patrolman downstairs to watch for him, while I got to sign my statement. As the steno typed in my vital statistics, Chief Steunkle and Mr. Devlin began to murmur quietly.

The Chief scratched his grizzled head. "Gotta wait for the lab report. She," the hand stopped scratching long enough to point in my direction, "puts the time between six and close to seven. No problem there, but until we get some prints, you know how it stands. Nothing's missing from what you can tell. Right? The safe wasn't touched. Maybe she interrupted the guy." He grimaced as he found a particularly itchy spot. "With that restaurant across the street, I'll get a hundred eyewitness reports. But you know what really . . ." He stopped scratching as the typewriter stopped clacking, then looked over and noticed the rapt expression on my face. "You all done now, Mrs. Gordon?"

I glanced at Mr. Devlin, figured I was, and bolted for my desk. Pulling the tote bag from the bottom drawer, I began stuffing my junk inside. The unused towel and smock were still folded with pristine neatness, but I slopped everything else on top of them, sunglasses, loose change, lipstick, blusher, extra Tampax, my purse too. As I was about to charge out of the office, a cool voice spoke behind me.

"Sit down a minute, Mrs. Gordon. Don't rush away just yet. I want to—" Mark Devlin broke off impatiently as someone called out to him. "Wait a minute. I'll be right back."

This was it. The axe falleth. I was hoping to get out of here before Mr. Devlin could fire me in front of half the city police department. I was feeling guilty enough without the shame of public dismissal heaped on my deserving head. Getting a reference after that would be brutal.

I hadn't wanted to drag Mr. Abbotts's name into it, but his disagreement with Ms. Busch would have come out anyway, and the blue Cadillac was something I had to mention. Regretfully, he had one fitting the description exactly: same color, same year, same white vinyl roof. An extenuating detail, aside from the fact that I couldn't make a positive identification, was that Mr. Abbotts never parked his expensive beauty on the street. He had reserved space number one to call his own.

Which brought me to Dennis. There were a hundred legitimate reasons for his being here at six forty-five: his car broke down, he was waiting for Godot, he came back to use the bathroom. I really didn't suspect him of murder, not lazy, bumptious Dennis Devlin. If he had been in the office, it was more likely that he accidentally stumbled over Ms. Busch's body, then ran away in terror. That would be in character.

As for my petrified reaction to Mark Devlin; the less said the better. I had behaved like a ninny, even allowing for intestinal problems and mental stress. It was the unnatural sound of the wheelchair that sent me over the edge. On reflection, I realized that a man in a sitting position would have a hard time overpowering anyone, much less a desperate woman fighting for her life. It was a relief that I didn't have to test that theory for myself, but Mr. Devlin had an alibi anyway. He said he was at his health club at the time of the murder. When I heard him, he had just come back to the office to go over some work for a court case in the morning. That explained the shuffle of paper I heard too. It was Sol Benjamin's deposition falling on the floor.

Explaining all of the above wouldn't win me my job back, but I'd have one consolation along with an unemployment check every week: the police weren't going to make an arrest based on my testimony. They'd check out everyone in the immediate world before zeroing in. That didn't just include people working here, but clients, ex-clients, every homicidal maniac who ever passed through town. Then there was the element who hated Katherine Busch on principle. They considered her cases, and her causes, to be antifamily, anti-American, and certainly anti-God. One of those pious souls might have decided to do the Lord's work for Him, and eliminate the libber. It made as much sense as the freaks who cry "guns don't kill, people do," then threaten to shoot if you try to take away their Saturday night specials.

Reverend Ritchie bordered on the lunatic fringe, if he hadn't already passed into it. Bible clutched in hand, he promised death to Katherine Busch with every hate-filled word out of his mouth. My fondest wish for him was that when he finally met his Maker, She be black, Jewish, and a charter member of NOW.

That applied to Mannie Blanco too. Ms. Busch said he was giving her a hard time because he resented taking legal advice from a woman. Today she'd finally counterattacked. I could understand Mannie's feeling chagrined at being put in his place, but was male chauvinism a reasonable motive for murder? Why not? It's part of the employee incentive plan on the corporate level. Only there, the killer is a whisper that the lady's best work is done on her back.

This was ridiculous. Why was I sitting here making empty speculations when I wanted to go home? If Mr. Devlin didn't get his butt out here and fire me already, I was leaving.

Then the elevator doors opened and Howard Busch stepped out. A young policewoman was holding his arm, but he hardly noticed she was there.

"There has to be some mistake. I'm supposed to be meeting my wife now. Where is she? Why can't you let me see her?"

"I'm very sorry, sir. If you'll sit down here, I'll get Chief Steunkle. He can explain everything."

The slightly built policewoman tried to equal in dignity the authority of her uniform, but Howard Busch kept advancing with her latched to his coat sleeve. "There must be somebody here I can see. Who's in charge?" Then he spotted me. "Mrs. Gordon . . . Ellie. What in the hell is going on?" He walked over with the officer still holding his arm. "They told me downstairs there's been a murder in here. I asked where Kathy is, and they said to talk to Chief Steunkle. Why can't I get a straight answer?''

The policewoman darted a glance down the hall, then looked at me for help. I knew what she meant. The medical investigator wasn't finished in Katherine Busch's office, and the husband had to be kept out.

''Mr. Busch, why don't you sit with me?'' I suggested. ''Chief Steunkle should be here in a minute to explain.''

But Howard needed no explanation now. ''Kathy's dead, isn't she? That's what no one wants to tell me.'' When I nodded my head, unable to find the right words, he sank into the chair, his eyes filling with tears. ''I should have guessed. I suppose I just didn't want to.'' Then he buried his face in his hands and began to shake with low, racking sobs.

It was a horrible sound, ugly, heartbreaking. The police-woman walked away and left me alone with him, but I didn't know what to say. My very presence seemed an intrusion. ''Would you like to be by yourself for a while?'' I asked gently.

He pulled himself together with an effort. ''No, please. I'll be all right.'' He blew his nose a couple of times then glanced around the room with red-rimmed eyes. His hands still shaking, he tried to smooth his hair, but the gesture seemed more a sign of his confusion. ''Can you tell me what happened? Did someone break in and...'' He stopped and cleared his throat. ''I presume the police called you down here for questioning.''

Poor man. He was making such a valiant attempt to come to grips with this nightmare. ''They didn't have to call me. I've been here the whole time...no, part of the time,'' I corrected, wishing Mark Devlin had given me my walking papers fifteen minutes ago. Now Howard wanted me to repeat everything I knew, except the version I gave him was edited slightly.

"So you found her." There was a catch in his voice. "And that's when Mark came in? Damn! Damn!" He smashed his fist into his hand. "Why did I wait so long? If only I'd gotten here sooner."

"Howard, don't." There was no comforting him, really. The shock was still too fresh, but I didn't want him to fall apart again. "Listen to me, you couldn't have arrived any sooner. I told that to Mr. Devlin when he tried to reach you at the plant. It was almost six when I placed the call to you from here. Even if you weren't due in until eight, you'd still have been on the freeway when it hap—"

"You tried to call me at Di-Con?" He was confused.

"No, Mr. Devlin tried," I explained again. "I'm the one who *did* call you. Remember, when you spoke to your wife earlier? That's what I'm saying, Howard. It was impossible for you to get here on time. Don't torment yourself with useless regrets."

Thankfully, Chief Steunkle made his belated appearance then, and Howard was ushered into Mr. Devlin's office. My heart ached for Katherine Busch's husband, but I had reached the end of my endurance. When Mr. Devlin wheeled over, I was beyond arguing with him. He didn't seem to be in the mood himself.

"I'm sorry to keep you waiting this long. Crap, it's been a—" He broke off and rubbed his bloodshot eyes. "Do you mind waiting a few more minutes? I know you could have been home a half hour ago, but I don't think you should be driving. How's the stomach? Look, the police won't be much longer. Will you wait for me?"

Mr. Devlin looked as though he'd been through a wringer and sounded worse, but he didn't appear to be a man bent on firing his office manager. I knew it a second later when the ambulance crew came through with Katherine Busch's draped body on a stretcher. He turned me around so my back was to the grim procession, while I gripped his hand for support. Afterwards, I saw my nail marks on his skin.

"Holding up?" he asked quietly.

I said I could hold up until he was ready to leave.

Chapter 6

Gulping a cup of instant coffee while I waited for Betsy to arrive, I scanned the morning paper. The *Chronicle* gave Katherine Busch's murder front page coverage, and the story had a Steve Tedesco by-line. Referring to his secret source, Steve speculated that her death may have been tied into the Blanco case. Without quite calling it a gangland killing, he ran around the issue, stopping short of suggesting why or how.

Betsy honked the horn and I dashed outside. She had offered to take me to work when I called her last night, the minute Mr. Devlin brought me home. I knew she must have been watching the on-the-scene television coverage, and I wanted to let her know I was still alive. We talked until past one A.M., but Betsy was reserving her judgment. The only comment she made was that after giving a statement implicating two members of the law firm and one of their clients, I was lucky Mr. Devlin dropped me off at the front door instead of the nearest ditch.

I meant to thank him again for his consideration the moment I got to the office, but when Betsy picked me up it was already eight-thirty; and when she let me off on Wilshire Lane, it took another ten minutes to elbow my way through the crowd on the parking lot. Some were there for a story— some just carrying signs. They ranged from *For God We Must* to *Nuke the Nukes*. The police officer at the door of the lobby assured me he'd have them all cleared away shortly.

As for my thanking Mr. Devlin right away, I found him already tied up on the phone, as were Josie, Maggie, and Barbara. The place was sheer chaos. Flexing my managerial muscles, I divided up the duties, leaving Josie at the switchboard and sending the others to cancel appointments for the day, court appearances, and the like. The office was officially closed, though at Mr. Devlin's request I had called everyone early this morning and asked them to put in a few hours. Normally Nancy Weaver didn't even come in on Friday, but she readily agreed to lend a hand today. Between the two of us, we accepted all the calls from Ms. Busch's clients, which ran the gamut from grief and shock to demanding an instant answer about their impending civil suits, divorces, judgments, and arraignments. I made a lot of soothing noises that seemed to work, until Mannie Blanco called.

He didn't want to be shuffled off on a secretary, he said. Give him the boss. Mr. Abbotts accepted his first two calls, but on the third I tried to take over again. Mannie balked vociferously, and as it turned out, he spoke to Mr. Abbotts a total of six times that day, despite my running interference. The only conclusion I could draw was that Mannie needed immediate help. His immunity trade wasn't such a pressing matter; he had already wasted three months. However, it was only a matter of hours since he made a statement to the police about Katherine Busch's death. As he was temporarily unrepresented, he could have spoken without the advice of counsel and now regretted the oversight.

No one was operating at peak performance. The murder had not only thrown everything into confusion, it had created a large black hole. In between their crying jags, the titty-tats tried to fill it.

Right before noon, I found them huddled around the coffee machine, with Andy and David to lend their judicial knowledge, discussing the murder. As one, the secretaries informed me that from now on, there would be no more overtime unless the firm hired a security guard to patrol the lobby downstairs and escort them to and from their cars. I asked what had been preventing them from working overtime before, but merely earned a dirty look from Barbara for my jab.

Josie was on her own wavelength. "The doors downstairs are always unlocked when somebody is still in the office. I think some freak wandered in last night, high on angel dust, and was making off with one of the IBM Selectrics when Ms. Busch tried to stop him. He strangled her, then beat it, scared out of his wits."

Fingering a pimple on his chin, David poked scornful holes in that theory. "No freak went out of his way to take that elevator ride up here, unless he was flying higher than four floors already. But if he did kill Ms. Busch because she tried to stop him, why didn't he tuck a typewriter under his arm on the way out. Besides, she wouldn't have risked her neck fighting some thug when all this stuff is insured anyway."

"Another thing," Andy reminded them, "there were no signs of a struggle out here, just in Ms. Busch's office. Seems to me she could have known the guy and invited him in herself."

The two future Supreme Court justices nodded wisely at each other then delivered the unanimous decision that whoever murdered Katherine Busch had simply walked into her office, strangled her, then calmly closed the door and strolled off.

"We know that, you duds," Maggie said. "The question is who, not how. And Ms. Busch didn't have to know the guy. He could have come in asking for legal help. I say it was the mob. Did you read Steve Tedesco's article this morning?"

"The mob wouldn't kill Ms. Busch," Barbara contradicted. "If they were worried, they would have gone after Mannie-baby. But why even do that? His deal is a secret. The mob doesn't know he's blowing the whistle on them."

"Don't be stupid," Maggie charged. "Do you really think that kind of thing can be kept a secret? The underworld has spies everywhere, even in the D.A.'s office. What about here? Maybe one of us let something slip to a friend."

David broke into the debate. "You're all forgetting the most obvious suspect—Ritchie. Could be he decided to take retribution out of God's hands and into his own."

Barbara lit a cigarette and blew the smoke out in a perfect ring. "I know somebody a lot more obvious than that." She smiled at their ignorance. "Mr. Mannie Blanco. Remember what Ms. Busch was like after he left? Now, that was one uncool lady."

"Yes, but she told Mr. Abbotts all about it; and if Mannie threatened to kill her, Mr. Abbotts would have said so." Maggie poured herself another cup of tea. "Anyway, why would he want to kill his lawyer?"

"Because she was a woman."

All eyes turned to Josie, who preened with the unaccustomed pride of having said something noteworthy. As the youngest and by far the giddiest of all of them, she had pointed out an issue they overlooked. Barbara was the first to put her in her place.

"We understand that, my child. A lot of people didn't approve of the great liberated Katherine Busch. She was a forceful woman who stepped on quite a few sets of toes."

Josie retaliated. "Your toes, you mean. Ms. Busch was okay until we got an office manager, then she wasn't so wonderful anymore. You're just sore because she liked Ellie better than you."

"Shades of the Smothers Brothers," David murmured.

"It's true," Josie said in hot attack. "Barb thinks *she* should be the big shot around here. Well, let me tell you something, Madame Hot Pants, when Katherine Busch turned over most of her work to Ellie, it could only mean that you weren't good enough."

"What's that have to do with her being killed?" Maggie stepped into the direct line of fire. "Barb didn't strangle Ms. Busch because Ellie took over some transcribing. Withdraw your poisoned darts, girls, and stick to the issue. Josie made a good point. Maybe it was a women's lib murder. Feminism Invites Fanaticism. So far we've got Ritchie, Mannie the madcap misogynist—"

"And Dennis Devlin." Andy leaned his six-foot frame against the wall, arms folded across his broad chest. "That's a classic example of male jealousy over female supremacy."

"Because she was a partner and he wasn't?" David took instant exception. "You're nuts. She was older and more experienced than Dennis. He understood that."

"Then why was he always making snide remarks about the token woman? You don't think he resented her?"

David gave his friend a scowl of disgust. "I think *you* resent Dennis. He got his L.L.B. along with a built-in practice, and you're going to be a one-shingle man."

"Only because my name isn't Devlin."

Before the Supreme Court could lose two hot prospects, I broke it up. "Enough, already. Josie, better get back to the switchboard. Barb, this is for Mr. Abbotts, and he wants it in triplicate. My future honorables," I said to David and Andy, "we appreciate that you cut class to come in today, so make the sacrifice count and go do something about that preliminary hearing on Wednesday."

Barbara made a face. "Simon Legree is cracking her whip again. Jump, everybody!"

So the day wore on . . . well past the few hours I'd expected. Mr. Abbotts came back from a meeting with the D.A. and asked for the Blanco case files. A little later, he buzzed me for the tape of yesterday's meeting. I had to report, as with so much other unfinished work, that it hadn't been transcribed yet.

"I didn't think it had." His voice crackled across the intercom. "Just get it for me."

I did everything in my power to obey, but the tape had been swallowed up in the chaos created by last night. It wasn't in my desk, nor in the file cabinet, and, after a brief search of corners and trashcans, it failed to make even a belated appearance. I went to Mr. Abbotts with the sorry news.

Ten minutes later a very unhappy office manager was walking out of his private sanctum, with her magic marker drooping between her work schedules. Mr. Abbotts wasn't precisely angry at me, especially as both of us agreed that the tape could be locked inside Ms. Busch's office, which was off-limits until the police unsealed the door. But I insisted that I had carried it out of there and put it on my desk. Neither one of us wanted to speculate on the possibility of someone swiping it from my box, though the police may have taken it as evidence. That was our best hope.

Driven by guilt, I organized a full-scale search party and forced an entire staff of professional office workers to get down on their hands and knees and sniff around on the floor like a pack of bloodhounds. The boys moved the copy machines in the storage room, while the titty-tats took out all the drawers in the file cabinets. Nancy Weaver scouted the lounge, while I emptied the trashcans. After an hour of this, the total receipts were plenty of dust and some loose change. I made a mental note to speak to the janitorial service.

The pinnacle of this inauspicious day came as everyone

was about to leave. A police officer showed up at two-thirty to escort the staff, one by one, down to headquarters for questioning.

Barbara went first, breezy and confident. On her dramatic return, she announced to the assembled staff that they could expect a third degree.

Josie's bottom lip began to tremble. "What did they ask you?"

"Not *they*. Chief Steunkle did all the asking. Where was I, who was I with, what time did I scratch my nose, how did I get along with the deceased, what was the general feeling about her in the office?"

"He asked you about us?" Maggie queried.

Barbara directed a meaningful glance around at everyone.

"Don't worry. I said we all loved her and couldn't imagine who would do such a horrible thing."

Of course, none of the titty-tats needed to worry. The inexhaustible trio had perfect alibis. Josie had spent the evening at the Rip Roarin' Round-Up, a western music stomping grounds, where she ate, drank, danced, and bucked the bull until midnight. She had a whole posse willing to swear on their ten-gallon hats to that. Maggie merely smiled secretly and said she had a date, but "he's married." I imagine the police were able to get more details than we did. And the inventive Barbara Beauchamp spent last night with her ex-husband, *à deux* and by candlelight, toasting the anniversary of their divorce. A rather inappropriate celebration, but no more incongruous than congratulating a loser for coming in last place. The idea is to be positive these days.

Andy and David were also quickly eliminated as suspects. They had left the office at four to go to class. The university was an hour away in rush-hour traffic, so they would have needed a helicopter to get back in time to do the dirty deed.

Gray-haired Nancy Weaver had the most prosaic alibi: she was home, cooking dinner for her gray-haired husband.

After listening to these tales, I felt as well informed as the police, and certain that no one on the staff had anything to do with the crime. Of course, the big bosses didn't come share their stories over coffee. I found out about Dennis only because it involved me.

Shortly before we were ready to lock up and get the hell out of the office, Chief Steunkle called to inform me that I had to answer a few more questions. He was on his way over, would I please wait? By the time he arrived, the others had gone, except for Dennis, who was all the way down the hall in his office. I was sitting at my desk ready to rehash all the alibis with him and more than willing to proffer my personal theories. It was somewhat of a letdown when Matt Steunkle sank his weary bones into Maggie's chair and asked me why I failed to mention seeing Dennis at Barney's last night.

According to the gentleman in question, he had meandered across the street about five-thirty for happy hour, and was in clear view when I walked in half an hour later. He even pinpointed the corner table where I sat, though he was on the other side of the room. After some cheerful imbibing, Dennis and friend left about six forty, passing right by me. Supposedly, I lifted my head and looked directly at them, but when Dennis waved, I ignored him and went right back to my book.

"He's sure it was me?" I asked ungrammatically. "Well . . . there's not much I can say, except that I didn't see him. As Dennis told you, I was reading. You know what it's like when you're engrossed in a book. It wouldn't surprise me if I left the restaurant without paying my bill."

"Nope. The time on your ticket is stamped six fifty-two on the register. You gave the cashier a ten-dollar bill, and she gave you four dollars and twenty-one cents change."

"Oh." The twenty-one cents made it sound so significant, as though one penny more and he'd have to call in the FBI. "Is that my alibi?"

"Partly. Other people saw you too, but right now it's Dennis's alibi I'm trying to check."

"Hey, Barney's was dark and noisy and crowded. So I didn't notice Dennis. Are you going to cite me for failure to wave?"

He sank several of his double chins onto his chest. "No, you're okay. It's Dennis who's in a corner. He was depending on you to corroborate his story. Nobody else knows exactly when he arrived or how late he left."

"That's impossible. What about the waitress, Barney himself, or the girl friend? Surely they weren't all reading."

A smile added one more chin to his collection, and he looked more like a basset hound than ever. "What was the book?"

"The Corpse on the Dike. A Dutch mystery," I explained, knowing full well he was interested despite the amusement on his face.

"Police procedural or thriller?"

"The kind you like, cops with souls."

He got to his feet. "That's it. No more questions."

"Wait a minute," I protested. "What about Dennis? Is he in trouble now?"

"Uh-uh. You would have been the easiest solution, but we'll turn up something."

"What about the cash register? Shouldn't the time be stamped on Dennis's bill too? I'm sure Barney keeps his receipts at least a day. If not, just go through the trash until you find one that says, scotch and water on the..." I slumped back. "Maybe he ordered a Singapore Sling with nuts on top. How did you know which check was mine?" I peered up at him.

"The waitresses always write the table number on food orders, so they know where to deliver them. Bar customers are easier to serve, and pay cash on the line. The girls make change right there. When the place is crowded, it can take a half hour before a waitress gets to the register, then she'll turn in a pile of receipts. The time on Dennis's paid bill won't mean anything.'' He walked to the elevator. ''As for the girl with him . . .'' He shrugged and pushed the down button. ''She was a pickup. Dennis doesn't know her last name.''

''Wait,'' I called as he stepped inside. ''What if nobody can prove Dennis's alibi? Does that mean he could be arrested because I was paying more attention to a fictional murder than a real one?''

''Don't worry about it.'' Steunkle smiled. ''As long as *I* don't make that mistake.''

The doors closed on that unbeatable finish. Cute, I thought to myself. Very cute. I should have called him Mattie-baby.

After a last-minute check that the office was ready to close up for the weekend—automatic light switches set, burglar alarm key in place, air conditioner off and telephone answering service on—I made a detour on the way to the elevator.

''Excuse me, Mr. Devlin. Are you busy?''

Dennis was in his shirtsleeves, tie loosened, sitting behind a desk littered with papers. ''What is it?'' he said, looking up.

For the first time I noticed a resemblance to his uncle, the same green eyes, the curve of his jaw, even the untidy look of being overworked. I apologized for seeming rude last night, but Dennis wasn't so much concerned with my manners as my memory. I explained that I hadn't forgotten his presence at Barney's; I never saw him to begin with. Dennis only grunted, decided against pursuing the issue, and went back to his work.

Naturally, he wasn't especially pleased that I had placed him at the scene of a murder, then left him dangling. But someone was bound to rescue him soon. Barney's was full of people last evening. How unfair could life be that not one of them noticed Dennis Devlin all decked out in a three-hundred-dollar suit with a fancy pickup on his arm. You'd think someone would have noticed the girl.

There were no new developments in the murder case over the weekend, at least not any reported in the papers, but Katherine Busch's funeral on Monday morning brought the wolfpacks out again. The chapel at the mortuary was filled to capacity. I shouldn't have been so cynical, but half the mourners were merely spectators who cried on cue when the lugubrious soprano burst into "Abide with Me," and the minute we stepped outside, flashbulbs shot off in our faces. It was a public demonstration of bad taste, not a funeral. I only hoped the family got some comfort from it.

To avoid the crowds streaming down the walkways, I took a shortcut across the grass and was almost to the parking lot, when Steve Tedesco sprang out from behind a bush.

"Ellie, wait. I saw you inside before, but I couldn't get near. How are you holding up after the shock of finding the body?"

"I'm doing fine, thanks, Steve, but that question sounds suspiciously like a lead-in. Have you got a tape recorder in your pocket?"

He held up his hands to prove innocence, then fell into stride next to me. "I keep all the facts in my head, a particular talent of my own. So tell me, how did you manage to keep your cool and be a heroine? Did you scream, faint, do any of those un-Ellie-like things first, or just go right into action?"

"As long as you're asking unpardonable questions," I snapped, "why don't you get Howard Busch's opinion on random violence in our fair city? Call your photographer so he can take some candid shots of the grieving widower. That ought to satisfy your morbid curiosity."

"Hey, what's biting you? Katherine Busch wasn't your sister. I'm sorry she'd dead, but news is news and it's my job to report it. You aren't going to stop office managing because she's not around anymore. In fact, that's the angle I want. The real human interest bit: how a woman employee felt about the wonderful Katherine Busch. Did she admire her, identify with her? What valuable lessons were learned?''

We stopped at my car when a breeze started to blow, scurrying bits of leaves and paper in the air and pushing Steve's cowlick straight up on his head.

"You look funny," I said, unlocking the door.

"Okay. You write the story. I'll pay you a hundred and fifty bucks for a two-thousand-word piece and a photograph of you looking sad and beautiful in front of the office. Right under a palm tree. The L.A. *Times* might even be willing to pay for a firsthand account.''

"*Chutzpah* should be your middle name. I'm not writing anything for anybody," I said in irritation. "Damn, where did I put my scarf?"

The ever-persistent Steve still wasn't giving up. "All right. Just give me a quote for today's paper. No story, just a line or two.''

My purse dropped onto the seat, spilling over upside down while I tried to disentangle my net scarf from the key ring. "Steve," I grated out, "leave me alone already. Go interview Mr. Abbotts.''

He sidled up to the car with a disgustingly vulgar smirk on his face, flicked an imaginary cigar while his eyebrows shot up and down, and in a damned good Groucho Marx voice said, "Would two hundred dollars change your mind, sweetheart?''

Steve wasn't talking about newspaper articles anymore, but when I turned around to give him a sharp no, there was Dennis Devlin standing right behind him.

"Good-bye, Steve," I said, looking at Dennis.

Steve glanced over his shoulder, grinned evilly, did a few more eyebrow gyrations, then walked away, still flicking his cigar. Dennis and I both stared after him a minute, a baggy little guy dropping invisible ashes on the parking lot.

I finally shook my head clear of Steve's nonsense and got back to Dennis. "Yes, Mr. Devlin. How are you doing?"

There was really no need to ask. Dennis was dressed immaculately in a lightweight gray suit, white shirt, and sober tie, but his face wore an expression my grandmother used to call *farplundgit*.

"Mrs. Gordon . . . Ellie . . ." He cleared his throat then started over. "About my alibi . . ."

"It's still up in the air? Well, don't worry too much. Barney's was a regular convention of non-abstainers. If you'll just hold tight, the police will find someone who saw you. They might be able to locate that girl—"

"Shirley," he filled in. "But I didn't catch her last name, so I don't know where to begin looking for her." He cleared his throat again and fixed his eyes on my left cheek. "In the meantime, I was wondering . . . would you tell Chief Steunkle that you really did see me there?" He hurried on before I could answer, this time staring directly into my eyes. "Look, Mrs. Gordon, I know you don't like me, and I don't blame you. We got off on the wrong foot because I behaved like a jerk, and if my apology wasn't enough at the time, I'm extending it ten times over. But please, let's end the grudge right here. I need your help. We both know you saw me at Barney's the other night. Just tell the police that. I could wait around for months before somebody else says so. Play fair, will you?"

If Dennis hadn't looked so genuinely sincere, I might have slugged him with my purse. But this was no act. He honestly thought I was withholding the truth. "Mr. Devlin," my tone was deliberate, "I would never put you in a position like this because of a meaningless disagreement. If I despised you, I wouldn't do it. But I don't despise you. I don't even dislike you. So when I claim I did not notice your presence at

Barney's, it means unequivocally and concisely that I did not."

Amazingly, even after that speech, Dennis still didn't believe me. Distrust flashed in his eyes, spread across his face, then spewed out with his words. "So you're going to stick to your story."

That about used up the last of my patience, a large portion of it already expended on Steve Tedesco. "It is not a story," I said, turning my back on him and climbing into the car. "It is the unvarnished truth. Now, would you kindly take your hand off the door?" He pulled it away as I started the motor. "And a good day to you, too, Mr. Devlin."

Chapter 7

The "women's lib" murder disappeared from TV and news-papers one day after the funeral, superseded by more recent atrocities. But while the world went on wagging, at the office it was an uphill struggle to function with two and a half attorneys and enough clients for twice that many. Mark Devlin counted for one and a half, but Dennis and Mr. Abbotts hardly made up a single lawyer between them. Dennis had always been a weak link, and Mr. Abbotts was running for Congress. Never mind that the primary was nine months away; he was already spending time in smoke-filled rooms talking to the power brokers, rounding up support from precinct chairmen, and, while he was at it, rounding up the cash it takes to run a campaign.

At the same time, the firm wanted to keep all of Ms. Busch's clients, which meant keeping up her good work. No problem; it would just take a little longer. Hampering our efforts was the fact that the police had sealed up Katherine Busch's office until all the lab results were back. And behind those locked doors were most of her clients' files. Since the Blanco tape had never shown up, we logically assumed it was in her safe with everything else we needed. In the meantime, schedules were juggled, excuses made for late appointments, and sweet apologies given to complainers who thought, with some justice, that they were being put off. A certain amount of relief pervaded the office when Mr. Abbotts's wife Marjorie started coming in a few hours a day to help, although her presence was a mixed blessing. I knew her from old, so it was no surprise when she sailed in that first afternoon, manicured, pedicured, dressed for a garden party but geared for combat. The titty-tats were no strangers to Marjorie's formidable personality either. The woman looked like the San Francisco socialite she was, but acted like a master sergeant.

No one ever could claim that Marjorie Abbotts wasn't in her husband's camp one hundred percent. All the energy she usually devoted to his campaign was now harnessed for office work, so when she offered to do any job that needed doing, I set her at it. Marjorie manned the switchboard, ran the copy machines for hours at a time, trotted down to the Court House, typed depositions, and through it all gave free advice on how we could improve our efficiency.

In the midst of all the hassles, there was a bright spot in my week. Michael called Tuesday night when he returned from his back-packing trip, stunned to discover that while he was gone his mother had stumbled over a dead body.

"Ma, are you okay? Jeez, I couldn't believe it when one of the guys gave me a four-day-old L.A. paper and asked if Ms. Eleanor Gordon is my mother."

I gave him the story, minimizing my involvement and assuring him I had nothing to fear from the murderer. It had been strictly an attack on Katherine Busch herself, for whatever reason. Michael offered to come home tomorrow so I'd have a strong male shoulder to lean on, but I told him to save his muscles for the weekend when he could put them to use moving boxes. With the house on the market and a couple of nibbles on the line already, we had to decide what, if anything, should be salvaged from the old homestead. Michael agreed to do all the heavy work while I filled him in on the details of my brush with murder most foul. It was a merger of filial affection, duty, and curiosity, plus a touching protectiveness. That was a new note.

An old one popped up that week too. But instead of contacting me at home, Daniel Gordon called the office on Thursday afternoon, while I was in the middle of indexing a file for Mr. Devlin.

"Ellie," he shot out in his staccato voice, "what's happening there? Why haven't you called?"

"Nothing is happening so why should I call?"

"Don't play games. How do you think I felt when I saw my wife's name in the newspaper, involved in a murder, yet?" I could almost see him pulling on his collar.

"It's ex-wife, Dan."

"What's that got to do with it? Would it have cost you to pick up the phone and set my mind at rest?"

Dan was a master at guilt trips, but this time I held my tongue. He wasn't expecting an answer anyway.

"Listen to me," he rattled. "I don't like that place. Quit. Get another job. I want you out of there."

"What do you mean, *you* want? My life doesn't concern you."

"Well it ought to concern *you*. There's a murderer loose in that office. Anyone with an ounce of brains would get the hell out. What is it?" he demanded. "Money? You need money? I'll send you money."

"Stop it, Dan," I hissed into the phone, catching a curious glance from Barbara. "This is a reputable law firm. I don't know what you read in the paper, but I'm in no danger. You're being ridiculous."

"Yeah? Then how come your reputable law firm is playing around with Mannie Blanco? And don't tell me he's just a client. I wasn't born yesterday. You haven't been out in the world enough to know what's what. But don't worry about it. You want to be a secretary? I'll call Harry Rosenblum. He's looking for a girl to answer the phone in his new showroom. The place is only a few blocks from here, so I can keep an eye on you. What else are you doing?" He paused, not receiving the silent message I was sending over the wires. "Oh, yeah. Mike says you signed a contract with Rickard Realty. No second mortgages, Ellie. I don't want to pay somebody for buying my own house."

"The house is mine," I said quietly. "It was part of the divorce settlement."

"This is stupid, Ellie, not talking to you for months at a time. I only live forty miles away. It's not like another planet. You ought to call me, ask when you need advice. I don't mind."

My hand was shaking so, I could barely hold the receiver, but the tone of my voice was a cool twenty-seven degrees below. "I'll make a deal with you, Dan. You tell Harry Rosenblum to find someone else to answer his phone, and I won't blame you if I get murdered. Fair enough? Just go take a valium, and if business is slow, slip out to the lot and have a quickie with your secretary in the back seat of a Chevy. Put me out of your mind completely. I insist. In fact, I give you an unconditional mandate never to think of me again."

"That's the thanks I get for trying to help?" The injury in his tones could have moved three mountains. It didn't last very long, though. Dan never could sustain dramatic impact. "I don't know why I bothered," he snapped. "You don't even appreciate it."

"Funny, I just had the same thought."

"Still a first-class bitch, aren't you?"

"Maybe. But I'm not domesticated anymore. Good-bye, Dan. Have a nice life without me."

Out of the corner of her eye, Barbara watched as I hung up the phone, made a face, then gathered together the file for Mr. Devlin. Not until I actually set it on his desk did I realize it wasn't completed yet.

"Sorry. I'm not usually this scatterbrained."

His dark face held a combination of concern and amusement as I retrieved the file but then just stood there looking at him.

"Anything wrong?" he asked.

"Well . . . no, to be truthful. Not anymore. I may have just exorcised a ghost." I gave him a chagrined smile. "Didn't mean to do it on company time."

"No problem." He reached over and took the folder out of my hand and set it on his desk. "It's too late in the day to fool with Grant *vs* Hemmingway. You can finish tomorrow. Don't worry," he teased. "I'll try to find it in my heart to forgive you, as long as I'm not one of your ghosts."

I wanted to hug that hunk of man, sitting in a wheelchair and watching upright humans trip over their own feet. It could have afforded him cynical amusement to see how people who have no physical limitations can't cope with emotional knots, but Mark Devlin was a saint who forgave people their trespasses. He did it every day, and no one ever noticed.

"Mr. Devlin, I think you are really terrific. That's permitted on company time, isn't it?"

"It should be a requirement." His admiring glance also flashed approval at my choice of a slim A-line dress with a cutaway collar. "Are you busy after work?" he asked. "Your excellent taste in lawyers deserves a drink at the very least."

"That sounds wonderful." I accepted promptly.

"Better still, let me take you to dinner. I've always been curious about exorcisms. You can tell me all about it."

Boy, did he let himself in for something. Half an hour later, at La Belle Suisse, one of Casa Grande's more exclusive restaurants, we had progressed to the intimacy of Mark and Ellie, and I was still explaining.

"It was so hard to break free of the old boundaries. Dan's attitude really scares me. I'm still more of a Jewish housewife than an office manager, and it wouldn't be difficult to fall back on a comfortable cushion because my chair at work isn't tufted. Sure, smile away, Irish overlord. You think it's easy to be liberated?"

"Not at all." He chuckled. "I've always wondered why no one appreciates the merits of a benevolent dictator. No, I'm just teasing. But it's not a threat to life, liberty, and the pursuit of independence to have someone worry about you. Liberation doesn't mean being separated from the human race."

"Of course not. I just want to be separated from the way I was before. There's a heck of a difference between tottering around on high heels and stomping across the mud in combat boots. Dan doesn't think I can do it, not that he'd come rushing back to take care of me if I took a spill, but he'd like to keep the leading reins on from a distance. Male ego or something, I don't know."

"Give him time to adjust, Ellie."

"What you really mean is I have to prove myself first. All right, you chauvinist, I'll give you an example of one of the 'manly' jobs I'm learning. Last week my car wouldn't start. Because I had always turned to Dan in times of mechanica crisis, this was the first time I had to cope on my own."

"Did you ask him to rescue you?"

"That was in the old days, Mr. Devlin. This time I called AAA *myself*."

Mark raised his glass to me in a toast. "Ms. Gordon, I see a very long tongue in your cheek, but on behalf of the yellow pages, I salute you."

"I realize you are highly amused by my miniscule progress." I started to laugh. "But where would lawyers be without a research library?"

"My point exactly," Mark replied. "Everybody needs somebody sometime."

"But the way the system is set up, most women need somebody all the time. Twenty years ago, I earned a college diploma, but that was incidental. My parents gave me an advanced education to improve my mind and, along the way, snag a nice Jewish doctor. Dan didn't quite come up to expectation, but he *was* taking over his father's car lot. Big money," I snorted, taking a swallow of the whiskey sour. "It didn't matter what courses we took, so most women whiled away their four years in classes that had no practical value. A friend of mine got her degree in Italian Renaissance Art with a Drama minor. It would have been a lot more sensible if she'd skipped Stanford and gone to Safeway. Checkers earn over ten dollars an hour, and Elaine can't get a job for that kind of money, even if she dumps the kids on her husband and goes to the Guggenheim."

"What are you saying, Ellie? Society deprived you? You got all the wrong advantages?"

"No. I'm saying we threw away our advantages. Girls were just going to get married anyway. Why study medicine when the only time you'd go to the hospital was when you had a baby?"

"Sure the world changed its rules, but women are now being compensated for history."

"You mean affirmative action?" I asked. "That's fine for the new generation, but for women my age who grew up on 'words are feminine, deeds are masculine;' legislation comes a little late. It still doesn't change the fact that you're the one with the law degree while I'm the lowly office manager."

Mark's green eyes twinkled. "Take your pick: med. school or pre-law. Nobody says you can't start now."

"Are you kidding? I'd be ninety-eight by the time I finished."

"So what? You would have asserted the right to do as you choose; independence isn't just making a good living, Ellie, it's also being responsible for your own actions."

"Ah, sure and it's a mighty fine sermon you preach, Father Devlin, but making up for lost time at this point in my life seems a waste of the few remaining years I have left. Besides, I don't want to go back to college. With my luck I'd end up in my son's class, and he'd get better grades than I would."

"And so," he sighed in mock defeat, "the educationally misdirected Eleanor Gordon is merely a victim of male chauvinsim. While she repines, men are doing all the things she never did and probably never wanted to."

I took the swizzle stick out of my glass and chewed on the end. "You're only partially right. There are a lot of things I never wanted to do. But if I had learned to be self-supporting at any job, I wouldn't have felt so powerless when Dan left."

The humor faded from Mark's face. He looked into the bottom of his drink, shook the few ice cubes still in the process of melting, and asked seriously, "Are you still in love with him?"

Slipping my fingers under Mark's hand, I gave a little squeeze.

"No, you sentimental sap. I'm mad at him. Please don't credit me with finer feelings than I'm capable of. You Irish have to learn not to cry at every sad song you hear. I wasn't doing 'Danny boy.' Can't you tell the difference between pathos and *kvetching*?"

From then on all serious conversation ceased, and we swapped ethnic jokes. Mark could do a great Yiddish accent, but I had trouble with a brogue. My attentive host made sure I didn't want another drink before dinner, and when the menu came, urged me to forget my diet and live it up. I took his advice. After weeks of living on celery sticks and cottage cheese, I dove into clams on the half shell, ate my way through Lobster Newberg and rice pilaf, took a sample of Mark's steak Diane, finished my own chocolate mousse, then garnished it with a bite of his pear Helene.

"You encouraged my gluttony," I moaned after a second cup of coffee. "Where was your pity?"

"I think you ate that too, but I'll tell you what. To make up for overfeeding you tonight, I'll overwork you tomorrow. Fair enough?"

"Only if you take me for a walk now. Either I move or spend the night here. Come on. I'll push and you can admire my muscles."

When the waiter came with the tab, I tried to pay for my half of the meal, but Mark was adamant. I gave in gracefully, and we left the rococco magnificence of La Belle Suisse's dining room for the fresh air of the patio. After inspecting the length of it a few times, admiring the fountain, we settled at a table where Mark signaled for the liqueur trolley. I leaned back in the large wicker chair, sipped Vandermint, and watched the moon glide through the clouds. Mark kept a companionable silence next to me.

"Thank you for a beautiful evening," I finally murmured. "It's been too nice to end."

"Agreed. These are the first peaceful moments I've had in a week. You're good therapy.

"When you gave me the first aid?" I shook my head. "But it has been a hell of a week, though it seems more like a lifetime since Katherine died. What a stupid tragic waste. She had so much to offer—talent, ability. With the world needing all the help it can get, Katherine Busch was one of the few who could have made a difference."

"That's a very lovely tribute," Mark replied.

"But it's no consolation to Howard. He had more personal

plans, I'm sure, than watching his wife do her bit for humanity. They hadn't even started a family."

"What makes you think they wanted children?" Mark took a sip of his drink.

"I got the distinct impression when I spoke to Katherine last week that the Blanco case had forced her to postpone a lot of things. She and Howard gave up their summer vacation, for one."

"That's not exactly the same as waiting to have a family. Kathy wasn't at all sure she could combine a busy law practice with raising children and do either very successfully. Didn't she tell you?"

"No, but I wouldn't believe it anyway. Katherine Busch could balance three juggling acts at one time and still have two hands left over. Just look how well she coped with the assorted idiocies of Mannie Blanco and Reverend Ritchie. Speaking of the devils, where do they stand in the police investigation?"

"I can't imagine, but I also can't imagine why either one of them would want to kill her."

"To assert male supremacy."

"That's an interesting theory," he said blandly. "Touches of reactionary politics, though."

"Wait until I turn militant," I warned him. "Then I send my army of titty-tats to destroy the enemy."

There was a short silence before Mark asked, "I'm sure it's x-rated, but who or what are the titty-tats?"

Grateful to be back on a lighter subject, I gave him an earthy account of his office staff as we rambled down to the parking lot. Mark waved away the doorman, and I pushed him to the large gray Mercedes, not even conscious of the fact that he never asked me to, and I never offered.

Just as naturally, I held the back of the wheelchair until Mark pushed himself upright, where, with one hand on the side of the car for support, he tossed the chair into the trunk with the other. This was his standard routine, and he did it effortlessly. The sideways gait he used, leaning from one leg to the other, got him just as quickly to the driver's seat, where he lowered himself down and swung his legs inside.

I bent to the open window. "I thought you couldn't walk."

"Are you trying to turn me into Superman?"

"Don't need to. You're already wearing the cape."

In a charming gesture, he raised my hand to his lips. "Eleanor Gordon, if it's permissible *after* working hours, I think you're wonderful too."

Chapter 8

When I dashed out of the girls' locker room and into the gym, tugging my leotard down at the crotch and up at the bust, Betsy was already lying on her mat, eyes closed. The 5:45 aerobic dancing class was held at the YWCA, a good fifteen-minute drive from the office, and it was always a race to get there. Sometimes I won. Patting my new, flat tummy, I spread my towel beside Betsy and stretched out.

"Ah, this feels terrific. I'll just curl up and take a nap while you do all the work. That reminds me," which of course it didn't, "I went to dinner with Mark Devlin last night."

One blue eye opened as she turned her head to me. "And?"

"I ate too much."

The eye closed again. "Figures."

I went on, unabashed. "Mark is a charming man."

"Does that mean he's beginning to reciprocate your crush? I wondered how long it would take."

84

I rolled over and leaned up on my elbow. "You miserable clod. I don't have a crush on him; you make me sound like a gushy fourteen-year-old."

"In some ways you are."

Betsy was saved by the opening strains of "Rocky." As it blared through the ceiling rafters of the gym, bounced off the basketball poles, and reverberated across the floor, our instructor pinned on her microphone.

"Ladies," her voice boomed, "shall we begin?"

One hundred groaning women got to their feet and started running in place. This was the warm-up. As soon as everyone was sweaty and shouts of "turn up the air conditioner" rang from all directions, it was time to actually begin.

Our leader, standing on an improvised stage so we could see her, was a slim perky young thing who taught about ten of these classes a week and in her spare time trained adolescents in wilderness survival skills. She was merciless. With a smile on her face, and a song in her heart, she prodded, yelled, pepped, and tortured in the name of physical fitness. About half the class kept up with her easily. Those were the skinnies who only came to annoy the fatties, I heard the lady in front of me say. She was a ballooning matron in a chrome yellow leotard, size forty, and when she jumped, her rear end bobbled like lemon jello. I had a sneaking sympathy for her, but she should have camouflaged the worst of her fat, the way I did when I started class, in a nice baggy gray sweat suit.

While we shadowboxed to the tempo of "Beat Me Daddy, Eight to the Bar," I got back to Besty with a swing at her jaw. "I resent your inference."

"I haven't inferred anything yet." She jabbed at my chin.

I ducked. "Oh, yes, you have. Ever since I crawled out of that muumuu you've been heckling me about dates...men..."

"You can say it." She laughed. "The word is *sex*."

The woman in yellow shot us a glance over her shoulder. My voice low, I threw a right to Betsy's middle. "You're not going to make me feel like a basket case this time—Forlorn Female Forsakes Fornication for Fellowship. If I want a roll in the hay, there's always Steve Tedesco. What's wrong with being friends with Mark Devlin?''

''Nothing, as long as you've got some other social life. And I don't mean jogging with me. Dan kicked you where it hurts and you're still sore, but a platonic friendship with Mark Devlin isn't the answer. And stay away from Tedesco. Married men are pure poison. You need to meet the right kind of man and have a normal relationship. The longer you put it off the harder it will be.''

I swung out with an upper cut. ''You think Mr. Right exists? How medieval of you. Why can't you just be happy that Mark and I enjoyed each other last night? So he's a nice man who's not on the make. Give me some time, Betsy. I'll work up to a real date eventually.''

The music switched to a Mac Davis hit. Hollering that we should listen to our bodies, even cheat if necessary, the instructor led us in a series of exercises that demanded the strength of a Marine sergeant and the flexibility of a Yoga master. On my hands and knees, I kicked my right leg in the air in a pale imitation of the gyrations being demonstrated on the stage.

''Is that the best you can do?'' Betsy chided. ''Or do you have to work up to high kicks here too?''

Gritting my teeth, I shot my leg halfway over my back. ''I'll have you know that I've been living a life of monastic chastity for months now, and it doesn't bother me at all.''

The lady in front of me farted.

After class Betsy didn't want to change clothes again, so I followed her to Madre's Mexican Munchies, a carryout restaurant shaped like a sombrero. We drove through the brim, picked up our food, then sat in Betsy's car and ate out of molded cardboard.

''You have to loosen up,'' she said, biting into a beef

burrito, and somehow not dripping chili sauce on her white tights. I was on my fourth napkin. "Nobody really lives *la dolce vita,* and women do not go to bed with a man just because he bought dinner. You're prepared for the ultimate, when most men don't expect that anyway, not if they're secure, sensible adults. Men are just people. They like to laugh, love a compliment, want to have a nice time with a nice person. Remember I told you about Barry Janish, the Hollywood script writer? He'd be perfect for you. No, you dope. Not to marry. To have fun with. He's divorced, lives in Laguna Beach, and I think you'd like him. I never went out with him myself, but I've met him at a lot of parties. He's fun."

"I'm sure he is, but what would a Hollywood script writer want with an ordinary housewife?"

Betsy shook her burrito at me. "First of all, you're nobody's wife. Second, you'll be moving out of that house soon, and third, what in hell makes you think you're ordinary? Who else would tell the Shakespeare Festival director 'Go fucketh thyself.' Barry would love that line."

"Is that how you're going to sell him on me?"

Betsy took a sip of her diet coke and gave me the benefit of her most supercilious expression. "My dear child, I shall tell him that you are an attractive, cultivated woman, a graduate of Stanford, and a lady to the marrow of your delicate bones."

"And when he finds out the truth?" I snorted, wiping chili off my chin.

She only laughed.

To my amazement, when Betsy called me at home an hour later and said Barry Janish was picking me up around ten o'clock to go out for a drink, I didn't scream in protest. Betsy had merely accepted my tacit approval of Barry Janish as a possible future date, and moved it up to the present. I gave in gracefully. A couple of drinks, some scintillating conversation with a writer—how hard could it be?

First I put on a pair of slacks and a sleeveless top, then decided that was too informal and changed into a pants suit. Vetoing that outfit, I finally settled on a wraparound dress in light blue, with spaghetti straps at the shoulders and a matching shawl. In case the man was over six feet tall, I slipped on my spike sandals. Wash and wearable hair in place, mascara not too thick, I only had to add a drop of eyeshadow, a dab of lipstick, and I was ready when the doorbell rang at five after ten. I wanted to make a last-minute dash to the bathroom, but that urge would disappear as soon as my stomach relaxed. A shining smile on my face, I opened the door.

My first date as a single woman of the eighties began at the Shanty, a hangout not far from my house, with plank floors, fish netting on the walls, and a free bowl of peanuts with every two drinks. Against the music of a rhythm and blues combo in the corner, Barry Janish told me the scenario of his new screenplay. It was X-rated on a mere technicality, though he was hopeful the director could tone it down to an R. As he explained why obscenity was essential to the plot, I felt as though I had stepped "inside" Hollywood.

If Barry didn't quite resemble one of the heroes in his films, he did look extremely intellectual: on the small side, hair thinning, face creased from hours of concentration. He said he wanted to write a novel someday. In the meantime, he was collecting material. When two bowls of the obligatory peanuts were empty, he was still telling me about the leads in his last movie who got carried away during a nude love scene. When the director yelled cut, they didn't. So captivated was I by this cerebral discussion of how the modern film writer plies his craft that when we got back to my house, I invited Barry in for a night cap, as though either of us needed one, and more talk.

He made himself comfortable on the sectional in the den, while I mixed him a bourbon and water and myself a glass of seltzer.

"Nice house," he commented, gazing around. "How come you're selling?"

"I don't need all this space anymore. My son is going to college, and there's only me left to rattle around eight rooms, two and three-quarter baths, an all-electric kitchen, and oversized garage. That's how it reads in the listing. Besides, my ex-husband says he has too many bills to keep up the house payment too."

"Tell me about it. I just dumped a twelve-hundred-dollar-a-month payment myself. It was eating me alive."

"How long have you been divorced?" I asked, sitting down next to him.

"Which time?"

"You've been married more than once?"

"This last one made four, but that's the end of the trail. Marriage is a thing of the past. From here on out, it's me first."

"Me first. That sounds nice for a change," I agreed. "My ex wanted me to stay home and cuddle his ego while he played games with his secretary. No more. Now it's my turn to play games."

"There's plenty of them to choose from." He smiled.

I took a long swallow of seltzer. "Any recommendations?"

"For a lady like you, I'd say strip Scrabble."

"Mmm. Sounds intellectually stimulating."

"That isn't all. Come on, I'll show you."

It happened so quickly that I was literally caught with my straps down. In one move, Barry slipped them off my shoulders, pulled the dress to my waist, and pressed his open mouth against mine. I tried not to spill the seltzer.

Then he drew back and looked. "Jesus, you've got great tits."

Next to my soft brown eyes, they were my best feature, but not ones I cared to put on public display. Barry was examining them so intently, he could have been checking for camera angles. "Barry, let's not—aaag." He cupped them in his hands. "Barry, stop. I don't want to be in the movies." He didn't even hear me. I snatched at a strap and set my glass on the table. "Why don't we skip to the word part of this game? I'll start with thanks, but no thanks."

"Doesn't fit. This is strip Scrabble, remember?"

Barry was too intellectual for me. I could barely spell *single,* much less *sex.* What he wanted was beyond my first grade capabilities. But the point of this date was to increase my vocabulary. How could I graduate to liberated if I stayed hung-up on a one-syllable word? As a Hollywood writer, Barry Janish had the ideal credentials to give me a Berlitz course on modern human relationships. They were his stock in trade. I let him push me back on the couch and lower the top of my dress again.

Five minutes later I was still counting the speckles in the ceiling. Either my ears were plugged, or Barry and I just weren't speaking the same language. Where was the hot, throbbing surge of passion that should have been invading my loins? With all the nuzzling and fondling, not one flicker of lust had been stirred. His mouth was firmly attached to my left breast, but as I looked down at the bald spot on his head, my only reaction was that his teeth were almost as sharp as Dan's.

"Hey, Barry." I squirmed. "Let's stop and talk for a while."

"Anything you say, baby," he croaked. "Just listen to this." Moving off me, he unzipped his pants and exposed the very topic I wanted to avoid.

The Scrabble game was down to the wire, and I only had two blank tiles left. Telling Barry they spelled *no* didn't help. He was using a different alphabet. Enough with words; it was time for action. As his mouth opened and aimed for my breast again, I shoved his head back and rolled off the sofa, landing in an undignified heap on the floor. Before he could move, I scrambled to my feet and dashed halfway across the room.

"What the hell are you doing?"

I hitched up the dress and yanked at my pantyhose. "I'm sorry. I tried to tell you, but this just isn't working."

"Since when? You were all hot to trot a minute ago."

I cringed at his dialogue. "Barry, please. You're a very nice man, only I'm not ready yet."

"Okay, let's go to the bedroom. I'll make you ready. Just tell me what you like. How about if I eat—"

"Barry! Listen to what I'm saying. I don't want to make love." This was ridiculous. How did I wind up standing in the middle of my den, begging a man with an erection hanging out of his pants to put it away and go home?

Barry wasn't thrilled about it either. "Look here, nobody said this is love. You invited me in and stuck your titties in my face for sex. Well, it worked, kid. I got a hell of a hard-on. If you don't want to fuck it away, give me a blow job. But I can't walk around like this tonight. Take a look at that thing."

I looked, but it left me unmoved. If Barry wanted sympathy, he'd have to go buy it somewhere. Couldn't he see I had my own problems? Still, I was polite. "I'm sorry, but I can't help you. Perhaps a cold shower would be beneficial."

His face turned bright red as he leaped off the couch and clutched his pants together. "You stinking bitch. You crummy stinking bitch! Don't tell me you can't. You *won't*." He struggled to pull the zipper over his bulge then finally gave up with a disgusted grunt. "Shit. You're nothing but a lousy cock tease."

The epithet hung in the air as the door slammed behind him. It was probably one of the best lines from his last hit.

What did I expect from a hackneyed writer of stale eroticism? Cleverness? Originality? Barry Janish was no D. H. Lawrence.

And I was no Lady Chatterley. Might as well be honest about the whole thing, although Mellors didn't have a mammary obsession and teeth like a shark's. Even so, I flunked tonight's crash course, verbal and otherwise. Maybe I should turn in my Scrabble set and take up skiing. I might have a chance there. Out in the snow, everybody's cold.

Chapter 9

Michael arrived shortly after three on Saturday in jeans and a sweatshirt with the sleeves cut off, but it was his hair that needed the trim.

"They don't have laundromats in L.A.?" I asked as he dumped a bag of dirty clothes at my feet.

"Sure, but nobody does it like Mom." He gave me a hug and an experimental pinch. "Hey, you're getting skinnier. Good work." The social amenities taken care of, he headed for the refrigerator.

Michael has a great mixture of genes from both sides of the family: my wavy hair and brown eyes, Dan's lanky build, my mother's European *savoir faire*, and the appetite of a peasant. As he satisfied the last of those with three salami sandwiches and a jar of pickles, I filled him in on what he missed by going back-packing last week. Naturally he had a ready answer.

"The Devlins did it."

"Not the butler? Oh, dear, and I was so sure."

"I'm serious," he protested, only giving up the argument long enough to dive into a thick wedge of cheesecake. "I talked to Dad this week, and he says those lawyers you work for are crooks."

"Your father's an ass . . . is assuming," I amended.

"Look, Ma, both the nephew and the uncle were there. The younger one doesn't have an alibi, and those guys in wheelchairs have arms like gorillas from pushing themselves around. He could have strangled her easy."

"What for?"

"How should I know? If he's a crook, he's got plenty of reasons. What does Mr. Abbotts say?"

"Not nearly as much as you. But don't forget the other suspects. Reverend Ritchie, Mannie Blanco, a homicidal burglar, or a hit man for the syndicate."

"You know what, Ma? You read too many mysteries."

The eminently practical Michael Gordon got down to work after that, emptying drawers and lugging filled boxes to the garage. At nine that evening, following a large pizza with pepperoni and onions, he declared it was time for a movie. I was pretty bushed by then and tried to convince him that television was just as bad and a lot cheaper, but he dragged me to a neighborhood theater, where we sat through a charming epic involving two car wrecks and three antiheroes whose idea of a fun time was to urinate in public. It must have been a Barry Janish production.

On Sunday, Michael woke me up bright and early to make him pancakes—"as only Mom can do it," he said, hand over heart. I gave him an instant mix and fortified myself with black coffee. Even that wasn't sobering enough.

"The piano, four Currier and Ives prints, and the ice cream maker? That's all you've decided to sell so far?" he asked incredulously. "What are Currier and Ives?"

In answer, I made him roll up the Tabriz rug and stand it in the corner of the garage. That and some Black and Decker tools were all Dan wanted. I regretted the rug, maybe the tools too, but no quibbling. Dan had let me have everything else, including the color TV and stereo.

While I was propping the rug against the metal shelving and trying to shove a burlap bag in between for protection, I noticed my tote bag sitting on the top rack. I had tossed it up there the night of the murder, when Mark Devlin brought me home. He offered to come in with me and check for bogeymen, but I was in fairly good shape by then. Coming in through the garage, I gave the house a once-over, then signaled him an all-clear from the front door. It was a needless precaution, but Mark understood the natural dislike of walking into a dark, empty house on that particular night.

Maybe it was a Freudian reaction, but I totally forgot about the tote bag. I had already taken out keys, wallet, and Tampax during the ride home and put them in my purse. Only the unused towel and smock were left in the bag. And the tape.

"Oh my God!" I shrieked, pulling it out from the folds of the towel. "I had it here the whole time."

"What's the matter?" Michael came tearing in from the yard. "Why are you yelling?" When he saw why, he was almost disappointed. "You found a cassette? Jeez, I thought something bit you. Give it to me. I'll put it with my other stuff."

"This does not belong to you, I'm happy to say. It's the private, personal property of Abbotts, Devlin, and . . . it belongs to the firm," I finished with less enthusiasm.

"Hey, it says Blanco on the front. Come on, let's listen to it."

"Not so fast. First of all, it's not for you to hear, and, second, we don't have a cassette player. You took it to L.A. with you, remember?"

"I'll borrow one," Michael answered.

"No, sweetie. This is really confidential. It's a tape recording Ms. Busch made with Mannie Blanco the day she was killed. All privileged talk between lawyer and client, nothing special.''

"So what's it doing here?"

"Your brilliant mother walked off with it by mistake. We've been searching the office for a week, but I had it hidden in the garage the whole time."

"You brought it home the night she was killed?"

"Yep. Never even transcribed it."

"Then how do you know it's nothing special?"

It gave me a glow of motherly pride that my son had inherited my deductive abilities. "A good try, Michael, but you still can't listen to it."

He tagged at my heels as I went into the house. "Ma, that tape could have some clues on it about Ms. Busch's murder. I think it's your duty to let me borrow Wayne's cassette so you can find out."

"I will do my duty at the office tomorrow."

"Suppose Blanco splits for Mexico tonight?"

"Blanco? You told me the Devlins did it."

Michael gave up the fight with a rueful grin, while I called Mr. Abbotts to report the find. He accepted my apology like the gracious man he was, and only requested that I bring him the tape in the morning.

I would have too, if I'd put it in my purse immediately, instead of leaving it on the desk in the kitchen where I'd be sure not to forget it. Running behind schedule as usual, I zoomed out of the house on Monday morning without pausing for a cup of coffee or even going into the kitchen.

Confessing that to Mr. Abbotts wasn't much fun. I did mention that my son had come home for the weekend and stayed until late last night, but still, I felt like a first-class fool. Office managers are supposed to be organized. The only thing I had coordinated was a lost and found and forgotten.

"Was he mad?" Josie asked me in mild curiosity.

"No."

"What did he say?"

"I'm overburdened."

"Really?" Her baby blues widened. "Are you?"

"I suppose so. He's cutting back my workload."

"That's nice of him."

"Barbara's got the Blanco files back."

No one could say Barb was a sore winner. She went around with a pleased smirk on her face all day, while I made a lot of "load off my mind" noises that office managers shouldn't transcribe notes when a typist was available. The worst of the dislocation was over, and I had more important things to do. Barbara could emulate my wonderful editorial style by studying the earlier transcriptions.

That's what I said, but I felt as though I'd been demoted. Mr. Abbotts was only thinking of me, as the song goes, but it seemed that I had reached my Peter Principle. Any more responsibility and I hit the level of incompetence.

With a vow to be reinstated as a person of extraordinary efficiency, I came home from aerobic dancing class with Betsy's little cassette recorder tucked under my arm. Unlocking the front door and stepping into the entry hall, I flipped on the overhead light, then bit back a scream.

In the living room, my precious Queen Anne desk had been rifled. The drawers were pulled out and the few things I hadn't packed yesterday were scattered on top—a box of stationery, recent letters. The velvet sofa wasn't slashed, thank God, but the cushions were on the floor as though someone had searched beneath them. Racing down the three steps into the den and flicking on every light switch along the way, I expected to find the TV and stereo gone, but all the intruder had done here was make another mess. The sectional was no longer one neat couch, and every lamp shade was crooked. What kind of burglar had broken into my house—a compulsive slob? Hoping against hope that all our hard work over the weekend hadn't been demolished, I stuck my head into the garage, but apparently my housebreaker stopped short of getting his hands dirty. Not a box out there had been moved.

A jewel thief! Mourning Grandmother Rappaport's pearls, I took the stairs two at a time. My jewelry box had been taken out of the bottom dresser drawer and the contents dumped on the bed, but everything was still there. In the closet all my purses were open and shoes turned upside down, but the intruder was too lazy to pull the clothes off the rack.

Even so, it was a mess. Every room had been given a thorough going over, at least the ones I'd seen so far, which brought to mind the rooms I hadn't seen yet. Who knew what evil lurked in them? I wasn't going to go blundering into trouble like some gothic heroine.

More cautiously I went to the door of my bedroom and paused. No sound but my stomach growling. Then I tiptoed into the hall and peeked into each room, listening for sinister noises. That was still gothic, but a little more adult than saying boo in the dark.

I made it to the kitchen without finding anything more sinister than a pair of ski boots Michael had left in his closet. It seemed logical to presume that the burglar ran off when he heard me coming. The jimmied lock on the back door explained how he had broken in and broken out, only the shnook had been too nervous to take anything with him.

I called the police and reported the break-in. They promised to send a squad car right over and asked me not to touch anything so they could get some prints. It was just routine. More than likely, the house was hit by vandals rather than a ring of inept burglars. Who else would have rummaged through the canned goods in the pantry and left the dishwasher standing open?

I couldn't clean up until the police came, in case a box of

Rice Krispies held an important clue, so I just sat down at the desk in the kitchen, keeping well away from the open top drawer, so as not to smudge any fingerprints on the handles. Staring at the disorder inside for a moment or two, I realized something had been stolen after all. It took me almost as long to miss it as it had for the thief to find it. Mannie Blanco's tape was gone.

An hour later, dressed in jeans and shoulder-hugging knit shirt, Mark Devlin was sitting in my kitchen watching me gobble ice cream. I called him when no one answered at the Abbotts's house, and he arrived shortly after the police got here. It was Mark who explained that the tape was the property of the law firm, and shifted the focus away from a residential burglary. The police took prints from the back door and a few other spots, and agreed to deal with Mark if anything came of it. That was very nice of them, but it didn't help with my problem. For an hour now, I'd been eating and arguing. Mark thought I was overdoing both.

"Think it out, Ellie," he said again with infinite patience. "You're putting too much importance on that tape. No one is going to care if you heard it or not."

"Sure, if it's a blank reel. But if it's not, I may become the most sought after girl in town." I started to choke on a nut.

"That's a lot of ice cream," Mark warned. "You're going to make yourself sick."

"Fine. You can let me have the wheelchair. I need it more than you do anyway. Look at me, Mark. I'm really scared. Blanco's trade is supposed to be a secret, but the way Mannie has himself barricaded like a princess in a tower is almost a classified ad. Everybody, especially his old pals, wants to know what he's hiding besides himself. So they break into my house and steal the tape. That's a perfectly reasonable, sensible move. I applaud their good judgment, but if they hear something they don't like, they might not like the idea that I heard it too."

Mark wiped his hands across his face and tried again. "Ellie, would it make you feel better if we released a press statement tomorrow proclaiming your ignorance?"

"Oh, that's funny." I took another chunk of ice cream. "Right this minute, some godfather probably has his ear glued to a cassette, wondering which hit man to send after me. He's going to believe I had the tape for a whole week and never got around to playing it?"

"You won't accept that this could have been an unorganized crime break-in?" Mark was getting sarcastic.

"You mean an ordinary thief saw more possibilities in stealing a tape than a pearl necklace? Bull. Can you picture somebody roaming around the house with a cost sheet in his hand, figuring which room offered the best returns? What did he think I kept under the living room sofa—the Hope diamond? Come on, Mark, you don't have to soothe me with baby-talk. This house was searched, and for one thing only."

"Okay, I'll buy that. It doesn't mean you're in danger."

"Stop being so calm about it. How can you be sure I'm safe?"

"Do you *want* to think the mob is after you?" Mark sounded wearied by the whole conversation.

"Some people think they were after Katherine Busch."

"And you see an immediate connection."

"No," I answered slowly, "but even a distant one frightens me."

"Believe me," he said in a gentler voice, "the distance is light years away. Do you think I'd let you be a sitting target for a UFO?" As usual, Mark's confidence was infectious. I handed him the bowl of ice cream. He took one look and gave it back. "Didn't even save me a nut."

"You have nerves of steel. What do you need with Dutch chocolate courage? That's the last of it too. Maybe there's some plain vanilla left, if Michael didn't polish it off."

"You sound back to normal now," he said with relief.

"But I don't want any ice cream, thanks. It's time to stop eating and go to bed."

"I can't."

"Indigestion?" The swine had a sarcastic grin on his face.

"Delirium tremens," I shot back. Actually, it was after-shock. My house had been violated, and I didn't feel safe in it yet. "Mark, would you stay here tonight? I don't want to be by myself. I know it sounds silly, but that chair propped against the back door doesn't seem like very much protection."

"He won't come back," Mark said. "And the police are going to patrol the street all night."

"Never mind. I'll call and make a reservation at the Hilton."

"You're going to walk in there wearing chocolate-flavored leotards and tights?"

I looked down at the reason for his amusement and had to admit I was as big a slob as my housebreaker. It was also a hell of an outfit to wear while entertaining the police. No wonder the cop kept staring at my legs. Aside from being blue, they were showing. "I'll change first."

"Don't bother." He smiled gorgeously. "Just grab a tooth-brush and a swimsuit."

"You going to scrub me in the ocean?"

"Not quite. Take your pick—hot tub or pool."

Chapter 10

The first item on the agenda at Mark's house was a shower. Looking like a used fudgsicle was one thing. Smelling like one was unpardonable. When I finally joined him in the living room, he had already changed his clothes and was wearing a bright blue knee-length terrycloth robe. His feet were bare.

"A drink first?" He held out a crystal brandy snifter.

"Absolutely. That's just what I need." Taking the amber-filled glass from him, I sank down on one of the man-sized chairs that flanked the fireplace. "You don't drink out of jelly glasses, I see. Another bachelor stereotype down the tubes." Raising the snifter, I toasted him, then took a sip.

No jelly glasses, I gazed around appreciatively, but a nice collection of contemporary art. It fit Mark as much as the house did. Clean, smooth lines, no kitsch, no frills. From the outside, it was California ultramodern, with chalet-style redwood beams sloping from roof to ground. A sweeping canopy stretched from high above the front door to the other side of the circular driveway, but when Mark got out of the car to get his wheelchair from the trunk, I realized the overhang was not merely for effect. It was an umbrella.

The house had been designed for Mark's convenience, from the seat and grab-rails in the shower to the extra-wide hallways and doors. The carpet was low pile for easy maneuvering, the light switches at a handy height, and all the entrances had ramps instead of steps. The main part of the house—living room, dining room, and den—was combined into one large area, separated by the arrangement of furniture rather than walls. A double couch and several oversized armchairs provided seating around the fireplace, with a spacious corner where Mark could get to the shelves of law books and pull right up to his antique oak roll-top desk. It was all very practical and imaginative, but it also demonstrated that Mark had not only money, but taste.

I was about to compliment Mark on his home, when a young man came out of the kitchen. "Can I get you folks something to eat before I crack the books?"

"Ellie, this is Luis Romero," Mark said. "When he's not helping me, Luis studies pre-law at the Irvine campus of U.C. He's my mainstay and chief bottle washer. Luis, this is Eleanor Gordon, a very hungry guest who'll be staying the night."

"I'm delighted to meet you, Luis, but forget the food. I'm full of ice cream."

Luis shook my hand politely. Golden skinned, brown eyed, and too handsome for his own good, the boy was charmingly dignified. I asked him about his classes and where he was from. His parents were old friends of Mark and had been reassigned to Kirtland Air Force Base in New Mexico. Colonel Romero did something with missiles and trajectory, while his son aimed for the law. Mark was just as much a mainstay to him—surrogate father, a home away from home, and a big help with homework.

When Luis went off to tackle that very thing, Mark suggested the two of us continue our conversation in the hot tub. Carrying the brandy snifter, I followed him outside to the deck.

Aside from bumping into movie stars on every corner, California's feature attraction is the ocean. When Mark switched on the outdoor lighting, there it foamed, thirty feet below us, breakers splashing up on the beach. Casa Grande is almost on top of the ocean, but from up here we had the best ringside seat in town. Even the hot tub was built-in near the edge of the deck, overlooking the water. The view couldn't have been better.

With almost the same movements he used to get in and out of the car, Mark locked the wheelchair, pushed himself up, then swung around to sit on the wide ledge of the hot tub. He took off his robe, then lifted one leg at a time over the top before easing himself down into the water.

Michael should only see the muscles on that torso. Mark looked as tough as a wrestler, with shoulders that would have done credit to a weight lifter. That's what he was in a sense, having to use the top part of his body to move the bottom half, too.

"Don't look," I ordered, starting to untie the belt of my coverup. "I don't want you to see me in a bathing suit until the worst parts are submerged. Turn your head."

"You have a beautiful body," he said after a moment.

"Cheater!" I was halfway into the tub, with one leg still straddling the ledge. "Aren't you gentleman enough to let a lady retain her modesty?" Sitting down beside him, that modesty almost fell out of the top of my suit. It was sizes too big and gaped indecorously as it filled with water. I sat straight up to combat the forces of nature.

"More tense than you thought, huh?" Mark poured me a little more brandy. "Hey, don't slug it. You're treating my Napoleon with rank indifference."

"Ooooh. And I thought I was the pitiful punster. You know what, Mr. Devlin?" I turned to him. "You are as tipsy as I am. Did you eat dinner, or was the empty ice cream bowl the closest you got to a meal tonight? Want me to make a tuna fish sandwich?"

"No, thank you."

"Sure." I pretended insult. "You think my tuna salad is going to taste like a chocolate parfait. Well, let me tell you something, Mr. Smug, I can eat *and* cook."

"Which comes first?"

Stretching out my pint-sized legs as far as I could still brought them a foot shy of Mark's, or I would have kicked him. "Why is it that no matter how hard I try to make it to the boardroom, I always end up back in the kitchen? From this point forth, I hereby remove myself to the boudoir. If I have to pick a room, it should be one more in keeping with my new position in life. In fact, I'm seriously thinking about a swingles condo. New image altogether."

The blue/green outdoor lighting gave Mark a blue/green smile. He reached around for the decanter of brandy sitting on the tile ledge of the tub, and poured me a drop more. "My prescription is working. The lady is intoxicated and informative. Tell me more."

"Mmm. This is good. The last time I was in a hot tub all we got was celery juice. Madeline Jacobson was on a health food kick, and she made everybody do deep breathing exercises too. I thought the object was to relax in the water. She claimed the body had to be prepared first."

"Is she married to Allen Jacobson? I thought so. He's the architect who designed this house."

"Really? They're nice people."

"Do you see them much?"

An interesting question. Actually I hadn't seen any of my friends in quite a while. During the initial stages of hibernation, all kindly overtures were rejected. After a few tries, people stopped calling. Even now I hated the idea of being the sore thumb in a crowd of couples. The men would have felt obligated to pick up the tab if we went out, and the wives would have felt obliged to matchmake like crazy. Not out of altruism especially; it's just safer to make sure a single woman on the prowl isn't hunting in your backyard. The Jacobsons weren't like that, but how could we resume our bridge foursome as a threesome? I sure as hell didn't want to spend the rest of my life playing dummy.

"I haven't had the time to see much of anybody," was my facile answer to Mark's question. "Between working, trying to sell the house, and now the murder investigation, I've hardly been able to keep up with my laundry." If Mark thought that was a cop-out, he kept it to himself. "Speaking of the investigation," I grabbed at a change of topic, "the police don't really suspect Dennis, do they?"

"I'm sure not. He's a little upset because we can't seem to locate the girl with him that night; but when we do, he'll feel a lot better."

This time, I was the one who held back. When Mark spoke about Dennis, the pronoun was *we*. I knew he cared for his nephew deeply, but without realizing it, he showed another side to that love—protection.

"Don't worry," I offered in support. "Dennis will be fine."

"I hope so. He's a bright kid, but my sister-in-law had a tough time of it with him after Bob died. I guess you know my brother was killed in Viet Nam. Phyllis remarried a few years later and then came stepfather problems. Anyway, I've tried to help Dennis. Maybe too much."

"You can never have too much of a good thing," I said, flicking a few drops of water on his chest. Mark reached for my hand, but I wriggled back in self-defense. "If Dennis tries to follow in your footsteps, he'll be headed in the right direction."

"Is that my Napoleon talking?" The good humor back on his face, he trickled a handful of water down my arm.

"Not at all, sir." I set down my glass and leaned back. "It's in the stars . . . I see it—Mark Devlin's astrology chart. Right over your head." I pointed. "It says he's a cross between Perry Mason and Ironsides, has a distinguishing mole on his right shoulder, never loses his temper, prefers meat to fish, and can really walk but uses a wheelchair to arouse sympathy."

"Does it work?"

"Well, let's put it this way. I give you an A for effort, but it only translates as admiration."

"I suppose I'll have to settle for that," he said with a straight face, "but I hope it isn't too much for a handicapped person to take sitting down."

I was still lying back in my star-gazing position, captured by the twinkle in his eyes.

"I don't believe you. How come you're not franchised yet?"

"Just waiting for the right terms. Interested?"

"Only if I can have the exclusive."

He started to answer, then changed his mind. Instead, he leaned over and kissed me.

What a kiss! Brandy fumes swam in my head, while something warm and wet moved against my tongue. Eyes closed and lips parted, I floated on a wave of liquid sensuality, feeling hands inside the gaping top of my bathing suit.

Only when I realized to whom the hands belonged, did I finally come to my senses. Confused and embarrassed, I pushed him away.

"My God." Struggling to sit up, I looked anywhere but at Mark. "Your liquor certainly went to my head."

"I hoped it was me," he said, watching my fumbling efforts to fix the top of the bathing suit. It was wet and sticking in all the wrong places.

When my decency was restored, I dared to look at him. "Yes, well . . . I didn't expect you to . . . I mean, you caught me by surprise."

"So I gather," was his unsatisfactory reply. "Is it a terrible shock?"

"That you kissed me?"

"Among other things."

"Yes . . . the other things." I licked my lips nervously. "Well, I'll admit you did a good job of hiding it up till now."

"I wasn't hiding it," he said in amusement. "You never looked in the right place."

"That's disgusting!" I shot up and eluded his grasp, climbing out of the tub in absolute fury. "You knew I misunderstood all along. Giving you all those soppy compliments . . . so wonderful, so brave . . . yuch!"

Trying to get the terrycloth coverup over my head and pull it down over the wet suit, I snarled at him through the folds. "What a line you have—play father confessor, lure a defenseless woman to your house, and when she's drunk with your cheap whiskey, you suddenly unfrock."

I heard Mark getting out of the hot tub; and by the time my face was free, the robe still sticking around my hips, he was sitting on the ledge, leaning forward to get the wheelchair. I had bumped into it a minute ago, and it was just slightly out of his reach. I made no move to help him, and he didn't ask. He only dropped his hand and looked at me. The aqua shades of the outdoor lighting cast him in a cold bronze mold. Not even his eyes held any warmth.

"I suppose you won't believe me if I say I wasn't trying to trick you. I only guessed tonight that you were under the wrong impression. Stupid of me. A man in a wheelchair—"

"Shut up!" I shouted. "Don't you dare put me down like that! Damn you, Mark. I'm not sure I can take your being a normally functioning male. You were a hell of a lot nicer as a man of the cloth."

"Yes," he agreed in a sober voice. "That's probably true. But I wasn't trying to put you down. Most people make the same mistake you did, and it's entirely my fault for not telling you the awful truth about me. I should have casually brought it up at dinner the other night, but it might have put you off the Lobster Newberg."

"Or the chocolate mousse."

"No. Nothing could have done that."

"You unchivalrous ass!" I flopped down next to him with my arms sagging between my legs. "How many more times will I make a fool of myself tonight? 'Let me count the ways.' First I cry the mob is after me..."

"An understandable error."

"Then I force you to bring me to your monastery..."

"Slightly inaccurate."

"Which, of course, gets me to screaming fraudulent deception. Here you come to my rescue like a knight on a charger, and I try to stab you with your own lance."

"That analogy makes me nervous. Can we skip Freud and proceed directly to the house? Come on. Forget about it."

"No. I owe you an explanation."

"That's not necessary. This was a bad night to throw you a curve ball. My timing was off, and I put out the wrong signals. That's the end of it."

"That's a lousy ending. At least, give me one curtain call. Mark, listen, you surprised me tonight, that's all. My reaction to you is how I always... your curve ball just hit me in the wrong place." I gave a nervous laugh. "My libido is in deep freeze, shall we say. I liked you as safe old Father Devlin because we could have a nice platonic relationship, and I wouldn't have to feel... inadequate."

His eyes narrowed in speculation, as though he didn't know whether to accept my story as truth or a burnt offering for turning him down. "You think you're frigid? Where did you get such a notion?"

The forthright way lawyers put things was a bit unsettling, but if I were going to convince him the fault was mine and not his, I couldn't fall back on maidenly modesty. For some reason, it seemed more important to salvage Mark's ego than mine. Maybe because he already had one handicap.

"Believe me, Mark, I'm not thrilled to admit that I have the ultimate character flaw. It's almost as terrible as confessing you haven't got a sense of humor. But it's true. Or at least it was," I said slowly, "until you surprised the pants off me."

"Don't pun around with me, girl. Ellie, stop."

I was trying to put my arms around his neck, and he was pulling them off.

"Not yet, Ellie. Another time. Get used to the idea first. I'm in no rush."

Obviously not. He was holding my hands down in my lap, kindly but firmly. If I had been in a state to think at all, I would have taken his advice and let things rest for a while, but the excitement of self-discovery was too much of a relief. I wanted Mark to kiss me now.

"You're being ridiculously noble," I told him. "You have perfected a cure, and there's no reason to withhold treatment."

"There are a lot of reasons," he argued with calm logic. "You can't switch me from Father Devlin to lover in five minutes."

"What's the matter?" I jumped up. "Are you afraid I'll genuflect?"

If Mark had laughed at that moment, I would have pushed him over backwards into the hot tub. He didn't. "Ellie, you're standing in front of the chair. Do you mind? I'm getting cold sitting here."

I tossed him his robe, then brought the wheelchair right up to the tub where he could reach it. He hauled himself up while I automatically held the handle bars for support.

"If you've changed your mind, Mark, just come out with it. Tell me I no longer appeal to you."

"You appeal," he shot over his shoulder as he headed into the house.

I almost tripped over my feet following him. "Then why are you being so stubborn?" I stalked him across the living room and down the hallway.

"You can sleep in here." He pointed to the open door of a bedroom but kept moving.

I only paused long enough to glance inside. It was obviously the guest room, decorated in green and white, with a single bed.

"How can you ask me to sleep alone? You don't care that I had a horrible experience tonight and need some comfort?"

Mark continued down the hall and into his bedroom. I padded after him, but stopped in the doorway. This room was much larger, with french doors to the deck at one side and an alcove with bookshelves and a TV on the other. Between was a king-size bed. Mark was parked in front of it, as if he were trying to block the view.

"Look, Ellie, I'm not going to take advantage of a vulnerable moment. I'm flattered by your generosity, but believe me, you don't owe me a thing."

"Oh, so that's it." I folded my arms. "Thank you, Mr. Devlin, for finally admitting what you really think of me—a neurotic who uses her body to pay off debts. It must make you feel very superior to refuse me on that basis. I presume you'd prefer I pay in cold, hard cash for the privilege of bedding you. Sorry, I don't have any money with me at the moment. All I have is a bunch of insecurities; and if you choose to think I feel guilty about mixing your motives in with my own problems, you're right. I could just send a check and an apology in tomorrow's mail and forget about it, but I'm trying to conduct my life with a bit more courage than I have in the past. Not everyone has your assurance. Some of us weren't lucky enough to overcome a severe affliction. We have to learn confidence the hard way. If I tripped over some of your spokes in the process, you know where you can stick them.''

I was proud as hell of that speech until I saw that under Mark's bent head, his shoulders were shaking. Then I could have bitten my tongue out. I crept over and touched his arm. ''I'm sorry. I had no right to say those things. Mark? Mark, say something.''

When he looked up, he was laughing. ''Do you really want me to stick them?''

''You goddamn bastard,'' I charged. ''I thought I had destroyed the last vestiges of your manhood. You think it's funny!''

''I think it's fantastic. In one hour I went from saint to sinner to selling my favors.'' He was still chuckling.

''So I'm not very perceptive. But you're not exactly the boy next door either.''

''Oh, no, Ellie Gordon. You're not going to run away now.'' There was devilment in his eyes as he reached for me. ''I'm convinced. 'Come on and kiss me, Kate.' ''

His hand was stretched out to me, and all I had to do was reach across the chasm that separated the weak from the strong. Only now that my bluster had died and the alcoholic haze was clearing, I started wondering why I wanted to go to bed with a perfect stranger. It seemed a fine idea when I talked Mark around, but at the moment the point escaped me. What was I trying to prove? That my cunt worked? That a man in a wheelchair didn't repulse me? That I could be liberated if I shut my eyes and wished hard?

Mark saw my hesitation, but instead of sending me away to think some more, he invited me closer. ''I don't do this with all the girls. They lose respect for a guy if he's too easy.''

I walked into the circle of his arms and kissed him on the cheek. Then in a bravado gesture, I began peeling off the robe and bathing suit as he watched. Taking down the heavy brown and white bedspread, I lay down on top of the cool, striped sheets. It was almost a shock to the skin. My body was burning from the tips of my blushing breasts to my tautly curled toes. It was some relief when Mark closed the door and switched off the overhead light, leaving the room a romantic blue from the glow outside. Then he sat down on the edge of the bed and slipped off his trunks.

"So how do you do it?" I blurted out.

"You mean you're still a virgin?" Lifting his legs onto the bed, he rolled over, looming next to me like an underwater predator ready to gobble me up. "Relax, Ellie. It'll be fine."

My toes began to uncurl as Mark traced a finger down my cheek. With tender consideration, he took it slowly, just kissing my face and lips until he could feel me responding. I had one brief moment of anxiety, worrying if his hand would falter when he touched the fading lumps of cellulite on my thighs, or if he would be put off by the stretch marks on my stomach. But when his tongue began licking the tip of my breast, I moaned in delight and forgot about trivia.

The ability to walk was another incidental, and my preconceptions about people in wheelchairs underwent several drastic reversals. Mark was a skilled lover and easily shifted us both into positions that offered the maximum benefits. They were nothing new in the scope of lovemaking, although it had been years since Dan went to so much trouble to ensure my pleasure. Mark didn't believe in rushing or stinting, but proved what versatile things hands and mouths could do. Even my own part in the proceedings was not as passive as the one I usually played. He guided my hands to touch and feel, until I went down on him without prompting. The final delight was riding on top, and we raced to the finish in a mouth-to-mouth heat.

Afterwards, I curled up in his arms, while his chin rested on the top of my head. "That was wonderful." I sighed. "And not as hard as I thought it would be. No," I put my hand over his mouth. "No jokes. For a change I'm being serious. Your cure worked, and nobody's happier about it than I am."

He kissed my fingers. "You sound as though you met the enemy and he's yours. Was it such a difficult feat?"

"May I say now for the umpteenth time, you're wonderful, but climbing over the wheelchair wasn't the barrier; at least, not after the initial shock. Climbing into bed shook my delicate equilibrium."

"My hand wasn't very steady either."

"I don't believe you." Turning my head to see if I could detect a smile brought me eye to eye with him. "You didn't seem nervous. If your hand was trembling, your aim was sure fine."

His teeth gleamed briefly. "I'm delighted to know you were pleased, but it wasn't a one-man show. A little realism, please."

I propped up on an elbow to see him better. "Let me tell you something, Mr. Devlin. No one is more realistic than I am. Maybe I wasn't half bad tonight, but you're the one who gets out there every day and copes with a real disability. Mine's only in my head."

"But it's a helluva head." He leaned up and kissed it. "And I like the way you cope with my disability too."

"You mean the way I insult you with it . . . threaten to take apart your wheelchair spoke by spoke?"

"And stick it," he said, pulling me down on top of him.

It was nice that Mark found my impudence appealing, but I wouldn't have dared be so facetious without a half a keg of brandy in me. In fact, I was nervy even for an out and out drunk.

"Mark, do you mind that I make jokes about the wheelchair?"

"As opposed to pretending it's not there?"

"How can anyone do that? It's in clear . . . I'm sorry."

"Come on, don't back down now. Of course, people don't see it when they prefer not to. Either they back away like the condition is contagious, or they're very careful just to look me in the eyes."

"But I'm sure you get plenty of rude stares, as though you're some kind of display."

"Sure, but I stare right back . . . at their crotch."

"Why, you evil voyeur. What an excuse to get a cheap thrill."

"I see the world from a different angle," Mark claimed, and backed it up with vivid descriptions of the rear ends he was forced to look at. That gave me a bad case of the giggles, and we finished in a laughing heap, my hands held over my head while Mark threatened to tickle me.

"If you do, I'll report you to the labor relations board," I warned him. What a complaint. "My boss got me into his bed under false pretenses, and I never want to get out."

He released me, but pulled the cover aside and ran his hands down from my wrists, along my arms, then slowly over my breasts. By the time his fingers reached my stomach, my legs were already spread apart.

The second time was even better.

Chapter 11

The view from the deck was just as spectacular in the morning when the sky was a bright blue and the ocean bathed in sunlight. The tactful and unobtrusive Luis served coffee, croissants, and freshly squeezed orange juice to the music of surf crashing on the beach, but my lover of the night before had his nose buried in the L.A. *Times* sports section. He only looked up to hand me the women's page. Biting down a crack about sexual stereotypes, I exchanged it for editorials and read Doonesbury.

Finally, a word from Mark. "A triple play took it to the tenth inning."

Beautiful. Lovely. Was I supposed to bat my lashes and ask the final score? I studied him over the rim of my cup, but the only emotion registered on his tanned face was joy that Detroit lost a doubleheader yesterday. Dare I hope to compete? I dared nothing. Maybe this was the protocol for waking up in a strange house, in a strange bed, with a strange man at your side. "Thank you very much for a nice roll in the hay last night, and would you please pass the butter before you close the door on your way out?''

How much easier to be a blissless wife than an uncertain paramour, I sighed.

At least, I was a cherished office manager. Mr. Abbotts showed tender concern for my well-being, claiming the only thing that mattered about last night was that I hadn't been hurt. He was referring to the burglary, but my mind was on Mark's casual peck on the cheek this morning, when he took me home to change clothes and get my car. It took some concentration to listen to Mr. Abbotts.

''Housebreakers aren't always thoughtful enough to wait until the owner is out of the house,'' he said with grim humor. ''Now don't worry about the tape. We can make another one.''

''I'm sure you can, but you ought to warn Mr. Blanco that this one's been stolen.''

''I called him as soon as I found out, but he said there's no cause for alarm.''

''Except that I have a broken lock on my back door.''

''Yes,'' he said, frowning at something over my head. ''Was there any other damage to your house?''

''I don't believe so. What *was* Mr. Blanco's explanation? Surely he can't think a simple cassette had more value to a casual thief than my color television?''

''That's all he told me,'' Mr. Abbotts said. ''Nothing important was discussed during that particular meeting with Ms. Busch. I'm sure he'd repeat any vital information to me. I'm not going to have much more luck with his case than Kathy had if he holds back. In any matter, the firm will pay for your door. Don't be proud.'' He squeezed my arm. ''I'll charge it to Mannie's account.''

We both got a little laugh out of that. I still wasn't convinced, but if Mr. Abbotts, Mark, and Mannie Blanco all considered it a mere bagatelle, then I might as well worry about my own problems instead.

Last night had resolved one anxiety; my hormones were all functioning adequately. But had my newfound sexual appetite been offered a one-time treat, or could I expect more of the same?

Mark had been admirably nonchalant all morning. I presumed that if he had fallen madly in love with me overnight, he would have mentioned it in passing at breakfast. Still, I hoped for some gesture of awareness . . . a special smile, a meaningful glance, a pat on the rear . . . a nooner on his desk. But when the hours passed without a word from him, I sank into an apathetic gloom.

After a late lunch with Nancy Weaver, where I pretended that everything was fine, thank you, Mr. Abbotts asked me to clean out Katherine Busch's office and send home her personal effects. It wasn't a pleasant task, though it would have been harder to take last week when the police first unsealed the room. Then all we did was get her case load sorted out and divided among the other attorneys. At least, by now, the janitorial service had vacuumed up the chalk marks that outlined her body, and washed away the fingerprint powder.

Taking a deep breath, I began with pencils and pens in the top drawer of her desk, working down to writs and procedural forms in the bottom left. When the office supplies were transferred to the storage room, I started filling a box with what had to be given to Howard. A twenty-four-carat gold inscribed Cross pen. A rain bonnet. Two solid leather attaché cases. The worst part was taking her framed diplomas off the wall. All those hard-earned certificates—State Bar Association, Federal Bar Association, special awards, honors. I put the color portrait of her husband on top of them.

Double-checking to make sure that nothing had been overlooked, I hesitated again over a large manila envelope. It was from an insurance company, addressed to Ms. Katherine

Busch rather than the law firm, but since it was in the file cabinet I assumed it was company business.

Wrong. It was Katherine Busch's business. A hospital bill and two forms, from an OB/GYN and an anesthesiologist, stapled to an insurance claim made out to her, for a medical termination of pregnancy. Not the flu after all. I stuffed the papers back intside the envelope and placed it in the box over Howard Busch's smiling face.

"Josie, give me an outside line, please. No. Never mind. Would you ring Di-Con and get . . . wait, let me see if I can remember. Yes, extension seven-oh-two." One quick call and the whole distasteful business would be over.

"Am I speaking to Howard Busch? Hello, how are you? This is Eleanor Gordon at the law firm. Very well, thank you. I'm sorry to disturb you at work, but there are some things here at the office that belonged to your wife, and . . . yes, I thought so. Would you be able to stop by after work this evening to pick them up? Oh, I see. Not until after eight. No. We'll be gone by then." I looked over at the boxes. "Not too much, really. A cab? That seems . . . wait a minute," I interrupted. "Why don't I bring everything over to you myself? It's no trouble. Honestly, I'd be glad to . . . all right. Thirteen-oh-six Sandy Cove Drive. Yes, I know where it is, in Sea View Estates. Not out of my way at all. At eight o'clock? See you then."

I jiggled for the switchboard at Di-Con to get back on the line, then asked for Betsy's extension. It rang six times before she answered.

"Hello?"

"You sound as though you were running. Is some demented physicist chasing you down the halls for scientific purposes?"

"No such luck. I just came from Howard Busch's office."

"That's funny. I was just talking to him."

"I'm glad you got a laugh out of it. His department is a

week late on my blueprints. That whole Seattle project is behind schedule. So what's up? I'm too busy to gab.''

"Will you go to Howard Busch's house with me tonight?"

"What for? You making a sympathy call?"

"A delivery. I've got some boxes and several drooping plants to move out of here, and I volunteered personalized door-to-door service.''

"Sorry, love. I'm in no mood to see Howard again, not until he shows me some finished work. Still want to meet me at Antonio's, or will that cut it too close for you?''

"No. It's okay. I just have to stop at the bank first, and Antonio's is halfway between here and Sea Views. But how about making it six-thirty instead of seven? Great.''

Great? What was so great? I wasn't in the mood for fish at Antonio's. I didn't want to go to Sea Views. And when the real estate agent called a little later to tell me she had a buyer for the house, I almost told her to forget it.

Why was I abandoning home and hearth on top of everything else? This business of career office managing, dealing with murder, police, and aerobic dancing was still unfamiliar territory. More times than not, I floundered like a backwards salmon trying to spawn downstream. At least I knew and understood what was in that tri-level on Ricardo Place: the foil wallpaper in the bathroom, the orange shag carpeting in the den, the patched hole in the ceiling of the garage. Even when I turned the kitchen into an asylum and made eating my occupational therapy, it was more secure than being a wandering Jew.

Where was I going anyway? Definitely not to a singles condo. Maybe Michael would like a bunky. How about a nice quiet retirement community?

The best idea was a halfway house for the semiliberated where I'd have my own room, but with a security guard posted at the door, a ten o'clock curfew, and nightly classes on the philosophy of equal opportunity, affirmative action, and the E.R.A. After I passed How To Take It on the Chin 101, then I'd be allowed on overnight field trips with men like Mark Devlin.

He was the cause of my old-fashioned megrims; why not admit it? Obviously, the man had decided in the clear light of day that what transpired in the dark last night wasn't worth repeating. I shouldn't have taken it personally. A lot of women were screwed and rejected in the space of twelve hours. By today's standards, it was an adult relationship. But I hadn't graduated the course on one-night stands yet. Mark warned me to take it slower, but I was too busy showing off. Look, ma, no hangups. If I had used my head instead of my *chutzpah,* I'd have noticed that while I was backing him up to the bed, he was trying to back away.

Trying to be realistic but finding no solace in it, I slumped through a period of self-pity, battled briefly with anger at the world, then settled into a firm resolve to show Mark I didn't give a damn. There was no time like the present, but since he was making himself scarce, I might have to wait until tomorrow before slaying him with massive indifference. But at five minutes past five, as the titty-tats were running the eight-yard dash to the elevator, he finally emerged from the back.

"Jesus, it's been a helluva day."

The poor dear did look tired, bless his fickle little heart, but I only made noncommittal noises out of a poker face, and continued clearing my desk. No need to sympathize unduly.

"I talked to three candidates about an associate position here. One wants junior partner or nothing." He rubbed the back of his neck. "I told him nothing. Phil has somebody in San Francisco he likes, but there's another one in L.A. who's interested, too."

"How nice to feel so wanted."

Mark grunted and flexed his shoulder muscles. The double message went right over his left bicep.

I smiled so brightly, it almost cracked my jaw. "Well, have a nice evening. I'm off. Oh, by the way, I think my house is sold."

"Did they sign a binder?" He yawned. "God, I'm tired."

"Absolutely. And for my asking price. They want to move in by the middle of September."

"Good." Then, as blandly as if he were ordering a cheese sandwich, he asked if I'd like to celebrate by spending the weekend in Las Vegas.

"Las Vegas?" I parroted.

Mark looked at his watch. "Damn, I've got to get out of here. That zoning commission meeting is in fifteen minutes. Aaron Stern is flying up to Vegas on Thursday night, and he wants me to come with him to check out the deal on some property he's buying. I'll arrange with your boss to give you Friday off, and we can make it a package deal. What's the matter? Don't you want to go?"

"No. Yes. I'd love to." How quickly a drowning woman grasps at straws.

"I won't be doing business all the time." He leered and gave me a long, hard kiss. While I was still recovering, he shot off to the elevator, saying he had to dash or he'd never make the meeting in time.

I almost asked what meeting.

My equilibrium was restored by the time I arrived at Antonio's, and I would have poured my news into Betsy's ear the moment I sat down, only she'd been doing some thinking since I spoke to her earlier, and immediately pointed a carrot stick at me.

"I know why you're making a sacrificial trip out to Sea Views. To do a little sleuthing."

"Don't be silly." Spreading a napkin on my lap, I took a carrot stick too. "Just because you're not feeling very benevolent toward Howard Busch at the present doesn't mean I can't be nice. Besides, I'm not sleuthing."

"At all?" she asked. "Come now. Modesty suits you, but it's even money who finds the murderer first, you or the police. I just presumed you were going to question the classic suspect. And I don't mean the butler," she added, biting off a chunk of carrot.

"Boy, you do have it in for Howard. Think maybe you're taking a jaundiced view of the guy? He was madly in love with his wife, remember?"

"So? They didn't live in an enchanted cottage."

"They came pretty close, Bets. But he has an alibi anyway, and I helped verify it. After his plane arrived from Seattle, he went to Di-Con, worked a while, then drove to Casa Grande, ETA, eight P.M. Satisfied?"

"Not really. Whatever work he did when he came back to the plant sure wasn't what I left for him. We're a whole week behind schedule now."

"That didn't happen in one night, superwoman. Come on, give the poor guy a break. It's not his fault his wife was killed."

"I know," she relented, "but that doesn't help my budget. This nuke project is an expensive baby, and my department is already running over."

"Speaking of babies," I said, "it seems Howard may have had two of them on his hands. Yours and his."

"What are you talking about?"

"Swear you won't repeat this. I probably shouldn't be telling you, but Katherine Busch had an abortion last month."

"So? Women do it all the time. Don't tell me you've suddenly become a right-to-lifer."

"Of course not." I bit into an olive. "It just struck me that a competent woman like her wouldn't hedge at a little more responsibility."

"Hold it a minute, pal. Those little responsibilities grow

up. It's tough to combine a career and motherhood, even for competent engineers," she added with a heavy hand. "And some people just don't think it's very nice to shove another unsuspecting kid into this overpopulated world. Maybe she was an environmentalist. Maybe she just wanted to wait."

"I know all that, Betsy. It's just that she seemed so ready to take on everything else."

"You know something, Ellie? You've got a fixation about Katherine Busch. As long as she was superwoman—successful, married, and happy—you made her your ideal. Now comes the revelation that she was as fallible as the rest of us, and it spoils the picture. It's okay for Eleanor Gordon to goof, but women like Katherine Busch better not forget to take their birth control pills unless they really mean it."

"Do I sound that bad?"

"Not really." Betsy smiled. "Just a bit of sloppy thinking from an otherwise astute person. It's that liberal arts education."

"As opposed to your superior scientific training. Yes, you've mentioned that before. But I still think Katherine Busch was an unusually strong woman. How many wives would have an abortion while hubby was out of town? I would have wanted a soothing hand on my fevered brow, and tea and toast in bed for a week."

"Some people don't like tea and toast."

As if the mention of food had worked sympathetic magic, the waiter finally appeared. I told him to forget the menus; we were sticking with the salad bar. Betsy didn't cavil at my decision, just asked me if I'd gained weight again.

With a smug smile, I informed her that Mark Devlin had invited me to Las Vegas and that I intended to drop another pound or two before I went.

"That's a good idea," she approved. "I always gain weight on business trips. Every meeting is conducted with a plate of food in front of you."

"This isn't all business."

"Really?" Her brows arched in a large question mark. "I detect a coy note under that innocent stare. What is the other point of the trip, if you don't mind my asking, which of course you don't, because that's why you brought it up."

"Pure pleasure," I said airily.

"Is that so? And why does Mark Devlin want to give you pure pleasure?"

"Well—" I delayed to open a package of crackers. "Last night my house was robbed and—"

"Your house was robbed? When? While you were sleeping?"

"No, no, cool down. Sorry I sprang it on you like this. It happened while we were at the aerobic dance class."

"Bastards! How much did they take?"

"Well," I hesitated, "actually, nothing of mine. Just a tape recording of Mark's."

Unbelievably, that was nearly all I could tell Betsy without breaking the confidentiality of the Blanco case. If I poured out my fears about the mob stealing the tape, it would be revealing Mannie's secret negotiations. Feeling isolated and oddly defenseless, I was limited to describing the mess in the house rather than the confusion in my head.

Betsy's well-trained mind was on the essentials anyway. "So what does this have to do with Las Vegas?"

"I'm getting there. A little background first." I smiled at her wry look. "Naturally I had to call Mark to tell him about the robbery. He came over and dealt with the police, then insisted on taking me home with him."

"You were in that bad shape?" she asked with concern.

"Terrible. The robbery had me really shaken, but I was staggering when we got out of Mark's hot tub, and by the time we tumbled into his bed, I was simply flat on my back."

Startling the worldly-wise Betsy Hanson into a state of speechless surprise was no easy feat. I knew this would do it.

"Why, you big shit," she said in fascination. "First a robbery, then flat on your back." Laughter bubbled up and came pouring out. "How do you go from crisis to crisis with such dramatic flair? And you even waited to tell me all at once. But I'm a mite bewildered. The last I heard, Mark was limited to spiritual communion."

"An error in judgment on my part," I said demurely.

"I won't ask how he presented the contradicting evidence." She started to laugh again. "So now it's on to Las Vegas and the main showroom. Quite a tour. May I offer my felicitations?"

At this point my balloon started to deflate a little. "The play could fold after a couple of performances. Remember, Bets, only yesterday the leading lady was an understudy."

"Seems to me you learned all the lines overnight. If Mark likes and you like, what's the problem?"

"I don't understand the stage directions." That's as close as I would come to admitting the agonies of ignorance I suffered today. "You're an old trouper, my friend. Tell me how to play it: cool, amused, sophisticated, with one eye on the wings?"

"By ear," was her short answer.

"I'm tone deaf and distrusting."

"Oh, Ellie love." She smiled sympathetically. "I understand exactly how you feel, but you can't use your body to test a man's integrity. Mark's only taking what you're offering."

"I realize that. But isn't there some way I can tell what he means by it?"

"Can he tell what *you* mean by it?"

I rested my chin on my hand. "Okay. As soon as I figure it out, I'll let him know."

Chapter 12

Sea View Estates was Casa Grande's newest prestige housing development, though the name was just the usual California hype. On the wrong end of town for ocean breezes, the "Estates" were an eighth of an acre with a choice of five house plans; the exterior trim either English Tudor, French Mansard, Spanish Hacienda, or Southern Antebellum. If the mixture couldn't be classed as architecturally pure, at least all the solar collectors were identical.

"You gotta have a gimmick." In the fifties it was fallout shelters in every backyard. Today it was an alternate energy source on every roof. Sea Views touted that, and the added benefits of small lots, authentically simulated Corinthian columns, plywood half-timbering, and a hacienda only lacking wrought-iron grillwork and a tile roof. These savings gave the hard-pressed homeowner some extra cash for the play-as-you-pay arrangement. For a nominal yearly fee, everyone shared the joys of mini-parks, racquetball courts, a fishing lake, volleyball nets, a putting green, and, of course, the obligatory olympic-sized swimming pool.

When hippies tried togetherness, they were booed out of town. Call it recreational community participation, pay to give up your privacy, and it's the American Dream.

Thirteen-oh-six Sandy Cove Drive was another mock-French, pseudo-mansard with a courtesy palm tree in the yard and an abbreviated driveway. By the time I trekked twice up the scalloped stepping stones to deposit everything at the front door, I fully expected the *fleur de lis* bell to chime "La Marseillaise." Howard answered immediately.

"Ellie," he began, then saw the boxes at my feet. "I didn't realize that there was so much. Why didn't you come get me?"

To make up for that oversight, I let him carry everything to the garage while I maneuvered the plants inside to the flagstone entry. They were a sad little bunch after a week of drought in Katherine's sealed office. The Boston fern was suffering from a nearly terminal case of dehydration, and the split-leaf philodendron was jaundiced by iron deficiency. Howard, I was happy to note, looked a lot better than the plants did. He was thinner and had lost his California tan, but at least he'd also lost the dazed, grieved air he'd worn at the funeral. Almost excessively grateful for my kind efforts on his behalf, he invited me to stay for a cup of coffee and a tour of his helio-tracker.

Personally I found the rock pit and the fabled solar collector a big disappointment. All that hullabaloo for ecology, and the thing still needed an electric motor. Apparently the Busches were a lot more impressed with their energy-saver than I was. It seemed to be the only thing in the house that did interest them. After living here for almost a year, they still hadn't gotten around to furnishing the living room or dining room. Howard said something about not having had the time to do things properly yet, but I could tell he was embarrassed. When we got to the den, furnished, but not in grand style, he made an unnecessary fuss about folding up one little newspaper and asking me to excuse a nonexistemt mess.

"I don't know how you feel, but I like everything in its place," he said. "Sit down and get comfortable. Coffee is on the way."

Whatever Howard thought about the rest of the house, he needn't have felt demoralized because of the den. It was a nice room. There were two matching easy chairs flanking the fireplace, a small gun cabinet and some old hunting prints against one wall, and floor-to-ceiling bookshelves filled with college texts, engineering manuals, thirty volumes of Legal Jurisprudence, and a ton of science-fiction paperbacks. Katherine told me she had a weakness for little green men and rogue computers trying to take over the world. I could picture her curled up in that chair, glasses perched on her nose, reading for a while, dozing over the television, challenging Howard to one more hand of gin rummy. How could he bear it in here without her?

I was sitting on the couch when Howard came back carrying a tray with a Melitta pot, plain white cups, and brown linen napkins. He set it on the table and made a formal presentation of pouring.

"I'm a coffee nut." He smiled. "This is part of the show. Couldn't do any less for beans grown in Colombia and ground by my own hands. This blend is called Supremo. Try it black first and see how you like it."

"Mmm. I like it."

While I drank, Howard continued his discourse on the importance of developing alternatives to fossil fuels, which led to the nuke project at Di-Con, then to Japanese automakers, and finally back to the house again.

"I admit this place isn't exactly what Kathy and I wanted,

but we had to start somewhere, and a house with solar has great resale value.''

"You'll make a profit, all right. I'm selling my house now, for almost three times what we paid for it fifteen years ago.''

"I'm not surprised.'' He lit a cigarette. "So what are you going to do? Buy a condominium?''

The idea still didn't sit well. "Maybe. What are you going to do?''

"Nothing right now. I can't even think until the investigation is settled.''

"Do the police have any leads yet?''

"Not that they've told me.'' He shrugged. "The only one I've heard from is Reverend Ritchie. He invited me to join his church. Said it would bring me comfort in my time of mourning.''

"The gall of that man,'' I snorted. "He couldn't convert your wife, so he's trying it on you. What a hypocrite.''

"I don't think so.'' Howard let out a big puff of smoke. "The guy's sincere, just kind of old-fashioned. You don't hear too many fire-and-brimstone sermons these days.''

"Is that what he gave you?''

Howard got up and walked over to the fireplace. "Not exactly. He only recommended that I learn from the sins of the past and begin a new life. Actually, he blames Kathy for my unhappiness.'' Howard tossed the half-smoked cigarette into the empty hearth, then crushed it out with his shoe. "Seems she brought retribution on herself by breaking God's laws.''

Ritchie certainly had a unique way of comforting the bereaved. But then, winning over Howard Busch would be a kind of final victory over Katherine. I didn't know if the police were still considering Ritchie a possible murder suspect, but he certainly wasn't on my list of the top ten innocents.

"Do you believe him?" I asked carefully. Lesser gurus than the Reverend Billy Joe have swayed people their way.

To my relief, Howard shook his head. "I don't believe anything, except that my wife's dead and Mannie Blanco is running around free."

"You think Mannie killed her?"

"No, no. I didn't mean that." Howard turned toward the fireplace and pressed his hands against the mantel. "It's the whole setup. The deal he's trying to pull. Every hood in the syndicate knows what he's up to, and Kathy had the information. She knew how to use it." He rubbed a hand across his eyes. "Sorry. I get a little carried away. It's so damn obvious . . . to me, anyway."

"I know. I wondered myself if the mob were responsible. In fact, that was my first thought when the tape was stolen from my house."

"What tape?" he asked. "Not one of Mannie's?" Howard was surprised when I nodded yes. "How did it get to your house? I thought Kathy kept them in a locked file."

"She did, but this one hadn't been transcribed yet. It was made that Thursday afternoon, and in all the confusion, I took it home with me by mistake."

Howard gave a short laugh and reached for another cigarette. "So what did the creep say this time?"

"Nobody knows for sure. I never did get to hear it; in fact, I didn't even know I had it until the day before the robbery. We thought it was in her office all along, locked in that file you mentioned."

Howard quirked a blond eyebrow. "This tape was made the day she was killed, then it was stolen before anybody got to hear it? How does Mannie explain that?"

"According to him, there's nothing to explain."

Howard started puffing furiously on the cigarette. "I don't believe it. The bastard never told the truth in his life. Living in that sealed-off palace, with those goddamned guard dogs.

He's running scared.'' Howard flung the cigarette into the fireplace. "I'll explain it for you. The D.A. was fed up. If Blanco didn't give him something soon, the immunity deal was off. Mannie had to come through to save his own neck from fifteen years in prison. Only one of his double-crossed pals didn't like the idea of being traded for Mannie's freedom, so he took his name off the bartered list. That's the secret of your missing tape,'' Howard said bitterly. "Try that on Blanco for size.''

"Maybe he was telling the truth for a change,'' I suggested. "You know he hasn't said anything yet that's the least bit damaging to anyone, including himself. Why should this tape be any different from the rest?''

Howard fixed me with a steady gaze. "Why was the only person who knew what was on it murdered?''

Coincidence, I wanted to say. Nothing more. But the coincidence made a terrible kind of sense. I half-believed it myself. Hood talks to lawyer, lawyer is killed, tape of their conversation is stolen. Howard made it sound *ipso facto*.

Mark hadn't. He saw no connection between the robbery and Katherine Busch's death, at least none he admitted. Maybe that was a polite deception to keep me from wetting my pants in terror. If Katherine Busch's death warrant had been sealed by what Mannie told her, then the cassette could have done as much for me.

No. We went over all that. Mark wouldn't treat me like a babbling idiot. If he thought my having the tape put me in any danger, he'd have warned me. I was just getting caught up in Howard's emotional reaction.

"Maybe the pieces do fit together,'' I said briskly, "but Mr. Devlin assured me they have no connection.''

Howard stared through the smoke. "I can understand him saying that. It'd be a helluva burden for him to think the case he gave her blew up in her face.''

Howard didn't choke on that but I almost did. He went on,

his mouth grim. ''Maybe it's as much my fault as Mark's. Sometimes you have a gut feeling about things, and mine was to steer clear of Mannie Blanco. But I didn't push it. Mark's the lawyer. He said the case was good for Kathy's career, and he had helped her so much already, who thought he could be wrong now? Mark is an extraordinary person. Look at how he made a comeback after that accident. You have to give him credit.''

''I give him plenty of credit, Howard, and you too. But your wife was an unusually capable woman. When she took the case, she understood the risks involved.''

Howard smashed the cigarette out in the ashtray, then stuffed tightly balled fists in his pockets and paced to the window. ''I saw the risks better than she did, but I still went to Seattle and left her here alone. I could have made an excuse to Di-Con; they wouldn't have fired me. But Kathy insisted. My job was as important as hers, and she wouldn't hear of my quitting the nuke project to stick around town. I wanted to at the beginning, but we didn't have that kind of marriage.'' Howard looked down at his feet and rolled back on the heels of his shoes. ''We each made our own decisions when it came to careers. I couldn't justify interfering with her work now, even if it scared the crap out of me. That's what I told myself, anyway.''

''Howard, you can't blame yourself because you respected your wife's freedom to make her own choices. My God, most women would give you a medal of honor for that. In turn, Kathy couldn't accept your sacrificing your career for hers. The two of you had a beautiful relationship. There's nothing to feel guilty about.'' He raised his head, and I continued more softly. ''It may not be much consolation right now, but she never could have piled up so many achievements in such a short time without your support.''

''I don't know.'' He gave a crooked smile. ''She was pretty special. Mark gave her the opportunity to show it, but Kath earned every star in her copybook. Nobody could match her for drive and brains. You saw all those awards. She was on her way to being one of the top lawyers in California.''

''I know. Just working in the same office with her, you could see that.''

His face fell. ''She paid a hell of a price trying to get there, didn't she? I'm learning to accept her death, but I can't forgive it. Not when she didn't even have a chance to live first.''

''No.'' I shivered. There was still an empty living room to fill, a couple of bedrooms down the hall. Howard lit another cigarette and let out a long stream of smoke. I had to wipe my eyes.

''Hey, is this bothering you?'' He waved ineffectually at the layer of smog around his head and put out the cigarette. ''Why didn't you say something? It's a stinking habit, but I seem to be doing it more lately.''

''No, I'm fine. Smoke doesn't bother me, but I've stayed way too long.''

''That's my fault, but you're such a sympathetic listener.''

''And you're a terrific brewmaster,'' I said, getting up from the couch. ''Tell me what that coffee's called again? Supremo? A perfect name. Can you buy it locally?''

Howard suggested a few places as he walked me to the front door, and when I saw the plants still sitting in a bedraggled huddle on the floor, I asked about them too.

''They're not worth saving.'' He shrugged. ''I'm just going to toss them.''

They ended up in the back seat of my car. It was an impulse to say I'd like them as a remembrance of his wife, but I felt a funny attachment to the dumb things. That night, with Jewish motherly love, I overwatered them, put a healthy dose of plant food into the soil, set them all by east windows, and promised they'd live to a hundred and twenty.

At least they were going to have a chance.

Chapter 13

By Thursday evening, full of excellent resolves to count on nothing beyond the weekend, I was in midair long before we boarded the private jet to Las Vegas. Aaron Stern was doing the co-piloting, one of his hobbies, leaving Mark and me alone to enjoy the luxury of the cabin. There was room for twelve to frolic comfortably, be refreshed at the well-stocked bar, read any number of magazines, or just listen to music. So much for Betsy's claim that no one lived *la dolce vita*. All I needed was a mink coat slung over my shoulder to complete the picture of a jet set darling.

In preparation for my first liberated liaison, I'd gone shopping last night and bought a seductive bikini with complete disregard for what it showed, two gorgeous nighties, and a couple of slinky evening dresses. Steve Tedesco wouldn't have believed it. I wasn't sure I did myself. The uptight, upright Eleanor Gordon had burst forth as a woman of the times. The titty-tats had nothing on me.

Thinking about them brought something else to mind.

"Mark, it might be a good idea if we didn't mention this trip to anyone in the office. A whisper of our going away together and the titty-tats will demand a complete rundown on where, what, why, and how long did foreplay last. Don't laugh. It's true. They have a competition going, and I'd rather stay out of their relay races."

"Whatever you say." He nodded agreeably. "If you want, we can book separate rooms at the hotel so even the desk clerk won't know. We'll just sneak over to each other every night."

"What about the house detective? Don't you think he'll wonder about a woman in a backless, almost frontless nightie, roaming the halls at three A.M.?" I gave him a full description in body language, and when we finally pulled apart, he said I had a graphic way with words.

So did he, for that matter. Mark's lovemaking, whether it was in a king-size bed or fifteen thousand feet off the ground, worked absolute magic on me. Only this time around, there would be no probing into the wiles and wherefores of his intentions. I had overcome my fear of flying. Now I just had to master the art of doing loop-the-loops without going into a tail spin. This weekend ought to do it. After three days airborne with Mark, I should qualify for a pilot's license.

How hard was it for him to get to this point? Granted, Mark had superhuman strength of mind, but it must have been difficult to make that first pass at a woman from a wheelchair. I wasn't going to ask mow many successes he had had; plenty, judging from *his* graphic way with words. But what had happened in the beginning? He told me that a lot of people were uncomfortable around his handicap. Was his wife one of them?

"Why did you get a divorce, Mark? Was it because of the accident?"

"No, not really." He withdrew his arm from behind me. "Our marriage started fizzling out long before that."

I was sorry I asked. My question had driven him back over to his side of the armrest and spoiled the mood. Why did I have to demand his life story? Just because I'd told him all about my marriage, my divorce, my insecurities, didn't mean he had to return the honor. "I'm sorry, Mark. It's none of my business."

"Worried that you've bruised my delicate feelings?"

"Did I?"

"Of course not. It's just that assessing blame afterwards is a waste of time."

"I know. It took me a while to figure that out for myself. But why did your wife leave just when you really needed her? If she stuck around until then, what made the difference?"

"I don't know if I can explain," he said thoughtfully, "but Christy's complaint always was that I worked too hard and didn't spend enough time with her. After the accident, she thought it would be different, but as soon as I was able I went right back to the same old pattern."

"I think that's marvelous. She should have been delighted that you weren't reduced to a helpless invalid."

Mark smiled wryly. "I'm talking mental, not physical, Ellie. Being in a wheelchair changed my life-style radically; it didn't change me. Whatever faults I had before, I still had, only in a sitting position. A physical handicap doesn't make saints out of sinners. Suddenly not being able to play racquetball doesn't endow you with the wisdom of the ages either. I neglected my wife when I could walk and did the same thing when I couldn't walk."

"That's a pretty big concession. Most men would just say their wives didn't understand them."

"No, mine understood me very well."

Satisfied that he had explained fully, Mark reached for a *Sports Illustrated* from the bulging rack while I accepted the fact that if there were more to the story, I wouldn't hear it from him. He had answered one question though: his wife hadn't left him because of the wheelchair; she left him in spite of it. Someday, when I had time, I'd really analyze that, but for now I only wanted to concentrate on the fun-filled weekend ahead.

Las Vegas is the ultimate fantasy. In one glittering oasis in the desert, they've gathered every absurdity ever invented for the pursuit of pleasure. There are no clocks in the casinos to remind the happy vacationer of home, so all he has to do is stand under crystal chandeliers, à la Versailles, and watch his money change hands faster than the champagne is flowing. There's no easy way to tell the rich from the nine-to-fivers either. Everyone acts as though fine wine, Frank Sinatra, and pheasant under glass is the norm for an evening's entertainment. The truth only outs when the guy who arrived in an eight-thousand-dollar Volkswagen leaves in a fifty-thousand-dollar bus. Old joke, but no lie. It's hard to remember that those little chips are real money, although they're tossed around like tiddleywinks by the Arab sheiks wandering around in Bond Street suits. I don't know why the Arabs are so easy to spot, but Vegas is filled with them. The only time it makes me nervous is when one of them has five thousand dollars riding on my number, and I roll a seven. Then I try very hard not to look Jewish.

At 3:00 A.M. Friday morning, I was tired but happy to be watching Mark clean up at blackjack. He was on a winning streak, and I wouldn't even twitch my nose in case it changed his luck. As another pile of chips was being added to his formidable collection, a short, stubby hand clapped him on the shoulder.

"Okay, buddy, that's it. The old wheelchair gimmick won't work here. Cash in your chips."

I froze. The man was dressed in a conservative black suit and his voice had the bark of authority.

Mark only grinned. "Finally throwing me out, Lou?"

"You betcha." Then he started to laugh and pump Mark's

hand up and down. "You son of a gun. Where you been hidin'? See you're winnin' as usual. Come on, give the dealer a rest. I'll buy us a couple of drinks."

Lou snapped his fingers and a young man materialized to scoop up Mark's winnings and take them to the cashier. Tokens then transferred back to real money again, we left the noisy casino to squeeze around a small table in the bar. Lou must have snapped his fingers again while I wasn't looking. Waiting there for us was a knockout blonde named Stacey.

Her tall, willowy body draped over the chair, Stacey blazed with sex appeal and diamonds. A simple little black dress accentuated the former, while several carats' worth of the latter hung from shell-like ears and circled dainty wrists. As for the long, tapering fingers, raising them must have been a Herculean task.

I finally dragged my eyes away from her and began to appraise her boyfriend. Lou had seemed sinister at first; now he was just a middle-aged, balding, stocky man, a good five inches too short for a six-foot showgirl. Their May–December romance had the trimmings of Mutt and Jeff.

"Is there really a wheelchair gimmick?" I asked him.

"You betcha. And it's a damned good one. A couple of years back, some guy almost broke the bank playin' blackjack. Bein' in a wheelchair, he was sittin' a lot lower than the regular stools, and his trick was to park himself at the end of the table, so when the cards were bein' dealt, he could see 'em from the bottom. Look, I'll show ya. If I'm a leftie, I deal with this side up. All you gotta do is sit over there, just a little lower down, and suddenly you got ESP. Watch now. A rightie does it from here, and if you're on that side, it's a peep show from another angle."

"It's an angle, all right," I agreed. "How did you catch on?"

"A couple a pit bosses finally spotted that the guy only switched tables when we changed dealers, and he was real particular about where he went next. Just as we was about to nab him, he stood up and ran out. Didn't take the wheelchair with him, neither.''

''What about his chips?''

''In a bag.'' Lou took a fat cigar from his pocket and bit off the end. ''He could cash 'em in any hotel on the Strip.''

I nudged Mark in the arm. ''Lucky you were sitting in the middle of the table or Lou might have you in handcuffs now.''

''Lemme tell you about luck,'' Lou said, lighting the stogie. ''Vegas wouldn't be here without it.''

''I thought all the odds were with the house. Even your slot machines are timed to go off. That's not luck, that's business.''

''You betcha, doll, and the business of odds is to make winnin' a lucky break. Gamblers like to play the chance, not the sure thing. They wouldn't be throwin' all those nickels in the slots unless they was figurin' on luck.''

''And the casino's got it down to a science. Just enough winners to keep the suckers coming back for more, right?''

Lou grinned. ''That's business.''

I couldn't help smiling back at him. He may have sounded like a thug from Brooklyn, but he had a funny kind of charm too. He also had plenty of street smarts. That helps when you're in the business of fleecing your fellow man.

Stacey put her beringed hand on his arm. ''Lou, honey. It's getting late. You go off at four. Can't we leave now?''

''Hell no.'' He frowned. ''I'm entertainin' my friends.'' Stacey kept her face completely expressionless, but her long nails tapped impatiently on the table. Lou ignored her and looked at Mark. ''You guys ready to call it a night?'' he asked.

''We'll finish our drinks first,'' Mark said.

''Yeah.'' Lou flashed a hard look at Stacey. ''You don't wanna get the bum rush when you're on vacation. So tell me, counselor, what's happenin' with Blanco's case? I hear tell he's got an ace up his sleeve.''

"No ace, Lou. We're just trying to work up a decent defense," Mark answered. "Don't believe everything you read in the papers."

"Okay, okay, I know. You gotta keep your trap shut." Lou puffed on his cigar. "But he's a real bundle of bad luck. Just watch yourself."

"Are you talking odds or business?" I couldn't help asking.

"Smart." Lou nodded his head at me. "You're real smart. But I'll tell you, doll, when you're a bad businessman, the odds are against you. Mannie's a punk. He never played it right. Everybody knew he was runnin' rackets, and don't tell me the police wasn't lookin' the other way. But like I said, Mannie's a punk. He leaned too hard on the wrong customer to pay up, or he used a marked deck. Whatever, bad business means bad luck, and them odds is a crapout in anybody's book."

"I'm sure Mr. Abbotts will take good care of him," I said, then added with a blank stare, "and Mr. Blanco may be innocent. Only the courts can decide that."

"Okay." Lou nodded. "I'll go along with that." His eyes narrowed behind the screen of smoke. "If Mannie ever gets to court." He pointed his cigar at Mark. "Just listen, counselor. You don't have to talk, but remember I told you that Mannie ain't even got a three a clubs up his sleeve. I know that guy, and he's always been small time. The best he can come up with is a two-bit gambler like himself and a bunch of worthless I.O.U.s. A jackpot'll turn out to be fingerin' a congressman who took a little payoff as a side bet. That's it, I'm tellin' you. Nothin's worth the price Mannie's gonna cost you." Lou sat back and smoothed his tie. "You pass that along to Phil."

And I said Lou wasn't sinister? How did he come by all that information? Not the newspapers. They were only guessing at the truth; Lou sounded as though he had an inside source. It was still a shot in the dark, though a seasoned gambler like him would know that trading information for immunity was a smart way to hedge a bet. But he also claimed Mannie had the goods on a congressman, and that item hadn't been broadcast in the Sunday edition yet. It wasn't even in the Blanco files.

Glancing around the room covertly, as though I expected to see a legion of lieutenants in white fedoras and black pin-striped suits, I tried to put some salt on that wild theory. Just because Lou looked like a gangster, talked like a gangster, and knew things only a gangster would know, did not necessarily mean he was a member of the fraternity. I had murder on the mind and a bee in my bonnet put there by Howard Busch. Mark's friend might not be a racketeer, just a street-wise con man. Then why did listening to him make me think of *The Godfather*?

Containing my rampant curiosity until Mark and I got up to the room, I asked the moment the door shut behind us, "Who is that character? Was he putting me on, or does he always talk like Nathan Detroit?"

Mark smiled and slid his hands up my dress. "You betcha."

"Hey," I said with a catch in my voice, "what are you doing down there?"

"Getting you ready for a bath," he murmured. His fingers caressed the sensitive skin on my stomach, then circled lower. "See? You're wet already."

Chapter 14

Friday's breakfast was served to us at the decadent hour of two P.M. This time Mark left the sports page on the nightstand as the waiter rolled a plastic-domed trolley into the room. In unison we turned down the young man's suggestion that we dine out on the terrace in the one-hundred-degree heat. There was a nice table right by the patio doors, where we could look at the sun instead of bake in it. Mark reached for a bagel before the waiter even pocketed his tip.

"Lox, cream cheese, tomato, *and* onion." He smiled, then hesitated.

"Go ahead," I prompted. "You can always use a mouthwash afterwards."

Grinning, Mark plopped a beautiful slice of juicy red onion on his sandwich and took a bite with a groan of pleasure. "You really aren't going to eat?" he asked. "I ordered enough for two."

"You ordered enough for four." I poured myself a cup of black coffee and walked away from the table.

"Have some creamed herring at least," he said with a twinkle in his eye.

"Don't tempt me! I'm not exactly on a diet this weekend, but I'm not tall enough to start out with all that Jewish soul food in the mornings. Do you want me to be five feet in all directions? Go on, *ess mein kind*. Grapefruit and coffee will do me just fine." Mark took another bite while I looked in the mirror and sucked in my gut. "Now, if I were built like Lou's girl friend, Stacey whatsherface, I could just store all the excess food in my legs. Did you notice how tall she is? I bet they don't even accept showgirls under six feet."

Mark choked on a piece of herring. "I hate to disillusion you, Ellie, but she's no showgirl. Stacey's a hooker." He immediately took another chunk of fish, still grinning.

"Aw, come on. You're just jealous because Lou's date was taller than yours." I sat down across from him and propped my chin on my hands. "Are you telling me she bought all those diamonds with her gratuities?"

He laughed. "Hookers make a hell of a lot more money than showgirls, and not on gratuities. They charge a set fee."

"That's a defamation of character," I objected. "Stacey looked perfectly nice to me. She didn't pick her nose at the table or slurp her champagne. In fact, she seemed very refined."

"You mean, she didn't say 'ain't.' Oh, Ellie." He wiped his eyes with the back of his hand.

"See?" I denounced. "You shouldn't make fun of people while you're eating." I handed him a Kleenex. "Okay, how do you know she's a hooker? There wasn't any scarlet A on the front of her dress. I would have noticed. Unless you saw it embroidered on her soul."

"Don't ask how. I can just tell. And I know Lou." That set him off again.

I had never seen Mark laugh so much. Or eat so much. Gluttony must be transferable. "All right, you smartass, Stacey is the most grammatical hooker in Vegas, but who is Lou . . . what is his last name anyway?''

"Smith. He owns part of the hotel.''

"Maybe so, but his name isn't Smith. That one's not even embroidered on his handkerchief. How do you know him?''

"The firm handled some legal work for him a few years ago. He has property in California, rentals, a couple of shopping centers.''

"There speaks the diamonds.'' I reached over and speared a tomato slice. "But he looks more like a gangster than a man of commerce.''

"Because he had his nose broken a couple of times? That could have happened while he was conducting business. Oh no. Forget I said that. You have a funny gleam in your eye. Let me just remind you that one of the more notable criminals of the age was called Baby-Face Nelson. He looked as 'nice' as Stacey.''

Mark ducked a flying wedge of lemon, as I glared at him in feigned indignation. "I challenge you to a test of perception—my female intuition against your male prejudice. We'll find out who has x-ray vision. The winner gets a bagel.''

Mark rose to the bait, and like two idiots we spent the rest of the day, between gambling (we lost), table tennis (he won), and a show that night, putting every woman we saw into pigeonholes. Aside from spotting ladies of the night, Mark swore he could tell whether a woman was an innocent tourist or married and having a fling with another man. We really fought about the fiftyish lady with dyed red hair and a bag of knitting on her lap. Mark said she was a madame on vacation; I claimed she was here for the Mah-Jongg tournament. When we discovered she was a shill in the casino, the contest ended in a draw.

On Saturday afternoon Aaron Stern came by the suite to talk option waivers, abstract titles, and restrictive covenants. He was ready to buy if Mark approved the mortgage agreements. I left them to it and took off for a couple hours. It was too hot to stick a nose outside, and I wasn't interested in the jai alai games, but there was plenty to do in the hotel. Bypassing the slot machines, the beauty parlor, and the Swedish masseuse, I headed straight for the row of boutiques that lined the mezzanine.

For anyone who still had pocket money after leaving the casino, the hotel shops were ready and waiting to correct the situation. Their prices were exorbitant and their wares tempting, the theory being that a tourist from Cleveland shouldn't gripe about paying more in Vegas for the same thing he could get at home. He might save a couple of dollars if he waited, but afterwards he'd still be in Cleveland.

Well aware of those applied mathematics, I had left my purse upstairs and come prepared to look only. The clerks were more than happy to let me browse, on the second theory that if a customer didn't produce her checkbook now, she might after another shot at the crap tables. One extremely hopeful saleswoman absolutely forced me to try on a full-length sable coat. I had to tell her regretfully that it was too much like the one I had at home.

The true test of my skills as a window shopper came at the jewelry store. On a blue velvet mat, next to a hunk of pink coral, lay a pair of diamond earrings that appeared to be replicas of the set Stacey had worn the other night. Curiosity was one of the reasons I asked the clerk to take them out of the case. The other was a perfectly natural desire to see how they'd look with the fur coat.

A perfect match. No question about it. I ought to recommend the coat to Stacey since she already owned half the outfit. Turning my head for a three-quarter view, I caught Lou watching me in the mirror.

"Hiya, doll. Buyin' a little trinket?"

"No. Just looking." I took the trinkets out of my ears and

handed them back to the salesman. "Sorry, they're the wrong color."

"How much?" Lou nodded at him. "Twenty-two hundred? That's chicken feed. Let the guy wrap it up for you. Devlin can afford it."

From the side of the mirror where I was standing, that remark could have been taken as openly insulting or optically flattering. I didn't like Lou's insinuation, but being put on Stacey's pay scale was definitely a complimentary view of my charms. Either foregoing that bagel had done wonders for my skin tone, or Lou's idea of chicken feed was very different from mine. Giving him the benefit of the doubt, I played it somewhere between blushing virgin and shameless hussy.

Lowering my lashes, I said demurely, "Oh no. I'm not that kind of girl."

"Yeah?" He gave a hoot of laughter. "Come on, I'll buy you a corned beef sandwich, and you can tell me what kind of girl you are."

Lou kept up the ribald kidding all the way to the coffee shop, while I discovered that sinister criminal types have their own fascination. Whatever he did could be interpreted on two levels. He could have been holding my arm protectively or to prevent me from escaping. The close-set eyes appraised my figure as though he were stripping off my clothes, but only to check for a hidden weapon. And when he began plying me with five thousand calories' worth of deli, it didn't have to mean hospitality, but a probe for my Achilles heel. I tricked him by eating everything on my plate.

"Lou, please," I finally raised my fork in surrender, "no more. I'm on the verge of being gluttoned to death."

"Here, take. A little cheesecake'll push the food down. Helps the digestion." He scooped a wedge from his plate and dumped it on mine. "Eat, don't just stare at it. You need some meat on your bones."

What a pro. Lou not only stacked the deck; he made an offer I couldn't refuse. The cheesecake was as delicious as his comments on women who only eat to live. "They don't get no fun out of life. Take a look at me. I'm havin' a great time. You don't see me munchin' a celery stick with my beer and pretzels."

"Thought you liked them tall, blonde, and scrawny," I teased.

"You mean Stace? Naw, she's a bimbo. You don't wanna look like her. You got brains."

"But look who's got the diamonds."

His jowls shook. "Gotcha, doll. That's good. That's real good. You're a regular wisecracker, huh?"

"A one-woman burlesque." I pushed the empty plate away. "And now that you've added some meat to my funnybones, tell me about yourself. Aside from the food, what brought you to Las Vegas? Your voice sounds pure Brooklyn to me."

"Then you ain't never been to Brooklyn, sweetie. The Bronx. I was born and raised in the Bronx. Can't you tell how I dot my *i*'s?"

"Sure, but it's how you cross your *t*'s that tricked me for a minute."

He laughed at that, then explained that he'd cashed in his East Coast chips and gone west for his health.

"Asthma." I nodded sympathetically.

That set him off again. Rarely had my humor been so appreciated. Before I could attempt another sally, he jumped in with a question of his own.

"How do you know Devlin? You a client?"

"I'm his office manager. Phil Abbotts actually hired me."

"Abbotts, huh? You friends with him too?"

"If you mean, do I sleep with both law partners, the answer is no."

"Sleep? Hey, who said anythin' about sleep? Maybe I'm nosey, but I didn't mean nothin' like that. No way, kid. I just figured since you work for him, you oughta know all about Blanco's deal."

"Who said there's a deal?"

"See! What did I tell you? Brains!" Lou slapped his thigh in admiration, though it didn't discourage him from sneaking around another corner. "Say, I was real sorry to hear about your lady lawyer. That's too bad."

"It certainly is."

"Did Mannie take it hard?"

"He's surviving." I wiped my mouth and put the napkin on the table. "You were right about the cheesecake. I feel a lot better now. Thanks for the feast, Lou."

"You betcha. But what's the rush? Where you goin'?"

"I told Mark I'd be back at three."

"Okay, okay. Eat and run," he grumbled, signing the tab and leaving a five-dollar tip for the waitress. "Devlin don't deserve to have it so good, but I'll do him another favor anyway. Come here." Leading me out of the coffee shop to a quiet corner next to the men's room, Lou hoisted his pants, then threw a look over his shoulder. "Listen, doll, when you get back home, tell Denny to watch his step. Nothin' critical yet, but he's in a little deep and I got a feelin' Mannie'll use it. Like I said, the guy's a creep, but he knows how to pinch where it hurts. I don't want to see Denny get it in the balls."

"Are you saying—?"

He pushed up my chin and closed my mouth. "If you want it spelled out, doll, ask somebody else. I'm only bein' a nice guy. Me and Mark go back a long way, and I owe him a couple of good turns. You take care of this one, and next time, he'll owe me. Got it?"

I nodded my head. "You betcha."

He winked and sauntered off, hands in pockets, weaving

around the dice tables and disappearing behind the slot machines.

Good old Lou. I should have known his surprises wouldn't end there. That evening, while I was fighting with the zipper of my blue dress and calling for Mark to come out of the bathroom to do something wonderfully masculine with it, my struggles were interrupted by a knock at the door of the suite. With one hand behind my back holding the dress in place, I opened the door to a uniformed bellhop. He asked for Ellie Gordon, then handed me a small foil-wrapped box. I wanted to tip him, but he said it had been taken care of already.

How sweet of Mark. Down to the last detail too. I perched on the arm of the sofa and tore off the silver paper. "You shouldn't have," I called out. Mark didn't hear me over the noise of running water, and three seconds later I praised heaven for that small favor.

On a bed of cotton wool lay a pair of twenty-two-hundred-dollar diamond earrings. The card said, "For a very bright lady, Lou."

The jewels gleamed up at me as the brains Lou admired turned to noodles. This couldn't mean what I thought. No. Impossible. It had to be a joke. But what kind of comedian spends this kind of money on a gag? I could take it as a hilariously expensive tribute to my scintillating wit, except diamonds aren't funny. They're gratuities.

I snapped the box shut and paced across the room in my stockinged feet. That would teach me to be charmed by balding gangsters. One corned beef sandwich and I was already in Lou's clutches. The bright lady wasn't very smart to go to lunch with him in the first place, but I thought I could learn something. It was exciting to pit my wits against a wily fox like Lou Smith. He pumped me for information, and I played cute, funny, and cleverer-than-thou. Now I was stuck with a payoff I had no intention of earning. Pass on a message to Dennis. Do Mark a favor. What kind of joke was that? Unless I missed the punchline, Lou was setting me up for a two-way communications satellite between Las Vegas and Casa Grande. Keep him informed about the Blanco case, and he'd keep me in diamonds.

Damn it! Mark would never understand. I could try explaining that it was all an innocent mistake, but my conscience was only reasonably clear. Not that Lou learned anything from me at lunch; I just never got around to telling Mark I went.

My heart almost stopped when he called from the bathroom.

"Ellie, is somebody here? Who are you talking to?"

"It's just the television," I yelled back. Already I was becoming a pathological liar.

And a panic-stricken sneak. I dashed into the bedroom to hide Lou's bribe in my suitcase, but before I got halfway to the closet, Mark came out of the bathroom. I stuffed my hands behind me and backed up to the dresser.

"What are you watching?" he asked, toweling his hair dry.

"Nothing."

"Sounds like a good show. Who's in it?"

How could Mark joke around at a time like this? Desperate to get rid of the earrings before he saw them, I leaned backwards over the dresser to reach for my evening bag, but as my fingers closed over it, a drawer handle poked me in the rear and I grunted.

Naturally Mark had to notice me the one time I would have appreciated a little inattentiveness.

"Any reason you're shimmying up the furniture?"

Glad *he* was in a good mood. Gritting my teeth, I flashed him a smile. "No reason. I like cracking my vertebrae and breaking both arms. Can't you tell I'm trying to zip my dress?"

"It wasn't especially obvious. Would you like me to help?"

"No. I've almost got it." Working faster, I opened the clasp of the purse, but Mark started toward me.

"Come on. Don't be stubborn. Let me see what's stuck."

As he reached me, I slipped the earrings out of sight, then spun around. "All right, big shot. Do something clever."

In one stroke, the zipper was up. "See how easy a man can do it?" he teased, patting the sore spot on my rear. "Just whistle when you want me next time." With that he went back into the bathroom while I sank my head onto my arms.

There was no turning back now. I was committed to a trail of lies and deceit. Somehow the earrings had to be returned to Lou without Mark becoming the wiser, but a half hour later, as we were seated in the hotel dining room, they were still in my evening bag, a ticking bomb that needed defusing.

"What would you like this evening?" Mark asked, handing me a menu. "An ordinary spinach salad, steak and lobster, baked potato, sour cream, rolls and butter, coffee, and strawberry cheesecake?"

The mention of cheesecake made me queasy. "I'm not very hungry. Just a steak."

"No lobster to wash it down?"

"A little maybe."

As Mark read over the wine list, I discarded one scheme after another for getting rid of Lou's unwelcome largesse, but it wasn't until the dinner plate was set before me that a magnificent idea dropped into my thick skull. Just do what Lou did.

Not putting it off a moment longer, I held my stomach and groaned realistically. "Mark, I don't think I can eat this. Excuse me while I run to the ladies' room for an Alka Seltzer. No, it's nothing serious. Just a tummy upset. I'll be right back."

In the powder room I found the same motherly looking attendant who was there last night. A pink bow atop her gray curls, she lolled in her chair, half asleep.

"How would you like to make a fast twenty bucks?" I

asked abruptly. There was no time for finesse. No need either. She just held out her hand.

"Take this package to Mr. Lou Smith in the casino. Sure you know him? Tell him that Mrs. Gordon says thanks but no thanks. He'll understand."

So did she. When I pressed the money into her palm, she didn't put it in the cup on the vanity with her other tips, but stuffed it in her bra. God knows what went on in these hotels. The service was prompt anyway. Just as I got back to the table, dinner arrived.

"I gather the stomachache is all gone," Mark said, watching me dig into the steak.

"Oh, yes," I answered cheerfully. "Must have been gas."

That satisfied Mark, but I was far from content, though I did manage to hold my raging curiosity in check until the following morning. Or rather, Mark's lovemaking that night pushed all thoughts of Lou Smith out of my head. In fact, they didn't return until after Sunday brunch in bed and a few other all-engrossing occupations.

"Come on, you lazy dog." I prodded Mark on the shoulder. "The sky is clear, the sun is bright, and the pool is waiting. Grab a towel."

With a grunt he rolled on his side and pulled the sheet over his bare bottom. "Uh-uh. The men's singles finals at Wimbledon are on TV. I thought we'd watch."

"Again? It's a rerun. You must have seen it sixteen times already. Believe me, Mark, the ending's not going to change. I'd rather sit around the pool and soak up some sun."

"Don't let me stop you." He clicked on the remote control.

I considered it, but decided no. We were here together, and therefore, we'd stay together. Putting on my bathing suit, I went out on the balcony and lay down on a chaise lounge with the L.A. *Times* crossword puzzle. After oiling my shoulders, legs, and stomach, I started with one across.

Fifteen minutes later I was stuck. "Mark, what's a nine-letter word for Persian hashish eaters, eleventh century?"

"McEnroe is serving. Wait a minute." After the prescribed pause, he called back. "I don't know."

Abandoning that reference source, I worked on my own. Seventy-two down was a weapon of the pampas. Easy. Bolas. Another ten minutes and the puzzle was almost complete; just one lousy corner had me baffled. The species of Brazilian tree was impossible without a crossword dictionary. I tried once more for a little cooperation.

"Mark, who dry-nursed King David in his dotage? Not Bathsheba. It starts with *A*."

"Abishag."

"Bingo. You're brilliant, you know that?"

"I wish you'd come watch this game. Borg has pulled it back from set point three times already."

"Sorry. Not interested." Two more blanks filled in and I let the paper slide to the floor. "Mark, guess what? Eleventh-century hashish eaters are assassins."

"You're missing some of the best tennis I've ever seen."

Maybe, but I was thinking about assassins. "Mark, how does Lou Smith know Mannie Blanco?"

"Ellie, take a look. Borg just aced him on the serve."

I went inside and plopped down on the bed next to him. "Were you listening to me?"

"Sure."

"What did I say?"

"Tell me again, and I'll tell you if it's right."

"Damn you. Take your eyes off that game and look at me." He did, but only because a commercial came on. I started to roll away when he pulled me into his arms.

"All right, I'm sorry. What did you ask me?"

"How come Lou knows so much about Mannie Blanco?"

"Does he? They are in the same business. Gambling."

"Don't you think Lou is worried about what Mannie might tell the D.A. about certain mob figures?"

"Where did you dream up a connection between Lou and the mob? Is every broken nose a sign of depravity?"

"Mark, listen. Mannie Blanco has never breathed a word about a crooked congressman, yet your old buddy Mr. Smith knows all about it. Maybe he found out from Mannie's last tape."

"Baloney."

"How do you know?" I asked, sitting up so I could get a good look at Mark's face. "He sure seemed interested in the topic the other night."

Mark had one eye on the screen, waiting for the beer commercial to end. "Lou doesn't know anything about tapes, Ellie. That's just our office procedure, not a worldwide practice. Ours are reused as soon as they're transcribed anyway."

"Well, obviously someone knew that one hadn't been recorded over yet."

"And you think Louie checked out our stock of cassettes before choosing the one he wanted." Mark turned up the sound. "Forget the tape, Ellie. I told you it's not important."

"Howard Busch thinks whoever stole the tape killed his wife," I said bluntly.

Mark frowned disconcertingly. "So that's it. Howard gave you a bone to chew on. He says the mob killed Katherine; you say the mob broke into your house and stole the tape. And you've got Lou pegged for both crimes? That's crazy. Drop it, Ellie. Howard doesn't know any more than you do. And I don't want you questioning Louie. I presume that's what you're leading up to. Let the police solve Katherine's murder. You stay out of it."

Mark hadn't raised his voice, but for him, that was angry. Thank God he didn't know about the diamond earrings. A little nervous still over that close call, I tried to sound perfectly disinterested in the entire affair.

"Of course, I'm staying out of it." I yawned. "Do you really think I'd go chasing after a murderer?"

Mark cocked an eyebrow at me. "As a matter of fact, yes. But if you keep it inside the pages of a mystery story, you'll be fine. Just remember that nosy, middle-aged ladies usually get bumped off in the fourteenth chapter."

"Thanks for the middle-aged," I retorted. "You may return to Wimbledon now with my compliments. I shall retire to the balcony and work on my tan." I hit him with a pillow to show there was still life in the old dog, then went back outside.

I needed to be alone for a moment anyway. Did Mark realize what he had just said? It changed the way I had been looking at Katherine Busch's murder, at any rate. Until now, I'd never thought about the fact that hardly anyone outside the office knew we taped Blanco's conversations with his lawyer. It wasn't standard procedure. As Mark pointed out, the underworld would need psychic tentacles to fish through that box of tapes in the conference room and then find the right one in my kitchen.

Besides, how could any hoodlum have discovered that Mannie finally talked turkey that particular afternoon? For one thing, Katherine wouldn't have discussed Blanco's revelation with anyone except her colleagues. Not only would that have been unethical, but there wasn't time enough for her to speak to anyone else. She was dead three hours later without ever leaving the office. The only other source of information was Mannie himself, and he would have slit his own throat first. That meant one of Katherine's confidants must have blabbed. Eliminate Mark and Mr. Abbotts, and the booby prize had to go to Dennis. Was that the favor Lou Smith wanted to pay back?

Chapter 15

The minute I set foot in the office on Monday morning, the titty-tats pounced.

"I wish I had a mysterious date who took me away for the weekend." Josie sighed wistfully.

"Who is he?" Maggie couldn't even wait for an answer. "Was it all moonlight and roses? Where did you go?"

Three pairs of eyes had me pinned. "That's for me to know and you to guess," I answered smartly, then shrugged in pretended defeat. "Oh, all right. I went to visit my mother."

"I wonder where Mr. Devlin disappeared to on Friday," Barbara had a provocative gleam in her eye. "Did you happen to run into him at your mother's?"

"She must be in love." Josie giggled. "Look how she's blushing!"

"Get to work, you bums," I ordered, hands on hips.

One whiff of sexploits and the titty-tats reacted like bloodhounds. They pestered me with questions, chased clues, and laid snares, but all they got out of me was age, rank, and serial number. Naturally that only confirmed their suspicions, and by lunchtime my guilt was sealed. The office manager and the boss were having an affair. With that tidbit to feast on, the terrible trio didn't have time to mouth off the usual blue Monday complaint that they were overworked, underpaid, and out-voted. It was just as well. Of all Mondays, this one really justified mass revolt.

Mark had left for San Francisco early this morning on business. We had to cancel all of his appointments through Wednesday afternoon, and Carolyn Brewster didn't want to wait. Mr. Abbotts returned from a hearing madder than hell at his witness who never showed, and neither of our trusty law clerks could come in until three o'clock. Not that it made much of a dent in the turmoil; surprisingly it was Dennis who offered to trot on down to the County Courthouse and file two motions for summary judgments, a writ of replevin, then skip over to District Court and sit in for his uncle at a pretrial conference. He squeezed all this in while finishing his own work and won everybody's approval when he sweet-talked Carolyn Brewster into shutting her big mouth.

It was a beast of a day from beginning to end, and I didn't blame my co-workers for wanting out of the cage at five sharp. I would have beat them to it, only Mr. Abbotts roped me into searching through the dead case files in the basement for a paper he claimed was very vital. That *non sequitur* kept me downstairs until almost six. When I came back up with the five-year-old terminated contract and two dusty knees, Dennis was waiting at the elevator.

"You're still here?" we echoed simultaneously.

Dennis's splendid show of industry today had left him looking only slightly less the worse for wear than I did. His suit jacket was slung over his shoulders, tie loose, top two buttons of his shirt undone, and he sagged with the weight of a bulging briefcase.

"How did the pretrial conference go?" I asked sympathetically.

"For two hours." He held the door of the elevator open for himself while I stepped out. "It was nip and tuck all the way whether or not Haskins's payment to Rosen was a general acceptance or a qualified acceptance."

"Sounds like a hung jury. But wait a minute. You said Haskins and Rosen. This antiquated rescission agreement must be for you." I dropped it into his briefcase. "They sure have been going at it for a while. If they can't get along, why do they keep doing business together?"

"They're brothers-in-law."

"How convenient."

Dennis only had enough energy left for a shrug. "Get your things. I'll wait and walk you out."

The lights were off and a hazy dusk filled the corners with shadows. Skipping a quick knee wash in the ladies' room, I accepted his offer rather than stay alone, although with the new safety locks on the door in the lobby there was nothing to worry about. Still, I felt better having a pair of strong shoulders to protect me. Interesting that they were Dennis Devlin's.

Today was the brightest and most shining example of his change in attitude. He'd been improving his entire performance for over a week now, and tonight he was showing me more courtesy than he had since I refused to substantiate his alibi. The elusive Shirley was still in limbo somewhere, so either Dennis was being influenced by his uncle, or I had charmed away his temper with my winning ways. Whatever the reason, the boy was becoming a man, and this growth deserved an acknowledgment from me—not necessarily a pen and pencil set, but some show of appreciation. He was Mark's nephew, after all.

Feeling wise and kindly, with clean hands and a pure heart,

I gave Dennis what I thought would be a highly appreciated Bar Mitzvah present. "By the way, I met a friend of yours."

"Really?" he asked politely as I preceded him into the elevator. "Who's that?"

"Lou Smith." The doors closed while I fished through my purse for car keys. "He wanted me to pass on a message, though I'm not sure what it means; but he said to watch out that Mannie Blanco doesn't try to collect where it hurts." When I looked up, Dennis was staring at me in amazement.

"Louie told you that?"

Oh, dear. Dennis wasn't overly pleased with my gift. I tried to exchange it. "He's an old family friend, I gather. Nice guy. He seems to know Mannie Blanco pretty well too. Called him a horse's patoot, though."

My attempt at levity didn't even crack the grim expression on Dennis's face. "You know Louie." I smiled nervously. "A joke a minute. He was probably just teasing me. Forget the message. I can't understand why he thought it would be a favor to your uncle. How could you and Mannie . . . Dennis! Stop! What are you doing?"

Flinging his jacket and briefcase to the floor, he thrust me back against the wall, his fingers digging painfully into my arms. "You goddamn fucking cunt. Don't even try it. Do you hear me? Not a word to my uncle or anyone else about me and Mannie. I'll kill you." His red face was only inches from my white one. "Just open your mouth, and I'll wring your fucking goddamn neck."

Here it was. Nightmare number one come true. Locked inside a barely moving elevator, I would be knocked senseless, strangled, my body flung down the shaft in a final burst of rage. What made me think Dennis Devlin and I were on our way to becoming bosom buddies?

The elevator came to a stop with a slight jerk, and in the brief moment of imbalance I shoved Dennis backwards. As he stumbled, trying to regain his footing, I flew through the opening doors and out of the lobby, not even pausing for a DON'T WALK sign on the corner or the squeal of suddenly applied brakes. I was the cat with nine lives walking into Barney's, life and limb intact.

After checking over my shoulder that Dennis wasn't behind me, I let out a long breath and went to the bar. It was an effort to climb onto the stool, but my legs wouldn't have lasted ten more feet to a table. Besides, I wanted to keep my eye on the entrance. Happy hour was coming to a cheerless close, when all drinks reverted to their regular price, and most of Barney's customers were leaving. A dark, secluded booth held no attraction. At the bar there was a chance that if Dennis did follow me in, Barney might stop wiping the counter long enough to save me.

What was I worrying about? Barney didn't have to save me. I had just escaped death and destruction without the aid of Barney, police, or James Bond. Me. Myself. Alone. No male had come to my rescue; no masculine help had been needed. I was my own Wonder Woman. Screw you, Dan Gordon. Take that for your eighteen-year umbilical cord. With a brilliantly resourceful combination of timing, quick thinking, and the fleet foot of a true jogger, Eleanor Gordon combatted the forces of evil. Who said she was only half-liberated? Hell, I was almost free.

I celebrated by ordering the famous two-olive martini. Barney was delighted to mix me a sample, though he looked at me a little oddly when I bolted it down in three swigs. My throat burning, I held out the glass.

"Play it again, Sam."

"Hey, take it easy. You trying to tie one on?"

"That's not a bad idea."

He made me another, but took his time about it while he kept one wary eye on my face. "Drink it slower," he cautioned. "It packs a wallop you ain't used to."

"You are a gentleman and a bartender," I told him,

"which is more than I can say for some lawyers around here."

"Yeah?" He went back to wiping the counter. "Who's suing you?"

"An erroneous conclusion, my friend. I shall probably bring an assault and battery charge against my attacker."

"Attack?" Barney stopped wiping. He looked over his shoulder, then leaned across the counter. "I knew you were in trouble when you asked for a martini. What happened? Wait, don't say anything yet."

He let two men who were paying their bills at the cash register leave before hunching over conspiratorially and whispering, "Who got you? One of those hoods?"

I stared at him and shook my head. "I was just . . . kidding, Barney."

He didn't believe me. "You don't want to talk. I get it. But you oughta be careful hanging around here alone this time of night. They already got one lady in your office." He leaned closer. "You said 'attack.' Did the guy . . . uh . . ."

"Rape me? No. It was strictly business."

"That's good." His eyes scanned the room in distrust. "You listen to me, Ellie. You go to the police. Get yourself some protection. How do you know he won't try again?"

I took another swallow of the second martini, then pushed it away, deciding I needed a clear head more than the drink. Would Dennis try again, and what would he try again? I still didn't know if he had murder or mayhem in mind, but I sure knew what triggered it. The Las Vegas Connection.

It didn't take omniscience to see that the name Lou Smith brought chills to Dennis's heart. Lou had the same effect on me, so I could appreciate the affliction. Only Dennis's sore spot looked a lot more serious than a pair of diamond earrings. He had gambled in Mannie Blanco's highly illegal gaming establishment, left his calling card on a few I.O.U.s, and the glad tidings had wigwagged through the crime syndicate's organized grapevine. That was just the kind of gossip they liked to hear. A man with something to hide is in a spot to be used. And when that man is positioned inside enemy territory and has access to classified information, it's too perfect for an honest crook to turn down.

Dennis didn't need me to tell him he was in trouble. Mannie Blanco held his unpaid gambling debts, but Lou Smith wanted to do the collecting. Sure Mannie could expose him as a law-breaking lawyer, which meant fines, disbarment, maybe a jail sentence; but Diamond Lou Smith and associates could see to it that the problem never came up. Not much choice, really. Only, how far would Dennis go to protect himself from retribution? Submit a weekly report on Mannie's progress? Steal a tape recording to show good faith? Commit murder?

The hell with Lou Smith's favor. I should have done one for me and left his message back in Vegas along with his earrings. Now, instead of just disliking me and distrusting me, Dennis thought I was conspiring with the mob against him. And instead of dismissing him as an immature boob, I was reconsidering my original assessment of him as a murderer. Both of us couldn't be right.

I must have looked a little strange, because Barney asked if I felt okay. "You're not going to puke on my floor, are you?"

"Not yet."

"Like I told you," he urged again, "go see the cops. They'll take care of you. I know a couple of guys who wished they took my advice and got police protection. One of them's dead." He nodded, looking ghoulishly satisfied.

I finished the drink. "What did you tell the police when they questioned you about the murder? I imagine they asked about witnesses, what you were doing at the time, all kinds of things. Were you able to help at all?"

"What gives? You turning into a dickless tracey? Sorry,"

he grinned, "that's my monicker for lady cops. Sounds like Mickey Spillane, huh?"

"To the hyperbole," I agreed. "So what did you spill to the fuzz?"

"Nothing." He sighed in regret. "It was so busy in here, I didn't get to see anything. The place was packed, and my new bartender was having trouble with the Harvey Wallbangers."

I patted his hand in sympathy. "I can never get them just right either. It's the orange juice." Then before he could comment, "Do me a favor, will you, Barney? Walk me to my car."

He loved it. Telling one of the others to cover for him, he escorted me chivalrously across the street. Dennis's yellow Corvette was gone, but Barney was watching for trigger men with .38s. After making sure I was safely locked in, he came back around to the driver's side.

"Listen, when you get to the station, ask for Chief Steunkle. Tell him I sent you. If that blonde busybody at the front desk gives you any static, you explain that you're a citizen of this country and you got rights. Steunkle knows what they are. He won't put you off. Just tell him Barney said you should come. He'll remember me, my last name is Ganderspensky."

Police stations are traditionally dank and cheerless, with paint peeling off the walls, water spots on the ceiling, and vintage 1932 linoleum coming up from the floor. There was none of that romance in Casa Grande's new city jail. Thanks to modern technology and a hefty bond issue, we now had a two-story architectural wonder of cement, steel, and unbreakable glass. Plenty of parking, but no charm. It didn't even look intimidating.

Neither did Chief Steunkle when I was ushered into his office. Perhaps my newly won assertiveness made the difference, but I extended my hand and said easily, "Matt, how are you? Working late again, I see. Whenever do you find the time to read?''

"Over my cold dinner." His sleepy eyes creased into a good-natured squint. "So what brings you down here so late? Sit down. Is it business or curiosity?"

"What a suspicious mind you have."

"Both, huh? Okay, what can I do for you?" He leaned back in the swivel chair and waited.

I leaned back in the straight chair and began. "Did you ever find out anything about the break-in at my house? It happened a week ago tonight."

"I remember seeing the report, but Frank couldn't find any prints. That's all we can do unless somebody owns up. Has there been much vandalism in your neighborhood? I can increase the patrol for a while. Get the kids a little nervous."

"You think it was kids?"

He scratched his chin. "You think it wasn't?"

That's what I liked about Matt Steunkle. Our minds were attuned to the same devious channel, only he was picking up the signal faster than I wanted. "You're the expert," I parried, flashing him a winning smile. "I don't think anything, except it took me two hours just to clean the kitchen."

"And the tape?"

"I beg your pardon?"

"The cassette that was stolen," he explained needlessly. "You never even thought about that?"

I conceded ruefully. "Now I know why you're the chief of police, and I'm just an ordinary housewife."

"Not ordinary." He grinned.

"Yes, I have a friend who once told me that. And not a housewife either. But to get to the point, now that we've skipped all the preliminaries, who did it?"

"Murdered Katherine Busch, you mean." He started scratching his head now—an especially propitious sign. "I don't know yet."

"Oh, hell." I slumped back. "You had me primed for the K.O. Obviously you agree with my theory about the tape and murder being connected, but until we discover who stole one, we won't know who committed the other."

"Hold it!" Like a bulldog he thrust his head forward and joggled his jowls. It was a fascinating move. "Where did the 'we' come into this case? I don't remember asking you to help. Cooperation with the police is one thing. You can't volunteer for the homicide squad."

"I have no such intention, believe me. My goodness, no." I gave a tinkle of laughter to show I was a scatterbrain who didn't know one pronoun from another, but Matt Steunkle wasn't buying.

"Tell me the truth," he said. "Something got you worked up tonight, or you'd be home with a good book by now, and I'd be sitting down to a cold supper. Don't play detective, Ellie. Tell me what happened. Who's the suspicious character?"

"Everybody."

He relaxed again. "The jitters, huh? Any reason in particular?"

"No," I lied. "It's just that everyone keeps asking me for the latest news, as if I'm investigating the murder myself. People think because I found the body, it makes me clairvoyant. At the least they wonder if I know more than I'm saying."

"Yeah. Amazing how many guilty consciences are roaming around. Run into any lately?"

"You're a devious man, Matthew Steunkle. I come here to find a cure for my paranoia, and you want to know who gave it to me. All right, I'll make you an even swap. The names of everyone you've eliminated as suspects, for my personal opinion of each one."

He looked at me shrewdly. "How about hearing your opinions first? The list may change after that."

"Uh-uh. I'm not incriminating anyone without your help.

They can do that all by themselves. The Reverend Ritchie, for instance. What's his alibi?''

"The Sports and Sorts Health Club. He arrived at six-ten, verified by your boss Phil Abbotts who was leaving for an appointment just then, spent fifteen minutes in the sauna while Mark Devlin was there, had a workout in the pool with Ned Wilson, and a couple of minutes in the gym. At seven-o-five, he was showered and dressed and walking out the door. If you're interested, I'll show you the names of the two men who left with him. It's right here in my file.''

"Don't bother. The file in your head is good enough. I'm glad to know so many people are on a physical fitness kick, but what's so healthy about Thursday night that half the town shows up for alibis?''

"A masseuse comes in from Laguna.'' He made another ostrich move. "Want to ask me about Dennis Devlin now?''

The man was patient, I'll say that for him. He let me beat around the bush for ten minutes, when all the time he was hiding inside of it. The irony was that he thought I knew what I was looking for.

"What's the use? I'm his alibi, and you know how much good that's doing him. Any closer to finding Shirley? Oh, well, maybe she'll crawl out from under her rock one of these days. Why couldn't Dennis have been at the health club with everyone else?'' I threw my hands up at the empty question.

Steunkle began tugging at his ear, a new gesture, and one I couldn't interpret. Not anymore. "I have a feeling you're holding out on me,'' he said with frightening accuracy. "Want to tell me what it is?''

"You read too many mysteries,'' I parried. "All I have are a lot of questions. That's why I'm here. Please don't think I suspect Dennis of murder. I just feel guilty because I can't get him off the hook.''

"You wouldn't feel so guilty if it were Ritchie, though.''

He stood up. "Don't get so hung up on alibis. Sometimes they're as dependable as an eyewitness."

"Thanks."

"I'm not the only one who reads too many mysteries," he hit back lightly. "But remember one thing from them—not having an alibi doesn't make you guilty. There's got to be a motive first."

"I learned that from Nancy Drew." I followed him to the door. "Except when the papers dub a case the 'women's lib murder,' it kind of narrows down the field."

"You mean the motive is professional jealousy?"

"Let's just say career-oriented. Well, thanks, Matt. I appreciate the time. Your dinner's liable to be a popsicle by now, but you've done your civic duty by me. I feel a lot better."

"Did you get the answers you came for?"

"Not really. There's still the stolen tape, and a few other matters, but we'll—sorry, I mean you'll—find the answers eventually. Just don't hold out on me, huh?" I smiled.

"As long as you don't go sleuthing on your own."

"Never," I promised. "And you won't mention to anyone that I was here?" He nodded his grizzled head. "Good. It might make things a little uncomfortable for me at the office if they thought I was sneaking to the police."

"Nobody'll find out from me," he said.

I turned at the door. "By the way, do you know Barney Ganderspensky? I didn't think so. Good night."

Chapter 16

Only in fiction are amateur detectives greeted by the police with open arms and invited to help solve the case. Matt Steunkle was the second person to warn me of the dangers of sleuthing. On top of that, he seemed to believe I was holding back evidence. He was right, but before I accused Dennis of anything, I wanted to talk to Mark. He might yell about the corned beef sandwich topped with diamonds, but he also might have some logical explanations for all my worries. Maybe it meant nothing that Dennis gambled with Mannie Blanco, received warnings from hoodlums, and had no alibi for the night of the murder. As for Dennis's promise to wring my goddamn fucking neck if I snitched to his uncle, I was depending on Mark to talk him out of it.

Thank goodness, Tuesday was peaceful. Dennis stayed out of the office most of the day, and when he was in, stayed out of my way. The titty-tats' heavy teasing didn't bother me either. Then came Wednesday.

"Why the long faces?" I asked cheerfully, back from lunch

with Nancy Weaver. "The noon-hour quickie gives you girls indigestion?"

"Mr. Devlin's here," Josie mourned.

"And those are tears of joy. How nice." I sat down. "Your sentiments are heart-rending."

"Then you already know about her," Maggie said hopefully.

"Her?" I turned slowly on the swivel chair. "Who's her?"

Barbara filled me in on the drama I missed by taking my lunch break at 12:30. "Mr. Devlin brought back an attorney from San Francisco, and it looks like she's going to be the new associate."

"Good. We can use some help around here. Aren't your feminist souls delighted that he hired a woman?"

My feminist soul was thrilled, though my ego felt a bit bruised. Mark had told me only that he was going to San Francisco on business. I knew the firm had some interest in an applicant there, but he neglected to mention that this was also a hiring trip. It wasn't important, yet it separated the office from our personal lives. A smart move, I decided abruptly.

That equivocation lasted precisely ten minutes, until Dennis, Mark, and Mr. Abbotts came down the hall and formed a color guard at the water cooler. As they smiled moronically, a vision of loveliness stepped forth and paused by the tank. A burp of air sighed tribute.

No wonder the titty-tats extended me their deepest sympathies. She was breathtaking. Coal black hair, flashing brown eyes, a wide luscious mouth, and all that with a figure to match. This was a lawyer? From under what rock had Mark unearthed her? And he'd had to go all the way to Frisco yet. I swallowed my instant antipathy and rose to greet her as she undulated across the room on high heels and a wave of false congeniality. Her retinue followed closely behind—or her behind closely, as you will. When they reached my desk, she took heartless advantage by standing right in front of me, so I had to look up eight inches just to see her nose. It was like the great unwashed not measuring up to the *haut monde*.

Mr. Abbotts made the introductions by order of rank, then proudly proclaimed Ms. Helen Ramirez as the firm's new associate member. She'd be starting work officially in September but was here now to become familiar with the office, look over the case load, and find an apartment. On all fronts, he beamed, the staff would be more than happy to give their utmost assistance. Lacking forelocks to pull, we pledged our servitude with warm wishes and felicitations. I told her *mazel tov*.

During all of this Mark sat in fatuous silence, taking unspoken credit for finding a woman of such exceptional beauty and rampant sex appeal. If she couldn't think, at least she was decorative. It wasn't until the eye-catching Ms. Helen Ramirez sailed into his office that I got hold of myself. I was thinking just like a titty-tat in the office squatters society. All newcomers keep out. I was here first, so take your brains and beauty and go threaten someone else's security. Where was my pride in the feminist sisterhood? I should be admiring the woman for having so much of a good thing. Katherine Busch didn't make me feel paranoid. Why let Helen of Troy shake me up?

For over an hour a do-not-disturb sign was posted invisibly on Mark's office; but when Carolyn Brewster arrived for her three-thirty appointment, Ms. Ramirez took a much-needed coffee break and went to Mr. Abbotts. I timed it perfectly and just happened to be walking down the hall when Mark's door opened twenty minutes later.

"Carolyn, don't get so excited next time." He soothed his ruffled client. "If your sister files an interlocutory, it doesn't mean the case is settled. That's just a temporary action."

"If she wins this, Mark, I'll tear every stitch out of her facelift. She did it on my money anyway." With that Mrs. Brewster patted her own rejuvenated cheeks and marched out.

I stuck my head in the door. "Hi. Did Caro the Lamb have another hair-pulling session with her sibling?"

Mark just shook his head. "Here, put these back in the file for me. This too." He added another paper then reached for the phone. "Oh, do me a favor and ask Helen to come in here. I want her to see this motion."

You mean, see *her* motion. I bit back the thought. "You look frazzled, Mark. How about dinner at my place tonight. I'll soothe your fevered brow with a mushroom omelet and white wine."

"Not tonight," he said flatly. "I'll be working with Helen." He spoke into the phone. "Oh, Josie, get me Brooks and Atkins. I want to speak with Al." He looked back over at me and told me with all the charm in the world that he was too busy to talk now. "I'll call you this weekend." His attention switched back to business. Or had it been anywhere else? "Al, where's that rescission agreement? No, I'm up to my neck."

I closed the door softly.

There's only one thing more frustrating than not getting your questions answered, and that's not even getting your questions asked. Suspicion of Dennis weighed heavily on my mind, but speculating about Helen Ramirez had my heart down in my boots. I tried not to think about what had happened during the two days Mark was alone with her in San Francisco. A man, handsome, single, lonely. A woman, young, beautiful, thin. It might have been "midsummer madness" under the Golden Gate Bridge, or "come kiss me sweet and twenty" at Fisherman's Wharf. Then there was Chinatown.

That evening, having worked myself into a state of acute travel sickness, I wandered around the house like a muse of tragedy, too restless to do any more packing and too unhappy to consider where I should go with all my boxes. After a week of bliss, I was back at square one, uncertain, untrusting, and unwanted.

Of course the last time Mark gave me his cool, disinterested shoulder, I had jumped to the wrong conclusion and bruised myself for nothing. But one hard knock was no lesson. I still didn't know whether it was time to mourn the end of a brief affair or wait calmly for a phone call. Maybe I'd try calm for a change. Optimism. Faith that Mark and I had a more meaningful relationship than sharing an electric blanket with a single control. Weren't we wonderfully compatible despite having opposite interests, diverse backgrounds, and contrasting personalities? So what if Helen were taller, younger, prettier, and better educated? On second thought, it might be better if she fell off her Trojan horse and had to be shipped back to San Francisco for a prolonged convalescence.

Unable to chase my blues with the latest Dick Francis mystery, I turned my rancor to the television, where there was always something worth vilifying. I found the perfect abomination on channel seven. ". . . male and female created He them." The voice was pontifical. It scratched at my nerves like chalk squeaks on a blackboard.

Well, what do you know? The Reverend Billy Joe Ritchie was a guest on our local low-budget, no-talent public affairs program. The moderator was a seriously underfed brunette with horn-rimmed glasses who always asked the questions written on her clipboard whether they followed the trend of the discussion or not. The cameras offered only two angles, both usually unflattering to the participants; and all this was compounded by an inadequate boomlight that revealed everyone's criminal tendencies. Ritchie definitely had them.

The left side of his face smiled unctuously at the camera until he remembered to swivel around. "Let's not fool ourselves. God created woman to be man's helpmate, to bear his children. Not to compete with him in the business world!''

The camera dollied back for a three shot and for the first time I saw that there was another guest tonight. Mr. Abbotts? What was he doing on the show? It wasn't on his schedule of appearances this week. Had the station called for a booking at the last minute? It was valuable publicity, but why had Mr. Abbotts agreed to appear with Ritchie? They disagreed on practically every issue; and though my boss was no slouch when it came to debate, it was awkward arguing with someone who could call in a heavy like God as his authority.

Mr. Abbotts's reply wasn't bad, though. ''That's surely a matter more of faith than fact. In the eyes of the law, men and women are individuals and citizens with equal responsibilities and rights for the most part. Of course the question of who is equal to whom has been a matter of discussion over the years, but legislation has tended to keep broadening the protection of the Constitution to all Americans, regardless of faith, sex, or skin color.''

Delighted with that riposte, I sat down on the couch, pleased with my boss. Billy Joe wasn't so happy.

''You're assuming that all these new laws are being made in the spirit of the Constitution. A lot of Americans think that they are corruptin' it. The E.R.A.—which the people rose up and rejected, praise the Lord—was an attempt to destroy the American family. To force women out of their homes and into factories. Then the government would take over child care, and we know the result of that! Godlessness, socialism, even Communism!''

Mr. Abbotts shook his head as if in disbelief. ''The question is moot, at the moment, but I would like to point out that all the proposed amendment said was that men and women would be equal under the law. Not such a frightening idea. Several states already have an E.R.A. as part of their constitutions and nothing terrible has happened."

Ritchie let out a bark of laughter. "Nothing terrible has happened? Have you seen the divorce statistics lately? Even you liberals admit the institution of the family's in trouble! And I'll grant you the E.R.A. sounded innocent, but we know how it would end up after those Washington lawyers got done interpreting it! Women drafted into the army, made to fight. That would be the best of it. The insidious spread of so-called secular humanism has to be stopped. Human fallible law cannot take precedence over Divine Law."

He was scary because he meant it. He wanted to push his particular beliefs down all our throats, no excuses accepted.

"I think you're speaking of ecclesiastical law, and that is not divine. Each religion has its own canons of faith. There is no way Constitutional law can favor one over another. Besides, judicial rulings don't interfere with religious doctrine. One guards freedom; the other is a choice."

I was on the edge of my seat, truly impressed by Mr. Abbotts's control. I would have been yelling by now. He was picking up the fight where Katherine Busch left off, though politically it could be suicide. Billy Joe might be a disgusting bigot; but as long as he spoke as a defender of the American family and quoted the Bible, his beliefs carried heavenly weight. Politicians had no such credibility.

Ritchie turned the full thrust of his anger on the man beside him. "How can you say that the law doesn't infringe on religious beliefs when the government has been in the business of killing innocent babies? It offends me and a lot of other people that our taxes have been used to fund abortions. It's time for a constitutional amendment to stop these murders!"

The moderator, who had been sitting in open-mouthed silence, interrupted finally. "I'm sorry, but we are running out of time. Mr. Abbotts, we only have thirty seconds. Would you care to respond to that?"

He tried, valiantly, but thirty seconds isn't very long. He managed to make the point that in a pluralistic society, the government cannot legislate morality, and that, given the diversity of belief in our society, the choice of abortion should be available to the individual woman. After all, anyone who wanted could have as many children as she liked.

When the moderator began thanking the participants, I snapped off the set, thoroughly annoyed by the realization that Ritchie's rhetoric had probably seemed very convincing. I was probably the only person watching who agreed with Mr. Abbotts. The people who had turned in to hear Ritchie wouldn't; that was sure. And Mr. Abbotts had just lost their votes.

The only good thing, from my point of view, about Reverend Ritchie was that he made it easy to stick to your guns. When someone hates you on principle, you don't feel guilty for hating him back. At least, I didn't.

Galvanized into action by the adrenalin of argument, I strode to the phone and called Mark at home. Even if he were going to work late, he should be done by now. Why should I wait until this weekend to ask my questions? He had plenty to answer for right now, and some of it was even about Dennis.

"Hello?" A breathy voice answered. "Hello? Is anyone there?"

"May I speak to Mr. Devlin, please?"

"He's busy right now. Would you like to leave a message?"

"Just tell him Mrs. Gordon is on the phone. I think he'll speak to me."

I heard her relay my words, and after a few seconds she came back on the line. "Mrs. Gordon, I'm sorry, but Mark—I mean Mr. Devlin—says he's tied up right now. He'll talk to you tomorrow."

"I see. Please tell Mark—I mean Mr. Devlin—that will be fine. Thank you."

There was no ice cream in the freezer, so I settled for

crackers, though I would have preferred to sink my teeth into Helen Ramirez's neck. Why hadn't Mark hired someone brilliant, middle-aged, and ugly? He wouldn't take her to his house for high-level business discussions. A handshake and a pat on her wart would be the closest he got. Helen Ramirez invited hands all over the place. I visualized her lying on Mark's bed, with the lights from the patio turning her skin to aquamarine, Mark's favorite color.

Naturally I had a lousy night's sleep, dreaming of blue lagoons, blue mermaids, and blue bells chiming at midnight. When the phone rang at six A.M., I rolled over and answered with a growl.

"Ellie, sorry if I woke you. What did you want last night?"

What did I want? Oh, just a vow of eternal love and undying devotion. To Mark I said more reasonably, "Did you and Helen have a nice time last night?"

Mark didn't find that so reasonable. "What do you mean, nice time? We were working."

"Don't sound so defensive. I wasn't accusing you of anything but patting her wart."

"What do you want, Ellie?" he said impatiently. "Make it fast. I have to be in court at eight."

Since the subject of his extracurricular activities with Ms. Ramirez wasn't getting anywhere, I switched to my other peeve. "I need to talk to you about Dennis."

"Not now. Later."

"When later?" I snapped. "Tonight? Tomorrow? Next Yom Kippur?"

"Saturday," he promised. "As soon as I put Helen on the plane to San Francisco." There was a voice in the background that could have been Luis—or Helen, and Mark said quickly, "I haven't got time to talk anymore. See you at the office."

I tried. I really tried to let him see me at the office, but five foot ten inches of body beautiful completely blocked me out.

I was willing to stand in line and wait my turn, but Mark's sights were raised too high to see me. I was Lilliputian, unimportant, small, and turning very mean.

"Oh, shit. What did you say, Maggie?" I put liquid paper on my typo.

"The boss wants to see you."

"Mr. Devlin?"

"No, Mr. Abbotts. You handled the report on the Yonemoto/Pulaski suit, and he needs information on one of the depositions."

I pulled the file and took it with me, marching past Mark's closed door without a glance, and greeting Mr. Abbotts with a wide smile. "I saw you on television last night. Great job. I don't know how you kept from punching that bigot, but your line about freedom versus choice was a terrific blow. What made you appear with Ritchie anyway?"

"To kill the opposition." He smiled. "I did all right, didn't I?"

"Do you want me to answer as an office manager or a campaign worker? The first says whatever you do is right. The second has some reservations. Katherine Busch couldn't lose anything by taking him on publicly, aside from a few chauvinistic clients. You might lose an election."

"Would you rather I curry favor with Ritchie?"

Mr. Abbotts was being facetious, but I had come a long way from naively believing that principles are a magic carpet to truth. Whose truth? Maybe Ritchie was right and we'd all be condemned to everlasting hell for not listening to him. Mr. Abbotts couldn't offer any alternate rewards for turning the other ear. It was a guess. One big, chancy guess. Personally, I'd risk it, but most people want to protect their flank, just in case.

"Let's put it this way," I answered him. "I'd lose respect for you if you suddenly turned toad-eater, but I want you to win the election."

"Oh, I will," he promised. "Don't doubt that for a minute. I'll win."

That was confidence. Not boasting, not hot air, but sheer self-determination. People like Mr. Abbotts were rare. And to be envied. While he coolly planned his strategy for the primary next spring, I feverishly vacillated about what to do in the next hour. One choice was to storm Mark's office and accidentally push Ms. Ramirez out the window, or stand on the ledge myself and threaten to jump unless she were dismissed instantly. I could see it now, my body bent and broken on the parking lot, with Mark murmuring down at me, "But I have an appointment."

Damn him! Surely he could spare five measly minutes to hear how his no-good nephew attacked me in the elevator. That might move him from impassive to interested. Certainly my attractions weren't doing it.

At one o'clock, having heard nothing from Mark, I decided that was it. If he wanted me, too bad. I was going to lunch. Josie and Maggie had already come back, and with Nancy Weaver spending her lunch hour at the dentist's, that left Barbara and me on the last shift. She wanted to go to the new Hungarian place a few blocks over on Twelfth Street. Goulash sounded masochistic on a ninety-degree day; but since the hair shirt fit the occasion, it was okay by me.

Barbara ordered wine to keep my gin and tonic company, and though I made a series of nonsensical toasts, smiling happily for her benefit, she wasn't fooled.

"Mr. Devlin dumped you, didn't he?"

"You're assuming again," I retorted. "What are you having? Goulash or moussaka?"

"Moussaka, and I'm not assuming. Take my advice, Ellie. Play it cool. Don't go back to the office half-soused because of that Latin lady."

"All right, I'll have moussaka too."

"And take a breath mint too before we go back." Then she

shook her head. "I don't believe it. Here I am giving you advice when last week I prayed you'd fall on your ass."

"So you were a week early." I shrugged. "Happy now?"

Barbara toyed with the large red hoops in her ears. "I guess we're on the same side after all. Funny, isn't it? You've got the same problems with men that I did. Before my divorce, that is."

"Past tense?" I queried. "You're still living with your ex-husband."

"Yeah, but not being married makes all the difference. I've got my freedom and a bed partner who pays half the rent."

"Charming setup. Does he cook too?"

"That's the problem with middle-class," she snapped. "A person's only supposed to have fun in captivity. Why should I be married to Jason when we get along better as live-ins? He dates as much as I do, and nobody feels cheated. What's to cheat when there're no promises in the first place?"

Barbara was echoing what I tried to tell myself but didn't want to hear. No commitment meant no commitment. She didn't have any problem switching from "till death do us part" to "bring on the troops." But then she was a titty-tat. I was the old-fashioned girl on the Valentine who asked for one man at a time.

"What do you do about conscience-raisers like fidelity, honesty, faith, hope, charity, et al.?" I asked.

"You think I've sold my soul to the devil?" She gave a short laugh. "Listen to me. You have more than one girl friend, right? Okay, if you go bowling with one, it's not disloyal to your tennis partner. And every time you have dinner with one group of people, it's not a stab in the back to any others. Not everybody enjoys all the same things. It's legal. We don't all have to be alike. But when it comes to men and women, suddenly they give seminars on how much you're supposed to have in common. Why? Why should people of the opposite sex have to be more identical than

Siamese twins? That's really asking the impossible. One man can't supply the moon and the stars and a little green cheese thrown in for extras. But people go ahead and get married anyway, and what results is a disgruntled wife who wants to go to the movies while loverboy is hooked on a football game. That has nothing to do with honor and fidelity. It's plain stupid. If she hadn't married the dolt to begin with, she could be at the movies with some other guy, and having a hell of a time. Instead, people become martyrs because of a wedding ring. And it's no different if you're just dating someone. Shit. Women would all be happier doing their own thing with any number of different men.''

Barbara made a lot of sense. Only an idiot would have whiled away a boring afternoon in a hotel room with a crossword puzzle because the man in her life was watching a tennis match. That sounded like the same cretin who gave up a museum tour for a hula show, then promptly got divorced. Was that commitment? A signup in purgatory? Surely I had more sense than to escape one hell with Dan only to jump into another with Mark. Besides, Mark wasn't jumping, not even wheeling in the right direction. Obviously he didn't want to get burned twice in the same frying pan. Who could blame him? Temporary didn't hurt . . . or last, I thought maliciously. Helen Ramirez may be his new playmate of the month, but that only gave her another three and a half weeks.

That was Barbara's kind of timetable. "No lifelong contracts." She tapped her spoon on the table. "You have to play it single in mind, with divorce decree in hand. Learn from your mistakes Ellie. Men are after one thing. Give it to them, but on your terms."

Barbara wasn't just a titty-tat. She was a sister-under-the-skin. Beneath her frizzy tresses and low-cut shirt was a heart that had been broken just like mine, but pieced together again with self-protective glue.

"One question, Barb. Playing the field sounds great, only

I'm still a rookie. Should I expect a date to end in the bedroom?''

''That's the general idea,'' she smiled, ''but if not, you can always suggest it.''

Chapter 17

The sun had been up a bare sixty minutes, but for the last fifteen Betsy had been running me through my paces. I dragged to a stop as the crosslight turned red. "Slow down, you fiend." I wiped the sweat that trickled down my cheek and dripped off my chin. "Who do you think you're jogging with, a marathoner?"

"No, a grouch. What in hell is the matter with you? Another headache this morning?"

Instead of answering, I dashed across the street, dodging two kids on a bicycle, and beat Betsy to the curb. "Now can we stop for breakfast?" I demanded.

She kept moving, past Bob's Diner, a donut shop, and a gas station with a coke machine outside. "No food until we finish two miles. Come on, grump, tell me what's bothering you besides the lack of protein."

"My leg hurts." I huffed and puffed and complained about incipient bunions, shin splints, and stress fractures all the way down Twelfth Street, but when we turned into the park and back on the jogging path, I let the bitter truth come pouring out.

"Mark and I are finished."

"Finished what?"

"Our affair. Our short-term relationship. It's over, kaput, fini, defunct, shuffled off this mortal coil."

It did my sore heart good to see Betsy miss her stride. She faltered, skidded on one Nike, tripped over the other, then came to an ungraceful halt. "You're joking!"

"I wouldn't joke about a headache."

She pushed up her sweatband and looked at me for signs of facetiousness. "Why did you wait a mile and a half to tell me?"

"I would have said something thirty feet ago, but I was afraid you'd fall under a truck."

Betsy closed her eyes, shook her head, then pulled me over to the grass, where we both flopped. An ant began crawling up my leg immediately.

"All right, begin at the beginning," she directed. "I can take it now. I'm sitting. What in the hell happened with you and Mark?"

"It can best be described as *Much Ado About Nothing*. Remember all those wonderful lines about liberated liaisons and leading ladies? Well, I could have saved myself the trouble of *Love's Labour's Lost*."

"Will you please bring it up four centuries and tell me why the show folded?"

"An understudy took over my part." I flicked the ant off my knee. "Mark brought her back from San Francisco with him, ostensibly to work in the office. It's just what the firm needs, a lady lawyer with a degree in S.A. This one's a tall, ravishing beauty, who purrs like a kitten and scratches like a cat."

"Oh, Ellie, I can't believe Mark would spring something like that on you without warning. Didn't he explain?"

"How could he explain? The workaholic hasn't had five crappy minutes to spare me since he came back with his protegée. Whenever I ask for a few seconds of his valuable time, he looks at his watch and picks up the phone."

Betsy wrapped her arms around her legs and looked at me sideways. "Then how did you discover the salacious details of Mark's hiring practices?" She was beginning to sound skeptical.

"From Helen Ramirez herself," I answered smartly. "That's right. Mark left it to his new inamorata to inform me that he prefers Latin lovers to Jewish princesses."

"He wouldn't."

"He did. The other night I finally lost patience at waiting around for him to remember me, so I called his house. It was relatively late, eleven o'clock. I figured he'd be in bed watching the news. My guess was only half-right. Helen the house cat answered, purring. When I asked for Mark, she hissed and told me he was busy working."

"Maybe he was," Betsy protested mildly.

"Naturally. I don't doubt her word. Would a lawyer lie? Besides, that's what he's been doing all week. He spent two days in San Francisco 'working.' Kept at it Wednesday, Thursday, and Friday in the office, and is obviously so dedicated to the job that he takes Helen home with him at night to 'work' some more."

"What is he, a superman?"

"No, a swine."

"Hold it, Ellie. You're convicting him on circumstantial evidence again. First you said Mark was impotent because he's in a wheelchair, and now you've got him pegged as a hog in heat. Wait for proof this time. Let Mark speak out in his own defense before you condemn him to the slaughterhouse."

"I don't need a brushoff spelled out in four-letter words. And I don't have to be fluent in Spanish to understand. Dan Gordon taught me everything I never wanted to know and won't ask again about the male animal.'' Betsy opened her mouth to speak, but I cut her off. ''Forget the lecture that husbands and lovers don't fall into the same category. I know all about no strings, no ties, no commitment, no expectations. But what about no dismissal without notification? What about no severance, no common courtesy, no balls? Damn it, Betsy, I gave Mark Devlin the best two weeks of my new life. I bared my soul and my bottom to that man. All I asked in return was some consideration, but no; he lets me find out the hard way that a black-haired Goldilocks is sleeping on my side of the bed. Typical,'' I snorted. ''Only women have the decency to send a Dear John letter. Men just grab their pants and run.''

''There must be a reasonable explanation,'' she said, standing up and brushing the grass off her legs. ''I think you should ask.''

Betsy certainly was careless with my damaged psyche. Asking for Mark's intentions could pixilate it altogether. I didn't need to hear that he had so much more in common with Helen than with me. What man wouldn't? She was younger, prettier, smarter, and probably better in bed. But if he swore their relationship was strictly platonic, despite all the above, I might believe him. Duped again or dumped again, there was no difference. I could be either one more reject in a long line of has-beens, or just wait my turn on the carousel. Helen on Mondays and Wednesdays and me on alternating Tuesdays. Bull on that. As long as the rides were free, I was picking my own merry-go-round.

''Tie your shoe, Ellie. Once more around the park and we're home. Come on. I'll make you a big breakfast. Eggs, bacon, pancakes, juice, the works.''

I couldn't help laughing. ''Some pal you are. When I wanted all that, it was *verboten*. Now that I don't need anything except black coffee, you offer me the whole enchilada. You're crazy, Betsy, but sweet.'' We looked at each other for a moment, then I pushed her onto the pathway. "Don't worry. I haven't broken my heart over the Devlin debacle, just bruised it a little." We started jogging at a slow pace, with Betsy still unsure of me. Every two steps she would turn her head and check for tears. "Will you stop that!" I ordered. "Thanks to you, this isn't the Ellie who used to dribble ice cream down her shirt. Can't you tell I'm me again?"

"Not really."

"Well, I'll prove it to you. If you promise not to fall all over your feet again, I will explain my cure for the habitually jilted. It's called, if you can't beat them or join them, unman them."

Betsy didn't falter for an instant. "Is this done surgically?"

"Uh-uh." I ducked under a low-hanging branch. "That would defeat the purpose, which is to screw the guy before he can screw you. It's the latest thing in self-defense. Everybody's doing it."

"It's as old as the hills and the name of it is retaliation. Don't confuse it with karate, unless you want to chop yourself in the neck."

"I won't. The two former men in my life taught me how to duck. Even Barry Janish gave me some helpful hints."

"Anyone else you want to kick in the balls while you're at it?"

"Yes, as a matter of fact. A zoology professor who lowered my grade ten points because I balked at the lab assignment. Never again, Betsy. No one's going to step on my face because I was dumb enough to put it under his foot. You told me I need experience. I'm going to get plenty."

"Hey, don't make me your excuse. I was encouraging normal relationships, including friendship. If you're thinking about revenge, take the responsibility for it yourself."

"I already have. Barbara has fixed me up with a new man, and tonight a whole new review hits the boards, with me as director."

At that moment the sprinkler system spurted on, shooting a fountain of water over our heads. Betsy jumped aside. "Damn it! Is this Barbara one of the titty-tats?"

"The tittiest." I ran through the spray.

A few days ago, before he became so conscientiously busy, and while I had him on the phone, Mark promised to call me as soon as he "put Helen on the plane this Saturday." Of course I didn't expect it after Friday morning's episode, when he asked for someone to take dictation, and, on finding out that I was the only one available, said he'd wait until Maggie was free. Granted, dictation wasn't one of my specialties, but I could have used a tape recorder. It had been building up to this anyway; me chasing and him scooting into doorways. My big disappointment, though, was never getting to tell him about Biff Bosworth. Mark was such a sports nut, he'd gnash his teeth in envy if he knew I was spending Saturday night with the third best rusher for the L.A. Rams.

When I saw Biff for the first time, I regretted not telling Helen Ramirez either. No question she would have gnashed her teeth. This guy was six-four, with California sun-bleached hair, biceps that flexed all over the place, and, for a rusher, had the cutest, tightest end on or off any football field that I'd ever seen. He was just as approving of my assets, and inspected the deep cut of my shirt as if it were an especially interesting vee formation.

We went to a country-western bar in Venice that was packed to the saddlebags with city slickers who strutted their stuff in designer jeans, Stetsons with feather hatbands, and four-hundred-dollar Tony Lama boots that had never kicked cow chips. An eight-piece combo howled about getting it on at the Alamo, but everyone was trying to do it right there on the dance floor. Biff and I were no exception. It's amazing what can be done in the name of Cotton-eyed Joe. Biff managed to get his cotton-picking hands around me as we danced, and I was stroked, patted, squeezed, and branded as a prize heifer. In return, I showed him all the down-home hospitality that he could have expected on the real range.

We only began to get acquainted in a less Biblical sense when the combo took a break. I ordered a Coors Light to match the ambiance, then listened in fascination as Biff told me a little about his career. At age thirty, the list of his job-related injuries included one knee operation, two concussions, and uncounted cracked ribs. With an empathetic shudder, I asked if playing football weren't more masochistic than macho. Biff smiled and admitted that perhaps you had to be a bit "into" pain, but he swore he loved the game, particularly the roar of the crowd at the lovely crunch of bone on bone.

"The real downer," he confessed, "is that the body calls it quits at the grand old age of thirty-five or so. Sometimes sooner, if you get unlucky. That's why I'm trying to play it smart. Sock away the cash investments while the cash keeps coming in, so I can plan for the future. Don't know what I'm going to do yet, but when the time comes that I hang up my cleats for good, I don't want to be one of those pitiful old jocks who can only talk about the glory days because they have nothing going for them anymore."

Before I could tell Biff how wise he was, a couple of giggling groupies in skin-tight Calvins interrupted us with a request for his autograph. I sat back, rather enjoying the reflected fame and admiring the way Biff handled the situation. Joking lightly, he signed his name in an illegible scrawl, making his fans quite happy, then got rid of them with practiced speed.

"Sorry, Ellie." He grimaced slightly as they left. "I was hoping to avoid that kind of thing. No need to bore you with the football scene."

"Do I look bored?"

"Of course not. Barbara said you're terrific, which is an

obvious understatement, but she did mention that you're not the greatest gridiron fan in the world.''

"That much is true," I admitted, not unmindful of his tossed-in praise. "I barely know a fourth down from a field goal. And as for stats, when the announcer mentions the E.R.A., I always think he's talking about the recently defeated constitutional amendment.''

That broke Biff up. "E.R.A. is a baseball statistic," he explained kindly.

Before I could regale him further with my complete lack of sports knowledge, another cheering section of autograph seekers approached our table. This time they were two husky men who kidded Biff about his gorgeous date. I almost turned around to look for her myself when it dawned on me that I was the dish they were ogling. Me, Ellie Gordon, who had nine years, at least, on Biff. Either it didn't show, or I was so enticing that it didn't matter. Bemused by both possibilities, it took me a minute to realize that Biff was suggesting we abandon ship.

"This can't be much fun for you," he said mistakenly as we moseyed out the swinging doors into the cool air.

I would have argued the point, but evidently scribbling his name on crumpled napkins wasn't Biff's favorite way to spend a Saturday night. To a celebrity like him, it was just another overdose of public adulation, another ho-hum appearance on the *Tonight Show*. But to a voyeur like me, that was just the kind of annoyance I'd find it a pleasure to suffer. Stale and flat, but oh-so-profitable.

Nevertheless, I agreed with Biff that privacy had its own rewards, and once back inside his low-slung Ferrari, he gave me a sample of the sort of reparation he had in mind. Despite the gear shift that separated the two seats, we managed a kiss that would have raised the roof if it hadn't been off already. Feeling an intoxication that owed nothing to the Coors, I suggested we go back to my house so I could further my football education. "Obviously, there's a good deal more to learn about how to play this game," I said coyly.

Biff, a good sport if ever I met one, loved the idea. Peeling out of the parking lot in a splatter of gravel, we headed for Casa Grande at speeds well over the legal and sanity limit.

It was an unforgettable journey. Biff almost drove off the road a couple of times because he kept trying to look at what he was touching. I conducted myself with only slightly more restraint, but when we arrived at the house both of us dashed in, ignoring all the proprieties, and charged straight down the hall to the bedroom, Biff wordlessly pulling off shirt and boots as he went. While I was still slipping out of my panties, he tackled me onto the bed.

"Hey," I protested with a laugh. "I know you're a rusher, but you aren't going to rush this, I hope."

"Not a chance." He grinned. "In this game, you're the quarterback. We'll take it as slow as you like." He licked one tingling breast. "I just can't decide if I like your jokes or your body more." And with that compliment ringing in my ears, play commenced.

No one could accuse Biff of leaving his technique on the football field. I wasn't so bad either. In fact, after executing some passes that left us both breathless, I scored my first touchdown. Then I threw Biff the ball, and he caught it in the end zone, tying the game. Within minutes we were lining up for another play. For this one, he stood and held me, while I wrapped my legs around his waist and clung to his massive shoulders.

"Don't drop me," I gasped.

"Nothing to worry about," he said with serious concentration. "I can benchpress three hundred."

That made me laugh so hard we had to call a time out.

Later, lying on the bed, cuddled with Biff, I felt elated. Also exhausted. This evening was a far cry from the embarrassing awkwardness of that encounter with Barry Janish, or even the comedy of errors that sent me leaping into Mark's bed. I had to give Barbara credit for her wise counsel. Recreational sex could be quite therapeutic. For sure, I didn't have any hang-ups about Biff.

"Thank you for a lovely evening," I said, giving my football hero a kiss along with the gentle hint that it was time for him to go.

"Can't I stay the night?" He sounded hurt. "Give me a chance to catch my breath, and we'll go into overtime," he coaxed.

Flattered, I hesitated. "Aren't you supposed to be in training?"

He laughed and kissed my bare shoulder, then nuzzled the hollow by my collarbones. "I appreciate your concern, coach, but I'm a big boy now."

"So it seems," I remarked dryly, noticing that he was growing even as I spoke. "Biff, really——" But my protest changed almost immediately into a moan of surprised pleasure. This rusher certainly knew how to keep the ball in motion.

Still, an hour later, I pushed him out the front door. Enough is enough, I told him firmly, blowing him encouraging kisses as he went down the walk so he wouldn't be tempted to turn around and invite himself back for breakfast. Then I shut the door and slipped the lock in place, returning to bed with a sigh of relief that I was going to have it all to myself. Was that one of the joys of being single? Having great sex without any unnecessary intrusions into one's domestic tranquility? After eighteen years of sharing a bed and bathroom with a man, it was delicious to have sole proprietorship. Funny how I never appreciated that before.

But then, there were a lot of things I didn't appreciate until tonight. Yawning, I snuggled under the covers and vowed to call Betsy first thing in the morning to tell her about the education I had acquired via Biff. I'd gone out with him for his great big gorgeous body, thinking I'd play the game the way men did. Of course, twenty years ago, my credo was that any man uninterested in the contents of a woman's head had no right to the treasures below. Yet this evening, in my vengeance, I was going to be macho matron, grab Biff by the balls and never look up. But instead of reversing a few trite stereotypes, I found myself relaxing, really enjoying his company, and in the process I charmed the pants off a very personable, bright, and successful young man. Betsy might say I-told-you-so, but I had needed a refresher course in basic human relationships. Up to now my vocational training had been rather one-sided, though tonight's extracurricular activity could qualify as a graduate seminar. It was a lot to learn all at once, but my date with Biff proved to be the perfect lesson for a down-in-the-mouth lady who was taking a little affair with Mark Devlin much too much to heart.

That was quite an admission, coming from me. After all, I was the intellectual who always dismissed her own poor judgment with the built-in copout that it wasn't my fault. If Dan had been a better husband, I wouldn't have gained seventeen pounds. If Barry Janish had been a serious novelist instead of an x-rated script writer, I wouldn't have kicked him out of the house while his fly was still open. And if my grandmother had wheels, she'd be a Greyhound bus.

Why did I insist on giving away all the credit for my mistakes? Surely I was capable of taking a pratfall on my own. I collected full honors for fifteen happily married years, then claimed to be an innocent bystander while Dan cocked up the last three all by himself. It was much more forgivable to be a hapless victim of male abuse than admit that some of my wounds were self-inflicted. But if I really wanted the liberated woman of the year award, I couldn't demand equal opportunity without accepting equal responsibility. It was time to acknowledge that some of my most spectacular swan dives were taken with both feet planted on *terra infirma* and my head twisted around in the wrong direction—like depending on Mark Devlin.

In my mind I listed all the excuses. Mark had come along at a vulnerable time in my life. My ego was battered by a divorce, no matter what else I may have done to it, and Mark's attentions were balm to my wounded spirits. The inexcusable excuse lay in my thinking that he was the cure for all my ills. If a handsome, intelligent man found me attractive, it proved I couldn't be a complete factory reject. But to consolidate my evidence, I enhanced his image by endowing him with good taste, keen judgment, and general all-around superiority over other men. Mark had tried to tell me on the plane ride to Las Vegas that his handicap hadn't made him a bigger or better person than anyone else, but I didn't believe his unflattering self-evaluation. I decided that Mark's reticence obviously hid pearls of unspoken wisdom; his absorption in the sports page merely showed a probing interest in current events; his neglect of me was a sterling example of high-minded restraint. How could I believe any less? Hadn't he defied his physical limitations to take his place atop Mt. Olympus with the other gods? I couldn't allow Mark to be a mere mortal; he was my personal messiah. By virtue of his affliction overcome, he would overcome mine too. It was so logical. All I had to do was pull the wheelchair out from under his ass and make it a halo over his head.

The vision had lasted for two or three weeks, which wasn't bad for a fantasy, but then Helen Ramirez showed up and showed the real Mark. Actually I should thank her for yanking the rose-colored glasses off my eyes so I could get an undistorted look at the scene. Funny, though, that it took Barbara, of all people, to make me see the light. And to think how I jeered at the titty-tats' philosophy, accusing them of indulging in casual copulation as another form of social intercourse. Yet going to bed with someone didn't have to be a promise for the future, or the first installment of a package deal. Two people could enjoy each other without getting that personal. Oddly enough, I found I liked the idea of being emotionally independent. I liked being a liberated lover, knowing that Biff was going to take me out again and it didn't mean I had to attend all the Rams' home games. Too bad I wasn't that smart about Mark, but at least now I knew that I didn't need him or any other man around to affirm my worth every minute of the day. That was a merit badge I could pin on myself.

Congratulations, Ellie Gordon, I thought sleepily. Maybe you've finally grown up.

Chapter 18

And then there was light. A perfect California day: no heat wave, no earthquake, no flood, just smog. Wearing the confident smile of someone who has solved her personal problems and sporting my new executive-woman rompers with tote for matching bathing suit and accessories, I walked into the country club dining room where Sunday brunch was in full cry. If the moment had been recorded for posterity, the only one heard applauding would have been me; but as I took a table by the window, Madeline Jacobson joined in.

"Ellie, you sneak. Why didn't you call? We could have had breakfast together." She rushed over with a hug and a smile of welcome back. "I am so glad to see you. Tell me everything. How's the job? Where did you get that fantastic outfit? Oh, Ellie." She hugged me again. "You look terrific."

"Compliment accepted." I laughed. "Where's Allen? He has to give me his share of praise too. How about having coffee with me?"

"I can't. We have a ten-thirty reservation for a racquetball court with the Warrens. But let's meet at the pool afterwards."

"Still the physical fitness queen?" I teased.

"How else can I combat middle-age?"

Phyllis Warren came up behind her. "Take a younger lover."

There was talk a couple of years ago that Phyllis had done just that, but now she let Madeline overrule her, and they hurried off, promising to meet me by the high dive at twelve.

The next familiar face materialized just as the Eggs Benedict arrived. A radar trap. Steve Tedesco took the empty seat across from me and half my English muffin.

"Hand me the butter, will you?"

"Of course. But as long as you've sold out to the pluto-crats and joined the country club, how about some jelly too? A taste of my eggs, perhaps. Don't forget the sauce."

Steve snatched a strip of bacon in return for my spurious accusation. "After all we've been through together," he grinned, "don't you know by now that I'm incorruptible? I only entered these hallowed portals because our sports writer is having a baby and I have to cover the tennis tournament for her."

"I always said a woman would be your doom."

"Yeah, I was kind of hoping the same thing myself." He treated me to one of his Groucho Marx leers.

Even without the funny faces, Steve looked comical next to all the La Coste types floating around. In his favorite baggy pants and Fruit of the Loom un-sports shirt, he was a dandelion in a bed of tulips. Knowing Steve, though, that was exactly the effect he wanted.

"So what do you think of the view from the top?" I asked him.

"It's claustrophobic, but I like the view across from me. With those new hollows in your cheeks, you remind me of a heroine in a Russian novel. Not planning to throw yourself under any trains, I hope.''

"Steve, you're the only person I know besides myself who can turn a simple 'how do you feel' into a literary allusion. But first of all, the gaunt look is what all the best models are wearing this season, and secondly, you know darn well that Amtrak's on strike.''

"I love you, Ellie.''

"Then put down that spoon. I hate sugar in my coffee.''

His hand was still raised over my cup, but his voice lowered. "Don't turn around, but here comes the Reverend Billy Joe. He's finished his Sunday sermon and a few of his well-heeled congregants are treating him to an afternoon of hosanna and hospitality on the golf links. They praise his form and he blesses their moral rectitude.''

"I thought our resident holy man converted you. The last article about Ritchie in the *Chronicle* was practically reverential.''

"Orders from above.'' He raised his eyes heavenward. "The editor wrote it. It seems that when I ran that column on Ritchie's convenient tax dodges, there was a lot of flak. Some of our readers have a hard time separating greed and gospel, so rather than lose subscriptions or advertisers, Ritchie is now treated as a sacred bull. I'm to confine my stories to politics and tennis.''

"So the hard world of commerce is infringing on your principles. Too bad. How about letting the doctrine of fairness infringe on your prejudice? That article you wrote last week was so full of bias, I almost drowned in the crocodile tears. Somehow you made the legal aid clinic seem like the only oasis for the poor, because wealthy lawyers in private practice are too busy defending clients with Swiss bank accounts and important Mafia connections. You forgot to mention that these same lawyers take court-appointed cases. And maybe even once in a while accept a client who's not rolling in ill-gotten gains. It might surprise you, Steve, but some of the people Mr. Abbotts represents are just the kind of criminals you like: underprivileged hold-up men, poverty-stricken pimps, illiterate arsonists who never learned how to read 'close cover before striking.' "

"Ellie, I love all your figures of speech, but you'll never convince me that Phil Abbotts deserves to be our next congressman. The man has no concept of what it means to be poor and Chicano in this state. You can't see beyond that fatherly smile and his support of the women's issues, but he's a long-distance liberal. All he'll ever do is cry about the environment, and work to reduce taxes for his friends who cry about how hard it is to manage on a lousy hundred thou' a year. They're his people, his financial backers; not the poor shnooks in the barrios. And poor shnooks like you are won over by that lacquered veneer. Wake up, Ellie. Face reality. The guy's ambitious. He'll do and say anything to get to Washington. So would his gentle spouse. You should see Marjorie outside right now. She even gave *me* one of her fake smiles. Believe me, Ellie, Phil Abbotts is no hero. He's a typical politician."

"Why do you make 'politician' sound like a dirty word? Is there no honor in Washington outside the press corps?"

"Just for that, give me the last bite of your egg." His fork got to the plate before mine. "I'll tell you again what I said a month ago. Abbotts is either crazy for taking Blanco's case during an election year, or has a good and private reason. That's my guess, and men with mob connections don't belong in public office. Too many of them are there now. That's what makes 'politician' a dirty word. I'm only trying to keep it clean."

"You're a wonderful guy, Steve. For three-quarters of my breakfast, you willingly share your biased view of mankind, morality, and tax shelters. I disagree with almost everything you said; but then you disagree with me, so I guess that makes us even. It's equitable prejudice anyway."

"How about testing the theory?" he answered seriously. "I think we could make beautiful mutual tolerance together."

Another radar trap. I bent my head so Steve couldn't see me smiling, and when I looked up again he was drinking my coffee, his face lit with mischief. "That was a good line," I admitted. "Aren't you going to follow through?"

"Too corny. It wouldn't have worked. I'm going to have to bowl you over with my dynamic personality and blatant sex appeal."

"Well, Steve, I hate to tell you, but you just blew it." I gave him the other half of the English muffin as recompense. "I was won over by your dynamic personality and blatant sex appeal years ago. All it needed was a good convincing argument. Mutual tolerance would have done it." The look on his face as I walked away was worth the price of a breakfast.

Donning my new bikini in the women's locker room, I headed out for the pool to soak up some sun. I'd planned a little nap on the deck but bunches of old friends kept wandering by and stopping to chat. Why had I stayed away so long? It was surprisingly easy to pick up the pieces. Everyone was happy to see me again and delighted to welcome me back to the world. I garnered invitations to three dinner parties, a beach bash, a Bar Mitzvah, and two promises to fix me up with the perfect man.

In return they all wanted to hear about the murder investigation, but only Marilyn Calander asked what the corpse looked like. I dodged that one by getting in some politicking for Mr. Abbotts. At least no one probed for details of my divorce; it was accepted as fact and finished. The only discomfort was keeping a smile on my face when Mark's name was mentioned. Yes, he was a terrific guy, marvelous to work for. Yes, I knew Allen Jacobson designed his house. I heard it's lovely.

After five laps of the pool, I left Madeline to finish her

twenty without my help, and went to the outdoor bar to get a cold drink. It was only after I sat down and ordered a Perrier and lime that I noticed the woman on the next stool.

"Hello, Mrs. Abbotts. How are you?" I inquired politely.

It was a foolish question. I hadn't seen her since she had been down to the office a few weeks ago, but Mrs. Phillip Abbotts was always marvelous. That was her stock in trade. Marjorie devoted her life to being marvelous at throwing helpful political parties, playing vicious bridge and genteel sports, and every once in a while she even managed a moderately marvelous intellectual conversation. Of course her greatest accomplishment was telling everyone else what to do and how to do it.

"Hello, Eleanor." She used the perfect tone for greeting a social acquaintance who was also a skivvy in her husband's office. The last time I heard that particular intonation, she was ordering me to bring back two salami sandwiches and a watercress on whole wheat. Still, my exclusive, expensive, executive-woman ensemble was every bit as elegant as her shell-pink maillot with matching jacket. In a battle of fashion plates, it would have been a draw. In a test of superiority, Marjorie was boss: When she picked up her gin and tonic and asked me to join her on the patio, I figured it was to assign me a few more office duties that I could take care of in my spare time. Her first words dispelled that notion. "I saw you with Steve Tedesco earlier," she said, a sting in her voice. "I hope you weren't indiscreet. As an employee, your opinions are taken as firsthand information, and people can get the wrong impression so easily."

And when I was a plain old volunteer, my opinions were taken as secondhand information? Money doth have a way of talking these days. "Trust me, Mrs. Abbotts, I'm quite careful not to give the wrong impression to the press. In fact, I once kept Steve from writing a story. It was one of his typical 'money corrupts' themes, but I didn't appreciate the innuendo before an election.''

To praise my efforts, Marjorie exhibited a tight smile that never got north of her lips. ''Then I'm sure you understand how important it is to clear up this business with Dennis. Bad publicity has a way of tainting the atmosphere, and it's crucial to remove all suspicion of murder from the office.''

''Of course, but there's nothing I can do about Dennis's alibi, if that's what you mean.'' This time the edge was to my voice.

''Are you so sure, Eleanor? Dennis claims you're nursing a grudge against him. If that's so, you've picked a regrettable way to foster it. But the situation still isn't irretrievable. People do have a way of forgetting things now and then. Say, in a week's time, you suddenly remember having seen Dennis at Barney's, I'm sure we can avoid repercussions.''

It was an effort not to toss my Perrier into her two marvelously made-up faces. Instead, I addressed one of them. ''This isn't a case of willful amnesia, no matter what Dennis says. I'm telling the truth.''

Marjorie's smile, frost-bitten as it was, became an icicle. ''I suggest you give it further consideration. It's amazing how under oath people recall the slightest details, especially if they've been accused of suppressing evidence.''

The sun disappeared behind a cloud, bringing on a sudden chill. Suppressing evidence. Goosebumps broke out on my arms as I realized how true it was. The tape had been in my possession for over a week. An accident? An oversight? What proof was there that I hadn't made a copy, spliced out a portion, even put it up for bids? One whiff of diamond eardrops and case closed.

It had been a big mistake to stop worrying about Dennis because he hadn't tried a repeat performance of his elevator scene. Apparently, he'd just switched from physical aggression to legal combat. My position was still underarmed. I knew enough to make him squirm, but not enough to protect myself. And with Marjorie on his side, I might as well charge at a Sherman tank swinging my purse. There was no use appealing to Mark for help—not in a battle between beloved nephew and discarded lover. And if I tattled to Mr. Abbotts about his wife and his junior associate, I'd be a discarded office manager too. Not that Phillip Abbotts would be party to coercion; he just wouldn't believe me.

"What exactly do you want me to do?" I asked, shivering in the hot sun.

Marjorie Abbotts stood up in a graceful movement and made a studied show of tying her belt. To anyone watching, we had just concluded a friendly chat. Do spiders and flies talk it over first?

"I think we understand each other," she said with nary a blush on her perfidious cheeks. "You were never a stupid woman, Eleanor. Just do the smart thing now. I don't have to remind you that this conversation never took place."

For a woman with a retarded sense of humor, Marjorie was hilarious. I was to recant my entire story to the police and throw myself on the mercy of Matt Steunkle's gullibility. Yes, sir, I truly had forgotten about seeing Dennis at Barney's. Then last night I had this truly remarkable dream, and it all came back to me. Truly. He was between the scotch and the sloe gin. I can't imagine how it slipped my mind.

If Matt bought that yarn, I'd take up writing fairy tales. Sure, from my prison cell maybe. Suppressing evidence made a much better story line.

Chapter 19

The stone walls stood twelve feet high and were topped with broken glass. For anyone who thought there might be an easier entry, the locked wrought-iron gates proved otherwise. And just in case the message wasn't getting through, three Dobermans barked hysterically as they tried to leap over the barriers, bent on ripping out my throat.

"Nice puppies," I muttered, only sidling close enough to the gate to press the buzzer. The box next to it squawked a response. "It's Eleanor Gordon, from Mr. Blanco's attorneys," I replied. "Is Mr. Blanco home?" I could barely hear over the barking. "What's that? Yes, it's a legal matter. No, Mr. Blanco isn't expecting me."

With the mad dogs snarling at me, I stood there like a dotty Englishman in the burning noonday sun, hoping I could carry this off. Shortly one of Mannie's bodyguards came down the drive, three leashes in hand. He snapped his fingers, and the dogs instantly shut up, trotted over to him, and slobbered lovingly as he hooked on their leads. The big lunk slobbered right back. I received a more formal greeting.

"Where's your I.D., lady? Nobody gets in without no I.D."

I showed him my driver's license and Sears charge card. After comparing the signatures, he pulled a disk from his pocket and electronically unlocked the small side gate. "No cars get in until we check the plates," he explained, gesturing for me to walk through.

"Have the dogs eaten yet?" I hesitated.

The barrel-chested weight lifter smiled down at them, revealing a touching fondness for the brutes and a similar set of fangs. "Naw, they won't hurt you. These babies are sweethearts."

Not convinced, I stepped through cautiously and held my breath while the darlings sniffed my legs. Satisfied that I was just as nervous as they intended, the dogs fell back, eyes aglow, tongues lolling out, and watched my every move as we proceeded up the graveled driveway.

Whoever said crime doesn't pay didn't know the least thing about real estate values in California. Mannie must have paid over a half a million dollars for this nineteen twenties mausoleum. It was built by one of the ranking movie queens of the day, whose career bottomed out suddenly when a jealous lover pushed her off the gold-domed roof. Broken hearted, her husband made a shrine to her memory by replacing the southwest patio where she landed with a small temple. According to local legend, the poor man worshipped there daily until he remarried and moved to Cleveland.

My escort led me around the house, past the fabled spot, and through a row of cypress trees. Then he pointed. "You go right down there. I gotta take the dogs back."

Breathing a little easier without the Dobermans slavering at my heels, I followed the brick path to the rear of the house, where a dazzling recreation of a Busby Berkeley set stretched from veranda to poolside. Fluted marble columns and curved porticos looped around a half a dozen terraces on as many levels. The design was ostentatious enough to satisfy the gaudiest of grandstanders, although noticeably lacking were a hundred singing showgirls. They were probably bused in from Burbank for special occasions.

The Hollywood glamor broke down with Mannie Blanco. He was sprawled on a lounger, his skinny, hairy legs protruding from a pair of Hawaiian print shorts, and a can of Coors in his skinny, hairy hand. When he saw me admiring the scenery, he called out.

"Hiya, doll. Watcha got? A hot flash from Phil?"

"No, Mr. Abbotts didn't send me. I came to see you about something else."

"Yeah?" Mannie looked surprised, but not unfriendly. "Okay, take a seat and tell me what's on your mind. How about a drink? This heat's a killer."

"No thanks. I only want to speak to you for a few minutes."

"Whatsamatter, can't you talk and drink at the same time? Hey, Jake! Bring the little lady something cold. She looks all hot and bothered. What's your tipple, doll? Scotch, bourbon, beer? Jake! She's off liquor. Bring her a Perrier and lime."

A tall, bronzed body stood up from the deck, clad in the briefest pair of briefs I'd ever seen. He rubbed his curly black hair, flexed every muscleplate in his torso, then made all of them ripple as he walked to the poolside bar and pulled a bottle from the refrigerator. As he bent over to get glass and ice, I gazed in fascination until I noticed Mannie grinning at me.

"Mr. Blanco," I cleared my throat, "you might—"

"Don't be in such a hurry. That cabana over there by Jake is full of swimsuits. Go tell him to pick out a number for you. Come on, aren't you dying to take off your clothes?'' He winked.

''Not really.'' I smiled blankly, keeping eyes averted as Jake vibrated over with my drink. ''Now, Mr. Blanco, if we could—''

Again, that's as far as I got. From out of the cabana stepped another distraction. This one was female, gloriously blonde, perfectly tanned, and completely topless. At first I thought it was an optical illusion, too much sun and Perrier, but when she reached behind her to tug at the bottom half of the string bikini, a match to Jake's, the truth stood out.

''Hey, Olga,'' Mannie called. ''Come here. I want you to meet somebody.''

That was some body, all right. As she walked, her upper portion bounced even more than Jake's lower portion. He was taking careful note of that, for comparison no doubt, but Olga seemed unconcerned and unembarrassed. In fact, she took a chair directly across from me and leaned her arms all the way back against the cushions so I could get the maximum effect. Her eyes were large too.

''What do you think of those tits?'' Mannie asked with personal pride in the accomplishment.

''Beauties,'' I came through nicely. ''What do you do with them, Olga?''

''She's a model,'' Mannie answered, his gaze clinging to her particular qualifications.

''This one was in an ad for black satin sheets in *Playboy*.'' She smiled, smoothing her right breast.

''It looks like a great seller,'' I replied. ''Does the other one do anything for a living?''

Olga giggled and stroked both affectionately, making sure neither felt slighted. Poor dumb bitch. Or was she laughing at me all the way to the bank? Mannie certainly had a smirk on his face, but damned if anyone in this ménage was going to disconcert me, not after last night. Since that game of the week, I was beyond blushing. Or being put off.

"Mr. Blanco, if you're busy now, why don't I come back another time? Actually our conversation shouldn't be delayed too much longer, as your case is coming up soon . . ." My words dwindled off into implication. "But if you'd rather wait," I set the glass of Perrier on a small metal table, "you can call me when you're ready."

"No, stick around. I'll talk to you now." He dragged his unwilling eyes from the sideshow. "Olga, beat it. We got business to discuss. Now. Pronto. Get your ass out of here."

She pouted but obeyed, and the moment her behind was out of earshot, I charged in. "This is on my own, Mr. Blanco. No one sent me, but I had to warn you that you're in grave danger."

"That's real nice of you, sweetheart, but I know all about it. See? I got protection." He waved a hand to indicate the fence, the guard dogs, and three live-in cutthroats, not to mention a nude model or two.

"I understand that, Mr. Blanco, but I'm talking about a different kind of danger. A double-cross kind."

Like the story of the trained mule who wouldn't perform unless his owner hit him in the head with a two-by-four, at least I had Mannie's attention now. He pushed his sunglasses up and peered closely at me. "What are you talking about? A flim-flam? Forget it. Nobody can make me a patsy. I got all my bets hedged."

The opening was so perfect I couldn't resist. "So does Lou Smith."

The last time I dropped that name, Dennis almost dropped me down the elevator shaft, but Mannie Blanco's reaction was a hoot of laughter. "Louie? That fat crook? Oh, shit, don't tell me you talked to him." Mannie raised his hairy arms to show off his hairy armpits. "Oh, dollbaby, sweetie, you've been had. Louie's a bunch of hot air. Sure, he'd like to cash me in, but hell, he can't do nothing but beef. Don't worry about it."

That wasn't quite the point. I wanted Mannie to worry about it. "Perhaps you're right, Mr. Blanco, but he seemed to know an awful lot that should be strictly confidential. And what he didn't know, he asked about."

"Yeah, Louie always did have a big nose. That's why I broke it for him once. But I'm telling you, he can't do nothing because he don't know nothing. Let him snoop around." Mannie shrugged. "What the hell?"

The hell was getting the wind knocked out of my top sails before I even got moving. "Look here, Mr. Blanco. What would you say if I told you that Lou Smith tried to bribe me? In return for . . . gratuities," I choked a bit over the word, "my job would be to keep him posted on the developments in your case—who, what, and how much."

If a freezing look from Marjorie Abbotts could turn the sun to ice, Mannie's scorching appraisal made it feel like an acetylene torch beating down on my head. "Did you take the bait?" he asked, giving me the perfect straight-line.

"Mr. Blanco, please. I'm not that kind of girl."

The heat wave broke with a burst of laughter. Mannie appreciated the gibe as much as Lou had. "Okay," he chuckled, "so you're not a spy for Louie, but you didn't come all the way over here out of concern for my health neither. Can't say I got your angle figured, unless you're some kind a do-gooder, only I'm not sure yet who you're doing good for."

"For you, Mr. Blanco, and, in a roundabout way, me too."

"Yeah, sure, now you're starting to come clean. Before it was all my hide, now it's two asses . . . in a 'roundabout' way. Nice word. I like it. So tell me how roundabout? Like you're up shit creek with no plunger and I gotta bail you out? Tough. You shouldn't've pressed your luck too far with Louie. Or did you just open your mouth to show smarts? You dames is always mouthing off.''

''Not this time, Mr. Blanco. It was your mouthing off on a certain tape recording that got us both into this predicament. You see, Louie knows all about your crooked congressman.''

Finally Mannie began to take me seriously. He didn't quite beg for more, but he did scratch his armpit again. ''You know,'' he said after a lengthy pause, ''I can't figure you out. Either you're running an inside game or you're nuts. But I'll tell you, doll, I don't play unless I know what's in it for me. Why don't you lay your cards on the table and maybe we can do some bidding?''

There were no odds in trying to bluff Mannie with a pair of deuces, so rather than expose my weak hand, I hit him with a four flush. ''Lou Smith doesn't need me on his bribe list; he's already bought someone in your organization. Signed, sealed, and delivered; how else do you think he found out what you told Ms. Busch? That's the double-cross, Mr. Blanco; an inside source who's leaking information to the outside. He has access to your files, the D.A., and those fences back there. And Lou Smith has him by the neck.''

''Where do you come into all this?'' Mannie asked, still plenty skeptical.

''He knows I'm on to him. Once he finds out I've been to see you, he'll have to do something, and it won't be nice. But don't panic, Mr. Blanco. I've figured out a way to stop him. We can protect ourselves and get to him before he gets to us. You have the upper hand.'' With all my cards face down, I went for broke. ''Just prove that he killed Katherine Busch.''

A hornet sailed by, changed its mind and circled back, hovered briefly over my glass, then shot off as Mannie called my hand and took the pot.

''No dice. Why should I rock the boat? I'm taken care of, baby.'' He poked a finger at me. ''I got my own angle to play on this 'inside source.' You come to the wrong place for help, toots; I can't do a thing for you. Not that I don't feel sorry for you." He shrugged with convincing disinterest. "It ought to be a lesson to you. In this business you gotta have finesse."

"I'm not in this business, Mr. Blanco. That's why you're the only one who can protect both of us."

"Not both. Just me. And it don't do me no good to bring a murder rap into this. As a matter of fact," he said thoughtfully, "it might be what you call, counterproductive. Yeah, that's it. Counterproductive. Sort of like 'roundabout.' Got my drift?"

"I'm catching on."

"Let me tell you what your problem is, kid. You can't come waltzing in here and deal yourself into the game unless you got something to trade. You got something?" He raised the sunglasses off his boney nose again and looked at me as if I carried whatever it was in my bra. "Naw. You got nothing! See what I mean? You didn't back the odds. You got no paper, no I.O.U. But I got a special private insurance policy on this here inside source, and he can't hurt me without hurting himself."

"A double indemnity clause," I said dryly, getting to my feet.

"Now you're catching on, toot sweet," he punned in execrable French. "Always hedge a bet coming and going, 'cause if you don't keep an extra card up your sleeve, the customer might try to welch. That's where you went wrong. You see, I got two copies of my policy, just in case. One's for me, natch, and one's for him to keep in a nice, safe place, so's he can tune in and check the fine print whenever his memory starts to go bad. Understand?"

"Yes, as a matter of fact, I think I do."

Mannie seemed pleased that his lesson in business practice took such quick root. "You got a lot of spunk, sister. I like that. Just remember to stick to your side of the fence. I want to keep liking you."

"Scout's honor," I assured him. "But one thing, purely an academic question. Accepting the fact that you're in no danger, don't you care that he killed Katherine Busch?"

"Academiclike," Mannie answered candidly, "I really don't give a shit."

Chapter 20

Chocolate cake with green icing and blue flowers is a vile color combination at any hour of the day. When one is expected to consume the spectrum at nine A.M., one turns one's head and pretends to be on the Beverly Hills diet. Not that I was opposed to morning office parties; I adore champagne with my bagels. But even spelled out in lox and cream cheese, the message on this cake would have turned my stomach: CONGRATULATIONS DENNIS.

Naturally he was to be congratulated. How many people make it from murder suspect on Friday to full law partner on Monday? Silly me thought promotions took more than two weeks of solid work, to say nothing of a solid alibi. But then, silly me forgot about clever Marjorie. She hadn't wasted a minute to start the big guns rolling. Once I'd been ordered to step into line, about face and forward march, it was all systems go. The victory celebration seemed a trifle premature, but apparently Dennis told the joint chiefs of staff that their renegade office manager had changed sides, hence the cannonade of chocolate cake. Now all I had to do was retreat to Matt Steunkle with my white flag.

The problem was that signing up with the unholy alliance might not be any guarantee of safety in the ranks. "What so tedious as a twice-told tale?" Once I spoke my piece, why keep me around? As an office decoration? Suppose I changed my mind? Suppose Dennis didn't want to take that chance? It seemed a clear case of damned if I did and damned if I didn't. I could just dye my hair red, change my name, and catch the next flight for South America, but thanks to Mannie Blanco's Machiavellian little heart and big blabbery mouth, I knew of another nice "safe" place. Lucky for both of us that the lessons of Watergate were lost on some people.

After the cake-cutting ceremony, Mark left for an appointment in L.A.; Mr. Abbotts took off for court beaming like a proud grampa; and Dennis sailed in and out accepting kudos and kisses from everyone but ungracious me. My excuse was overwork. I started by piling my desk with papers, losing two folders, and only finding them again after Maggie typed new ones. This was followed by groans about being way behind schedule. Late in the day I made a half-hearted attempt to enlist titty-tat help, which fell on typically deaf ears, so when I griped about having to stay late, no one was too sympathetic, or more to the point, surprised.

The only hitch came when Mr. Abbotts had me rearrange his evening schedule. He was speaking to the League of Women Voters tonight at Civic Hall, and instead of driving all the way home and back, decided to move his regular health club visit from five to six, change and shave there, then meet his wife for dinner at Antonio's. It was a perfectly sensible plan from his point of view, but it meant he'd be in the office for an extra hour, and I had to stall around until he left. It would take more *chutzpah* than I possessed to look for a copy of Mannie's collateral right under the boss's nose.

Of course, there was still Contingency Caper No. 2.

Dennis had announced he'd be partying late tonight, celebrating his notable achievement. That provided a clear field for an exhaustive search of his bachelor apartment on Truman Street. I wasn't eager to try it. Though I'd dressed for the part of cat-burglar just in case—dark pants and shirt, sure-footed espadrilles—scaling the rooftop of a four-story apartment complex and wriggling down the air-conditioning ducts seemed a bit ambitious for an apprentice criminal. Much better to start with something easy, like cracking Dennis's safe. A pricking of my itchy thumbs told me that was the right place to start anyway. He wouldn't take a chance and leave the tape in the kitchen like I did.

When Mr. Abbotts wandered out of his office for the fourth time and asked how work was progressing, I smiled wanly and wiped my sweating brow. It was tough going. So far I had dusted off everyone's typewriter, moved the pens and pencils in my top drawer from the right side to the left, washed out the coffee pot with scouring powder, and checked the file cabinet for mites. There didn't seem to be much more that demanded my immediate attention, so when the phone rang, I almost danced for joy. If I spoke slowly enough, maybe it would use up two or three minutes.

"Good evening. This is Abbotts, Devlin and Devlin. Office hours are over for the day, but if you'd care to leave your name and telephone number, someone will return your call in the morning."

"Ellie? This is Howard Busch."

"Oh, hello, Howard. How are you?"

"Fine, thanks. Listen, I've been trying to track down Mark all day. Is he there?"

"No. He went into L.A. this morning and hasn't been back since. I doubt he'll show up this late. Have you tried his house?"

"Yes, but Luis doesn't know when to expect him either."

"Anything wrong?"

"No, it's just business, but I'm flying to Seattle on Wednesday, and Mark said he'd get together with me before I left and go over some stock transfers. Never mind. I'll catch him tomorrow."

"Good luck. He's got the Brewster hearing and that'll take all day."

"Great."

"What about Mr. Abbotts? Can he help?"

"Phil's there? All right. Let me talk to him."

Howard was in the process of terminating Katherine's interest in the firm and was understandably impatient to be done with it. Di-Con was transferring him to the Seattle office in October, regardless of the murder investigation. He'd have to come back for the trial, of course, but now he was needed at the nuke project. Most of the push for this transfer was Betsy's doing, or rather she voiced a weighty opinion about missed deadlines, projected overcosts, and the value of making Howard an on-site consultant. It was probably a kindly attempt to get him away from all the pain-filled memories of Casa Grande as well. I wanted to do my bit for Howard, too. If Mr. Abbotts would just hurry on out of here, I might even get it taken care of tonight.

The next phone call should have been left for the answering service, but I was too intent on looking diligent to think of defenses. With a lilt in my voice and a block in my head, I got as far as "Good evening, this is—" when Marjorie interrupted.

"Eleanor, you're still there? Please check the calendar on the far left corner of Josie's desk and tell me if the meeting tonight starts at seven-thirty or eight."

"Eight o'clock," I answered without having to look.

"And my husband's appointment at the spa is for six?"

A glance at the wall clock showed that was a bare five minutes away. *Déjà vu* raised the hairs on the nape of my neck. At a little before six o'clock on the night Katherine

Busch was killed, I was in the same spot, doing the same thing, with Howard Busch on the phone then too. A psychic would have called it an omen. Of what?

"Eleanor, did you hear me? I said let me speak to my husband."

"Sorry," I answered quickly, "he's on another line right now."

"Very well, I'll wait. Do you know how to put my call on hold and transfer it to one of his extensions? I realize it's a complicated console, but Josie must have explained the system to you by now."

"Oh, yes, she showed me all the tricks."

"Good. But first, Eleanor, have you thought over what we discussed yesterday?"

"Absolutely," I said with perfect honesty. "In fact, I'm going to take care of it right now."

"I'm very glad to hear that. You're doing the sensible thing, and I'll make sure Phil doesn't forget."

When Marjorie was reduced to a blinking red eye on extension 15, I thought over that comment. How could Phil forget if Marjorie hadn't told him what to remember? Yesterday at the country club she indicated our arrangement was strictly private. I believed her. Mr. Abbotts was too honorable a man to stoop to threats and trickery. That was Marjorie's special department. So how did that rate me a reward? My boss might appreciate the fact that I was going to free Dennis from all suspicion, but even if he gave me a bonus for telling the "truth," he'd add a dismissal notice for not telling it sooner. Could Marjorie talk him into doing better, or was she only trying to keep me quiet until Dennis could take care of the problem permanently?

The lady knew how to push people's buttons, all right, but thanks to Josie's expert tutelage, so did I. When Howard hung up, I transferred Marjorie's call, and with the practiced ease of an authentic switchboard operator, turned on the main line and held my hand over the receiver, so that Phil and Marjorie couldn't hear my bated breath.

"Why are you still in the office? Don't you realize it's almost six? Damn it, Phil, we're going to be late, and for once, it won't be my fault."

"I'm leaving right now."

"You should have left ten minutes ago. And what's she doing there?"

"How the hell do I know? Working."

"Get rid of her."

"Marjorie, please . . ."

"Why don't you ever listen to me? I warned you she'd be trouble. Suppose someone questions you tonight about that whole business? What are you going to say?"

"Will you stop panicking? Mark and I are taking care of Dennis, so you don't have to worry about Eleanor."

"Are you and Mark going to take care of Steve Tedesco too? And Mannie? You're crazy, Phil. She could blow everything sky high."

"Calm down, Marjorie, will you? Go take a valium and let me finish up so I can get out of here. It's late."

As carpet-muted footsteps rounded the corner of the hall, I was sitting at my typewriter pounding out "the quick silver fox killed the lazy brown dog all for the sake of the party." Mr. Abbotts grunted good night, and I nodded, my fingers flying at an all-time record of sixty words a minute. My speed slowed to a more normal forty as he went to the elevator, and, after the doors closed behind him, it dropped to thirty. When Mr. Abbotts landed on the ground floor, my dexterous digits were barely pecking out ten words a minute, and by the time he was out of the building and climbing into his blue Cadillac, I was out of the chair and reaching for the combination to his safe.

The first part of the tape was sheer letdown. Mannie complained about everything from the high cost of living to the odds on the Steelers-Cowboys preseason game. Then he began complaining about his lawyer.

BLANCO: How come you're just sitting there? Don't you care what happens in the world? You never talk; you just stick that snooty nose in the air. Christ almighty, why can't you act human, for shit's sake?

KATHERINE: While you're paying me by the hour? That can get expensive, Mannie. I suggest we limit our conversation to business. Your counteroffer's been rejected by the D.A.'s office and unless you come through with something, and soon, Ed Weiss is pushing for a trial date. Care to talk about that?

BLANCO: No. I told you already. I don't talk unless I get guarantees. Why should I give away collateral when nobody's giving me nothing back?

KATHERINE: You're never going to get anything back if you don't stop playing games. The government doesn't just hand out a half a million dollars on demand, and the Witness Protection Program isn't going to protect you from Weiss. If you want immunity and a free trip out of the States, you're going to have to show cause why you deserve it.

BLANCO: That's your job. You convince them I know plenty.

KATHERINE: How? Just tell me how, when I don't know any more about your secret associations than they do? You haven't given me one name, date, fact, figure; not a damn thing to work with.

BLANCO: You don't need nothing. All you got to do is make a deal.

KATHERINE: Forget it, Mannie. I can't make a deal that will get you off with less than ten to twenty.

BLANCO: I knew I shouldn't have let no dame take my case. You libbers ain't worth shit. If you wasn't so prim and proper, you'd have already gotten somewhere with Weiss. Jesus, you been playing footsy with him for three months. Can't you make it pay yet? Hell, I could've slipped him a C-note under the table and done better than you.

KATHERINE: I hope you're not serious.

BLANCO: Damn right, I'm serious. Weiss ain't no pure lily. You get him in his back room real privatelike, and show him how you're such a hot-shot lawyer. Hell, he'll be eating out of your hand in no time. A few other places too.

KATHERINE: Get out of here, Mannie.

BLANCO: Whatsamatter, you too good for that? You above the rest of the world? Well, let me tell you something, miss hoity-toity lawyer. When you're strutting your ass in front of a judge, all he's looking for is a piece of it. He don't give a damn what ten-dollar words is coming out of your mouth, 'cause he's too busy peeking down the front of your dress. So hell, unbutton the damned thing and let him see your god-damn tits. He gets a thrill and you win the case.

KATHERINE: Shut your vile mouth and get out of my office.

BLANCO: Uh-uh. I paid you five grand already and I want some results first. If you can't talk me a deal, play it the other way. Here, I'll give you a lesson how it works. Hey, you don't wear no bra, huh?

KATHERINE: Get your fucking hands off me or I'll kick you right in the balls.

BLANCO: Yeah, that's the place. I was afraid you didn't know where they were.

KATHERINE: You bastard! Let go of me. I'll kill you for this, Mannie.

BLANCO: No, you won't. For five thousand bucks, you owe me. I gotta get something from my lady lawyer, and this is all you're good for. Come on, lay on the floor real quiet and let me get my money's worth. Hey. Shit! What the hell . . . You goddamned bitch! You could have killed me with that thing.

KATHERINE: Too bad it's only a letter opener, because I'd like to castrate you. But you'll never get that close again. The firm is dropping your case.

BLANCO: You can't do that.

KATHERINE: I just did it. Any of the undocumented evidence you wish transferred to another attorney will be supplied, along with a notice to the District Attorney's office. You can expect a bill from me at the end of the month, which is to be paid in full within thirty days. Charges will be itemized as to expenses and hourly fees. Look for it to run about fourteen thousand dollars, not five.

BLANCO: Hold it!

KATHERINE: That will cost you an extra hundred.

BLANCO: Okay, now that you had your fun, sit down and cut the crap. I won't touch you. Just put down that blade.

KATHERINE: Didn't you hear me, Mannie? I said get the hell out of here.

BLANCO: Whatsamatter with you? Nobody explained the arrangement? You still ain't wised up? Well, do yourself a favor, honey. Go talk to Phil before you stab somebody with that thing. He'll tell you I'm here to stay. And he'll tell you I'm a real valuable client you don't go waving knives at.

KATHERINE: Just what are you trying to say?

BLANCO: Not trying, I'm saying it. Your partner's into me for thirty grand. A little loan from his last election, but it's not going to do this one no good if the news leaks out. See what I mean?

KATHERINE: You shmuck.

BLANCO: Hey, come on. You're getting plenty out of it too. Hot-shot libber proves women are as good as men in the courtroom; lady lawyer against male chauvinist pig clergy-man. You don't like those headlines? You don't like being a feminist celebrity? Well, I did it for you, toots, remember that. A lowdown gambling man put you on top of the heap, so don't complain about the smell.

KATHERINE: Are you threatening me?

BLANCO: Uh-uh. I don't make threats, just a little helpful advice on how things stand.

KATHERINE: And if I still say no?

BLANCO: Well, let me put it to you this way, nice and simple. Phil ain't going to let you quit. See the drift? He can't afford to give me up. Now put away that blade and button your shirt.

The tape clicked off. I pushed the forward control, but that was the end of the reel. The thirty-minute Memorex had played itself out on Mannie's final shot. There wasn't even a murmur of what Katherine might have said to him. It was just too bad she didn't cut off his balls while she had the chance. Never mind. I'd do it for her. By the time I finished with Mannie Blanco and Phillip Abbotts, neither one of them would be able to stand straight again. The bastards. And to think I'd blamed Dennis. It was Mr. Abbotts who had everything to lose.

Steve Tedesco asked me why the eminent counselor would involve himself with someone like Mannie Blanco in an election year. How about because they were already involved to the tune of thirty thousand dollars? With a pal like that, Mannie wouldn't go to a stranger for legal aid; and with a debt like that, Mr. Abbotts couldn't say no. He had to keep Mannie happy in order to keep him quiet. If it came out that they had financial dealings, the silver-haired SOB could forget about a career in politics. "Aspiring Congressman in Hock to Racketeer" is not the headline to win votes, or advertise a law practice, for that matter. Mr. Abbotts had managed a certain distance by fobbing Mannie off his shoulders and onto Katherine's, but finally the burden got too heavy for hers.

That afternoon, as soon as she kicked the slimy little hood out of her office, Katherine stormed in to see her partner and told him she was through. No more Blanco case. After that attempted rape, she wouldn't have defended Mannie's right to choke on smog. Mr. Abbotts made a valiant effort to change her mind; his angry voice carried right through the panelled walls, but Katherine's protests were just as loud. She wasn't the kind of woman to cower under a blackmailer's threat, and she had too much integrity to cover for Mr. Abbotts. If he couldn't own up to his own deeds and take the consequences, he deserved what Mannie dished out. Otherwise, he'd better make some new arrangements. Mr. Abbotts had the rest of the day to think of another strategem, but Mannie wanted his lady lawyer, and what Mannie wanted, Mr. Abbotts had to supply. He came back to the office that evening, hoping to talk Katherine around, but obviously tempers flared again. Strangulation *is* a crime of passion.

The feeling of "having been here before" crept up my spine again. But then, as the saying goes, people who don't learn from the past are doomed to repeat it. That's why, when the door of the conference room opened behind me, I knew who was there before I turned around.

His eyes narrowed as he took in the tape recorder, the cassette on the table beside it. "You just had to do it," he said wearily. "I might have guessed."

"*Et tu,* Mark?"

Chapter 21

It made an interesting tableau: man in wheelchair with tie undone confronts woman in conference room with damning proof at hand. The rest spoke for itself.

"I'm sorry you found it," was his pithy comment.

"Is that so? Well, I can certainly understand, but you should have warned your partner to pick a better hiding place. My first attempt at safe cracking and *voilà*. Almost as easy as breaking into houses, don't you think?"

"I think they just about equal out," he said with a grim look at me. "Now put it back and forget what you heard."

"Forget? As in out of sight, out of mind? Forget the way a member of the bar forgets about concealed evidence?" I picked up the tape and flipped it over in my hand. Restraining myself from throwing it in Mark's miserable face, I threw more sarcasm. "Gee, I don't know. Instant amnesia seems a lot harder than total recall. Or don't you have any problems with criminal malpractice?"

"Not leaving me a loophole, are you?" He said that

calmly enough, no emotion either way, but his five o'clock shadow was two hours late for a shave, his hands were grimy from pushing the wheelchair, and the Monday Night Game of the Week was half over. I didn't feel one bit sorry for him.

"Who actually jimmied my back door open, Mark? Mr. Abbotts in his three-piece suit, or one of his accomplices? Seems he had many, but none more loyal than you. Just imagine being called by the very person you robbed and having to soothe her fevered brow."

"If you're accusing me of masterminding the crime, Ellie, I only found out about it the next day."

"Pardon me. Then you're merely an accessory after the fact. Secondary liability, shall we say. You dumbo," I railed at him. "That makes you *in pari delicto*, which happens to be illegal, in case you forgot the law and which happens to make you as guilty as your partner. My God, Mark," I waved the tape, "when they play this in court, how will you explain keeping silent about a felony? You'll be disbarred, ruined."

"I appreciate your optimism," he said with a twist of lemon in his voice, "but even if you press charges of breaking and entering, of which crime you too are guilty at present, you can stop swinging the tape around like a battering ram. It won't be played in court."

"What are you talking about? It's proof of motive."

"It's proof of nothing," he contradicted. "First of all, you came by it illegally, during the commission of a criminal act. Secondly, tape recordings are not considered the best evidence, because they can be doctored too easily. But most important, Ellie, and you should know this by now, what you're holding in your hand is a privileged communication between lawyer and client. Barring all the other complications, that means without Mannie's express consent, it's inadmissible evidence in any court of law."

"I can't even show it to Matt Steunkle?"

"You can't even tell it to Matt. Use your head, Ellie. You're an employee of a law firm. The same restrictions that apply to me cover you too. We have to uphold a client's confidentiality. It's the law."

"What about justice?"

Mark sounded almost sorry for me. "Put the tape back, Ellie. It's not going to do what you want."

Only in America could telling the truth be declared unconstitutional. I had it all right here, neatly encased in a nice black package, but because of a legal technicality, I couldn't repeat a word without bringing the wrath of the courts on my head. What a judicial system. "Fair is foul, and foul is fair." It didn't matter who won or lost, only that the good guys didn't play by inadmissible rules of evidence. The bad guys just hired lawyers. And Mark said I didn't leave him just a loophole; he had the Grand Canyon of escape hatches, privileged communication. The lawful sanctioning of the unlawful. My only protection was irrelevant, irregular, and immaterial.

"Very well, Mark. You win this round. It seems I have no choice but to obey the law that shields the guilty. It's not my favorite clandestine activity, but I'll just muzzle my conscience and pretend it's for the betterment of mankind. After all, you've found silence to be very golden, haven't you?"

"Not always." He glanced at his watch and started to back out of the room. "Today I proved that 'speech is silvern.' Do me a favor, Ellie, switch an outside line to my phone. I have to call Matt Steunkle."

"Don't tell me you're going to confess."

"I'm sure that would please you," Mark answered, starting across the hall. "But maybe you'll be almost as happy to hear that I've found Dennis's witness. Does that put you in a more forgiving spirit?"

I followed right behind him. "Repeat that, please. I find the tape, and you find a witness just like that? Tonight?"

"It wasn't quite that simple. I've had a private detective on her trail for weeks now, and he finally caught up with her today."

"Where?" I demanded.

"In L.A., on a street corner, on her way to work."

"Very funny," I scoffed. "What is she, a hooker?"

"She bills herself as an exotic dancer, among other things." Mark smiled. "Which is one of the reasons she's been so hard to trace. Naturally she tends to be a bit leary of the law, even when she's on the right side of it. Shirley Le Fleur is nothing if not cautious," he explained, reaching for the phone only to find that it was turned off at the switchboard. "Ellie, get me an outside line, please."

Ignoring that request, I pursued my own train of thought. "This witness, is she really the girl whose last name Dennis couldn't remember?"

"I get the distinct feeling you thought Dennis was lying about her."

"Not exactly." I hedged. "It was just such a farfetched story. But obviously you crossed her palm with 'silvern' and she's consented to do her civic duty and vouch for Dennis. But what did she witness besides your nephew that should make me so happy?"

Mark looked at me impatiently. "I'd hoped that the mere fact that I located her would act as some kind of character reference for me; but never mind, just put back the tape and get me an open line before Shirley changes her mind and flits back to L.A. I'm supposed to be at the police station this very minute protecting her rights."

No one could pull rabbits out of hats the way Mark sprang lightning bolts from the invisible. Suddenly there was a private eye I never knew about, a hooker who flags down business under a lamppost, and in one magical swoosh Mark expected a pat on the head for doing something right for once.

"Why didn't you tell me all this when you got here instead of reading me the riot act about the tape?"

"You never gave me a chance."

That was no excuse, but there wasn't much point in arguing about it. The only thing left for me to do was retrace my useless steps, unplug the recorder, push the chair back in place under the conference table, and wonder why I ever considered myself a detective.

It shouldn't have been any surprise that Mark caught me with the tape in my little red hands. A sleuth worthy of the title wouldn't have conducted an undercover search with the drapes wide open and the lights turned on. She wouldn't have left her car blatantly sitting in the parking lot to advertise her presence either. Frailty, thy name is Ellie Gordon. How could I have been so careless? But then, I was the original slipshod shamus. An entire conspiracy is hatched under my bloodhound nose, and I go chasing my tail. Of course I was up against a wily crew of schemers, every one of them playing a con game with me, including Mark. No, change that to especially Mark. As long as both of us were covered by the same rule of ethics, which was really completely unethical, he could have told me about the tape long ago. Instead, he waited until I followed the yellow brick road all the way to Oz, then handed me a writ of estoppel.

After reluctantly replacing the tape in Mr. Abbotts's safe, I paused in the hallway as Mark's voice, sounding oddly flat, carried out his open door.

". . . so she identified him from the photo. What about the time? Does it match? And the car . . . you got verification? Well, I guess that answers who belongs to the blue Caddy. No, I'm not surprised . . . sure . . . no problem, you go ahead and get her statement typed, and I'll be down in a few minutes. No, I know she won't sign anything without me there . . . she wants to Mirandize you first?" There was a long pause. "That's the way witnesses are . . . sure, I appreciate it . . . no, his meeting won't be over till around ten . . . yes, he'll be surprised, all right." Another pause. "Thanks, Matt."

As Mark hung up the phone, he saw me standing in the doorway. "Are the wheels of justice finally slipping into first gear, thanks to you?" I asked, feeling strangely unelated at the prospect of Mr. Abbotts's arrest. But if Shirley identified him and his car, my soft-headed regret wasn't going to change anything. When Mark didn't answer, I turned my back on him and continued down the hall to my desk. There was no reason to let sympathy get the best of me now, just because Mark's legal loophole turned out to be a noose. Too bad that in finding a witness to save his nephew, he seemed to have trapped his partner with nary a technicality in sight. That was his problem, though I was sure if Mark had known in advance that Shirley Le Fleur was going to talk her way through the barrier of privileged communication, he would have paid her double for the privilege of half the communication. But *caveat emptor.* Now it was too late.

After tossing the evening's worth of typing into the trash can and covering the Selectric, I remembered that I'd left the light on in Mr. Abbotts's office. Then I decided I didn't give a damn and went straight to the elevator, where Mark was waiting for me.

"What would you like me to say?" he asked.

"Nothing." I stared straight ahead. "Why change things now?"

"I really didn't have much choice, Ellie. Besides," he said, trying to cajole me and not succeeding, "Brutus *was* an honorable man."

"So were they all," I reminded him aptly. "And you know what my answer is? A fig on your honor." I threw him one, then quickly started rapping on the elevator door. "What's the matter with this thing? Why isn't it opening?"

Mark looked at me, then at his watch, back to me again, then unsnapped a key from his ring. "Here. Take this. I want you to go to my house and wait. The business at police headquarters shouldn't take more than an hour, maybe until nine, and there are a few things I'd like to explain before you never speak to me again.'' The key dangled from his fingers.

I left it hanging. ''There's no need to do a post-mortem for my benefit. You were only doing your duty, and far be it from me to question the law of the land.'' My haughty answer was the perfect rebuff, and, as he started to put the key in his coat pocket without even a protest, I filched it smoothly and dropped it in my purse. ''Maybe you do owe me some explanations.'' Then I pounded on the elevator again. ''Why won't it open?''

Mark pushed the down button.

That was the end of any more conversation between us; not that we'd had such an illuminating talk, but it seemed as though a moratorium on speech was in effect until the big summit conference later. There was plenty I could have said in preparation, just to get him into the mood for the upcoming battle, only I wanted to hear his strategy first. Apparently Mark had the same idea. We completed the brief elevator ride in silence, merely grunting something like ''see you later'' when we stepped outside, then got into separate cars and drove off in different directions. A meeting of the minds, it wasn't.

When was it ever? Mark and I communicated as well as a carrier-pigeon talking to an unmanned radio receiver. From the beginning I couldn't penetrate his bland mask. He played it cool, and I played a guessing game. Even now I didn't know the point of tonight's invitation. Was ''go to my house and wait'' the equivalent of ''meet me at the Casbah''? Or did it mean ''don't talk to the police until we get our stories straight''?

If Mark were in the throes of a reawakened desire for me, his attitude was certainly more tepid than torrid. On the other hand, my conduct resembled the girl chasing the boy until he catches her, which was exactly how I had trapped myself before. Trapped? What an oddly descriptive word. It was either a Freudian slip of the psyche, or another premonition, but since this was the night for ghostly portents, the spirit of Mark Devlin was bound to rattle his chains. I had left the attic door wide open, and here was the same situation, the same order of events as on the night of Katherine Busch's murder, but now his presence was materializing into a disturbingly clear shape.

It had never occurred to me before, or at least not with any significance, that Mark discovered a passion for my body after the murder, only after the tape was stolen from my house and after I indicated it held all the answers. An affair would be a convenient way to keep tabs on a nosy, lonesome divorcée and keep her too grateful to ask awkward questions. That might be considered an unusual mix of business and pleasure, if much pleasure could be gotten from such business; but I was a very willing victim. Mark said nothing; I said everything. He looked interested, and I took it personally. The only place he slipped was on top of Helen Ramirez. Since her entrance on the scene, Mark had been noticeably unpassionate, leaving me free to poke and pry without his knowledge or consent. In fact, he hadn't made another move on me until tonight, after I found the tape, after I discovered his culpability, after I threatened exposure. Coincidence? True love? Or another manifestation of time, motive, and opportunity? Mark's revived interest could be nothing more than a labor of lust. Sexual strategy, a few plausible lies whispered in my ear, several hours of hard diplomacy, and once again I'd be duped into credulity and bed at the same time.

So if I didn't trust the smooth-talking shyster, why was I driving ten miles over the speed limit to get to his house?

With Mark's key still clutched in my hot little fist, I turned onto Beachside Drive and parked in front of 170. The lights were on in the kitchen, and there was a note on the refrigerator from Luis, saying he'd be back before midnight. If Mark got hungry, the pot of chili stew only needed warming, and inside the vegetable crisper, in a green Tupperware bowl, he'd find a tossed salad. Luis's directions were easily followed, although the bottle of Robert Mondavi burgundy I added to the menu on my own initiative. Whetting my whistle for moral support, I carried the wine into the bathroom with me like a talisman, then turned on the ruthless overhead light and stared into the mirror.

Did Mark want me for my mind or my body?

That I knew plenty had doubtless made me interesting, but did the enchanting vision with the wine bottle in her hand have enough sex appeal to stir a man's libido, to wean him from the arms of Helen Ramirez? My face had more character than hers. My teeth were whiter. My nose was bigger. And I had a good personality too. Another swig of Robert Mondavi improved it. Hell, she had nothing over me. Could the immature Ms. Ramirez boast of such speaking laugh lines around her eyes? Did she understand the advantages of dry skin? Where was her other chin? Damn! I was a magnificent specimen of thirty-eight-year-old womanhood. What more could Mark want?

After another swallow of burgundy from the bottle and another glance at my flat stomach, I went into the living room, got a long-stemmed goblet from the buffet, then sat cross-legged on the couch and began flicking through a copy of *Newsweek*. Reading about what the president was up to these days ought to take my mind off being sad and hungry. He had only the weight of the world on his shoulders, lucky duck. So I filled the glass and commiserated with our leader; and every time my stomach grumbled for sustenance, I thought about the starving children in India, and had some wine instead.

A little while later inside the Oval Office, the hot line started ringing. It was the Russians calling to warn us that one of their runaway missiles was headed for Casa Grande. The president asked me to take care of it.

"Hello?" I said in a groggy voice.

"Eleanor? Is that you?"

Only a few glasses of home-grown burgundy and my head felt as though it had been stamped on by an army of migrant grape pickers, but I wasn't that far gone.

"Mr. Abbotts?" I asked faintly.

"Yes. Sorry, I couldn't hear you for a moment. May I speak to Mark, please?"

"He's not back yet." I glanced at the clock. Ten after ten. Mr. Abbotts must be calling from jail. Unsure of the proper tone to use with an employer just arrested for murder, I settled for neutral. "Is there anything I can do?"

"No. Just ask Mark to call me. I'll be at the office for about another hour."

The office! What in the hell was going on? No, don't panic. There must have been a delay, that's all. Just pretend you don't know a thing. Too late.

"By the way, Eleanor. What kind of work were you doing before that took you into my safe?"

"What kind of work?" I thought frantically. "In your safe? Oh, I didn't go there. Let's see, I did some filing. A little typing. And I filled the copier. Yes, that too. It was out of ink."

"Don't bother trying to deny it. I just want to know why you were looking for the tape and what made you think I had it."

Oh God, he knew everything. Where did I slip up? I took care not to touch his papers. Don't tell me he was one of those people who always kept the zero on the dial of his safe at twelve o'clock high. No, the light. I left the light on in his office. Careless, careless. Twice tonight I left a shining tribute to my activities. First for Mark, now for Mr. Abbotts.

But I couldn't confess, not until he was safely in custody. Maybe pleading the fifth would help.

"What tape?"

"Very well, Eleanor," he said briskly. "We shouldn't discuss this over the phone anyway, so as long as you're at Mark's, and I have to speak to him tonight, I'll just come over now and get this matter straightened away with you first."

"No, you can't do that. I mean, I can't do that." A well-developed instinct for self-preservation inspired me to lie with unusual fluency. "Sorry, Mr. Abbotts, but I stopped by here only to fill in for Luis temporarily. Howard Busch is coming to dinner, you see. Matt Steunkle too," I added for good measure. "And with Mark being so late—oops, there's the doorbell. Must be Howard. As soon as the chili is heated, I'm off. Nice talking to you, Mr. Abbotts."

I dropped the receiver as though the hot line literally burned my hand. Would he believe the shaggy dog tale about reinforcements? Probably not. Ten-fifteen was late for dinner. Besides, Mark wouldn't schedule a party on the eve of his partner's arrest.

Flying into the kitchen to snatch my purse from the counter, I halted with the car keys in my hand. Where was I running? If Mr. Abbotts didn't find me here, he'd just go to my house; and if I tried driving to the police station, he might intercept me on the winding two-lane highway along the beach. No thanks. But there weren't too many other choices. I could dig a hole in the sand outside and hope he didn't notice the hump, or maybe just lock myself in the bathroom and swallow the key. The polite thing would be simply to invite him to join us for supper, but he'd already had dinner. Diving for the phone, I dialed 911.

"Police emergency." The girlish voice was sharp and wide awake.

"I need to speak to Chief Steunkle immediately."

"Dial 247-3011."

"No, wait. Don't hang up. Can't you transfer this call?"

"No, ma'am. This is police emergency. You'll have to dial 247-3011. Thank you."

The empty line buzzed in my ear. Damn the police. Didn't they realize there are all kind of emergencies? I tried the other number. This time the voice was bored and masculine.

"Sergeant Ortiz, night desk."

"Chief Steunkle, please."

"Sorry, he's not in."

"Are you sure? He's supposed to be there with Mark Devlin. The attorney? You know, the man in the wheelchair."

"Chief Steunkle went home at six as far as I know. You want to leave a message—"

I interrupted him. "Would you just check for me? Chief Steunkle and Mr. Devlin were interviewing a witness tonight. A Miss Le Fleur."

"Lady, slow down. You want to talk to Miss Le Fleur?"

I hung onto my patience. "I want to speak to Chief Steunkle. It's extremely urgent."

"Your name?"

"Eleanor Gordon."

With a maddening obsession for the irrelevant, he asked, "How do you spell that?"

"I don't give a damn how you spell it. Will you please connect me with the chief?"

"I already told you, he's not here."

"Then why do you want my name? Never mind," I snapped impatiently. "What about Miss Le Fleur or Mark Devlin? Are they still there?"

"I don't know."

"Then check. Find out. Surely you keep a list of witnesses. It's spelled L-E F-L-E-U-R, Shirley."

"Geez, lady. Hold your horses." He rifled through some

papers on his desk. "Nobody by that name was here tonight. I got a Nora Nablinsky—"

Rudely I cut him off again. "Forget it. Can you get a message to Chief Steunkle immediately?"

"That depends. If it's an emergency—"

"Yes, it's an emergency. The man who murdered Katherine Busch is on his way over here right now. I'm at one seventy Beachside Drive, and you might tell Chief Steunkle that I'm alone."

"Busch? The women's lib murder? Why didn't you say so in the first place? I'll get right on it." There was nothing slow about his reaction now. He shot out orders to me. "Lock the windows and doors. Don't let anybody in. Keep out of sight." His last command was meant to be reassuring. "And stay calm."

Why shouldn't I be calm? Mr. Abbotts had only escaped a police dragnet and was out looking for me. Big deal. When you're a successful sleuth, that's the kind of thing that comes with the case. It didn't worry me. Not at all. No, sir. You gotta be tough in this business.

I slammed the phone down and ran for the front door first; locked and double-locked. The French doors off the patio were the next step, and after pushing the latch closed, I pulled down the wooden blinds for extra protection. Those glass panes were so easy to break through. Halfway back across the living room, bounding for the back of the house, two things struck me at once. You can't lock a window pane, and someone had just pulled up in the driveway.

It couldn't be the police that fast, and Mark wouldn't be walking up to the front door. He wouldn't ring the bell either. On the second peal I was ready to go hide under the bed, but after the third time a voice called out, "Ellie, are you in there?"

Of course. I left my car right out in the open again, except this time, it had been a brilliant idea. I unbolted the door as quickly as possible, grabbed a handful of sports coat, and yanked.

"Howard, what a lucky coincidence. You're just in time for dinner."

Chapter 22

Moments later I was at the kitchen table cuddling a hot mug of coffee with chilled hands. Outside the temperature may have been 75 degrees, but I felt as shivery as I had yesterday sitting across from Marjorie under the sunny skies of an August afternoon. I still hadn't explained the dramatic reception except to babble about a telephone call from Mr. Abbotts. Howard, arriving innocently in the hope of catching Mark and faced with a paranoid office manager instead, probably thought I had blown up the word processor and my irate boss was after my scalp. If only it were that ordinary.

In any case, being patient and supportive, Howard poured me a cup of coffee first, then went to fix one for himself; instant, but he didn't shudder in distaste. When he tilted the kettle, though, a little water splashed onto the counter, which he deftly blotted up with a wet sponge. Precise to the marrow of his mathematical bones, he then flipped the sponge over to the dry side, brushed a few spilled grains of freeze-dried coffee into his hand, tossed them down the disposal, rinsed off his hand and wrung out the sponge, then carried his filled mug to the table, holding a paper napkin underneath. Mesmerized by this dedication to detail, I didn't notice for a moment that he was waiting for me to speak.

"Where's Mark?" he asked, bringing me out of my reverie.

"On his way home, probably. He should have been here at nine. Only an hour late, but you will stay until he gets here?"

"Of course, but what's all this about Phil?"

"I really don't know how to tell you this, Howard. In fact, I don't even want to tell you, but you're here, so I guess I have no choice." His smile was so encouraging, it seemed heartless to wipe it off his face. "This is terrible." I turned my head away.

"Nothing's that terrible," he soothed with unsuspecting assurance.

"Yes, it is."

"Then take a deep breath first."

"You're still not going to like it," I warned him.

"Tell me anyway."

Primed for gasps of shock and heart-wrenching fury, I explained the situation, but Howard didn't even rattle his coffee cup in mild agitation; he didn't believe me.

"Where did you hear that story?"

"You don't understand, Howard," I said, trying to be civil about it. "It's no story. It's proven fact. I found the evidence myself."

Skipping over Mark's contribution might have been unsporting, but it was the end result that counted. "The important thing is," I repeated, "Mr. Abbotts knows what I did, and if the police don't catch him first, he's coming over here to kill me too."

Again Howard's response was something less than quivering alarm. "Are you sure you're not imagining things? No, no, Ellie, I don't mean that you're making this up, but how could you possibly find out if Phil mur . . .'' He cleared his throat, but I saved him the trouble of finding an easier way to say it.

"Listen to me, Howard. I didn't use a Ouija board. Somehow my involvement in the case turned into a search. Do you remember my telling you about the tape that was stolen from me? How we both agreed that the murderer must have taken it to hide his identity? Well, I found the tape tonight, although to be honest with you, I wasn't thinking of Mr. Abbotts when I started. Dennis was my real suspect. He didn't have an alibi for the night of the murder; and when I refused to give him one by changing my statement, he threatened me. Then I learned from a mobster that Dennis owes Mannie Blanco a few gambling debts.''

If Howard still wasn't buying, at least he looked impressed. "You actually went to the mob? That's pretty risky. They're dangerous people.''

"You should see Dennis in action. But my only other hot prospect was Ritchie. Don't gape. Even if he is a man of the cloth, he hated your wife. Katherine made him sound like a fool every chance she got, and he gave her plenty. Unlike Dennis, though, the reverend had an airtight alibi. At least a dozen virtuous witnesses could offer vows that he was toning up his blubber at the health club. Mr. Abbotts could vouch for that too, except that Phil was leaving the spa at six when Billy Joe was arriving. By the way, did you know that Ritchie was never ordained anywhere? He just went into business for himself.''

Howard tore a strip off his napkin and rolled it into a ball. "Seems you conducted a thorough investigation," he commented, "but didn't it ever occur to you that looking for a murderer might be a good way to get yourself killed?''

"That's what I've been trying to tell you.''

He digested that home run for a moment, then hit me a bunt. "All right. You obviously came across something. What is the damning evidence?''

I gave it to him in one pitch. "Katherine was going to quit the Blanco case; but Mannie and Mr. Abbotts had transacted a private deal, and your wife was their negotiable instrument."

This time Howard wadded the entire napkin into a ball. "She wanted to quit? That's not what I—"

He didn't finish, but it was perfectly obvious he hadn't known that bit of information. Katherine was probably saving the happy news for when they went to dinner. Her prelude would have been crab legs at Antonio's, and the coda, a night of love. Howard couldn't have asked for a better celebration for a better reason. He had begged Kathy to get off the case months ago because of the danger involved. It was a twist of black irony that taking his advice was the death of her.

Howard looked a little green around the edges. "The whole thing is preposterous," he understated. "Crazy. What did the police say when you told them?"

This was going to be tough. I had just barely convinced Howard that the tape was proof, and now I had to explain that it wasn't. It would have been simpler, though not as meaningful, to tell him about the eyewitness first, then dazzle him with my erudition. However, when I tried going backwards now, it was like pedaling a bicycle uphill in reverse and upside-down.

"Let me get this straight," Howard said when I was through. "Mark caught you breaking into the safe, told you he had a witness, and you put back the tape. The police don't have it."

His summation was as tight as the knot developing in my stomach. "They can't use the tape," I repeated. "But they do have Shirley Le Fleur, and in this instance, that's all anybody has. 'One eyewitness is of more weight than ten hearsays.' Do you think I would have given up my evidence otherwise?"

Taking a moment to review the situation before commenting, Howard went to get a coffee refill, but changed his mind and rinsed out the cup instead, put it on the drainboard, then took a dishtowel and wiped his face with it. That didn't seem to clear his mind either. "Did Mark actually tell you that Phil was to be arrested tonight?"

"Not in so many words," I admitted defensively, trying to remember the little Mark did say. "But I distinctly heard him tell Matt Steunkle that Mr. Abbotts's meeting would be over around ten o'clock. Apparently Mark wanted the police to wait, so his partner wouldn't be arrested at a public gathering of the League of Women Voters. That would be a horror."

"You didn't hear anything more specific?"

"I was only eavesdropping, Howard, not listening in on the extension, but this Shirley Le Fleur identified Mr. Abbotts from a photograph, and was able to tie him to the blue Cadillac that was parked in front of the office at the crucial time. Wouldn't you say that's damning enough, or that it at least provides an adequate reason for the police to pick him up for questioning?"

"I guess so." Howard still looked puzzled, as if he couldn't quite imagine Phil Abbotts as a murderer, witness or not. "I know the blue Cadillac was there," he murmured finally. "I saw it myself." Then, with the incisive speed of a logical mind, he began to break down the rest of my story. "But assuming the police were going to nab Phil as soon as the meeting was over, what was he doing in his office at ten o'clock, calling you? If Mark went to the police station at seven-thirty, I can't imagine what caused such a delay, unless Shirley Le Fleur changed her mind, or was mistaken."

"Or there is no Shirley Le Fleur," I said harshly.

"That's not necessarily—"

"Let's eat." It seemed like a good way to shut him up, but when I lifted the lid off the pot of chili, beans, meat, and sauce were still congealed in a crust of fat. Appetizing it wasn't, but I had a knack for swallowing the inedible; for example, the garbage Mark had fed me tonight. Covering the pot and turning up the flame, I announced glumly, "Dinner isn't ready yet. Want some cheese and crackers?"

"Don't jump to conclusions, Ellie. There's probably a perfectly simple explanation."

"Okay, let's pick one. Who was Mark talking to from the office tonight?" I cocked my head in a pose of whimsical concentration. "Not the police, but what about the time service? That's a nice recording. Or the weather bureau. Or dial-a-prayer. Yes, I like that one. It has the ring of truth, don't you think?" I punned humorlessly. "Besides, how sinful could a person feel if he's having a fake conversation with the twenty-third psalm? On-the-spot absolution."

The expression on Howard's face almost unwomaned me, but I battled on in defeat. Using the principle that tearing off a bandage quickly somehow makes the pain more bearable, I ripped every last figment from my imagination in one excruciating yank.

Mark didn't have the decency to dial a prayer. While I was obediently hiding the evidence again, he was busy reporting my find to Mr. Abbotts. How else could the murderer know which dirty rat was going to squeal on him? There wasn't any witness, that's for sure, nor any proof, and pretty soon, if Mr. Abbotts got his way, there wouldn't be any me. Did Mark realize this possibility, or had he been practicing illegal ethics again with his eyes closed? Mine certainly weren't very open. In fact it seemed a lot clearer in retrospect, as were most of my flashes of brilliance, but he must have set up the scheme with malice aforethought. While I bumbled to the doorway of his office like an ineffectual Inspector Clousseau, the light from Mr. Abbotts's foolishly forgotten desk lamp was casting my shadow directly in front of me. That would have given Mark plenty of time to gauge my petty pace, all the way to his last syllable.

Chapter 23

The clock ticked loudly in the silent kitchen. Howard had made a complete reconnaissance of the house and grounds ten minutes ago, finding nothing. Now he would check his watch every other second, rap his fingers on the counter, then give me a long stare before starting the procedure all over again. I merely stirred the chili and waited for the Swat Squad to burst through the door.

So where were my dinner guests? The fire burned and the cauldron bubbled, but no one was rushing over to eat. Matt Steunkle should have been burping on his last bean by now, while the emergency boys in blue polished off the tortillas. I sprinkled some oregano in the chili, then added another pinch on the theory that if a little is good, a lot is better. But after four more uneventful laps around the pot, I began to consider the onion salt, a clove of garlic, an incantation. Maybe an eye of newt and toe of frog would do the trick. This recipe certainly wasn't conjuring up any policeman, spiritual or otherwise. In fact, the whole situation was getting weirder by the minute. After so much double toil and trouble, was everybody going to stand me up? Even Howard looked ready to cancel his reservation.

I turned off the burner and slammed the wooden mixing spoon into the sink. Missing hors d'oeuvres might be considered fashionably late among *haute* officialdom, but skipping the entreé was socially unacceptable in the best law enforcement circles. Either my dinner invitation was sitting on the bottom of the desk sergeant's trash can, or he hated Mexican food and had sent everyone off to capture a runaway egg roll at some Chinese restaurant on the other side of town. Why else would the police forego a meal like this? The entire Swat Squad couldn't have joined Weight Watchers right after I called. Of course, a nameless person with a disguised voice might have told them that the party was postponed due to technical difficulties. I had informed Mr. Abbotts with my own big mouth that the Chief of Police was coming to dine, and it didn't take the eye of a newt to see what a sharpie like my boss would make of that. But surely it was the *modus operandi* to give the hostess a procedural R.S.V.P. about a change in plan. Or don't they teach good manners at the police academy?

It was past time to call the police again and start the bureaucratic ball rolling once more: name (spelled correctly), address (is that 117 or 170?), and this time would I please supply the unlisted telephone number of the alleged killer, along with his astrological chart? I'd rather take it on blind faith that a platoon of modestly hungry plainsclothesmen was staked out in the palm tree across the street, poised for the dinner gong. Maybe if I closed my eyes and wished. That was the way you got Tinker Bell to show up.

Calm. The important thing was to keep calm. Howard already thought I'd gone crackers, standing by the stove and stirring the magical brew of the ultimate stew. I couldn't let him catch me chewing on the ladle. Very quietly and calmly,

I would call the police again and renew my request for help. If Howard made any noises about leaving before they got here, I'd simply tie him to the refrigerator and stuff a tomato in his mouth. As long as he stayed with me, I was safe. Mr. Abbotts wouldn't attempt a physical assault on a man twenty years younger and ten pounds heavier, and there was no other way he could storm this locked fortress, pry me from my stalwart protector, and get me alone. At least, I thought so until Howard turned from the window.

''Mark's here.''

Now why should that send a chill down my spine? Because he was unexplainably late? Because he had lied about going to Matt Steunkle, made up a nonexistent witness, used a convenient letter of the law to protect a murderer? The list could go on *ad infinitum,* but what came next concerned me at the moment. Mark had a key to my fort, deed of ownership, and eviction rights. Did he also have a vested interest in getting Howard out and Mr. Abbotts in? My knowledge of the law was not profound, but I did know that concealing information about a felony after the fact was tantamount to committing the crime. Mark had been his partner's keeper, but how close was their touching relationship? Good buddies, or murderer and accessory?

I wasn't the only one with a lot of unanswered questions. Howard didn't know what to think either. According to my scenario, Mr. Abbotts should have been the one arriving, breathing fire and brandishing a pitchfork. Instead, it was the innocent householder himself parking in his own driveway, taking a dangerous wheelchair out of the trunk, and coming in the front door as if he couldn't think of anything more exciting than going to the bathroom. As the wheelchair rolled to a stop in the kitchen doorway, Howard cleared his throat, stared at his highly polished shoes, and in general seemed as guilty as a kid caught with his hand in the cookie jar. I, in contrast, was well in control of the situation.

"Hello there, Mark. You're just in time for my last supper. Chili anyone?"

Ignoring my gibe with a convincing show of innocent forgetfulness, Mark immediately apologized to Howard. "Sorry I didn't get back to you today, but as you can see, I've been tied up since this morning. Did you bring a copy of the contract with you?"

"Yes, but I don't want to intrude if you and Ellie have already made plans for this evening," Howard offered cravenly. "We can get together some other time."

"I'm sure Ellie won't mind waiting until tomorrow, will you?" Mark asked me. "Howard is leaving town for a few days, and I know he'd like to get some minor details settled before he goes. I'm sorry, Ellie." Mark sounded almost sincere.

"That's a comfort," I replied, crossing my arms and leaning back against the counter. "Your remorse is something I'll always treasure. But rather than have you suffer it at all, why don't I just stick around and save you the agony?" No way was he getting me to walk down the garden path without a police escort.

"Ellie," Mark tried again. "Howard would like to go over private business matters with me. I don't mean to kick you out—"

"Oh, yes you do."

"All right," he allowed through gritted teeth, "but I'm trying to do it politely."

"Your manners are impeccable," I flashed at him, "but if you really want to show a little consideration, you might try explaining a few things, like your mysterious witness and the disappearing, reappearing tape."

"Let up for now, ' Mark said testily. "This is not the time to discuss office problems."

"Office problems?" My voice dripped hostility. "Howard and I thought it was a police matter."

Mark swung his head around to Howard, but my defender of life and liberty wasn't so sure he had to defend those things anymore. "Ellie's a little upset," he said in a cowardly desertion of his post. "She thinks Phil—"

"I don't *think* Phil. I *know* about Phil," I interrupted. "And not fifteen minutes ago you agreed with me, Howard."

"Yes, it all seemed very logical, but just because he and Mannie Blanco—"

This time it was Mark who cut him off. In a lightning-swift parry, he unsheathed his ever-useful rulebook and swung it at me. "Damn it, Ellie, I thought you could be trusted," he said angrily, "but obviously, you're waging a vendetta. Did you also mention to Howard with everything else you shouldn't have said that the information you gleaned from the tape is privileged, and you violated the law by repeating it?"

What a charmingly logical way to shut me up. Instead of a supersleuth in possession of criminal evidence, I was a criminal in superbig trouble myself. "What are you going to do about it?" I asked acidly. "Sue me?"

Mark gave me a baleful stare, then turned to Howard in a crafty move. "Do me a favor, Howard. Let me settle this business with Ellie before she gets herself into any more hot water. I don't know how much she told you, but I'd appreciate it if you'd keep it under your hat. The Blanco tape is supposed to be confidential."

What a stellar performance. Without straining the shamrock in his lapel, Mark made himself smell as sweet as the hay on the hills of Killarney. If he really got going, he could make all my accusations sound like the ravings of a hysteric on the verge of menopausal dementia. Unfortunately, Howard had no desire to hang around and see whether I was carted off to the booby hatch or the state pen. In fact, now that Mark had shown him the way to go, he couldn't wait to be gone. With an embarrassed smile and sheepish glance in my direction, Howard grabbed his briefcase.

"No problem, Mark. This can wait. I picked a bad night to come barging in. No, don't apologize. Just give me a call at the end of the week. I'll be back from Seattle on Friday. You just go ahead and do what you have to do. And Mark," he paused, unable to look me in the eye, "I won't say anything, okay?"

Mark's below-the-belt blow had left me too stunned for instant recovery, but Howard's defection brought me panting to life. *Calm* was the password, only there was so much twisted truth in Mark's broadside that it called for just as much cunning in the counterattack.

"Howard, don't you dare walk out that door!" I ordered.

As he hesitated, his nice, honest face torn with indecision, Mark hit me with another love-tap in the solar plexus. "Leave him alone, Ellie. Howard promised he wouldn't say anything about what you did, but I suggest you contain yourself before you get Howard into trouble."

In desperation I used my mother's favorite ploy, the guilt trip. "Howard, if you walk out that door and leave me like this, you may never see me alive again. And if I die, it will be on your head," I prophesied darkly.

"Will you stop that!" Mark charged in a tight voice. "You're acting like a lunatic."

Feeling on the verge of menopausal dementia after all, I railed at him. "What do you expect me to do, play shrinking violet while you convince Howard to let me wither on the vine? For heaven's sake, Mark, your partner can't wait to get his hands around my neck, and you're trying to make it easy for him."

"What in the hell are you talking about? You think Phil's going to kill you because you heard the tape?"

"I believe that's a fairly accurate estimation," I replied bitterly. "After all, he killed Katherine for pretty much the same reason. She too discovered something she shouldn't have known."

"Are you accusing Phil of murdering Katherine?" Mark demanded, wheeling toward me. "That's insane."

"Oh, no it's not," I backed away. "His prerecorded motive is right on the tape."

"Don't be ridiculous. Mannie's blatherings don't prove any motive."

"Then why did Mr. Abbotts go to such lengths to steal the tape from my house and hide it from me?"

Mark hesitated for a moment, then came up with a winner. "Because he was afraid you planned to take it to Steve Tedesco."

"And you fell for that excuse? You really thought I was some kind of media spy who sells stolen cassettes to enemy reporters? Oh come on, Mark. Nobody would buy a dumb story like that, not even the *National Enquirer*. Or is this just something you made up now?"

"Why would I lie to you?"

"It sure beats telling the truth, especially since the police are on their way here right now, and you stand a good chance of being hauled off in the paddy wagon along with your partner."

The expression on Mark's face was indescribable. "May I ask of what crime I'm to be accused?"

"Put that in the plural, counselor. First there's aiding and abetting a robbery cover-up, then withholding information of a crime, concealing evidence, and plotting to get rid of one pesky office manager."

"What is that supposed to mean?" he asked quietly.

"You tell me. Did you or did you not call Mr. Abbotts tonight and tell him I found the tape?"

"Yes, I told him," Mark admitted.

"And then did you inform him that I'd be at your house, alone and temporarily unsuspecting?"

Mark sighed. "He only wants to talk to you, Ellie."

For a moment I couldn't speak. Then I spun around and

leaned over the sink. "You bastard," I choked. "You supreme bastard."

Confession may be good for the soul, but Mark's didn't improve mine one bit. To my shame, I'd been much happier just suspecting him. Hearing him admit his treachery was not very satisfying at all. In fact, I would have greatly preferred if he'd put up some decent pretence of innocence, said he was tricked by Mr. Abbotts, lied to, had his feet boiled in oil. I was ready to accept any number of poor excuses. A fine time he picked to be honest. Still, I should have known he'd never protect Dennis at the cost of endangering his partner, not when there were other options available. And even supposing that Mark did have a soft spot for me in what passed for his heart, murder had been done before without personal attachments getting in the way. Now it was just a matter of "the trodden path is the safest."

"You're crying, Ellie," Mark noted clinically. "Save it for the courtroom, and maybe they'll reinstate the death penalty just for me."

"You deserve the very best," I said sarcastically, reaching for the towel Howard had used to wipe his face. With a corner of it, I dried my wet eyes.

"Did you convince Howard that I'd set you up to be killed?"

"Stop playing games." I sniffed. "You've been trying to isolate me for that very purpose ever since you arrived home. Just step into the oleanders, my dear, and see how far you can get. And when I refused to leave, you tried to get rid of Howard." Discussing the details of my scheduled death was such a novel experience, I could hardly bear to stop. "Your pattern is always the same, Mark, only this time you couldn't be a johnny-come-lately. You see, Howard," I explained with a hard edge to my voice, "if you hadn't come along and screwed things up, Mark could have made a more heroic entry, late as usual, but broken-hearted that the mob had claimed another victim, yet stoically silent because my body was inadmissible evidence. However, circumstances forced him to take a more direct approach. Too bad I didn't see it coming. But since Mark's involvement in Mr. Abbotts's past crimes had been limited to turning his head the other way, I assumed he'd do at least that little for me. My error. After the elaborate deception he staged to get me here, it should have been obvious he wouldn't be spending the night at the Y.M.C.A.''

The wheelchair creaked as Mark shifted position. ''You're building quite a case against me.''

Forcing myself to face him, I babbled on. ''Don't blame me because you slipped up, though I should offer my congratulations for that cleverly rigged phone conversation. You have a brilliant talent for improvisation, especially when your audience is a prize patsy like me, falling for every word of your inspired monologue. I must admit that inventing Shirley Le Fleur was a masterstroke.''

''There's not much point in trying to defend myself,'' Mark's tone was harsh. ''Your motto is 'my mind's made up; don't confuse me with facts.' ''

''That's not true. I'm very open-minded. I understand how you felt constrained to help your partner out of a jam. In fact, I think you two ought to plea bargain loyalty as your defense. That ought to win the jury over. They may be so impressed that they'll let you accompany your confederate in crime all the way to jail. Won't that be comfy-cosy?'' I jeered.

Howard, who had been listening to our argument with understandable fascination, interrupted with the sixty-four-dollar question. ''So is there a witness or not?''

Obviously, expecting an engineer to accept my unsupported word was like depending on the police to show up on time. ''Of course not,'' I snapped. ''Aside from her unusual timeliness, do you think any self-respecting hooker would call herself 'Shirley Le Fleur'? Only a man could concoct such a preposterous name. That man.'' I pointed. ''But then he has a habit of using rather trite figures of speech. Never overstate, Mark. What does this Miss Le Fleur do to earn her extravagant title, peel off the petals one by one until there's only a red hibiscus rooted up her rear?'' I wadded the towel into a ball and tossed it on the counter. Then I thought for a moment, picked the towel back up, and refolded the damp, dirty thing into the same neat square that Howard had made. My next throw sent it sailing into the sink. ''Can't very well call herself Naked Nora Nablinsky, can she?'' I glared furiously at Mark.

He glared right back. ''No, that would be much too original, but don't bother to apologize for maligning my creative abilities.''

''Don't worry,'' I replied in a weak attempt at humor. ''I never admit it when I'm wrong.''

One of the things I deplore most in a mystery is when the heroine discovers the truth while hanging by one hand from the edge of a cliff as the villain is about to crunch her fingers under his boot. The only saving grace to my sudden gestalt was that it proved the years I'd spent solving crossword puzzles had not been in vain. It was a simple palindrome that turned on the light switch in my head. If Nora and Shirley spelled the same thing forwards and backwards, then all the other letters I had been placing in the blank squares were out of order. Probably looking as dumb as I felt, I stood by the kitchen counter and thought about red herrings, red lights flashing on switchboards and the red badge of courage. I couldn't fall apart now, but was it too late to backtrack to a safer position? Could I erase all my dangerously wrong answers and start over again, or had I played this double anacrostic in indelibly red ink?

Turning toward Howard with a sick, fake smile on my face, I said, ''What do you say we blow this joint and leave Mark on his own to entertain Mr. Abbotts? I'm tired of waiting for him.''

But apparently Howard had been doing some thinking too, and my abrupt about-face was a little too abrupt. ''I don't know if it's a good idea to leave the house,'' he said with a nervous glance at Mark. ''I thought I just heard a noise in the yard.'' Going to the window, Howard peered outside toward the pool, and when he turned around there was a gun in his hand. ''Don't panic, Ellie. Phil won't try to force his way in here while I have this aimed at his partner.'' Howard raised the barrel slightly. ''Don't make any funny moves, Mark. I'd hate to—'' He stiffened. ''Did you hear that? Someone just stepped on a dry twig.''

Falling coconuts would have been a more appropriate sound effect in Southern California, and a lot better for me if made by an eager policeman climbing out of a palm tree. Howard's nerves were just overcoming his locale. So were mine, for that matter. I took a step nearer to Mark and gave him a warning shake of the head.

''Be careful, Ellie,'' Howard said. ''Keep your distance from him. If Phil is wandering around outside looking for an opening, Mark could pull you in front of him as a shield. I don't want to shoot you by mistake.''

Some mistake. In the same breath he swore to protect me, Howard was predicting my early demise. The possibility certainly existed, but why did I have to die in a kitchen, of all places? It took me long enough to get out of one. Surely I deserved better than to be found sprawled on the floor in front of the garbage compactor, with only a dirty dish towel to cover my face.

''Where are you going?'' Howard demanded.

''Oh, nowhere. Just to get an apple from this bowl. See? Apple anyone? Nectarine?'' Smiling inanely, I grabbed an orange, dropped it on the floor, then chased after the rolling fruit until it came to a stop in front of the wheelchair.

Casually I bent down and retrieved it, then took two paces back, which brought the handle of the oven door jabbing into my spine. Perfect. I had made a complete tactical maneuver across the room, and now the telephone was only an arm's reach away. Howard didn't notice the advantage of my new position because he was busy deciding how much I knew. Naturally it made him nervous. In fact, one more dry twig and he'd be the one to snap. At that point the official version of the ensuing tragedy would follow the story line that Mr. Abbotts tried to assault me; Mark came to his aid; and I accidentally stepped into the path of one of the bullets meant for them. An unfortunate mishap, but the end result would be that Howard would somehow manage to do away with the entire law firm of Abbotts, Devlin, and Busch.

"I know what you're thinking," Howard said, moving the gun in my direction.

"I would never think that."

"It's written all over your face," he insisted.

"So that's why I always lose at poker."

"But I couldn't have done it," Howard said defensively. "I was in Santa Monica when it happened. You said so yourself."

"Right." I smiled brightly. "I provided you with an airtight alibi."

"Only you remembered, didn't you?" Howard shook his head. "Was it something I said?" He wrinkled his brows in concentration. "Of course. Abbotts's car. I couldn't possibly have seen the blue Caddy unless I was at the office twice that night." He choked back a shaky laugh. "Not very bright of me to admit it, huh?" Howard seemed almost determined to prove his own guilt. After successfully hiding it for so long, I'd have thought he'd put up a better fight against the facts. Criminals usually do. Scientists, though, can't seem to escape them.

Mark, who had silently watched Howard's metamorphosis

from heroic to homicidal, now spoke in the soothing tones of a psychiatrist trying to coax a patient off a tenth-story window ledge. "We can work this out, Howard, I promise you. Just put the gun on the table and we'll talk. Let me help you."

"A nice try, Mark, but I don't think anyone can help me now. Seems I've backed myself into a corner. It's a little late to come up with another alibi, or are you going to find a new witness? Got anybody who'll testify that it was only an accident? That I didn't mean to do it?" With the gun still clenched in his white-knuckled hand, Howard groped awkwardly to pull a handkerchief from his inside pocket and wipe his forehead. "I didn't, you know. I never meant to kill her." He looked at me. "It was an accident. She just got me so damned upset."

"Of course she did." I tried to put a lot of warmth and sincerity into my voice, but it was tough when the phone was so near yet so out of reach.

"Listen to me, Howard." Mark diverted his attention away from me, along with the point of the gun. "We'll explain that you didn't plan things in advance. It's not as though you carried out a premeditated action. There are extenuating circumstances that will put everything into a different perspective. The first step is to get those in order, prepare our case. But I can't do it without your help."

We all needed help, but nobody was throwing out any lifejackets. Where were the police anyway? If Mr. Abbotts hadn't rescinded the invitation, somebody had certainly goofed.

"It won't work," Howard said finally. "Take a look at Ellie. She doesn't believe in any extenuating circumstances. Kathy was the front-page libber of the year. How could she do anything wrong?" He gave a bitter laugh. "Just put one woman on the jury and I'll be lynched."

"What happened?" Mark asked quietly.

Bit by bit, the glorious facade that was Howard Busch cracked into a million pieces. "You ought to know," he began in a slightly shaky voice. "Everything had to be her way. I was supposed to postpone my life until she found fulfillment. She seemed to think I had volunteered to atone personally for several thousand years of sexist oppression. That wasn't the original deal. It was fifty-fifty, share and share alike in the beginning. Only, in the last few years, Kathy needed more. She swore things would even out, but after she finished law school, after she got established with a good firm, after her partnership came through, after the Blanco case. And I fell for it, like a sucker." His hand trembled as his voice rose a pitch. "When was it going to be even? After she was made queen? Goddamn, Mark, I gave her every little thing she wanted. I ate a million lousy restaurant meals so she wouldn't have to cook, spent my vacation working in the backyard because she was too busy to go to Hawaii, passed up the promotion of a lifetime so she wouldn't have to leave Casa Grande . . ." Howard stopped on a ragged breath.

Poor suffering man. So if life were so unbearable with the liberated lady lawyer, why hadn't he asked for a divorce years ago? To hear him tell it, he was the human sacrifice on the altar of Katherine's ambition, and only murder could even things out.

"Do you want to know what made the worm turn?" Howard asked, with the gun wavering in Mark's direction. "You'll love it. It was what you lawyers like to call an extenuating circumstance. I came home after two weeks in Seattle, and my loving wife calls to say she's working late. So what else is new? All I said was, 'Shouldn't my little mama be taking better care of herself?' and she tore into me. 'Will you stop with the little mother routine? This has been the all-time fuck-up stinko day, and I don't need to hear that garbage.' Nice, huh, Mark? No 'how was your trip' or 'glad you're back.' Forget 'I missed you.' " Howard clenched his fist. "I guessed right away, but she wouldn't admit it. Said we'd talk over dinner, another lousy, overpriced restaurant meal. But I got it out of her finally. I wouldn't hang up until she told me. Ready for this, Mark? While I was out of town, my wife had an abortion. She did it behind my back.''

Mark started to say something, then thought better of the idea. Howard was still too wound up.

''Having a baby was another thing we had postponed,'' he said angrily. ''But when she got caught, we agreed it was providential. She could take three months off, and then go back to work. I thought we had that settled. She knew what it meant to me, Mark. To have a family. But you should have heard how she told me, as if everything I wanted didn't mean shit. 'There's not going to be a baby, Howard, so just shut up,' '' he mimicked harshly. ''Oh, she apologized for losing her temper, but how could she apologize for killing my baby? It wasn't just hers. It was mine too. She had no right!''

''Kathy felt she did have the right,'' Mark said reasonably, ''but it wasn't an easy decision for her.''

Mark meant to be comforting, but Howard's pale face was suddenly suffused with color. ''*You* knew? It was a secret from me, but she discussed it with you? Of course,'' he threw back his head. ''She wouldn't do anything without Saint Mark's approval. I should have known. So you gave her your blessing to kill my baby, with a pat on the back for knowing her duty to the firm.''

''I did not advise her,'' Mark said carefully. ''I merely listened. You should know better than anyone that Katherine made her own choices.''

''Don't give me that bull,'' Howard spit out. ''Her choices were always what you wanted, what you told her to do. She fawned over everything you said, like you were God Almighty. One command from on high, and she obeyed.'' His face crumpled into a grotesque mask of anguish, as though he had accepted the final iniquity but couldn't withstand the blow. ''You could have stopped her,'' he choked. ''One lousy word, and she wouldn't have done it. Not for me. For you.''

I was standing against the curve of the counter, the sink almost directly behind me, the pot of chili on the stove to my left. Howard raised the gun and aimed it at Mark's head. I shot first.

Three pounds of beans, sauce, and chopped meat hit Howard broadside only microseconds before the gun went off. After that everything happened at once. Mark lunged forward and pinned him against the refrigerator. One of the plaques fell off the wall where the bullet sailed clear through the fastener. I ran for the phone again. And the police burst in.

Chapter 24

Not many self-styled detectives could start off on the wrong premise, follow false leads, miscalculate alibis, then catch the murderer with a pot of chili. Luis was scraping it off the kitchen walls right now. A couple of policemen were swabbing it off their uniforms. Mark went to change clothes entirely. As one of the few not wearing tonight's dinner, I was curled up on the couch, watching the rag-tag remnants of the parade pass by.

The main part of the procession had marched off some time ago. After striking with lightning force, they slapped Howard in handcuffs, wiped him down, then led him away. He never said another word, although the police had picked up most of it already. While I was wringing my hands in despair of them, they were quietly stepping on dry twigs and getting into strategic positions around the house. That was thanks to the sergeant, after all, who had passed on my SOS and had help speeding to the house a mere half hour later. Of course when the calvalry arrived and found me hermetically sealed in with both Mark and Howard, Chief Steunkle decided to play it safe. Instead of ringing the doorbell and asking for an explanation of why I'd cried bloody murder, he sent one of his boys to reconnoiter. Maybe because we were a little preoccupied, we never noticed him peering in the breakfast nook window just as Howard began waving the gun at Mark.

Concerned for our safety and enthralled by Howard's confession, the police waited for just the right psychological moment to announce their presence. Frankly, I thought they'd waited a bit too long. Did Steunkle have to hold out for a cliffhanger? But then, I had contributed my fair share to the evening's excitement. After being told explicitly by Sergeant Ortiz not to let anyone in the house, I invited Howard to dinner then proceeded to trip from *entrée* to *faux pas,* ready to serve the wrong person his just desserts. Of course, a lot of the credit for that *tsimmes* Mark dished up on his own plate. If he hadn't been so closed-mouth about the truth all along, he wouldn't have sounded so convincingly false tonight. That two-way conversation we had at the office was enough to lead anyone astray. While Mark was talking about hiding a robbery, I was haranguing about covering up a murder. Of course if I hadn't spent so much time conducting a private investigation into every crime but the right one, I would have known the difference. Luckily, in the middle of my tirade against Mark, I realized that the flowery Le Fleur and the Naked Nora were one and the same. From there logic and memory took over. Still, it was a blooming miracle, after starting out at such cross-purposes and picking up all the wrong cues, that Mark and I finally got our act together. Thank God and Luis, I brought the curtain down in time.

But there was no point in shivering over "what ifs" when there were so many "how comes" to settle. To start with, how come I never suspected Howard? How come I assumed he had a perfect alibi because I gave it to him? How come I gave it to him?

Some allowances could be made for the fact that this was my first case, but unlike complex mysteries where heretofore unseen footprints are trotted out in the last chapter to answer questions no one thought to ask, the clues in this murder should have been a dead giveaway from the beginning. I knew Howard disliked Mannie Blanco, thought Katherine was too absorbed in her career, wanted to spend more time with her, buy some furniture, make a home life, a family. I even knew about the abortion. But with my academic insight into criminal psychology, I recognized from the start that Howard Busch didn't fit the profile of a wife killer. He was such a wonderful husband.

I had read enough police procedurals to appreciate that when someone turns up dead, check out the nearest and dearest. But I'd also read all the latest marriage manuals, and Howard Busch checked out as the nearest and dearest model of a perfect spouse. He and Katherine did everything the way it was supposed to be done, according to *Garp, Good Housekeeping*, probably Masters and Johnson too. *The Working Wife and Working Husband Working at Working It Out; Managing Matrimony While Maximizing Two Careers*. They were the glossiest full-color image of wedded bliss I'd ever seen, the stuff of which dreams are made, especially mine. But for the fate of being born twenty years too soon and divorcing twenty years too late, I also might have made a "marriage of true minds."

For the Busches, however, the sweet accord of equals had soured. It wasn't women's lib that drove them to destruction, but an inability to compromise as they began to want different things. Whose turn came next? Having a family was Howard's fondest desire, but his wife's immediate goals had nothing to do with children, diapers, two A.M. feedings, and a leave of absence from the firm. Mark had told me quite a while back that Katherine felt she couldn't handle a career and a family simultaneously and do justice to both. But as Howard saw it, this was reneging on their agreement, though there wasn't much he could do about the situation. The baby was in Katherine's body, and Howard only had visitation rights. Could there be a solution that was fair to both parties? Probably not, but the decision ended in a dead heat for the Busches. The liberated wife-cum-attorney, who dressed out of *Vogue*, spoke out of turn, and outdid almost every man on the block, decided that abortion was the right answer. Her husband contested that verdict, and in the scrap of conversation I overheard between them, Katherine had just broken the bad news and was hoping to placate her enraged spouse with a romantic dinner *à deux*. It might have worked if Howard had gone to Di-Con from the airport as planned, then talked to Kathy from a safe distance of sixty miles or so. His temper might have cooled on the long ride home. Perhaps not, though. Katherine hadn't just aborted a fetus. She'd killed a dream.

No assessments. I refused to hold an inquest on what happened to the Busches, mostly because my own actions might not hold up under scrutiny. Not only had I been a poor judge of character and a disloyal employee, but I was an unlicensed detective who stuck her nosy snout where it didn't belong. If Mark didn't fire me for conduct unbecoming an office manager, Matt Steunkle would cite me for failure to leave the scene of a crime. As to forgiving the way I forgot Dennis's alibi, and forgetting about the way I remembered Howard's, he'd have to be dizzier than I was right now.

The reason for my light-headedness was not merely lack of nourishment, although I'd set a new personal record by going without food for ten hours straight. It was the sight of Mr. Abbotts coming in the front door. Thank God, Marjorie wasn't with him. As I sank lower in the couch, trying to disappear entirely, he disappeared down the hall to look for Mark.

Smart idea to get their stories together before saying

anything on the record. Shame I didn't have time to do that for myself.

Matt Steunkle had said good night to the last chili-covered policeman and was ambling across the room. "I guess congratulations are in order." He sat down with a tired grunt.

"Are you angry?"

He gave me the benefit of one bloodshot eyeball. "Because you captured a murderer single-handed and held him till I got here? Hell, I was going to give you a medal."

"You are angry."

"I'm not overjoyed." He yawned and rubbed his face. "Where'd you get the chili?"

"Luis made it."

"Too much oregano."

"Will you stop that. Here, arrest me." I stuck out my wrists. "Go on. I must have committed thirty or forty infractions of the law tonight, not to mention giving false information on my police statement. Please, throw me in the clinker and get it over with already."

"Mad at me, huh?"

"Darn right." I punched a pillow and stuck it behind my back. "Aren't you guys supposed to check everybody's story? I'm such a great investigator, you believe everything I say?"

"Of course not," Steunkle said, making no effort to spare my feelings. "We double-check everything, but we start out with the given information. Want to tell me what happened?"

"No. I'd rather be arrested for gross negligence than admit to gross stupidity. But since you asked." Matt rested his head on the back of the couch while I leaned forward and thought about *déjà vu*.

"Did you ever get the funny feeling of reliving an episode in your life with no recollection of ever having lived it to begin with? It's like a sense of nostalgia with no memory. That's what happened to me tonight, but I finally did remember. It was being in the office late, having to answer the switchboard, hearing Howard's voice, noticing the time. Are you still with me? All right, I'll skip the metaphysical. Here's the story with all the fancy taken out and the gaps filled in. At a little before six on the night she was killed, Katherine Busch asked me to place a call to her husband at Di-Con. She was on the phone herself at the time, stuck on hold and waiting to get off. I dialed the number in Santa Monica, but at that very moment my son felt the urge to contact his mother and reverse the charges. Caught between duty and two dollars for three minutes, I transferred Howard's call while it was still ringing and had a typical conversation with Michael. That was the gap. I presumed Katherine reached her husband on that call, especially since I overheard them talking a few minutes later. Not that there weren't enough red lights flashing on the switchboard to explain what happened, but I didn't read the signals correctly. It had to be due to the inexperience of the operator that the Busches could begin speaking on one extension, then hang up on another. What I overlooked was that two outside lines were connected to Katherine's phone. When there was no answer to the one ringing at Di-Con, she simply switched over and called home. Of course, that's where Howard was; not an hour from here, but ten minutes. You like the alibi I gave him?''

"What'd your son want?'' Steunkle asked.

"Huh?'' I turned to see if he were interrogating me in his sleep. "I don't know what Michael has to do with it, but he wanted money.''

"Don't they always.'' He smothered a yawn and sat up.

"Oh, come on. You aren't going to let me off that easily.''

"How old is your son?''

"Eighteen.''

"You got my sympathy.''

Matt had forgiven me, but I wasn't so ready to excuse him. The police aren't supposed to make mistakes. "Why didn't you ask for the record of long distance calls at Di-Con?''

"We did. It's a WATS line. They don't keep records. Everything else was inconclusive too. No one could say Busch was there after hours, but nobody could say he wasn't, either."

"Did you suspect him all along?"

"Sure. It's standard procedure to suspect everyone. We talked to Mark about him, to Phil, but they thought the Busches had a good marriage. No money problems. No affairs on the side. I don't know." He scratched his head. "Abortions are so common these days, it would have taken us a while to figure that as a motive."

I could sympathize. With all the drama in her life, a model husband seemed the least of Katherine's problems. "What will happen to him?"

"If he shuts up and gets a good lawyer, the charge could be reduced to voluntary manslaughter. He could even plead temporary insanity." Matt looked down at his watch. "Just don't get involved in that part. I know you'd like to see him hung by the toenails, then drawn and quartered, but you did your share already. Take it easy tonight, then come down to headquarters in the morning and make a statement."

"Wait a minute," I said as he got to his feet. "Tell me, whose Cadillac was it parked in front of the office? Did you ever find out?"

"The Nablinsky woman's. What's the matter? You don't like that answer?"

"I like it fine. I just wish I'd known that little detail two weeks ago."

Matt shook his head and smiled. "You think you could have solved the case faster? Oh, you're pretty smart, I'll admit that. You even corrected your own mistake and followed through on it. But it would have been a hell of a lot smarter, not to mention safer, if you'd never let Busch in the house at all. We were damn lucky things turned out the way they did."

"You're absolutely right, Matt," I agreed, praying he'd never discover just how right he was.

As the front door closed behind the Chief of Police, Mr. Abbotts took the vacated seat next to mine. Apparently he had concluded a satisfactory caucus with Mark and was now prepared for the little talk he promised me two hours ago. Mark, I assumed, was hiding in the bathroom picking beans out of his ears. The miserable chicken. He just didn't want to sit in on the axing. Actually Mr. Abbotts didn't seem too thrilled at the prospect himself.

"Eleanor, about tonight—"

I didn't let him finish. "I'm sorry, Mr. Abbotts. I never should have taken the tape from your safe." If he were about to jump all over me, maybe that would soften his mood.

"I understand, Eleanor."

"You do?"

"Yes, Mark explained how you were trying to help me, though I regret you were caught in the middle."

Prudently silent for a change, I only smiled. Evidently, Mark had done some fancy footwork around the truth, and it would behoove me to hear his version before modestly declining any kudos.

"That tape caused a lot of unnecessary fuss," Mr. Abbotts continued smoothly. "It shouldn't have, of course, but unfortunately the entire matter was blown way out of proportion. As I told Katherine weeks ago, Mannie's threat to misrepresent a perfectly legitimate business arrangement was sheer bluffing. No question but he could have hurt the campaign, but Mannie can't afford that kind of publicity either. If it came out that he tried to blackmail his attorney, it would suggest to everyone that he had no information to trade and was getting desperate. I explained that to Katherine, but like you," he nodded benignly, "she didn't want to take the chance. After Mannie behaved so improperly, I told her she had my full support to drop the case; but she insisted on keeping it for my sake. You may have heard us arguing that afternoon,'' he reminded me, as though I'd forgotten. Now he was citing it as proof of innocence.

"If you and Mannie understand each other so well, how did the business with the tape get so 'blown out of proportion' anyhow?'' I asked pointedly.

"Yes.'' He understood immediately. "The break-in. I'm afraid that was at least partly my fault. You found the tape, but you hadn't brought it back, so I asked Dennis to stop by and pick it up. He was a bit overzealous.''

"That's one way to put it. But why would Dennis overreact like that? I don't imagine he makes a practice of smashing in people's freshly painted back doors. For that matter, why send Dennis at all? I told you I'd bring it in the next day.''

"Yes, well, Dennis wasn't sure you would. No, no, Eleanor, please. It was a mistaken impression on his part. Nothing important. Just something he saw at Katherine's funeral that he misinterpreted.''

"What do you mean misinterpreted? What did he see?'' I flared up angrily. "I don't believe it. You mean he saw me talking to Steve Tedesco and thought I was going to sell the tape for a lousy two hundred dollars?'' Mr. Abbotts cleared his throat uncomfortably. "How could Dennis be such an asshole,'' I fumed. "And you,'' my disgust turned on Mr. Abbotts. "How could you have swallowed that? Where all his idiocies sacrosanct because he was doing them for you, or did you just feel sorry for him? For crying out loud, I wouldn't have pressed charges against the dumbo. A hit on the head maybe, for scaring the life out of me. But all you did for my peace of mind was replace the lock on my back door. I think I've never been so insulted in my entire life.''

"It was a regrettable error,'' Mr. Abbotts murmured.

"You bet it was. But why didn't you enlighten Dennis? He already had it in for me because of that stupid problem with his alibi. All you had to do was explain that I'm wonderful, trustworthy, the best damned employee you've ever had.''

Mr. Abbotts looked me straight in the eye. "I wasn't so sure of that, my dear. Not then. That's why I took you off the Blanco case and gave you a raise. As insurance. Then when you said you'd found the tape and were bringing it back, it seemed I was right and you'd simply decided that I could offer you more than Tedesco.''

"How could you believe such a crummy thing about me?" I asked indignantly. My hurt feelings were not at all appeased by the fact I had thought worse things of him.

"Why take a chance? On the surface, your actions could be read either way. In fact, everything was beautifully ambiguous. It could have been the slickest bit of blackmailing I'd ever encountered; especially when I took into account the way you asked for a job, reminding me how involved you were in my last campaign, hinting at a close association with Steve Tedesco. I hardly knew you well enough to rely on your integrity . . ." He paused at the horrified expression on my face. "Forgive me, Eleanor. I should have known better than to rely on circumstantial evidence.''

"Oh, that's okay," I managed weakly. "I've jumped to a few wrong conclusions in my time.''

"In any case, Mark explained what you did this evening; I do appreciate it, even though your methods were a bit unorthodox.''

"What exactly did Mark explain?" I asked, immune now to shock.

"How you wanted to get rid of the tape for my benefit.''

"Of course," I agreed. "But I still don't understand why you didn't just erase it.''

"Because it's evidence," came the pat answer. "Not the best," Mr. Abbotts defined as he stood up, "but Mannie was one of the murder suspects and a recording of his assault on

Katherine would have been important if he had been brought to trial.''

So Mr. Abbotts wasn't the devil's advocate in matters financial and fraudulent; not that his private arrangement with Mannie didn't reek of political expediency, but it wasn't the stench of murder. The sweet scent of truth lay somewhere between the *eau de sans reproach* with which I had been sprinkling him for years and the *essence of evil* I had poured all over him tonight. That probably meant he was no more or less human than the rest of us.

''Since you were saving the tape to use against Mannie, if need be, and considering that Steve would have used the tape against you, if he ever got hold of it, I think you deserve lots of credit,'' was my final analysis.

Smiling an all's well that ends well, Mr. Abbotts returned my commendation with praise for my daring and bravery in the face of great danger. ''You brought a murderer to justice,'' he said grandly, and I didn't argue the point.

That signaled the end of the parade. One by one they'd marched through and out, leaving me to bring up the rear. Always the first to arrive and the last to go. Not this time. While Mark and Mr. Abbotts were still saying good night at the front door, I squeezed around them.

''So long, everybody. It's been a great evening.''

Mr. Abbotts nodded abstractedly. ''See you tomorrow, Eleanor.''

''Make that Wednesday. I'm taking off tomorrow to recuperate.''

Neither one of my bosses protested; they could tell it wouldn't do them any good. Instead, Mark caught me by the wrist. ''Don't go. We haven't had a chance to talk yet.''

Since that was the idea, I tried to pull my hand away. ''Not tonight. I'm really tired. Maybe sometime next week.''

His grip on my wrist tightened. I gave another yank, which got me nowhere, then pretended to relax. That didn't work either. A loyal partner, Mr. Abbotts chose sides in this tug-of-war and told me I should stay as he was leaving immediately. When I suggested that he allow me to escort him to his car, the staunch defender of women's rights winked at Mark, then leaned over and whispered in my ear, "Why don't you just kiss and make up?" Then, with a silly cupid's smirk on his face, he walked out the front door, chuckling softly to himself. The stinker. I'd never vote for him again.

"That's enough, Mark," I hissed as the door closed. "Let go of me. I want to go home."

He patted my imprisoned hand. "All in good time. You had a busy night, and Luis is replacing the dinner you tossed away. Bacon and eggs," he enticed, "with lox and bagels. Hungry?"

What a dirty trick. Two hours ago it could have been called hunger. Now my stomach was plastered to my backbone and was whimpering for food. Still, I wouldn't give Mark the satisfaction. "I couldn't eat a thing," was my lofty answer as I twisted my arm in one more undignified attempt to free myself.

"Liar." He held tight. "I can feel you quivering with starvation."

"That's rage." I glared at him. "And if you'll let go, you won't feel it anymore."

"That's what I'm afraid of," he said, releasing me abruptly. "All I wanted was to thank you for saving my life tonight."

"Ah, ha!" I challenged now that freedom was only a doorknob away. "And after you thanked me, you were going to yell at me for putting your life in danger to begin with. Right?"

"Right." He turned around and wheeled into the living room.

"What do you mean right?" I followed him to the television set, where he tuned in to the end of the sports news.

"And if so, whose fault was it?" I demanded. "Were you ever open and honest with me? No, not once. In fact, you barely spoke to me at all. Admit it. The morning after Dennis broke into my house, when you knew damn well he did it and how worried I was about the mob, you just buried your nose in the paper, too engrossed in box scores to pass me the marmalade, much less explain what had happened. Remember that morning? It was the day after Detroit lost a double-header, and the Dodger game went to a tenth inning."

"I remember," he said, not taking his eyes from the television.

"And the day you started lying to me and never stopped."

Mark pulled his gaze from the screen. "I did not lie to you. I just didn't tell you everything. There's a difference, Ellie, and I don't appreciate the accusation. First of all, the tape should never have been at your house, and, secondly, it was none of your business."

"So you let me think I was on the verge of being murdered by the mob."

"I told you there was nothing to worry about," Mark defended himself. "Why wouldn't you believe me?"

"Let me see if I can count the ways." I held up my hand. "Katherine was killed. Mr. Abbotts had a motive. You helped him hide it. Dennis threatened to wring my neck. And Marjorie threatened to send me to jail. Shall I continue, or is that enough? Oh, and tonight you neglected to tell me the real name of the star witness so when I called the police station, no one ever heard of a Shirley Le Fleur."

"You jump to the craziest conclusions," he barked at me.

"Maybe so, but I didn't leap without a little shove from behind. If you hadn't told me to put back the tape because you had a witness—"

"I did not say *because* I had a witness."

"No, you just strung your sentences so close together that I didn't hear the silent semicolon. Besides, you had just admitted knowing all about the tape and what it could mean to Mr. Abbotts politically. I thought you understood I was talking about murder, not a robbery. Your cryptic phone conversation with Matt fit right in . . . saying now you knew who the blue Caddy belonged to . . . that Shirley Le Fleur made a positive identification from a photograph . . .'' I paused for a breath. ''Naturally I thought she had nailed Mr. Abbotts, though I should have realized that everyone suspected me of dirty doings, and just turned myself in to the police. Now you can go right back to the sports news and put me out of your mind the way you always do. I certainly wouldn't want you to miss a home run on my account. And the next time there's another replay of the Wimbledon matches, you can roll over ten other women to get to that too.''

''Goddamn it.'' Mark snapped off the television. ''What in the hell are you digging at?''

''Isn't it obvious?''

''Nothing about you is obvious, Ellie. Not the way you solve murders or the way you reason.''

''I'm not the clam. My feelings have always been up front, unlike the secretive cogitations of some other people I know . . . or thought I knew.''

''I don't believe it. You think you're easy to understand? One minute you're reciting Shakespeare and the next second you lock yourself in the bathroom with a bowl of ice cream. That's supposed to be a revelation?''

''Did you ever peek in the keyhole?'' I demanded inanely. ''No. You just turned off your ears while the water was running.''

''Will you please speak the Queen's English?'' Mark said in irritation. ''I know you love the sound of your own wit, but try to say something straight for a change.''

''I hate you.''

''Now you're starting to make sense. What else?''

Over the sound of my heavy breathing, I heard a door

leading from the kitchen click discreetly shut. Luis. There went our audience, and our bacon and eggs. Now I was really mad.

"You're a typical man," I said with infinite scorn. "Trite, laughable, and oblivious to everything except your own needs. The word *communication* isn't in your dictionary. You never explain yourself, never set a woman's mind at ease, assume she knows what you're thinking, put everyone else in front of her, and you never sent me flowers."

"I'm going to kill you, Ellie."

"Seems to me I've heard that line before. Does it run in the family?"

It must have. Mark started inching closer to me, with a deadly glint in his eye. "You had a good idea before. I should have strangled you in the bushes instead of having to listen to this crap. When did you want flowers, Ellie? On the only two days out of the past week you were speaking to me? Where was all your openness and honesty then? If you were angry, you could have ripped out my spokes and stuck them someplace. You threatened that once, but it was just more cleverness, wasn't it? It's easier to hide and sulk than live up to campaign promises."

"You didn't make any to *me*!" I shouted. "You didn't even act as though your hat were in the ring."

"What in the hell . . ." He made one long furious move nearer, while I tossed my purse on the couch. It was guns blazing at high noon. "What did you think I was doing, playing fast and loose?" Mark attacked. "You thought I'd go to bed with you for another notch on my belt? How did you come up with such a flattering opinion of me? Sitting in the bathroom counting the tiles on the floor?"

"Stop shouting!" I yelled, then lowered my voice. "There's no need to shout. We can discuss this sensibly, like two clear-thinking adults."

"How, when you can't think?" Mark said grimly.

"You don't have to be vindictive," I flared up again. "Just tell me what I should have thought when you brought Helen Ramirez back from San Francisco, and spent the next four days and nights with her, and every time I tried to come near you, you said you were busy working. Even a wife wouldn't fall for that."

"Wait a minute," he said in the coldest tone I'd ever heard from him. "You thought I was having an affair with Helen? That after spending a weekend with you in Vegas, I rushed off to bed another woman? Impossible," he commented to himself. "There aren't that many tiles on a floor."

Mark's freezing anger was worse than his unusual show of temper. I combatted it with the best logic in the world. "Well, you didn't call when you promised."

"On Saturday night? I certainly did, but there was no answer at your house. I called again on Sunday, but you were gone all day. Apparently I was wasting my time, since you spent the entire weekend solving crimes."

"Not the entire weekend," I said, thinking of Biff Bosworth. To tell or not to tell, that was the question. Was it better for Mark to suffer the slings and arrows of outrageous jealousy, or let conscience make a coward of me? It certainly seemed a shame to make him feel any worse.

"Everything fit right into the pattern," I explained instead. "You wouldn't listen when I tried to tell you that Dennis took ten years off my life during one three-minute elevator ride. And after the whole thing with Lou Smith... well, if you must know," I finished, since this route was wandering into a maze, "it seemed Dennis was guilty and you were protecting him."

"Backtrack a minute. What's Louie got to do with this?"

"You mean, your old friend Louie the legitimate business-man with not a larcenous bone in his body? I love how you lawyers consider a crook innocent because there wasn't enough evidence to prove him guilty."

"As opposed to one-woman juries who make everyone guilty on no evidence. So what about Louie?"

"As a close personal friend of yours and one who wanted to do you a favor, he told me about Dennis's gambling debts with Mannie. Louie's first thought was for you and Phil, of course, so you wouldn't be hurt by it. And on the off-chance he could find out what other top-level arms Mannie was twisting, Louie offered me a pair of diamond earrings to keep him posted on who, how, why, where. You get the picture. As the only dumb, but honest member of the conspiracy, I sent them right back. The corned beef sandwich he bought me I kept, of course."

"You are really stupid," Mark said quietly.

"I beg your pardon?"

"You can't tell the difference between a bribe and a proposition. Lou Smith is not a criminal, as I tried to point out on several occasions, and his gratitude to me stems from my separating him from one. That was his income tax evasion problem: Mannie Blanco. They were partners once in a—"

"Please, spare me the details."

Mark didn't seem to think my mistake was so funny, but I found it hilarious. One middle-aged nongangster tries to buy a roll in the hay with one almost middle-aged non-Venus, and the sagging siren doesn't have the courtesy to thank him for lunch. Maybe I should send him a bread and butter note. Maybe I should reconsider the diamonds too. At least Louie appreciated my worth. Mark wasn't even offering cheesecake.

"Where are you going?" he asked.

"Home. If I'm lucky, there'll be some ice cream left and I can take it in the bathroom with me."

"Will you please sit down and cool off?"

"I'm as cold as marble, for your information, so you can return to the boob tube while I go home and stick pins in your wax effigy."

"You know, you're beautiful when you're angry."

The sudden switch from exasperated to trite set off alarms in my head.

I hitched the purse over my shoulder again in readiness for a hasty retreat. "You have an odd way with compliments," I snorted. "Only a minute ago you showered me with brainless and uninformed."

"I said that?" He raised his brows in exaggerated surprise. "Impossible. You're brilliant. Witty. Sharp as a tack."

"Right. And the punch line is, you could get really stuck on me. Future tense indefinite. Drop me a line when you've decided."

"I decided."

Out of the corner of my eye I saw the crafty move coming, but before I could negotiate a clear passage between the moving wheelchair and the solid four-hundred-pound oak table, Mark had me pinned. He took hold of that same abused wrist, pulled me close, then slipped his other arm around my waist.

"Don't rush off," he whispered softly, as if he weren't holding me in a vise. "As soon as Luis hears we're not arguing anymore, he'll come out and finish cooking."

That was an interesting olive branch to someone on the verge of malnutrition, but I had willpower. "No, Mark. There's no point. It just won't work. We're too different. You're the great Sphinx and I'm the little chatterbox. You're calm, cool, collected, and I operate in high gear. Don't you see? It's bigger than both of us. We have nothing in common."

"We both like bagels."

"Nice try, but you're reaching."

"Look who's talking. Bigger than both of us?"

"Let go of me, Mark. You're spoiling what could be a delightfully poignant renunciation scene. It's supposed to end with, 'Good night, good night, parting is such sweet sorrow, that I shall say good night' until it's Wednesday morning when I come to work as usual."

"Does that mean we're not going to screw now?"

"Right on, McDuff."

" 'A man, I am, crossed with adversity.' "

"You'll survive." I looked over his head. " 'Men have died from time to time and worms have eaten them, but not for love.' Besides, 'Misery makes strange bedfellows.' "

"Let's take one step at a time, shall we? 'I do desire that we become better strangers.' Save the worms for last."

I lowered my gaze. " 'What! Wouldst thou have a serpent sting thee twice?' "

He thought a moment. " 'I had rather a fool to make me merry than experience to make me sad.' "

" 'That was laid on with a trowel,' " I couldn't help the sarcasm, "and the most unromantic offer I've had all week."

"I swear, the first thing in the morning, I'll send you a dozen red roses."

A door clicked open, tentative footsteps crossed the kitchen floor, then Luis stuck his head around the corner. Seeing no fatalities on the battlefield, he relaxed. "A midnight feast will be ready in five minutes. One egg or two, Ms. Gordon?"

"Three," Mark answered, a slow smile lighting his face, "and give her an extra bagel. If there aren't enough," he offered nobly, "she can have mine."

So I stayed. After all, a woman can resist only so much temptation.

Mystery . . . Intrigue . . . Suspense

__BAD COMPANY
by Liza Cody
(B30-738, $2.95)

Liza Cody's first mystery, DUPE, won the John Creasey Award in England and was nominated for the Edgar Award in 1981. Private detective Anna Lee, the novel's heroine, was hailed by Michele Slung of National Public Radio as "the first worthy successor to Cordelia Gray in a decade." Anna Lee returns in BAD COMPANY, another fine mystery in the P.D. James tradition.

__DUPE
by Liza Cody
(B32-241, $2.95)

Anna Lee is the private investigator called in to placate the parents of Dierdre Jackson. Dierdre could not have died as the result of an accident on an icy road. She had driven race cars; the stretch of road was too easy. In search of simple corroborating evidence, Anna finds motives and murder as she probes the unsavory world of the London film industry where Dierdre sought glamour and found duplicity . . . and death.

The MagPi ESSENTIALS

CONTENTS

[LUCY HATTERSLEY]

Lucy is the Editor
of The MagPi – The
Official Raspberry
Pi magazine. Her
first computer
was a Sinclair
Spectrum, but
Commodore was
her true love.
First with the
VIC-20, then the
C64, and finally
the adorable
Amiga. Lucy
learnt to code
at school using
Acorn computers;
then learnt it all
again with MITx.
Lucy has been
making computer
magazines since
she left school.

The
MagPi
ESSENTIALS

CHAPTER ONE
MADE BY YOU
WITH Google

The AIY Projects team chats to us about
the making of this incredible Raspberry Pi kit

"Natural Human Interaction is this idea of being able to communicate with an electronic device the same way you and I are talking right now," says Billy Rutledge, Director of AIY Projects at Google. We've caught up at Raspberry Pi Towers to discuss the AIY Projects kit, and the future of artificial intelligence with the maker community.

"We're all familiar with graphical user interfaces (GUI)", notes Billy. "Well, building a VUI is now the big thing." Voice has become "very popular" in the last year, says Billy. "Not just with consumer products, but also as a set of tools for device makers."

Google wants to help makers familiarise themselves with voice interfaces, but it's also really keen to tap into the creative prowess of the maker community.

"We're excited to put the kits out into the world and see what people make with them," says Kristine Kohlhepp, a User Experience

Researcher working on AIY Projects at Google. "We've done a lot of research to make sure people can assemble the kit and figure out how to make it work."

"The initial project is just an opener," reveals Blaise Agüera y Arcas, Principal Scientist at Google. "It's fun to be able to make a cardboard kit that uses the Google Assistant, but this is about a lot more than just making a lower-cost DIY version of Home."

The future belongs to intelligent devices. Billy says: "At some point soon, we'll see a new generation of devices that you can just walk up to and ask 'what are you and what do you do?' Then you'll have a conversation with it, to use its services in a very easy-to-understand way."

Natural Human Interaction is the term used for this kind of interaction between humans and devices. "A generation or two ago, all of our devices had analogue dials and knobs," explains Billy. "Then there was a shift to digital buttons and displays. Now we are moving to a human interface where you simply have a conversation with the device."

It's also important to ease people into AI as part of their natural interaction with electronic devices, alongside touching buttons and screens. "We can easily become distracted by personification of these kinds of systems," says Blaise.

It's important for makers to realise that VUIs are something they can create, and use, in their projects. "I think letting the makers see how easy it is to put AI, specifically Natural Human Interaction capabilities, into their projects will be a great thing," says Kristine.

"We want to show you how easy it is to use AI, and then share back with us to inspire new project ideas and keep the whole cycle going," Kristine continues.

> # We want to show you how easy it is to use AI

"My top-secret plan is to build more engineers," discloses James McLurkin, Senior Hardware Engineer of AIY Projects at Google. "Getting kits like this out into the world with Raspberry Pi allows us to build the things that then create more engineers." AIY Projects enables young makers to explore the possibilities with AI. "So this is very exciting for us," says James.

"What's interesting about the maker environment is what happens when we shut up, and listen, and see what people try," says Blaise. Historically, there have been many 'Hello World' types of starter projects for various programming languages and platforms, and in recent years we've seen exciting new hardware like the Raspberry Pi emerge. Now there is AI, another technology for makers and developers to add to their projects. AIY Projects brings these three things together, which will be "super interesting," reckons Blaise.

"I don't know what will come out from the mixture of those, but I'm very keen to see."

"I view this as an essential component in a maker's toolkit," Billy tells us. "We want makers to see that using AI is not hard or complex."

The Australian artist Stelarc has said that technology constructs our human nature. "We would not be who we are if we hadn't invented fire and woven clothes and built Raspberry Pis," says Blaise. "That is what being human is all about, and that's what distinguishes us from the other animals. So I don't like this idea that talks about AI as a competitive landscape of human exceptionalism, and ways that it is being eroded. That really misses the point of what all this is about."

"This first kit showcasing voice is just the start of our effort to bring Google AI to the maker community," reveals Billy. "Our projects will largely focus on Natural Human Interaction." Following voice, we intend to feature projects with vision, motion, and learning."

Google wants makers to add AI to their own projects, and share their results with others. "We want to learn what this community needs," says Billy, "and then work with them to build the tools they want."

Below The Voice HAT hardware

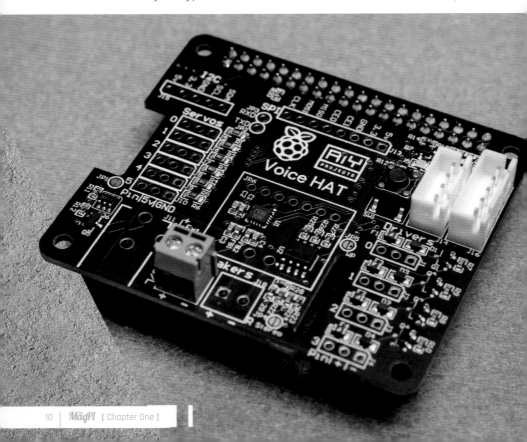

CHAPTER TWO
YOUR
AIY PROJECTS
VOICE KIT

Construct your AIY Projects voice kit and explore natural language recognition

nside the kit will be the components you need to build a voice-capable device with Raspberry Pi.

Open the box and you'll find two pieces of cardboard, an arcade-style button, a speaker, and some cables, along with a HAT (Hardware Attached on Top) board and another narrower board. One is to connect all the accessories together; the other is a stereo microphone.

All of these components fit together to build the AIY Projects kit: a small cardboard device with a colourful button on the lid. You press the button, or clap your hands (or create a custom trigger), and speak out loud to ask the device a question. The speaker, at the front, then announces the answer.

Use the Bill Of Materials list below to check you have all the components.

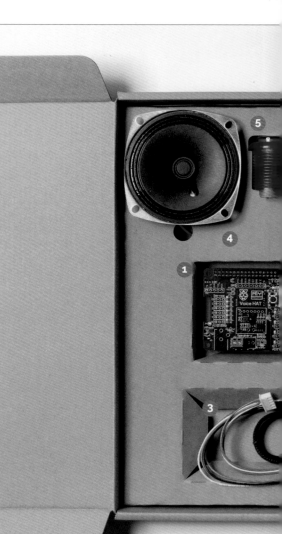

BILL OF MATERIALS

1 **Voice HAT accessory board**

2 **Voice HAT microphone board**

3 **2× plastic standoffs**

4 **3-inch speaker (wires attached)**

5 **Arcade-style push button**

6 **4-wire button cable**

FOLD UP

8

9

SPEAKER HERE

2

1

RASPBERRY Pi

GOES HERE

FOLD 4

6

7

7 **5-wire daughter board cable**

8 **External cardboard box**

9 **Internal cardboard frame**

CHAPTER THREE
ASSEMBLE THE KIT

Put the parts together to build a voice-enabled device

You'll Need

- Raspberry Pi 3
- Small, needle-nose pliers
- Phillips 00 screwdriver
- Two-sided tape

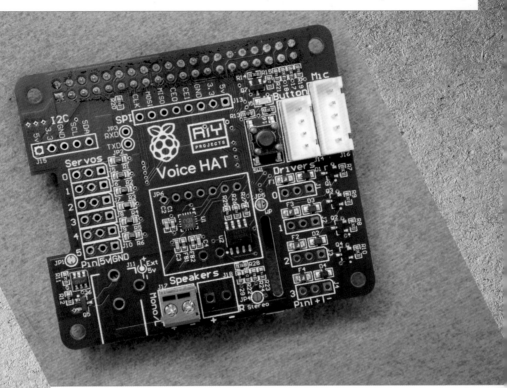

 ith all your parts ready, it's time to build the AIY Projects voice kit. The aim is to assemble all the included parts (and a Raspberry Pi board) and create a small cardboard device with a button on top.

This project is a relatively easy build, and you won't need to solder any of the components. Be careful to line up the wires correctly, especially the wires for the button. It's also a good idea to take a close look at the Voice HAT accessory board (the larger board). The Voice HAT is the heart of the AIY Projects kit, and everything connects to it. It also provides breakout GPIO pins, organised into two blocks: Servos and Drivers.

You'll connect the Voice HAT accessory board to your Raspberry Pi via the GPIO pins. The Raspberry Pi is the brains of the outfit: it connects to Google's cloud services through a local Python application. The Python source code is provided with the software image, as well as on GitHub.

Also take a close look at the smaller microphone board, which enables the device to hear you speak.

But first, we need to get it all assembled. The first step is to mount the Voice HAT accessory board to your Raspberry Pi, and then connect the speaker and microphone. Then you'll move on to folding the cardboard case and placing the components inside. Finally, you'll assemble the arcade-style button and secure it (and the microphone) to the case.

Ready? Let's start building your kit.

SET UP THE VOICE HAT

1 INSERT THE STANDOFFS

Start with the two standoffs. These are the small plastic cylinders, and they fit into the yellow mount holes on the Raspberry Pi board. Insert the standoffs into the two yellow holes on the opposite side from the 40-pin GPIO header (on the same side as the HDMI connection). Push them firmly, and they will hold in place.

SECURE THE HAT

Now get the Voice HAT accessory board and attach it to the GPIO pins on the Raspberry Pi board. Carefully line up the GPIO connector on the Voice HAT accessory board with the pins of the GPIO header on the Raspberry Pi. Gently press down to make sure the Voice HAT accessory board is secure. Press down on the spacers on the other side of the board to snap the boards together.

3 ATTACH THE SPEAKER WIRES

Take a close look at the Voice HAT accessory board and find the blue terminal with two small screws. This terminal is the speaker connection (it has 'Speakers' printed above it on the board). Each of the two connections has a small '+' and '-' symbol printed below. Find the speaker with the red and black wires attached. Insert the red wire into the positive '+' terminal on the Voice HAT accessory board. Now add the black wire into the negative '-' terminal. They won't be fixed yet, so hold them in place.

④ SCREW IN THE WIRES

At this point, the two wires will be sitting in the sockets unsecured. Hold the wires in place, and gently turn each screw in the socket using a Phillips 00 screwdriver. Gently tug on the wires to make sure they're secure. Now place the speaker to one side of the board so you can access the other components.

THE BUTTON CABLE

Find the 4-wire button cable: it has a white male connector on one end and four separate wires with metal contacts on the other. Insert the white plug into the matching white socket marked 'Button' on the Voice HAT accessory board (it is the one nearest to the red button). The cable will only go in one way around, so don't force it. Check that the colours of the cable match the image. Don't worry about the four separate wires with metal contacts; we'll come back to these later.

⑥ THE MICROPHONE CABLE

Find the Voice HAT microphone board and the 5-wire daughter board cable. The cable has matching white plugs on either end. Both ends of the cable are identical, so take either end of the 5-wire connector cable and slot it into the Voice HAT microphone board. It will only fit one way around. Snap the cable in, but don't force it.

7 CONNECT THE MICROPHONE

Take the other end of the 5-wire daughter board cable and connect it to the Voice HAT accessory board.

It is the second white socket, marked 'Mic' on the board. This connection is the larger socket, closer to the edge of the board.

The 5-wire connector only fits one way around. Look at the colour of the wires in the image, and the shape of the connector and socket, to line both up. It should snap cleanly into place.

ASSEMBLE THE BOX

8

FOLD THE CARDBOARD

Now let's move on to the box. Find the larger cardboard piece with a bunch of holes on one side (as shown in the image). Fold along the creases, then find the side with four flaps and fold the one marked FOLD 1.

9 ## SECURE THE BOX

Do the same for the other folds, tucking FOLD 4 underneath to secure it in place. Now set it aside.

10 FOLD THE FLAPS

Find the other cardboard piece that came with your kit (as shown in the picture). This piece will build the inner frame to hold the hardware. Fold the flaps labelled 1 and 2 along the creases.

RASPBERRY PI
GOES HERE

11 PUSH IT OUT

The flap above the 1 and 2
folds has a U-shaped cutout.
Push it out.

12 FOLD OUT THE FLAP

Then fold the rest of the flap outward. Fold
the section labelled FOLD UP so that it is
flush with the surface you're working with.
There's a little notch that wraps behind the
U-shaped flap to keep it in place.

⓭ CHECK THE FLUSH

The U-shaped flap should lie flush with the box side. At this point, the cardboard might not hold its shape. Don't worry: it'll come together once it's in the box.

⓮ ADD THE SPEAKER

Find your speaker (which is now attached to your Raspberry Pi 3). Slide the speaker into the U-shaped pocket on the cardboard frame.

⑮ SLIDE INTO THE RASPBERRY PI

Turn the cardboard frame around. Take the Pi + Voice HAT hardware and push it into the bottom of the frame below flaps 1 and 2 (pictured). The cardboard frame should expose the USB ports of the Raspberry Pi.

⑯ PUT IT ALL TOGETHER

It's time to put the build together. First, remove the SD card from your Raspberry Pi to prevent damaging it. Now take the cardboard box you assembled earlier and find the side with the seven speaker holes. Slide the cardboard frame and hardware into the cardboard box. Ensure that the speaker is aligned with the box side that has the speaker holes.

17 CHECK THE WIRES

Once it's in, the Raspberry Pi should be sitting on the bottom of the box. Make sure your wires are still connected.

18 CHECK
THE PORTS

Check the holes in the
cardboard box. The Raspberry
Pi ports should be clearly visible.

The AIY Projects voice kit is
designed to work without
a display, but you can
access the HDMI socket for
troubleshooting. This hole
also provides access to the
power socket.

One hole provides access to the
USB ports. These ports enable
you to hook up a keyboard
and mouse to the AIY Projects
kit, although it is designed to
be controlled hands-free with
your voice.

19 ADD THE BUTTON

Insert the plastic button into the top flap of the cardboard box from the outside in. The pushable button side should face outward, with the larger screw on the inside; i.e. the side marked 'BUTTON.'

20 SECURE THE BUTTON

Now, screw in the washer nut to secure the button to the cardboard lid. Carefully screw the plastic nut around the thread of the button to firmly hold it in place.

㉑ FOLLOW THE CROWN

Look inside the button and you will see a crown-shaped logo (as shown in the image). Make sure the crown points in the logo are pointing upward, and use this guide to connect the wires.

The black wire connects to the top right.

The white wire connects to the top left.

The blue wire connects to the bottom left.

The Red wire connects to the bottom right.

22 CHECK THE WIRES

Locate the four coloured wires with metal contacts that you previously connected using the crown logo. The blue and red wires should be attached to pins embedded in red plastic (or the colour of your button). The white and black wires are attached to the pins protruding from grey plastic.

The white and black wires connect the button switch response mechanism.

MIC BOARD

BUTTON

The blue and red wires control the LED light on the button.

㉓ TAPE THE MICROPHONE

Next, we use two-sided tape to secure the Voice HAT Microphone board to the top flap. You can also use a spot of hot glue if you don't have two-sided tape. The board sits below the button on the top flap, with the two microphones aligned with the two holes. Check that the holes, on the other side, are aligned with the two microphones before fixing down the board.

24 CHECK THE MICROPHONE

Turn the flap around, and double-check that the microphones match the cardboard holes. Correct alignment ensures that the Microphone board can clearly hear you when you start issuing voice commands.

25 THE FINISHED BUILD

That's it. Your voice kit is assembled, and you can now start installing the software and using the Google Assistant to answer your questions. Fold the top flap down to close the box up and admire your handiwork.

The MagPi
ESSENTIALS

 Google Assistant SDK

[CHAPTER FOUR]

SET UP THE
SOFTWARE

Download and set up the AIY Projects software
and connect your device to the internet

You'll Need

- Assembled AIY Projects Voice Kit
- USB keyboard
- Mouse
- HDMI monitor
- HDMI cable
- MicroSD card
- AIY Projects image file

Info & Updates:

aiyprojects.withgoogle.com/voice

You now have a fully assembled cardboard device that is almost ready to respond to your questions. Now that your box is assembled, we will begin the process of turning it into a Voice Assistant, and an intelligent voice-powered interface for your own projects.

To do this, you'll set up a Google Developer project and activate the brand-new Google Assistant SDK.

But first, you need the base to work with. And that's a custom operating system designed especially for the AIY Projects kit.

>STEP 01
Download image

First, you need to download the AIY Projects image from **magpi. cc/2x7JQfS**. Please check the website for any updates to this process. AIY Projects software is routinely updated. Click the Get the Voice Kit SD Image link. The image file is saved to your Downloads folder.

>STEP 02
Copy image

Burn the image to a microSD card using a program like Etcher (**etcher.io**) on a Mac, Windows, or Linux computer.

Etcher software copies the image to the SD card (see 'Burn SD cards with Etcher', **magpi.cc/2fZkyJD**, if you're unfamiliar with the process).

>STEP 03
Plug in peripherals

Now that your box is assembled, plug your peripherals in:
1 **USB keyboard**
2 **USB mouse**
3 **HDMI monitor**

>STEP 04
Insert SD card

Insert your SD card (the one with the Voice Kit SD image) into the slot on the bottom side of the Raspberry Pi board. The SD card slot should be accessible through a cutout provided in the external cardboard form.

The SD card can be tricky to remove after it's been inserted. We recommend using either small, needle-nose pliers to remove it, or attaching tape to the SD card before inserting so you can remove it by pulling the tape.

>STEP 05
Power up

With the microSD card inserted into the Raspberry Pi, and the peripherals (monitor, keyboard, and mouse) connected, plug in the power supply. The Raspberry Pi will begin booting up, and you should see the AIY Projects desktop.

>STEP 06
Check LED lights
Once booted, the small LED in the centre of the Voice HAT and the
LED inside the arcade button should both indicate the device is
running.If you have any problems booting, check the troubleshooting
guide in the appendix. If you don't see anything on your monitor, or
you see 'Openbox Syntax Error', check the troubleshooting guide at
the end.

>STEP 07
Connect to network
Click the network icon in the upper right corner of the Raspberry
Pi desktop. Choose your preferred wireless access point. Enter the
wireless LAN password in the Pre Shared Key box and click OK.

>STEP 08
Check network
Double-click the Check WiFi icon on your desktop. This script
verifies that your WiFi is configured and working properly on the
Raspberry Pi board.

If everything is working correctly, you'll see a confirmation message.
Press **ENTER** to close.

>STEP 09
Check speaker
Double-click the Check Audio icon on your desktop. This script verifies
the audio input and output components on the Voice HAT accessory
board are working correctly.

When you click the script, you should hear "Front, Centre" announced from the speaker. An LXTerminal window opens with 'Did you hear the test sound? (y/n)'.

Enter **y** if you heard the sound. Now press **ENTER** to test the microphone.

>STEP 10
Check microphone

Say "Testing, 1 2 3" out loud. It will play back your voice with the message 'Did you hear your own voice (y/n)'. Again, enter **y** and press **ENTER**. Press **ENTER** again to end the test.

If you see an error message, follow the message details to resolve the issue and try again.

TROUBLESHOOTING TIPS

- A red LED on the Raspberry Pi near the power connector should light. If it doesn't, unplug the power, unplug the connector to the microphone, and power-up again. If it lights after powering-up without the microphone, then the microphone board may be defective.

- If the lamp in the button doesn't light up, it might be the wrong way around. Take the lamp out of the button (see Chapter 3), turn it 180°, and put it all back together. If it still doesn't light, check that the wire colours are the same as the picture in Chapter 3 step 12.

- If you don't see anything on your monitor, make sure the HDMI and power cables are fully inserted into the Raspberry Pi.

- If you see 'Openbox Syntax Error', you'll need to rewrite the image to the SD card and try booting the device again.

Google Assistant SDK

CHAPTER FIVE

BUILD A VOICE RECOGNIZER

Use the Google Assistant SDK to create a device that answers
your questions and helps you get things done

ongratulations on assembling your voice recognizer device – now, let's bring it to life! We're going to build a voice recognizer that uses Google Assistant, much like Google Home.

The voice recognizer uses the Google Assistant SDK to recognise speech, along with a local Python application that evaluates local commands.

Your voice recognizer will let you talk to the Google Assistant, and it will respond with smart answers to your questions.

>STEP 01
Google Cloud Platform
To try the Google Assistant API, you need to first sign into Google Cloud Platform (GCP) and then enable the API.

Quick Tip

Use your Google account to sign in to the Google Cloud Platform. If you don't have one, you'll need to create one. Trying the Google Assistant API is free to use for personal use.

>STEP 02
Log into GCP
Using AIY Projects on your voice recognizer device, open up the Chromium web browser (click on the blue globe icon in the top bar of the desktop). Go to the Cloud Console (**console.cloud.google.com**). Enter your Google account ID and password.

>STEP 03
Create a project
GCP uses projects to organise things, so you'll need to create a new project for your AIY Voice Kit. In Cloud Console, click the drop-down button to the right of the Google Cloud Platform logo (in the top-left of the screen). Now choose Create Project.

>STEP 04
Name the project

Enter a project name, such as 'Voice Assistant' and click Create. After your project is created, make sure the drop-down has your new project name displayed (if not, click on it and choose it from the list of projects).

>STEP 05
Turn on the API

Click Product & Services (the triple line icon) in the top-left of the GCP. Choose APIs & services and Dashboard and click Enable APIs.

Enter 'Google Assistant API' into the Search box and click it from the list below. Now click Enable.

>STEP 06
Create credentials

In the Cloud Console, create an OAuth 2.0 client by going to APIs & Services > Credentials.

Click on 'Create credentials' and choose OAuth client ID.

If this is your first time creating a client ID, you'll need to configure your consent screen. Click 'Configure consent screen'. Enter a Product Name, such as Voice Assistant. Click Save.

>STEP 07
Name credentials

Select Other. It will have the default name 'Other client 1'. Change the name to 'Voice Recognizer' to help you remember the credentials. Click Create.

>STEP 08
Client ID and secret

A window will pop up, named 'OAuth client', with 'Here is your client ID' and 'Here is your client secret'. Don't worry about memorising the long numbers, just click OK.

>STEP 09
Download JSON

In the Credentials list, find your new credentials and click the Download JSON icon. If you don't see the download icon, try expanding the width of your browser window or zooming out (**CTRL+-**). A JSON file starting with 'client_secrets' is saved to your Downloads folder.

>STEP 10
Find credentials

Open a Terminal window (click Terminal in the taskbar) and enter:

```
cd Downloads
ls
```

…to view the client secret file. It will have a lot of numbers and end with .json.

>STEP 11
Rename the credentials

You need to rename the file to **assistant.json** and move it to your home directory. Enter:

```
mv client_secret
```

…and press the **TAB** key. This will fill out the rest of the letters in the file. Now add **/home/pi/assistant.json** to the end of the file and press **ENTER**.

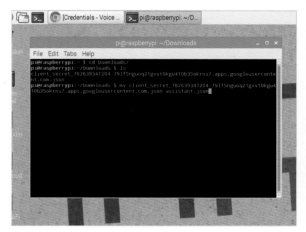

androidthings

Android Things is a new OS for connected devices that is fully compatible with the AIY Projects Voice Kit.

Developed by Google, it is a ready-to-use solution for building connected devices.

Developers can use existing Android development tools, security updates, APIs, resources, and a thriving developer community. It also includes new Android framework APIs that provide low-level I/O and libraries for common components like temperature sensors and display controllers.

In addition, a wide range of Google APIs and services – such as Google Play services, TensorFlow, and Google Cloud Platform – are available on Android Things. Developers can push Google-provided OS updates and their own app updates, using the same OTA infrastructure used on Google's own products.

To get started on building your kit with Android Things, visit the AIY Projects website (**aiyprojects. withgoogle.com/voice**). More information about Android Things is available on the developer website (**developer.android.com/things**).

This is how the full command looks on our AIY Projects voice recognizer (your client secret file will be different):

```
mv client_secret_782639341204-791f
5nguoq21gvvt0kgu410b35okrni7.apps.
googleusercontent.com.json /home/pi/
assistant.json
```

>STEP 12
Activity controls

Return to Chromium and visit your Google Activity Controls at **myaccount.google.com/ activitycontrols**. Make sure to log in with the same Google account as before.

Turn on the following by ticking the slider to the right, so they appear blue:

- **Web and app activity. Make sure the 'Include Chrome browsing history and activity from websites and apps that use Google services' checkbox is ticked).**
- **Device information**
- **Voice and audio activity**

GOOGLE DEMO APPS

Demo App	Description	Raspberry Pi supported
assistant_library_demo.py	Showcases the Google Assistant Library and hotword detection ("Okay, Google")	2B, 3B
assistant_grpc_demo.py	Showcases the Google gRPC APIs and button trigger	2B, 3B, Zero W
cloud_speech_demo.py	Showcases the Google Cloud Speech APIs, button trigger, and custom voice commands	2B, 3B, Zero W

>STEP 13
Start the voice unit
Double-click the 'Start dev terminal' icon and enter:

`src/assistant_library_demo.py`

A 'Request for Permission' window appears. Click Allow and close the web browser window. Return to the terminal window and you will see 'Say "OK, Google" then speak, or press Ctrl+C to quit…'

>STEP 14
The demo apps
In the Assistant Library demo, you can use the AIY Projects kit as a voice assistant. Say "OK Google" and ask a question out loud, such as "what is the weather in Cambridge?". Press **CTRL+C** when you're done.

Google provides three demo apps that showcase voice recognition and Google Assistant with different capabilities. They may be used as templates to create your own apps.

POWER OFF CAREFULLY

Take care to always turn off the Raspberry Pi using **Menu > Shutdown > Shutdown** or **sudo shutdown -h now** in Terminal. If you want to use your AIY Projects kit without a screen connected, you should add the **shutdown_demo.py** code from Chapter 7 and issue the "shut down" voice command before disconnecting the power.

Google Cloud Platform

[**CHAPTER SIX**]

CREATE A
VOICE USER
INTERFACE
FOR YOUR PROJECTS

Swap out traditional interfaces with a custom voice control
using your AIY Projects Voice Kit

You'll Need

- Google Cloud
  Speech API

B y now, you have built a device that embeds the Google Assistant. That's cool, but it's just the beginning. With Google Cloud Speech API, you can create an interactive, custom voice-user interface (VUI) for your project.

This enables you to explore a new generation of devices that you can have a conversation with, without the need for remote-control devices (such as joysticks or smartphone apps). Let's reconfigure the kit to use the Google Cloud Speech API.

> STEP 01
View the source

The source code for the voice recognizer app is part of the image that you've just installed. You can view the Python source code in the **/home/pi/AIY-voice-kit-python/src** directory. Alternately, the project source is available on GitHub: **github.com/google/aiyprojects-raspbian/tree/voicekit**. It is released under the 'voicekit' branch.

>STEP 02
Create service account

Head to Google Cloud Console in the browser and click Create Credentials. This time choose 'Service account key'. Click the 'Service account' menu and choose 'New service account'. Give it a name, such as 'AIY Projects', and change the Role to Project > viewer. Make sure the Key type is JSON and click Create. The key is downloaded to your computer.

>STEP 03
Create credentials

Find the file you've downloaded. You need to rename the file to **cloud_speech.json** and place it in your home folder.

```
mv My Project-[123etc].json /home/
pi/cloud_speech.json
```

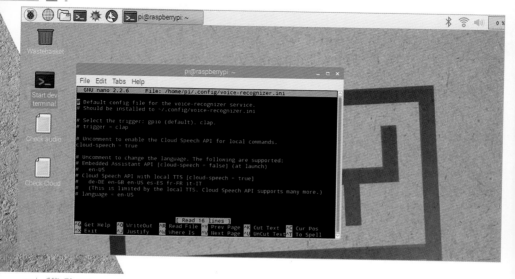

TensorFlow

TensorFlow is an open-source software library for machine learning. It was originally developed by researchers and engineers working on the Google Brain Team within Google's Machine Intelligence research organisation. You can learn more about TensorFlow, and how it can be used to add intelligence to your own projects, at **tensorflow. org**. To see how you can use TensorFlow to enable on-device audio detection, visit the AIY Projects website at **aiyprojects.withgoogle.com/voice**.

> STEP 04
Check Cloud Speech API
You need to have the Cloud Speech API enabled to use the service. In Cloud Console, go to API & Services > Library. Click on Speech API and click Enable (then follow the prompts to set up a billing account, or follow the instructions in step 6, then click Enable again).

> STEP 05
Check billing
You need to have billing set up with Google to use the Cloud Speech API. Open Cloud Console, click 'New billing account' and go through the setup. Check your project is selected in the Projects menu at the top. Click Products & Services > Billing. To connect or change the billing account, click the three-dot button, then select 'Change billing account'.

NOTE FOR EU USERS

At this time, the Cloud Speech API is not available to use with the AIY Projects Voice Kit. In the European Union, Google Cloud Platform services can be used for business purposes only, including the Cloud Speech API. Learn more here: **cloud.google.com/free/docs/ frequently-asked-questions**.

>STEP 06
Check Cloud

On your desktop, double-click the Check Cloud icon. Follow along with the script. If everything is working correctly, you'll see this message: 'The cloud connection seems to be working.'

If you see an error message, try restarting your Raspberry Pi with **sudo reboot**. Then follow the instructions above, or take a look at the instructions on the AIY Projects page (**magpi.cc/2q5SSF7**).

> STEP 07
Start it up

Open 'Start dev terminal' and enter:

```
src/cloudspeech_demo.py
```

You can now issue a limited number of commands:
- **Turn on the light (turns on the LED on the Voice HAT).**
- **Turn off the light (turns off the LED).**
- **Blink (the LED blinks).**
- **Goodbye (the program exits).**

Press **CTRL+C** to quit the interaction.

GETTING HELP

With so many options to explore with this first AIY Project from Google, you should make good use of the vibrant Raspberry Pi community. The Raspberry Pi community is on hand to help you with any issues, and make suggestions for your projects. Head to the Raspberry Pi forums and find the new AIY Projects page: **magpi.cc/ 1NlH5rQ**

>STEP 08
Create a new activation trigger

An activation trigger is a general term describing the condition on which we activate voice recognition or start a conversation with the Google Assistant. Previously you have seen two different types of activation triggers:

- **Voice activation trigger: This is the "Okay, Google" hotword detection in the assistant library demo.**
- **Button trigger: This is when you press the arcade button.**

You may design and implement your own triggers. For example, you may have a motion detection sensor driver that can call a function when motion is detected:

motion.py

```python
import aiy.audio
import aiy.cloudspeech
import aiy.voice


def main():
    '''Start voice recognition when motion is detected.'''
    my_motion_detector = MotionDetector()
    recognizer = aiy.cloudspeech.get_recognizer()
    aiy.audio.get_recorder().start()
    while True:
        my_motion_detector.WaitForMotion()
        text = recognizer.recognize()
        aiy.audio.say('You said ', text)

if __name__ == '__main__':
    main()
```

PYTHON API REFERENCE

Module	APIs Provided	Description & Uses in Demo Apps
aiy.voicehat	get_button() get_led() get_status_ui()	For controlling the Arcade button and the LED. See uses in any demo app.
aiy.audio	get_player() get_recorder() record_to_wave() play_wave() play_audio() say()	For controlling the microphone and speaker. It is capable of speaking some text or playing a wave file. See uses in assistant_grpc_demo.py and cloudspeech_demo.py.
aiy.cloudspeech	get_recognizer()	For accessing the Google CloudSpeech APIs. See uses in cloudspeech_demo.py.
aiy.i18n	set_locale_dir() set_language_code() get_language_code()	For customizing the language and locale. Not used directly by demo apps. Some APIs depend on this module. For example, aiy. audio.say() uses this module for speech synthesis.
aiy.assistant.grpc	get_assistant()	For accessing the Google Assistant APIs via gRPC. See uses in assistant_grpc_demo.py.
google.assistant.library		The official Google Assistant Library for Python. See the online documentation at developers. google.com/assistant/sdk/ reference/library/python/

Google Cloud Platform

CHAPTER SEVEN

CONTROL

AN **LED**

Create custom voice commands for AIY Projects

You'll Need

- AIY Projects voice kit
- Cloud Speech API
- Breadboard
- LED, resistor, and cables

 ow that you've switched from the Assistant SDK to the Cloud Speech API, you'll want to know what you can do with it. You add custom commands to your own Python files.

There is a selection of example voice commands located in cloudspeech_demo.py. We're going to modify this file to see how they work, then create our own Python programs to control circuit components attached to the Voice HAT.

>STEP 01
Backup first

You can create new actions and link them to new voice commands by modifying src/cloudspeech_demo.py directly. First, backup the file:

```
cp src/cloudspeech_demo.py src/cloudspeech_demo_backup.py
```

Open the cloud speech demo using

```
nano src/cloudspeech_demo.py
```

>STEP 02
Expect phrase

To add a custom voice command, you first have to make it explicit what command is expected to the recognizer. This improves the recognition rate.

We're going to add a new recognizer.expect_phrase method to the cloudspeech_demo.py code:

```
recognizer.expect_phrase('repeat after me')
```

The program now expects to hear "repeat after me" along with the other commands.

>STEP 03
Handle phrase

Next we add the code to handle the command. We will use aiy.audio.say to repeat the recognized transcript.

```
elif 'repeat after me' in text:
    to_repeat = text.replace('repeat after me', '', 1)
    aiy.audio.say(to_repeat)
```

You'll find the full modified code in the **cloudspeech_demo.py** code listing. Use **src/cloudspeech_demo.py** to run the modified program. Now press the button and say 'repeat after me 1, 2, 3' the AIY Projects voice kit should say '1, 2, 3'.

cloudspeech_demo.py

```
01.  """A demo of the Google CloudSpeech recognizer."""
02.
03.  import os
04.
05.  import aiy.audio
06.  import aiy.cloudspeech
07.  import aiy.voicehat
08.
09.
10.  def main():
11.      recognizer = aiy.cloudspeech.get_recognizer()
12.      recognizer.expect_phrase('turn off the light')
13.      recognizer.expect_phrase('turn on the light')
14.      recognizer.expect_phrase('blink')
15.      recognizer.expect_phrase('repeat after me')
16.
17.      button = aiy.voicehat.get_button()
18.      led = aiy.voicehat.get_led()
19.      aiy.audio.get_recorder().start()
20.
21.      while True:
22.          print('Press the button and speak')
23.          button.wait_for_press()
24.          print('Listening...')
25.          text = recognizer.recognize()
26.          if text is None:
27.              print('Sorry, I did not hear you.')
28.          else:
29.              print('You said "', text, '"')
30.              if 'turn on the light' in text:
31.                  led.set_state(aiy.voicehat.LED.ON)
32.              elif 'turn off the light' in text:
33.                  led.set_state(aiy.voicehat.LED.OFF)
34.              elif 'blink' in text:
35.                  led.set_state(aiy.voicehat.LED.BLINK)
36.              elif 'repeat after me' in text:
37.                  to_repeat = text.replace('repeat after me', '', 1)
38.                  aiy.audio.say(to_repeat)
39.              elif 'goodbye' in text:
40.                  os._exit(0)
41.
42.
43.  if __name__ == '__main__':
44.      main()
```

Use code to control GPIO pins via your assistant. This short program turns an LED light on or off

>STEP 04
Control on LED

Now that we can add custom commands, we're going to use the AIY Projects kit to control some hardware. Set up an LED circuit using a breadboard – follow the diagram shown on page 58. We are connecting the LED via the pins on Servo 0. Connect the live wire to Pin (on the left). This is GPIO 26 using the BCM numbering system. Connect the ground wire to GND (on the right). The middle pin provides a constant 5V of power. You can see the reference for each pin underneath the Servo 5 rail (check the diagram in 'Voice HAT hardware extensions' at the back of this book).

We have found that it will work by connecting wires directly to the through-holes on the board. For a more reliable circuit, carefully solder the pins supplied with your Voice HAT.

>STEP 05
Enter LED code

Create a new file using **nano src/led_demo.py** and enter the code from the **led_demo.py** listing. Notice the first line: **#!/usr/bin/env python3**. This enables you to run this code from the command line.

>STEP 06
Run the code

We need to make the file executable to run it from the command line.

```
chmod +x /src/led_demo.py
```

Now run the code using:

```
src/led_demo.py
```

Press the button and say "turn on the light". The LED on your breadboard lights up; say "turn off the light" to switch it off.

VOICE RECORDER

If you get a message that says: "Server error: Audio data is being streamed too slowly or too quickly. Please stream audio data approximately at real time." Then you've forgotten to turn on the voice recorder:

aiy.audio.get_recorder().start()

led_demo.py

```python
#!/usr/bin/env python3

import aiy.audio
import aiy.cloudspeech
import aiy.voicehat
import RPi.GPIO as GPIO

def main():
    recognizer = aiy.cloudspeech.get_recognizer()
    recognizer.expect_phrase('turn on the light')
    recognizer.expect_phrase('turn off the light')

    button = aiy.voicehat.get_button()
    aiy.audio.get_recorder().start()

    GPIO.setmode(GPIO.BCM)
    GPIO.setwarnings(False)
    GPIO.setup(26,GPIO.OUT)

    while True:
        print('Press the button and speak')
        button.wait_for_press()
        print('Listening...')
        text = recognizer.recognize()
        if text is None:
            print('Sorry, I did not hear you.')
        else:
            print('You said "', text, '"')
            if 'turn on the light' in text:
                GPIO.output(26,GPIO.HIGH)
            elif 'turn off the light' in text:
                GPIO.output(26,GPIO.LOW)

if __name__ == '__main__':
    main()
```

SET UP AN LED CIRCUIT

CIRCUIT

Connect an LED to the breadboard and create a circuit (with the longer leg connected to live and the shorter leg connected to ground). Don't forget to use a resistor (around 330 ohms) to protect the LED

GPIO 26

Connect the live wire to GPIO 26, the leftmost pin on Servo 0, and the live rail on the breadboard. See the GPIO layout guide from the previous page for guidance

GND

Connect the ground wire to the GND pin on the Servo 0 rail and the ground rail on the breadboard

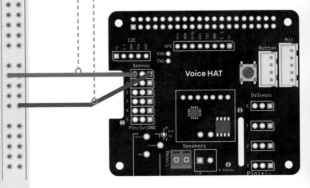

SAFE SHUTDOWN

One script that's well worth knowing is shutdown. This will safely turn off your AIY Projects kit. The **shutdown_demo.py** code uses the subprocess modtule to run a shutdown Unix command. Simply say "shut down" to turn off your AIY Projects kit.

shutdown_demo.py

```python
#!/usr/bin/env python3

import aiy.audio
import aiy.cloudspeech
import aiy.voicehat
import subprocess

def main():
    recognizer = aiy.cloudspeech.get_recognizer()
    recognizer.expect_phrase('shutdown')

    button = aiy.voicehat.get_button()
    aiy.audio.get_recorder().start()

    while True:
        print('Press the button and speak')
        button.wait_for_press()
        print('Listening...')
        text = recognizer.recognize()
        if text is None:
            print('Sorry, I did not hear you.')
        else:
            print('You said "', text, '"')
            if 'shutdown' in text:
                subprocess.call(["sudo", "shutdown", "-h", "now"])

if __name__ == '__main__':
    main()
```

The MagPi
ESSENTIALS

[CHAPTER EIGHT]
ATTACH A
SERVO

Servo motors are used to perform fine motor functions, and with AIY Projects you can program them for voice activation

You'll Need

- 9 g micro servo
- AIY Projects Voice HAT

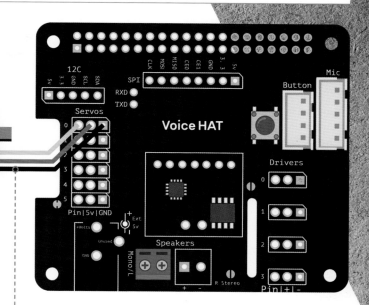

MOTOR CONTROL

Servo motors are controlled using pulses generated by a GPIO pin on the Raspberry Pi. The arm is moved between a high and low position.

SERVO WIRES

The three wires from the servo are connected to row 0 on the Servos rail. Make sure you connect the Pin, 5v, and GND wires in the correct order.

O ne of the big hopes for AIY Projects is that Raspberry Pi owners will integrate the kit into their own projects. In our last tutorial for AIY Projects, we looked at hooking up the hardware to control an LED light (a typical first hardware project). Here, we're going to take things up a notch and hook up a servo to the AIY Projects board.

On the Voice HAT hardware you will see two columns of pins. The one on the left (marked Servos) is for servos, and has a 25 mA drive limit. The one on the right, marked Drivers, is typically used for motors and has a 500 mA limit. You can connect wires directly to the Voice HAT hardware, but it's easier to prototype your circuits by soldering the pins (supplied with the kit) to the board.

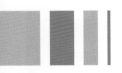

GET YOUR AIY PROJECTS KIT

>STEP 01
Servo motors

Servo motors move in a circular motion to a set position. They are often used to control robotic arms and legs, grippers, and the position of surfaces (like elevators and rudders on an RC plane).

It is relatively easy to hook up a servo motor to a Raspberry Pi, but the AIY Projects Voice HAT board makes it even easier, with a dedicated column of pins designed to control servo motors. Connecting your servos using the Voice HAT allows them to be controlled using voice commands and the Cloud Speech API.

>STEP 02
Servo control

Servo motors are controlled using pulses generated by a GPIO pin on the Raspberry Pi (we're using GPIO 26 on the AIY Projects Voice HAT board). The servo motor expects a pulse (the GPIO pin to be turned on, or high, and then off again) every 20 milliseconds. The length of the pulse determines the position of the servo arm. If it's 1 ms then the servo arm is rotated towards the left; 1.5 ms puts it at the mid-point; 2 ms and it's all the way to the right. The code for detecting these pulses and moving the servo around is provided with the GPIO Zero library. Install using:

sudo apt install python3-gpiozero

>STEP 03
Connect the servo

We're using a standard 9 g micro servo in this tutorial. These are tiny 5 V servos with an operating voltage of 4.8 V. Each servo comes with three wires: usually these are red, brown, and orange. Red and brown provide power to the servo, and are live and neutral respectively, while the third wire detects the pulse. Make sure your Raspberry Pi is powered down, and connect the servo wires directly to the Servos 0

A servo motor has three wires. Two provide power, while a third is used to control the position of the servo

row on your AIY Projects Voice HAT. Many servos have all three wires bundled into a JR connector; this can be plugged directly into the Voice HAT board. Be sure to fit it the correct way around, with the orange/yellow cable in the GPIO pin on the left.

>STEP 04
Power the servo

The 5 V running through the GPIO pins on the Raspberry Pi is enough to power two to three very small servo motors. We're only using one here in our tutorial, so we aren't going to add additional power.

>STEP 05
Test it out

Before coding the servo to respond to your voice commands, you can test the circuit using GPIO Zero in Python. Open IDLE 3 and enter the code from **servo_test.py**. Save the code and press **F5** to run it. The servo will move from its minimum position to the mid-point, and then to the maximum position with a pause between each step. Press **CTRL+C** to quit the program and stop the movement. If the servo doesn't work, double-check your connections.

>STEP 06
Integrate with voice

Now that the servo is working, it's time to integrate it with the AIY Projects code using the **servo_demo.py** script. Open Start dev

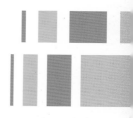

Right: A servo motor measures the length between pulses (a GPIO pin being turned rapidly on and off). When the pin is on for 1 ms, the servo moves to the low position. When it's on for 2 ms, it moves to the high position. Other pulse lengths are used to set it between low and high

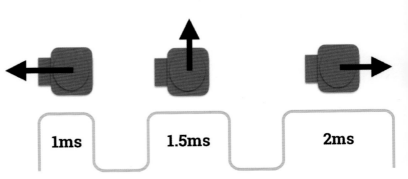

1ms   1.5ms   2ms

terminal and use **nano src/servo_demo.py** to create the empty text file. Don't forget to use **chmod +x src/servo_demo.py** afterwards to make it executable.

Run **src/servo_demo.py** and press the button on your AIY Projects Voice HAT board. Now say "change to minimum" or "change to maximum" to move the arm up and down. Saying "change" and any other command moves the arm back to the middle.

Now everything is working, you can attach the servo to the side of the kit's cardboard box. On the side of the kit, you'll see an arc-shaped hole. Most small servos will fit in this space. Twist the servo to lock it in place. Try adding a wooden or 3D-printed arm to the servo so you can clearly see it moving.

servo_test.py

```python
from gpiozero import Servo
from time import sleep

servo = Servo(26)
while True:
    servo.min()
    sleep(1)
    servo.mid()
    sleep(1)
    servo.max()
    sleep(1)
```

server_demo.py

```python
#!/usr/bin/env python3

import aiy.audio
import aiy.cloudspeech
import aiy.voicehat
from gpiozero import Servo

def main():
    recognizer = aiy.cloudspeech.get_recognizer()
    recognizer.expect_phrase('maximum')
    recognizer.expect_phrase('minimum')
    recognizer.expect_phrase('middle')

    button = aiy.voicehat.get_button()
    aiy.audio.get_recorder().start()

    servo = Servo(26)

    while True:
        print('Press the button and speak')
        button.wait_for_press()
        print('Listening...')
        text = recognizer.recognize()
        if text is None:
            print('Sorry, I did not hear you.')
        else:
            print('You said "', text, '"')
            if 'maximum' in text:
                print('Moving servo to maximum')
                servo.max()
            elif 'minimum' in text:
                print('Moving servo to minimum')
                servo.min()
            elif 'middle' in text:
                print('Moving servo to middle')
                servo.mid()

if __name__ == '__main__':
    main()
```

CHAPTER NINE

CONTROL A
DC MOTOR

Connect a motor to your AIY Projects Voice HAT board

You'll Need

- **DC motor**
- **4×AA battery pack**
- **Breadboard and jumper wires**
- **Utility / Stanley knife**

DC motors are used to control wheels, arm joints, and moving components. They are often found in robotic projects

n our previous AIY Projects tutorials, we've looked at how to move beyond using the Voice Assistant, and towards using your Voice HAT with basic electronics.

If you've been following our tutorials, you will have discovered how to connect the Voice HAT hardware to simple circuits. So far we've looked at how to control LED lights and servo motors, but in this tutorial we'll look at something a little more complex: using the AIY Projects Voice HAT to control a motor.

DC MOTOR

The DC motor connects to the positive and negative voltages via two wires. The direction in which the motor moves depends on which way around the two wires are placed.

EXTERNAL POWER SOLDER JUMPER

You need to cut the external power solder jumper, located just to the left of Servos 5 on the board. This isolates the Voice HAT power from the Raspberry Pi.

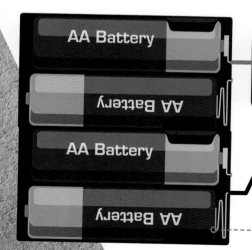

AA BATTERY PACK

The DC motor draws more power than the Raspberry Pi can safely provide, so a 4×AA battery pack provides power for the DC motor.

>STEP 01
Cut the power
The first thing you need to do is isolate the Raspberry Pi's power supply
from the power on the Voice HAT board. This will prevent the DC motor
from draining too much power and shorting out your Raspberry Pi. Locate
the external power solder jumper marked JP1 (just to the left of Servos 5
on the Voice HAT board). Use a utility knife to cut the connection in the
jumper (you can always re-solder this joint if you wish to share the power
between the board and the motor again).

>STEP 02
Power off
Make sure your Raspberry Pi and Voice HAT board are powered off. Now
connect the positive leg of the DC motor to the middle pin on Drivers 0.
Notice that at the bottom of the Driver pins is a '+' symbol.

>STEP 03
Wire for power
Next, connect the negative wire of the motor to the '-' pin on Drivers 0
(the pin on the right). You may have noticed that we're not connected to

motor_test.py

```
from gpiozero import PWMOutputDevice
from time import sleep

pwm = PWMOutputDevice(4)
while True:
  pwm.on()
  sleep(1)
  pwm.off()
  sleep(1)
  pwm.value = 0.5
  sleep(1)
  pwm.value = 0.0
  sleep(1)
```

the GPIO Pin on the left (which is GPIO4); this doesn't matter as it also controls the negative '–' pin that we have just connected to. This allows us to turn the motor on and off.

>STEP 04
Power up

Finally, connect the 4×AA battery pack to the +Volts and GND pins at the lower left-hand corner of the Voice HAT. This pack will ensure that the motor has enough power when you are using the Voice HAT, which will prevent your Raspberry Pi from crashing. Connect the power and turn on the battery pack.

>STEP 05
Turn on the Pi

Now turn on the Raspberry Pi and boot into the AIY Projects software. Enter the code from **motor_test.py** to test the circuit. We are using **PWMOutputDevice** from GPIO Zero to control the motor. This enables us to manage the speed of the motor (**magpi.cc/2tnAGrz**). We can use the **.on()** and **.off()** methods to start and stop our motor. Alternatively, we can set the value instance variable to a value between 0.0 and 1.0 to control the speed. These techniques are shown in the **motor_demo.py** code. You can also use **pwm.pulse()** to pulse the motor on and off.

>STEP 06
Use voice control

Now that we've seen how to control the motor using GPIO Zero, it is time to integrate it with the Cloud Speech API. Push the button on your Voice HAT board and say "motor on" to start the motor running; push the button again and say "motor off" to stop it

You can add more motors to your AIY Projects kit using the four rows of Drivers on the Voice HAT board. These can be used to build robots and other motion projects. Discover more project ideas for your Voice Kit at the AIY Projects forum (**magpi.cc/2wuTMMW**). We hope you've enjoyed this guide and build many great things with your AIY Projects Voice Kit.

motor_demo.py

```python
#!/usr/bin/env python3

import aiy.audio
import aiy.cloudspeech
import aiy.voicehat
from gpiozero import PWMOutputDevice

def main():
    recognizer = aiy.cloudspeech.get_recognizer()
    recognizer.expect_phrase('on')
    recognizer.expect_phrase('off')

    button = aiy.voicehat.get_button()
    aiy.audio.get_recorder().start()

    pwm = PWMOutputDevice(4)

    while True:
        print('Press the button and speak')
        button.wait_for_press()
        print('Listening...')
        text = recognizer.recognize()
        if text is None:
            print('Sorry, I did not hear you.')
        else:
            print('You said "', text, '"')
            if 'on' in text:
                print('Turning motor on')
                pwm.on()
            elif 'off' in text:
                print('Turning motor off')
                pwm.off()

if __name__ == '__main__':
    main()
```

VOICE HAT HARDWARE EXTENSIONS

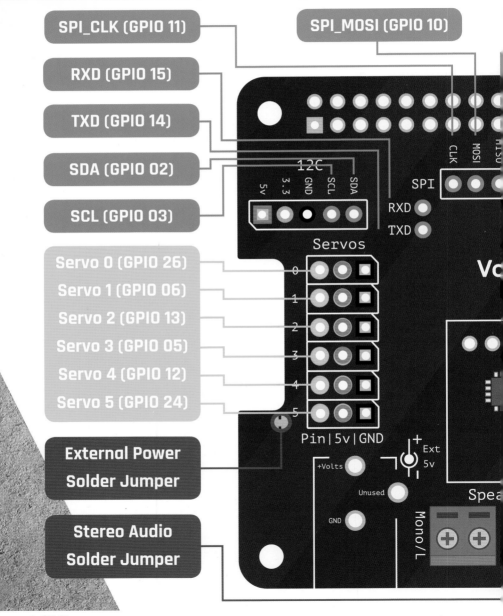

SPI_CLK (GPIO 11)

SPI_MOSI (GPIO 10)

RXD (GPIO 15)

TXD (GPIO 14)

SDA (GPIO 02)

SCL (GPIO 03)

Servo 0 (GPIO 26)

Servo 1 (GPIO 06)

Servo 2 (GPIO 13)

Servo 3 (GPIO 05)

Servo 4 (GPIO 12)

Servo 5 (GPIO 24)

External Power Solder Jumper

Stereo Audio Solder Jumper

I2C · 5v · 3.3 · GND · SCL · SDA

CLK · MOSI · MISO

SPI · RXD · TXD

Servos

0 1 2 3 4 5

Pin | 5v | GND

+Volts

Unused

GND

Ext 5v

Vo

Spea

Mono/L

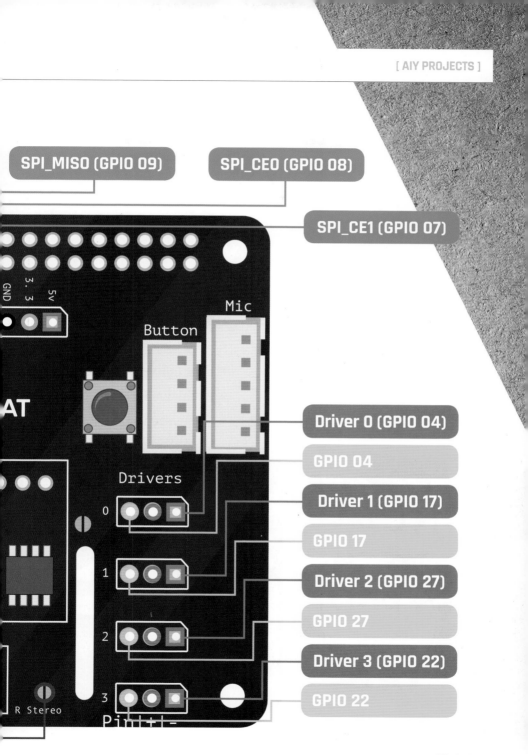

SPI_MISO (GPIO 09)

SPI_CEO (GPIO 08)

SPI_CE1 (GPIO 07)

GND

3.3

5v

Mic

Button

AT

Driver 0 (GPIO 04)

GPIO 04

Drivers

0

Driver 1 (GPIO 17)

GPIO 17

1

Driver 2 (GPIO 27)

GPIO 27

2

Driver 3 (GPIO 22)

3

GPIO 22

R Stereo

Pin+ -

The MagPi Magazine

raspberrypi.org/magpi

SUBSCRIBE TODAY AND RECEIVE A

FREE
PI ZERO W

Subscribe in print for 12 months today and receive:

- A free Pi Zero W (the latest model)
- Free Pi Zero W case with 3 covers
- Free Camera Module connector
- Free USB and HDMI converter cables

Other benefits:

- Save up to 25% on the price
- Free delivery to your door
- Exclusive Pi offers & discounts
- Get every issue first (before stores)

SAVE UP TO 25%

WELCOME TO AIY PROJECTS

G oogle AIY Projects brings do-it-yourself artificial intelligence (AI) to the maker community.

AIY Projects is a series of open-source designs that demonstrate how easy it is to add AI to your projects.

We are thrilled to present the very first project, a kit that lets you explore voice recognition and natural language understanding.

You will build a cardboard device that uses the Google Assistant to answer questions, like "how far away is the moon?" or "what is 18 percent of 92?".

Then you will learn how to add voice commands to your own projects. For example, you can register commands, such as "turn the lights on" or "robot, turn right and move forwards". In the kit, Google has included a microphone, a speaker, and an accessory board called Voice HAT, that is loaded with breakout pins to wire up a variety of sensors and components.

Google can't wait for makers to build intelligent devices that solve real-world problems and share them back to the community using the #AIYProjects hashtag on social media.

Your kit is a fantastic way to add voice control to your projects, and start exploring what's possible with AI.

Lucy Hattersley

FIND US ONLINE raspberrypi.org/magpi   **GET IN TOUCH** magpi@raspberrypi.org

EDITORIAL
Publishing Director: **Russell Barnes**
Editor: **Lucy Hattersley**
lucy@raspberrypi.org
Sub Editors: **Rachel Churcher and Phil King**

DESIGN
Critical Media: **criticalmedia.co.uk**
Head of Design: **Dougal Matthews**
Designers: **Lee Allen, Mike Kay**

DISTRIBUTION
Seymour Distribution Ltd
2 East Poultry Ave, London
EC1A 9PT | **+44 (0)207 429 4000**

THE MAGPI SUBSCRIPTIONS
Select Publisher Services Ltd
PO Box 6337, Bournemouth
BH1 9EH | **+44 (0)1202 586 848**
magpi.cc/Subs1